AVENGERS OF GOR

AVENGERS OF GOR

GOREAN SAGA * BOOK 36

John Norman

Distributed in 2021 by Open Road Distribution
180 Maiden Lane
New York, NY 10038
www.openroadmedia.com

AVENGERS OF GOR

CHAPTER ONE

It is Night; I Visit the Village of Nicosia

"Put away the knife," I said. "Do not lift it against me. I am then permitted to kill you."

"The codes?" he asked.

"Of course," I said.

"How do I know you are of that caste?" he asked.

"You do not know," I said.

"Why should I believe you?" he asked.

"That your life not be jeopardized," I said.

"My life," he said, "what does it matter?"

"One must decide such things for oneself," I said.

He replaced the knife, a kitchen knife, not finely ground, not hilted, not a war knife, not a killing knife, in his belt.

I looked about.

"What has been done here?" I asked.

"Is it not obvious?" he said.

It was obvious enough, but I wished my haggard, hollow-cheeked, wretched, despondent interlocutor, who had now sunk wearily to his haunches, not looking at me, to speak. One who speaks freely, unthreatened, of his own will, with no obvious motivation to lie, is more likely to tell the truth, even in its miserable plenty, than one intimidated, or one seeking profit by means of its distortion or concealment.

"A sudden disruption in the crust of the earth," I suggested, "a spillage of fire from ovens or hearths, uncontrolled, sweeping even to the *pomerium*, eating away the palisade with red teeth?"

We were within the blackened shell of what had once been a hut, a simple village dwelling. I could see my interlocutor, he now crouching, in the light of the yellow moon. His hair was blond, long, and uncombed, his beard poorly cut, his clothing little more than a wrapping of rags. I thought him weak, exhausted, and possibly starving, though such things may be easily feigned.

Things are not always as they seem.

That is well known.

"Do not spring up," I said. "I would act without thought. I could not help myself. We are trained so. There would be no time to think, to reason or understand. Forgive me, but your neck would be broken."

He then sat back, leaning against the wall behind him.

"You are a stranger," he said, bitterly.

"I am unknown to you," I said, "but I am not a stranger."

It is difficult to translate this into English, for the same word in Gorean is used for a "stranger," in the sense of someone not known, and an enemy. Literally I had said, "I am a stranger who is not a stranger."

"You wear the field garment, the trading garment, of the Merchants," he said.

"Think of me so," I said.

"But you wear a sword, sheathed, on a single strap, the leather not fastened across your body, but loose, over your left shoulder," he said.

"Thus," I said, "the blade drawn, the scabbard and belt may be instantly discarded, no longer constituting a perilous, graspable snare or encumbrance."

"You are of the scarlet caste," he said.

"I wear the garb of the Merchants," I said.

"Look about you," he said.

"Your time of troubles is some days gone," I said.

Ashes were damp. They had been rained on, perhaps several times, surely once recently.

"The smell of smoke lingers," he said.

"It will do that, for days," I said.

Wood lay about, charred, and broken. I saw little or nothing of value in the wreckage. There was no food, at least as far as I could tell. Even clay vessels were missing, or shattered, many apparently trodden underfoot in some intended thoroughness of havoc. Planks of what must once have been a portal were sundered, broken apart and splintered. On a stanchion, to the right, were deep marks testifying to the blows of an ax.

Everything spoke of an attack, a ravaging, a hurried, ruthless looting and burning. What had been done in this place, as it had been done, seemed pointless. It exhibited an inexplicable ferocity. The raid which had wrought this destruction was untypical of the work of common corsairs, pirates, and thieves. When one wishes to steal fruit from a tree one does not destroy the tree. One may wish to return, for new fruit, return when there is a slowly accumulated, renewed wealth, when there is a declined vigilance, when the prey thinks itself safe, when there is a new harvest, freshly reaped, to be gathered in, a new generation of females to be fastened in chains, ripe for delivery to the markets.

My eye roved the desolation, within and about the hut, the residue of carnage and burning.

This spoke not of economics and profit but of calculated destruction. It spoke less of men than of designing monsters, less of piracy than policy, less of spoil than extermination.

"The village is burned," I said. "Even the palisade is gone. How is it that you did not contain the flames?"

"Who was there to contain them?" he asked. "Those slain, those fleeing, those seized? The roasted beast, turning on its spit, does not extinguish the flames in which it cooks. Its dripping grease feeds the fire."

We were on Chios, the closest of the three 'Farther Islands', Chios, Thera, and Daphna, those islands beyond Tyros and Cos, once taken as marking the end of a world, beyond which lay only terror and mystery, and the devouring, waiting, stirring vastness of turbulent Thassa, the sea, fierce summoner of winds, raiser of storms, caster of fire, player with ships, jealous of her secrets. Were there not rumors of monsters, behemoths, the strike of whose thrashing tails could shatter hulls, of watery countries of impassable, seeking, floating, thick, clutching vines, avid to ensnare travelers, of inescapable spinning wells in the sea, capturing and sinking even the largest of vessels? And what of the abyss, beyond the brink of Thassa, where ships fell, plunging a thousand pasangs down, perishing? Who would wish to go there? Who would dare to look upon such a place? Who would wish to be swept over the edge of a world?

"You are one of them," he said.

"One of whom?" I said.

"Those who did these things," he said, "those who came with axes, flaming brands, swords, and chains."

"No," I said.

"You have come to see the work done," he said. "You have come to confirm horror. You have come to see if a pole of dried fish was missed, if a conical granary lies undetected, if an *amphora* of paga, buried in the sand, was overlooked."

"No," I said.

"Perhaps you search for survivors, some now crept back, as I, sorrowing, frightened, worn, hungry, from the mountains," he said, "to hunt and kill them."

"No," I said.

"Report to your commander," he said. "The work was well done, organized, swift, and thorough."

"I am not of those who assailed this place," I said.

"Now kill me," he said.

"Are you hungry?" I asked.

I took a bit of bread from my pouch and tossed it to him.

He held the bread to his mouth, tearing at it, not taking his eyes from me. Had it been poison, he could not have dealt with it more recklessly, less desperately.

"You suspect me," I said.

"You come at night," he said. "Merchants do not come at night."

"If I meant you harm," I said, "I would not have worn this raiment, white and yellow, easily seen. I would have dressed like the night, have come in stealth, as the sleen."

"You have no cart, no wagon, no pack," he said.

"No," I said.

"You are not of the Merchants," he said.

"Perhaps not," I said.

"One came before as you," he said, "days ago, seemingly, too, of the Merchants. We welcomed him, we regaled him, we entertained him, we shared paga, our maidens danced before him, we showed him hospitality. Two days later, following his departure, they came, with fire and chains. They took even the trinkets, precious to us, for which we had traded."

"He was a spy, a scout," I said. "He counted men, and huts, he assessed women, he ascertained goods, and locations, he identified strengths and weaknesses, he familiarized himself with habits and customs, studied the palisade, and marked the gates, the openings and closings."

"You seem familiar with such doings," said the man, thrusting the last of the bread into his mouth.

"Given certain ends, who would do things otherwise?" I said. "One does not raid blindly. Only a fool rushes into a lair within which a larl might repose."

"I think you are of them," he said.

"No," I said.

"You seek to join them," he said.

"No," I said.

"You are late," he said. "They have gone."

"Yours is not the first village," I said. "There is a pattern. The scouting, the attack. Then there is the disappearance, the vanishing. At least four villages were destroyed on Thera, and two on Daphna. Ships, too, have been waylaid at sea."

"How do you know?" he asked.

"It is not difficult," I said. "Things become known. Often there are survivors, sometimes perhaps spared that they may speak. Perhaps you are one such. Word spreads, swift, like the wind."

"How did you know of this place?" he asked. "How came you here?"

"A rumor, aflight in a tavern in Sybaris, high town of Thera," I said, "overheard nine days ago."

"Impossible," he said, "the attack took place but five days ago."

"I set forth immediately," I said.

"You arrived too late," he snarled.

"Five days ago?" I asked. "The attack took place five days ago?"

"Yes," he said.

I had surmised something of this sort, shortly after my arrival, from the condition of the village, it muchly surprising me, it muchly exciting me. My search, until now, had been long and fruitless. The predator, sought in vain, had left no trail. He struck, and then was seen no more, until he struck again. Long had I cast about in vain. Now, in the vast darkness of failure and disappointment, I glimpsed a tiny light. The predator had erred. He had left a trace. I now knew where to begin.

"I seek them," I said.

"To join them, to partake of theft and arson."

"No," I said.

"Beware," he said. "You are but one man."

"There are others," I said.

"I do not know your accent," he said, suddenly.

"It is from faraway," I said. "Do not concern yourself."

"It is not of Cos," he said, "nor Tyros."

I myself could not distinguish between the accents of Cos and Tyros. I suspect few could.

"This is Nicosia, this village, is it not?" I asked.

"As you well know," he said.

"How should I know?" I asked.

"Were you not here before, with blades and fire?"

"No," I said.

Nicosia was a shoreline hamlet of south Chios, within the hegemony of Cos, as are Thera and Daphna.

"What resistance was offered to the raiders?" I asked.

"What could be done?" he asked.

"The bow," I said, "the great bow, the fletched long shafts. On the continent, there are thousands of villages, sovereign and proud, prosperous and free, too costly to attack, defended by flights of the birds of death."

"We once had the bow, long ago," he said. "But Cos outlawed them, for our own safety, so that we would have little to fear from them."

"So that you would be at the mercy of those with arms," I said.

"Supposedly none would have arms," he said.

"Only those who recognized the advantages and power of ignoring the law."

"We are denied arms for our own good," he said.

"For someone's good," I said, "scarcely for yours."

"I do not understand," he said.

"And Nicosia is looted and burned," I said, "with impunity."

"Cos is supposed to protect us," he said.

"And where was Cos?" I asked.

"Elsewhere," he said.

"Perhaps Cos will one day arrive, to weep with you over the ashes," I said.

"Perhaps we should have retained the means to defend ourselves," he said. "It is hard to know. One wishes, of course, to obey the law. One wishes to be good citizens, to do what is right, to preserve civic peace."

"Have you not considered the possibility that your most dangerous enemy may not be thieves and brigands, bandits and killers, but Cos itself, the state?"

"I do not understand," he said.

"Who will control the state?" I asked.

"What are you saying?" he asked, bewildered.

"The state has power," I said, "and the ambitious, covetous, and unscrupulous seek power. Thus they gravitate to the state. They seek the state. Every tyranny seeks to disarm those it rules, to better have them at its mercy. Nothing is more clear. They need only dissemble and lie, need only trick the populace. They need only convince the ruled that being helpless is desirable, that it is in their own best interest, that a desire to protect oneself is benighted and shameful, an evidence of civic distrust, of moral ignorance and iniquity, even that an inability to defend oneself is rightfulness and salvation. Lies gilded pass easily as golden truths."

"Such words would be denounced as treason," he said.

"Treason to tyranny is fidelity to freedom," I said.

He was silent.

"In any event," I said, "be things as they may, dark things have been done here. Nicosia is wounded, ravaged and burned."

"Thanks to you and your kind," he said.

"Where is your Home Stone?" I asked.

"So that is why you are here, mysteriously in the night," he said. "You and your sort have not done enough? You come for the Home Stone!"

He half sat up.

"Do not draw your knife," I said. "The codes, the codes."

He removed his hand, reluctantly, from the hilt of the knife.

He sat back.

"The Home Stone was taken," he said, "taken and destroyed."

"That is unlikely," I said.

"Even if it were not," he said, "I would not reveal its conceal-ment. I would die first. I will never betray the Home Stone."

"Keep it hidden," I said.

"You have not come to steal it, to destroy it, to wipe Nico-sia from the earth, to make her be as though she never was?" he asked.

"No," I said.

"The Home Stone is safe," he said.

"I trust so," I said. "Do not tell me its location. I do not wish to know."

"Nicosia will rise again," he said, "though from the ashes. She will once more be green, be strong and grow, and flower."

"Let her be, as well," I said, "defended and dangerous."

"Then you are not of them," he said, "not of the killers, the arsonists and looters?"

"No," I said.

"But you seek them," he said.

"Yes, but not to join them," I said.

"But you have business with them?"

"Yes," I said, "the business of blood."

"Then you are not alone?"

"No."

"They vanished," he said. "They were here, and then gone. You will never find them."

I had heard this sort of thing before, on Thera and Daphna.

Ships had struck, burned and looted, and then disappeared. Whence then the raiders? How can such things be? How can ships disappear?

"For the first time," I said, "they have left a trail."

"Ships leave no trail in water," he said.

"The trail has been left," I said.

"I do not understand," he said.

"You have given me the clue I have long sought," I said.

"What clue?"

"That of nine days and five days," I said.

He was silent, sitting in the darkness.

"Their identity is obscure," I said. "I would know it."

"They made their identity well known," he said, "in cries of war and shouts of victory."

I had heard, too, this sort of thing on Thera and Daphna. It was common in my investigations. Reports and allegations were rampant. Wherever news of the mysterious raids was broadcast, it was the same. The rumors of responsibility spread from village to village, from port to port, from island to island, spread like the wind, spread like raging flame through straw. As unpredictable and terrible as might be the raids, as anomalous as might be the vanishing of ships, as elusive as might be the raiders, one thing was sturdily, unmistakably clear, he against whom blame was levied.

"Their identity," said he, "is no secret."

"So I understand," I said.

"They roundly and repeatedly proclaimed the glory of their vile, fierce, merciless, scarlet-haired captain," he said.

"You saw him?" I said.

"From afar," he said. "But, even so, no doubt could adhere to the recognition."

"There were three ships?" I said. I had heard that, from the accounts.

"No," he said, "six ships, four larger and two smaller."

This was an unwelcome intelligence, indeed.

"And men," I said. "Far more than oarsmen, than of mariners." I had heard that, even in the reports of only three ships.

"Yes," he said.

"And the ships reputedly hail from afar?" I said.

"From distances the mind must strive to grasp," he said. "Even from east of far Cos and Tyros, from a shore so dreadful and far that even Thassa herself will go no further."

"A shore so appalling?" I asked.

"Yes," said he, "where lies a citadel of ruthless cunning, of envy, violence, wrath, murder, and greed, of arrant ambition, a lawless, bestial port, feared from Torvaldsland to Schendi, a port the scourge of turbulent Thassa, a den of thieves and cutthroats, a lair of pirates, near whose walls fish dare not swim, over which birds refuse to fly."

"You have been there?" I said.

"These things are well known," he said.

"What place is this, so far and terrible?" I asked.

"It is called Port Kar," he said.

"I have heard of it," I said.

"It is from there the raiders ultimately derive," he said, "they and their pitiless, monstrous captain, with hair so wild and red, like blood and fire, he whose name even strong men may hesitate to speak."

"What is his name?" I asked.

"Bosk," said he, "Bosk of Port Kar."

"He it is," I asked, "who is responsible for such unconscionable horror and terror?"

"Yes," he said.

"I am Bosk of Port Kar," I said.

CHAPTER TWO

What Occurred that Night,
on a Remote Beach on Chios

"Thurnock," I said, "this is Aktis, of the village of Nicosia."

"A Cosian," said Thurnock, not rising.

"No," I said, "of the village of Nicosia, here on Chios."

Others had risen to their feet.

"A Cosian," repeated Thurnock.

"This is not Cos," I said, "though the weight of the spears of Cos are felt here."

"Tal," said Aktis.

"As we feared," I said, "the *pomerium* of Nicosia was recently, illicitly, crossed."

"Those we seek, the intruders, have struck," said Thurnock.

"With blades, fire, and chains," I said.

"How is it then," asked Thurnock, "that this scrawny verr, clad in filthy rags, perhaps ill fed, is still here, not slain, not chained like a girl, not carried off for the benches or quarries?"

"I fled, large one," said Aktis.

"Why, small one?" asked Thurnock.

"At the time it seemed the thing to do," said Aktis.

Aktis was not a small man, but Thurnock was unusually large, a boulder of a man, with arms like oars.

"Aktis," I said, "those on their feet here, greeting you, honoring you, standing about the fires, are my men, my friends." I then introduced Aktis to several of the men about, including Clitus, master of the trident, and handsome Tab, gifted with the sword. Several others stood aside, in the darkness. In the presence of a stranger, in a lonely place, many Goreans will not step into the firelight.

"Aktis," I said, "as is Thurnock, is of the peasants, the most fundamental of all castes, the ox on which the Home Stone rests."

"He is too small to be of the great caste," said Thurnock. "His voice may have changed, but I doubt he can yet grow a true beard."

"At least," said Aktis, "I do not have a large tooth, misshapen, which hangs over my lip, like a fang."

"It is a sign of force and power," said Thurnock. "Many a larl might envy it."

"Doubtless it appeals to women," said Aktis.

"They learn to kiss and lick it quickly enough," said Thurnock.

"I trust you will be friends," I said.

"I am not the stranger here," said Aktis.

"I beached the *Dorna* and *Tesephone* upwind," said Thurnock, with a look at Aktis, suggesting this decision might have been judiciously motivated.

"That was wise," I said. "The smell of smoke lingers long in the memory of ashes, as does as that of devastation and harm in the memory of men."

"He is a spy," said Thurnock.

"If so," I said, "congratulate him on his courage, for he, in our midst, is now in mortal danger."

"I am not a spy," said Aktis.

"Perhaps you are merely too clever to admit it," said Thurnock.

"It is clear you will become great friends," I said.

"How many intruders did you personally slay?" asked Thurnock.

"None," said Aktis. "How many did you slay?"

"And how many," asked Thurnock, "did the braver folks, the true men, of your village dispatch to the Cities of Dust?"

"None that I know of," said Aktis.

"There were no bows in the village," I said. "They were forbidden by Cos, lest they be misused, lest the population be endangered."

"And the village was sacked and burned, the inhabitants slain or carried off," said Thurnock.

"They came unexpectedly, swiftly, with violence, chains, and fire, and swept all before them," said Aktis.

"Perhaps," I said to Thurnock, "you could teach the bow to Aktis."

"He could not even draw the bow," said Thurnock.

"I am strong," said Aktis.

"The intruders knew the village lacked the bow?" asked Clitus.

"One supposes so," I said.

"We would not have known that," said Clitus.

"No," I said.

"But some of Cos would know," said Tab.

"That point," I said, "has not escaped me."

"What state would be so mad as to deny the means of self-defense to its citizenry?" asked Clitus.

"Any state which fears an informed, armed citizenry," I said, "any state which wishes to own, manipulate, and exploit its citizenry with impunity."

"Public reasons often conceal private plans," said Tab.

"I cannot believe such things," said Clitus.

"I know a place," I said, "where it has taken place, again and again. The citizens suspect nothing, and later, when they do, it is too late."

"As I understand this," said Aktis, "you are Bosk of Port Kar, and your fellows are of Port Kar, as well."

"Yes," I said.

"And you have come to find, and deal with, impostors who burn, loot, slay, and seize in your name?"

"Yes," I said.

"Why should they do so?" asked Aktis.

"I do not know," I said.

"To conceal their own identity, to mask themselves beneath a plausible, fearful reputation, to precipitate an escalation in the war between Port Kar and the island ubarates, Cos and Tyros?"

"Perhaps," I said.

"If you are truly the dreaded Bosk of Port Kar," said Aktis, "why do you object to intrusions and raids which cause you no harm and can do little but enhance your own reputation as a pillager and menace?"

"Perhaps because I am pleased to do so," I said. "Perhaps because I disapprove of deceit. Perhaps because I will not have others choose how my name will be heard."

"You are in danger here," said Aktis.

"Possibly," I said.

"Yet you have come."

"Yes."

"And these men, your fellows?" asked Aktis.

"Each a volunteer, a friend, not sought, not pressed."

"You are in unfriendly waters," said Aktis.

"If I contact your intruders," I said, "it is they who will find themselves in unfriendly waters."

"I do not think you are truly Bosk of Port Kar," said Aktis.

"How so?" I asked.

"Your hair," he said. "Bosk of Port Kar has red hair, like flame and blood. I saw him at Nicosia."

"Perhaps you should introduce me to him," I said. "I would much like to meet myself. Few people, I am told, meet themselves. It is hard to meet oneself. One is often, it seems, a stranger to oneself."

"Do not mock me," he said.

"The impostor dyed his hair, or wore a wig," I said. "Most likely a wig."

Thus, I supposed, he could most easily don, and remove, a disguise, an identity.

"Your hair is dark," he said, "brown or black. It is hard to tell in the light."

"It is a dark brown, surely bordering on black," I said. "I have often dyed it so, when it seemed judicious. In this way one minimizes the likelihood of recognition or discovery. Too, to be frank, so simple an artifice also tends to reduce unpleasant observations, insults, jokes, altercations, and such, sometimes seeming to require attention, with or without the sword."

Indeed, even from my boyhood in far Bristol, I had occasionally felt it incumbent upon me to make clear, with split lips, bloody noses, and such, my disapproval of such disparagement.

In any event, I was not to be held accountable for my hair. I had not chosen it in some vestibule on the brink of existence. Such things are managed, for well or ill, by the hereditary coils. It came with my skin, teeth, bones, blood, and brain. If I could stand it, others might do the same, or, upon occasion, accept the consequences.

"As I understand this," said Tab to Aktis, "you survived the attack on Nicosia."

"Yes," said Aktis.

"You assessed the enemy?" said Tab.

"I was there," said Aktis.

"State his strength, his resources," said Tab.

"Six ships, four larger and two smaller," said Aktis. "And many men, men far beyond oarsmen and mariners, perhaps six hundred."

"And there may be more," said Clitus.

"True," said Aktis.

"Raids have taken place," said Tab.

"Several," I said.

"And may again," said Tab.

"I fear so," I said.

"Cos patrols the shark roads," said Tab.

More than once we had lowered our masts and sails, and our low ships, painted green, the pirate color, difficult to detect in the waves of Thassa, had lain almost flat in the water.

"How can such forces indefinitely, at least six burdened ships, coming and going, venturing out and returning, time and time again, elude patrol ships, sightings?" asked Tab.

"One may speculate," I said.

"Ships require berthing, maintenance," said Tab. "Men require stores, water, supplies, tenting, housing."

"How then, with what ease," I asked, "can ships and men vanish?"

"Precisely," said Tab.

"Perhaps the Priest-Kings, with their mysterious and mighty powers, have some hand in this," said Clitus.

"That seems unlikely," I said.

"Thank the Priest-Kings," said Aktis, "that you have not encountered the intruders. Indeed, hire Initiates to petition the Priest-Kings that you do not do so."

"But we have come from afar," I said, "precisely to do so."

"You are outweighed, outnumbered," said Aktis, "in both ships and men."

"We are not vulnerable, unarmed villagers," said Clitus.

"You are far overmatched," said Aktis. "Do not seek the intruders. Do not meet them. You would be destroyed."

"Perhaps we need only locate them," I said, "and then let the justice and vengeance of Cos, armed with fleets, inimical to piracy, sweep them from the sea."

"Cos is at war with Port Kar," said Aktis.

"But not with Kenneth Statercounter, Merchant of neutral Brundisium, concerned for the safety of trade routes," I said.

"You would enlist Cos?" he asked.

"Why not, if practical?" I asked. "What robust polity tolerates piracy?"

"Cos, perhaps," said seated Thurnock.

"The weight of the enemy, his formidable nature, was not made clear to us in Port Kar," said Tab.

"We may have been misinformed, deliberately," said Clitus.

"Let us not carry suspicion to the point of madness," I said.

"It is possible," said Clitus.

"Many things are possible," I said.

News on Gor was often delayed, incomplete, haphazard, distorted, or spurious, even altogether unavailable. How might one separate idle rumor from sober truth; how might one tell fact from fable, fear, and fancy? This had much to do with the technology laws of the Priest-Kings, who, it seemed, recognized the danger, both to themselves and other forms of life, of sharing a planet with human beings, belligerent and short-tempered, curious, greedy, selfish, skilled in waste, exploitation, thoughtlessness, pollution, and war. Did the Priest-Kings not regard us as an interesting, but simple, primitive, short-sighted species? Who knows what might come of putting matches, bombs, and dynamite in nurseries, and madhouses?

"Go home, while you can," said Aktis.

"Shall we go home, lads?" I asked.

"We have scarcely arrived," said Tab.

"Clitus," I said, "if you will, see to the feeding and clothing of our guest, Aktis, he of the village of Nicosia."

"I want nothing from those of Port Kar," said Aktis. "I will have nothing from those of Port Kar. I will have nothing to do with those of Port Kar."

"Then you are not with us?" I said.

"No," he said.

"Tell me, Aktis," I said. "Do you not want Nicosia avenged?"

"I would give my life for that," he said.

"Then," I said, "you are with us."

He regarded us, evenly, his eyes moving from face to face, in the darkness, on the beach, about the fires, two vessels nearby, in the background, only shapes in the night, a larger and a smaller, drawn up on the sand.

"I am with you," he said.

"I will teach you the bow," said Thurnock, rising, and clasping his hand.

CHAPTER THREE

We Set Course for Thera; I Speak with Aktis; We Encounter a Surprise at Sea

I stood on the stern castle of the *Dorna*, Builder's Glass in hand, above the twin rudders, the small, swift *Tesephone*, shallow-drafted, capable of negotiating rivers, abeam.

I took us now to be far enough from shore that a change in course could not be detected.

I returned the Builder's Glass to its sheath at my belt.

"Course," I called to Thurnock.

The large peasant ascended the steps of the stern castle.

"Whither," he inquired.

"Thera," I said. "To the Cove of Harpalos."

This instruction was called down to the helmsmen.

From the Cove of Harpalos on Thera, I might take the *Tesephone* to the harbor of Sybaris. The *Dorna*, even disguised, even temporarily divested of its ram and shearing blades, still appeared too much a ship of war, which, indeed, it was, a knife ship. Few would take her as a "round ship," a cargo vessel, with its somewhat broader beam, higher gunwales, and capacity for freight. Too, I feared the *Dorna*, even disguised, might be recognized. It was not unknown on Thassa, particularly in the contested waters between Port Kar and the major marine ubarates, Cos and Tyros. It was my pretense that the *Dorna*, now referred to as the *Korinna* on the Cove of Harpalos papers, was a knife ship converted to freight duty, a pretense now accepted by the Cove authorities, due I suspect, first, to a judicious distribution of gold amongst them and, two, due to the fact that Therans, as well as those of Chios and Daphna, commonly failed to hold the insolent, exploitative, hegemonic tyranny of Cos in warm regard. To be sure, the influence of Cos was far more pervasive and powerful in the larger towns and ports, such as Sybaris on Thera, Mytilene on Chios, and Pylos and Naxos on Daphna. Indeed, in such towns, high administrative, military, and naval offices were largely staffed by Cosians. The theory seemed to be that cities command the country and, thus, those who command the cities command the country. The *Tesephone* was small, light, and clean-lined. It was like a whisper on the water. It was inconspicuous, helm-responsive, and swift. Few vessels on Thassa, I thought, could match its speed, or close with it at close quarters. Indeed, in its capacity to outrun and elude patrol ships, it was the sort of vessel which is often favored by clandestine traders, or, say, to speak more frankly, smugglers.

"After the Cove of Harpalos?" asked Thurnock.

"To Sybaris," I said.

"By means of the *Tesephone*?"

"Yes," I said.

"I thought so," said Thurnock.

It was there, in Sybaris, that I, in the guise of Kenneth Stater-counter, Merchant of Brundisium, in the tavern oddly named *The Living Island*, had heard the statement that Nicosia had been destroyed, several days before its actual destruction. This anomalous claim was the only clue, if it were a clue, I had so far managed to find as to the nature and whereabouts of the mysterious raiders perpetrating slaughter and rapine in my name. Who could allege, or know of, or confidently state, the destruction of a village or town prior to the event, unless one were somehow privy to the intentions of raiders contemplating such an attack?

"How is Aktis doing?" I asked Thurnock.

"He draws a good oar," said Thurnock.

"Relieve him, and send him to me," I said.

Thurnock then descended the stairs to the helm deck.

Once we were another Ahn from the coast of Chios, in the open sea, I would have the mast raised, with its long yard, and let the fore-and-aft rigged sail, the swelling, triangular sail, a lateen sail, now the fair-weather sail, take the wind. I thought this a politic delay, as shipping tends to be heavier in the vicinity of a coast, and a high-masted sail, swollen with wind, is easily detected from a stem castle, even by eye, at more than five pasangs.

"Captain?" asked Aktis.

"How go your studies with the bow?" I asked.

Thurnock had arranged a target on deck, of layered leather, backed with wood.

"It is a fearful, terrible weapon," said Aktis.

"It is supposed to be," I said.

"I love it," he said.

"Now you see why Cos does not wish to put it in your hands," I said.

"Clearly," he said.

"Could you recognize, again," I asked, "the small goods, trinkets and such, which you received in trade from the confederate of the raiders, the spy and scout of the intruders, he a merchant or in the guise of a merchant, and which were soon stolen back by the raiders?"

"Some, I suppose," he said. "I could doubtless more easily recognize larger items, of greater value."

"Larger items of greater value," I said, "gold plate and silver vessels, if you had them, and women, and such, would not be disposed of locally. I doubt even that they would be sold on Cos or Tyros. The risk would be too great. But smaller items, say, a ring or buckle, regarded as negligible or paltry, might very well have been kept by, or distributed amongst, the raiders."

"Its possessor, then," said Aktis, "might be a raider."

"Or one known to a raider," I said. "Even finding such an object in a market might be important. From whom did the seller obtain the item?"

"I see," he said.

"Perhaps you could recognize a raider," I suggested.

"I do not think so," he said. "The rush, the flight, the distance. Much happened quickly."

"They were helmeted?" I asked.

"Yes," he said.

I had expected that.

The common Gorean helmet, with its narrow Y-shaped opening, conceals much of the face.

"Save for the one proclaiming himself to be Bosk of Port Kar," he said.

"Do you think you could recognize him again?" I asked.

"Not without the hair, or wig," he said. "In a sense, I saw little more."

"Perhaps," I said, "one does not stop to peruse intently the features of those from whom one runs for one's life."

"I fear not," he said, wryly.

I did not think the raiders would be common brigands. I suspected, from the number of ships involved, that they were not only numerous, but well equipped, well organized, and well led. Perhaps, even, they might be mercenaries, professional soldiers.

"There were no uniforms," I said, "no flags, no pennons, no banners, no identificatory marks on helmets or shields?"

Surely the raiders would seek anonymity.

"On the contrary," he said, "banners were flourished and emblems and signs were boldly displayed, both on helmets and shields."

"Those of Port Kar, and of Bosk of Port Kar," I said.

"Yes," he said.

"Of course," I said.

How better could one achieve anonymity than under a false identity?

How better could one loot and slaughter with impunity than under the name of another?

"I fear I will be of little help in these matters," he said.

"One does not know," I said. "Perhaps you will be of great help."

"I should return to the oar," he said. "Thurnock has promised me an arrow for each extra shift I row, to the filling of a quiver."

"I shall speak to Thurnock," I said. "I do not wish you to die at the oar."

"I do not wish to receive goods for which I have not labored," he said, "goods which I have not earned."

This view was typically Gorean.

On Gor existence was seldom seen as an entitlement to security, success, and good fortune.

The Peasants, in its way, might be the humblest of castes, but, in another way, it was amongst the proudest of castes.

"Even so," I said, "I shall speak to Thurnock. I would have your quiver soon filled."

"One does not know what one will meet at sea," said Aktis.

"Or on land," I said.

"I would return to the bench, if I may," he said. "I am reluctant to have another draw the oar in my place."

"Have you ever been in Sybaris?" I asked.

"No," he said. "In all my life, I have never been more than a few pasangs from Nicosia."

I nodded. This was not unusual for many Goreans. It was not simply a matter of Home Stones. Travel could be arduous and dangerous. Nicosia, being on Chios and Sybaris on Thera, it was like Sybaris was a world away from Nicosia.

"Last year," he said, "the Fair of the Farther Islands was held in Sybaris."

This was the first I had heard of such a fair.

"Sybaris has rich fields inland," I said, "and a fine, busy harbor. In Sybaris there is much luxury and wealth, broad, prosperous streets, many of which are lit at night, colorful bazaars and variegated, well-stocked markets, ample inns, and hundreds of shops, restaurants, and taverns. The city is brighter and more alive at night than in the day. Even at the First Ahn, taverns thrive, and, on the streets, crowds bustle about, and gamblers gather on corners, breathlessly attentive to the rattle of cast stones, while flautists play and silken slaves dance on their leashes, coin pans at hand."

"And when do they sleep?" asked Aktis.

"Some at night," I said, "and some when the lamps need not be lit."

"It is a busy place," said Aktis.

"One crowd during the day, another at night," I said.

"How odd that seems," he said.

"You will find it far different from Nicosia," I said. "You will tremble with amazement, your blood will race, your eyes will be filled with wonders."

"There are women there?" asked Aktis.

"Yes," I said, "free women, some of whom decline veiling."

"They are so brazen, so shameless?" asked Aktis.

"Surely the maidens of Nicosia did not go about veiled," I said.

"It was a village," he said. "Everyone knew everyone. And there was much work to do, by both men and women."

"Put aside thoughts of free women, greedy, troublesome creatures," I said. "There are slaves, as well, some eager to please lest they be lashed, others, whose slave fires have been kindled, they then the helpless victims of their needs, begging to please, even for the slightest caress."

"I am not to think of free women?" asked Aktis.

"No," I said. "It is not worth the bother of pursuing them, except to get them stripped and in chains, that they may be redeemed and learn their womanhood. Think rather of slaves."

"Are there many slaves in Sybaris?" he asked.

"It is a rich city," I said.

"There were no slaves in Nicosia," he said.

"So much the worse for Nicosia," I said.

"Free women are exalted and priceless," said Aktis.

"Precisely," I said. "That is why they are such a bother. A free woman is priceless because she has no price, and without a price she is worthless. A woman has no value until she is a slave and her value then is what the free will pay for her. It is only then a woman learns what she is truly worth, when she is taken off the block, when she is sold. Until then let each think she would bring a thousand gold pieces."

"We are days from Sybaris," said Aktis.

"Yes," I said.

"I shall look forward to Sybaris," said Aktis, "and I shall hope I may prove to be of service to you there."

"I shall hope so," I said.

"May I, Captain," said Aktis, "return now to the bench?"

"Do so," I said.

"Ho!" cried Clitus, from the stem castle, where he stood lookout. "Land, land to port!"

"Thurnock!" I called down to the benches. "Rest oars!"

"What land is here?" I asked Aktis, who was partly down the steps to the deck.

"I have heard of none here, Captain," he said.

I hurried past him, down the steps, and, in my passage to the stem castle, was joined by Thurnock, who seemed as puzzled as I. In a moment we had climbed to the deck of the stem castle, and, shielding our eyes, looked across the bright, gentle water, in the direction Clitus indicated.

The *Dorna* rocked softly.

One could hear the water lapping against the hull.

Overhead a broad-winged sea kite wheeled in the sky.

"There can be no land here," said Thurnock.

"None is indicated on the charts," I said.

"It is tiny, not noted," said Clitus. "It was overlooked."

"This was essentially our course to Chios," said Thurnock, "our previous course retraced. Where was it when we came from Thera?"

"It is small," said Clitus. "Obviously it was unnoticed."

"How could that be?" asked Thurnock.

"It is small," said Clitus, "flat without mountains, easily missed."

"That could easily be," I said. "It seems no more than a skerry, a gray prominence. Consider the color, suggesting a volcanic origin."

"It is barren," said Thurnock.

"It seems so," I said. "There is some clutter, some brush, debris, dried sea weed, driftwood, such things."

"We may have missed it in poor light, even passed it at dusk, before beaching," said Clitus.

"Perhaps it was not here before," I said. "If it is volcanic, it might have recently risen from the sea."

I removed the Builder's Glass from its sheath at my belt, slid open its sections, and adjusted the focus.

"It is hard to assess its dimensions," I said, "but it is small, ovoid in shape, perhaps with a long axis of eighty paces, a short axis of forty paces."

"It is from a subsea volcano, erupted, magma coming to the surface, cooling and solidifying," said Clitus.

"But there is no open center, no lagoon," I said.

"It seems to tremble," said Thurnock.

"It is an illusion," said Clitus. "It is as on the Tahari, where air shimmers, rising from a heated surface."

"The air is cool," said Thurnock.

"Here," said Clitus, "but perhaps not there. The surface may still be hot."

"I do not think so," I said, adjusting again the focus of the Glass. "Our tiny islet is inhabited."

"Visitors, fishermen?" asked Clitus.

"I suppose so," I said. "They have seen us, unfortunately. I would have preferred that not to be the case. They are launching small skiffs away. They are fleeing the islet."

"Why should they flee?" asked Thurnock.

"Perhaps they do not recognize the ship," I said. "Perhaps they have had unpleasant dealings, unwelcome interactions, with others. In any event, they are not eager to make our acquaintance, and, clearly, they are in no need of succor, rescue, water, supplies, or such."

"How many are there?" asked Thurnock.

"Perhaps a hundred," I said, "now emerged from the cover of the driftwood, debris, and such."

I could see some twenty to twenty-five small craft departing from the islet.

"What would a hundred men be doing in such a barren and desolate place?" asked Thurnock.

"A hundred individuals," I said. "They are not all men. There are women and children, as well."

"Families?" asked Clitus.

"It may be," I said. "I do not know."

"How could they live there?" asked Thurnock.

"Doubtless they do not live there," I said. "Presumably they paused there, temporarily, on their way to some further destination, say, Pylos or Naxos, even Sybaris."

"Somehow I do not think so," said Thurnock.

"Nor do I," I said, "but I do not know why."

CHAPTER FOUR

What Was Encountered Later; Three Women; I Decide Against Performing an Act of Mercy

"These should now be frequented waters," said Thurnock, standing beside Clitus and myself on the stem deck.

We were now two days beyond the small, dark, uncharted, mysterious island whose unexpected presence had so surprised us.

"Yet we have seen no shipping," said Clitus.

"Perhaps," I said, "the depredations of Bosk of Port Kar are feared."

"I should like to have the false Bosk of Port Kar within range of my bow," said Thurnock.

"I should like to fish for him with my net and trident," said Clitus.

"How proceeds Aktis in his lessons?" I asked Thurnock.

"Excellently, as would be expected," said Thurnock, "since he is of the Peasants."

"Even though of Chios?" I asked.

"It is true that he is ignorant and stubborn," said Thurnock. "He is reluctant to overcome his primitive antecedents. He thinks a shabby village on Chios is worthy of a Home Stone, not merely that it has one, but that it is worthy to have one. Too, I struggle to correct his speech."

"It is Cosian," I said.

"He claims it is different," said Thurnock.

"He is probably right," I said. I thought it judicious to defer to the view of a native speaker on such matters. "But his lessons proceed well?"

"Brilliantly," said Thurnock.

"I suspect," I said, "that such things are possible only with a great teacher."

"I suppose it is only just to acknowledge that," said Thurnock.

"To be sure," I said, "the greatest of teachers cannot supply the strength to draw the great bow, the eye to mark the distant target, the mind, which instantly, without thought, processes the subtleties of distance, the moisture of air, the stir of wind."

"The student must contribute something," said Thurnock.

"I have heard it said so," I said.

"The *Tesephone* signals," said Thurnock.

"I hear it," I said.

Our mast and that of the *Tesephone* were raised. We were astern of her, and she was to port.

The sound of the drum carried across the water.

On the stem deck of the *Dorna*, surmounting the stem castle, we counted the beats. Commonly the same drum used by the *keleustes* to adjust and regularize rowing serves for signaling. There are many differences in how this is done, given the desiderata of clarity, speed, secrecy, and such. Most commonly, cyphers are involved, as opposed to signals for words or commands, such as 'enemy sighted', 'prepare for battle', 'convene', 'withdraw', 'return to port', and such. The cyphers, substitution cyphers naturally, are correlated, in one way or another, with letters in the Gorean alphabet, a long beat followed by two short beats, say, standing for a given letter, and so on. In some signaling, visual, utilizing flags, pennons, lanterns, torches, or such, and auditory, utilizing a drum, trumpet, or such, a different arrangement is used, which is generally thought to be easier to read, particularly by unsophisticated readers. The alphabet is divided into a limited number of groups, and each group contains its letters in sequence. Let us suppose that we take the twenty-five most common letters in the Gorean alphabet and divide them into five group of five letters each. Then, for example, sounding two beats or lifting the torch twice would indicate the second group. Then, say, there are four beats or the torch is lifted four times. That would correspond to the fourth letter in the second group, and so on. If one wishes to take the message out of the clear, then it is a simple matter to mix the groups and letters about. The particular groupings may be changed daily. Naturally both parties, the sending and the receiving party, have the same cypher schedules. Given appropriate visual conditions, the sender may elect to indicate group by utilizing one hand, usually the right hand, and the letter within the group by utilizing the other hand, usually the left hand.

"Debris has been sighted," said Clitus. "There may be survivors."

"These are dangerous waters," said Thurnock.

"Have the *Tesephone* heave to," I said. "Request bearings to the sighting."

Thurnock called these instructions back to our *keleustes*, whose post was close to the foot of the steps leading down from the stern deck, his drum on its stand between the two helmsmen.

Shortly thereafter, with the Builder's glass, I could make out what had occasioned the communication from the *Tesephone*.

We then proceeded further on the bearings provided by the *Tesephone*, which now fell astern.

"I can make it out," said Clitus. "Wreckage, listing, hull damaged, seared by fire, gouged planks, something alive, clinging to the stump of the mast."

"Three individuals," I said, lowering the glass, "slight figures, half veiled, in soiled robes."

"Free women?" asked Clitus.

"Seemingly so," I said.

"It seems that Bosk of Port Kar has struck again," said Thurnock.

"It would seem so," I said.

Surely we had heard in Sybaris, and elsewhere, that the sea lanes between the maritime ubarates, Cos and Tyros, and the Farther Islands, were being terrorized by the supposed Bosk of Port Kar. Yet, interestingly, the navies, and patrols, of both Cos and Tyros had failed to make contact with the six or more ships of the supposed Bosk of Port Kar. How could six or more ships, in essence a small fleet, continue to elude discovery? It seemed indeed, as though they vanished, only to reappear again, unexpectedly, with ravaging and carnage.

At this point, a narrow object, with a shrill whistle, its trail laced with smoke, ascended high into the air from the midst of the planks and timbers.

"The survivors have sighted us," said Thurnock.

"They try to attract our attention," said Clitus.

"They have done so," said Thurnock.

We watched the object, trailing red and yellow smoke, from ignited powders, reach its zenith, and then it seemed to slow and pause, and then, still trailing smoke, and whistling, fell into the sea.

Such an object is fired from a bow. The arrow, or quarrel, as the case may be, is designed to whistle and smoke. They are used as, in a sense, flares. They are not unknown in Gorean waters. I had encountered something very similar at the World's End. Pani warriors sometimes used whistling, smoke arrows to initiate and coordinate attacks. Occasionally a colored ribbon was affixed to the arrow to make it even easier to mark its passage.

"They mark their position," said Thurnock.

"And ours," I said.

"We must take on the survivors," said Clitus.

"Do you think so?" I asked.

"Surely," said Clitus. "They are without succor. They are stranded, lost at sea, helpless, only women, three women, free women, perhaps even of high caste. They will die of thirst or hunger. Thassa becomes restless. Timbers may part. They could be washed from their refuge. The fragment of their vessel lists, it takes on water, it sinks."

"Interestingly," I said, "it has not sunk yet."

"Creatures of the sea encircle them," said Thurnock. "We cannot let them die, drown, or be eaten. Would you have them devoured? Honor inveighs against it. Codes do not permit it. We must take them aboard."

"Signal the helmsmen to approach," I said. "Then rest oars."

Slowly we drifted toward the wreckage.

"Where are the men?" asked Thurnock.

"See the marks of fire, the ax-stroked timbers," said Clitus. "There was fighting. The men were slain, or taken to be galley slaves."

"There must be at least one man," said Thurnock. "What woman could fire an arrow to such a monstrous height?"

"There is scarcely room for the three crowded women," said Clitus.

"It requires only a cocked crossbow," I said. "A child could ignite the signal powder and discharge such a weapon."

"Yes," said Thurnock, satisfied. Then he added, "I do not care for crossbows."

"It is an ideal assassin's weapon," I said. "It is patient. It can wait, and then strike when it wishes."

"I still do not like it," said Thurnock.

"I know one who is a master of such a bow," I said.

"Its rate of fire is far inferior to that of the true bow, the great bow," said Thurnock.

"He of whom I think," I said, "would not expect to fire more than once."

I recalled a grayish cast of features, and eyes like glass.

We were now within a few yards of the scarred, smoke-stained timbers, these awash amongst the waves.

"Mariners, noble mariners," cried one of the women, extending her hand piteously, "succor, succor!"

"Glory to the Priest-Kings that you have seen us!" cried another.

"We are helpless!" cried the third. "We have no food and water. Footing is dangerous. Our vessel sinks!"

"We are saved!" said the second, a wild, relieved, gladness in her voice.

"I fear!" wept the first.

"Do not tremble," called Thurnock. "You are safe, all safe. We will have you aboard in a moment."

"Draw the port oars inboard," said Clitus.

"Do not," I said.

"Captain?" asked Clitus.

"Noble ladies," I called to the three women. "It is fortunate that your vessel remains afloat."

"Take us aboard, noble Master," urged the first.

"Recount your travail," I suggested.

"We are not slaves," said the second. "We are free. Take us aboard, we beg you, soon, and without demur."

"How is it we find you in such sore straits?" I inquired.

"Our poor vessel, the *Doris*," said the first, "was beset by pirates, two days ago, by the dreaded corsair, the merciless Bosk of Port Kar, rogue of Thassa!"

"The crew was slaughtered," said the second. "We three alone escaped, unnoted in the fighting, hiding below. Take us aboard!"

"I shall take the matter under consideration," I said.

"Captain?" asked Thurnock, puzzled.

"Rescue us," called the second. "We are not slaves, we are free women, noble free women, of good caste, of Naxos. We are helpless, and desperate! You cannot leave us here! We will drown or thirst to death! There are dangers in the water. Creatures stir. Take your oars inboard, that, assisted, we may clamber aboard."

"Prepare to back oars," I said.

"Surely not, Captain," said Clitus.

"Hold, noble Masters," called the first woman. "We have wine with us!"

"Ta wine?" I asked, "from the terraces of Cos?"

"No," she said. "Falarian."

Clitus whistled in astonishment.

"It was our secret cargo," said the first woman. "Save us. We offer it in exchange for our lives."

"Two bottles," said the second.

"Excellent," I said.

Falarian was a wine some thought to be a matter of mere legend. It was rumored, amongst certain collectors, that it actually existed. Its cost, it was claimed by some, might purchase a city.

"Keep your wine, your liquid treasure, noble ladies," said Thurnock. "We are not the sort to require payment for a deed incumbent even on the honor of a sleen."

"It was fortunate it was not discovered by Bosk of Port Kar," I said.

"We hid it," said the first woman.

"One would expect so practiced a pirate as Bosk of Port Kar to be less careless, more meticulous, more thorough," I said.

"Take us aboard!" said the woman.

"The Falarian is yours," said the second woman. "Enjoy it, share it amongst your crew."

"Fetch a cord, and basket," I said to Clitus.

"Then bring us aboard, generous, noble masters," said the second.

Very shortly thereafter, by means of the cord and basket, we had drawn the two bottles aboard.

"Back oars," I said. "Pull away. Resume course."

"Captain?" said Clitus.

"No!" said Thurnock.

"Do not leave us!" cried the first woman.

"Stay, stay!" cried the second, her ankles awash. "Take us aboard. Save us!"

"What are you doing?" said Thurnock.

"Attempting to stay alive," I said.

"Come back, come back!" cried the first woman.

"Stay, stay!" cried the second. "Stay, merciful masters!"

"Beasts, heartless beasts!" wept the third, her voice now drifting from behind us. "Bosk of Port Kar himself could not be so cruel!"

"You cannot abandon these poor women!" said Thurnock.

"They are not in jeopardy," I said. "It is we who are in jeopardy."

"I do not understand," said Clitus.

"Even now," I said, "the net is closing about us."

CHAPTER FIVE

We have Eluded Pursuit; Two Bottles of Wine; Much Remains Unexplained; The Cove of Harpalos is Sighted

"Would we had had our ram and shearing blades mounted," said Thurnock.

"That would bespeak our identity," I said. "It would compromise our guise as a merchant ship."

"I do not care to flee from enemies, as though we were frightened vulos," said Thurnock.

"A time may come when we will mount the ram and blades," I said. "That time is not now."

"We slipped between the two nearest pursuers," said Clitus.

"We had time," I said.

"Before the circle could draw tight about the decoy vessel," said Thurnock.

"How did you know it was a trap?" asked Clitus.

"I did not know," I said, "but indications were plentiful. It was alleged the attack had occurred two days ago. But it is not likely that a vessel in its seeming condition could have remained afloat for more than an Ahn. The ax strokes in the gunwales were not fresh; the burned spots were wrong; a ship fire burns in sheets, not splotches; I conjecture a lighted torch had been held to the hull here and there, and briefly, for the resin and tar between the planks had not run. Too, if you looked closely, you would have noted a submerged towing ring just below the water line at the supposedly damaged prow. I suspect that our supposedly pathetic derelict has been placed athwart the course of more than one vessel."

"I fear we only looked upon the distraught women with compassion," said Clitus.

"Would that not have been suspicious in itself," I asked, "three women, to be pitied, so distracting, and not one man?"

"Why would a pirate not have seized them for slaves?" asked Thurnock.

"Precisely," I said.

"They claimed to have hidden," said Clitus.

"Such a vessel is not a holding, not a city," I said. "They would have been shortly dragged forth by the hair, to be stripped and chained."

"I think," said Clitus, "we should perhaps not imbibe the Falarian."

"It is not clear that Falarian even exists," I said. "It may be a matter of myth."

"Well then," said Clitus, "perhaps we should not imbibe whatever wine it was."

"It seemed a cheap Ta wine," I said, "and, judging by a dipped finger, one oversweetened."

"To conceal the presence of some foreign ingredient," said Thurnock.

"I suspect so," I said. "I did not deem it judicious to subject it to further testing."

"Poison," said Thurnock.

"Doubtless," I said.

"Had we roundly shared the bottles with the crews, one bottle with us, the other with the folks of the *Tesephone*—" whispered Clitus.

"—we would all have perished," said Thurnock.

"It was a supplemental plan," I said. "If the trap of the decoy ship went awry, and we were not apprehended at sea, perhaps heartlessly and dishonorably abandoning our needful, lamenting damsels and absconding with the liquid treasure, they need only wait a bit, follow us, and obtain two fine prizes, adrift and unmanned."

"The she-sleen," said Thurnock.

"They were minions," I said.

"But free minions, responsible minions," said Thurnock.

"I fear so," I said. "Perhaps we shall meet them again."

"I am uneasy," said Clitus. "What of the wine?"

"I considered breaking the bottles and casting them overboard last night," I said.

"But you did not do so?" said Clitus.

"No," I said.

"It is a dangerous, treacherous beverage," said Thurnock. "Get rid of it."

"The bottles are subtly and quaintly marked," I said, "doubtless to make them easily recognized by those aware of their contents."

"Get rid of them," said Thurnock.

"I think not," I said. "They may prove to be of use."

"How so?" asked Thurnock.

"What would you do, dear Thurnock," I asked, "if you saw a tiny serpent, one which could fit in the palm of your hand, with bright orange scales?"

"I would avoid it at all costs," said Thurnock.

"Why?" I asked.

"It is an ost, the most venomous serpent on Gor, the deadly ost," said Thurnock.

"Precisely," I said. "And that is why I am reluctant to destroy the bottles."

"I do not understand," said Thurnock.

"Let us not concern ourselves with the matter at present," I suggested.

"There is something I do not understand," said Clitus. "We slipped between the two nearest ships, but they did not immediately turn and pursue us, but waited for four more ships, and then the six ships, together, began the pursuit."

"I think that was wise," I said. "The *Dorna* has the lines of a knife ship. A judicious commander wishes to assure himself of victory, and that is best assured, where practical, by bringing an overwhelming force to bear."

"We outdistanced the pursuers easily," said Clitus.

"The *Dorna* and *Tesephone* are sleek and swift," I said. "I think few vessels on Thassa could match their speed. And the pursuers, if they wish to remain together, are no faster than their slowest ship."

"The six ships were undoubtedly the fleet of the false Bosk," said Thurnock.

"I think so," I said. "Aktis once spoke of six ships in the attack on Nicosia, four large ships, and two smaller. Four of our pursuers were fifty oared and two were thirty oared."

This had been determined by means of a Builder's Glass, from the ringed lookout post on the raised, socketed mast. In battle conditions the mast is lowered. This protects the mast, yard, rigging, and sail, and minimizes any possibly adverse effect the wind might have on maneuverability.

The rowing arrangements mentioned were common rowing arrangements, a single rowing deck, with twenty-five oars to a side or fifteen oars to a side. Commonly there would be two or three men to an oar. Usually a compromise was sought between speed and maneuverability. A ship with two or three rowing decks favored speed over maneuverability, but, in battle conditions, would be likely to find it difficult to turn and close with smaller ships, lighter and more responsive to their helms. A prairie sleen in the Barrens, for example, has little difficulty in avoiding the charge of the lumbering kailiauk. Larger ships are most comfortable and successful when doing battle with vessels in their own class. A single prairie sleen could bring down a kailiauk, but, given the size and danger of the kailiauk, the menace of its strength and horns, it will commonly attack one only in a pack. The *Dorna* was a fifty-oar ship, commonly using three men to an oar; the *Tesephone* was much smaller, a twenty-oar ship, using two men to an oar. It, light and shallow-drafted, could navigate and come about easily, even in most rivers.

"We have seen no sign of the pirate fleet in our wake since early morning," said Clitus.

"We are now in Theran waters," I said. "Traffic would be expected. I think our pursuers have chosen to vanish, as seems their wont."

"Six such ships must have a base, a port," said Thurnock. "How could so many ships be concealed? Surely they, purportedly ships of Bosk of Port Kar, must be hunted relentlessly by Cos, a power at sea, an inveterate foe of Port Kar."

"Do you, my friends, enjoy speculating on likelihoods?" I asked.

"Speak, Captain," said Clitus.

"What is the likelihood," I asked, "that in the wide and open waters of mighty Thassa one might encounter a tiny, listing fragment of a shattered vessel, with three passengers, free women, in desperate need of succor?"

"Little likelihood, indeed," said Clitus.

"Such things can occur," said Thurnock.

"But more interestingly," I said, "that one should encounter a towed bait ship, so designed, so equipped, on one's course?"

"Likelihood increases," said Thurnock.

"A coincidence, one supposes," said Clitus. "A trap is set, some-where between Chios and Thera, and one then waits to see if an unwary vessel bound from Chios to Thera, or from Thera to Chios, will happen by."

"That might never happen," I said. "Consider the expendi-tures of time and effort. A wise corsair would do better to range the waters more broadly."

"Unless," said Clitus, "the corsair was informed, if it knew the vessel, the time, and course."

"One could then lay such a trap profitably," said Thurnock.

"Precisely," I said.

"Even if our course had been somehow noted," said Clitus, "how could information be supplied to corsairs so quickly?"

"By flighted vulos," I said. "Pani lords, at the World's End, frequently communicate by such means."

"But the cots, the homes of the flighted vulos, are on land," said Thurnock.

"They need not be," I said. "All that would be required would be ships which share regular coordinates at the time of messag-ing."

"Perhaps even ships recognizable from a great height," said Clitus. "The homing circles of a flighted vulo can cover hundreds of pasangs."

"Perhaps," I said. "One does not know."

"But where could we have been seen at sea, and our course noted?" asked Clitus.

"We passed a small island, did we not?" I asked.

"Yes," said Clitus.

"It could still all be a coincidence," said Thurnock.

"That is true," I said.

At that point, our lookout, armed with a Builders Glass, from the small, ringed platform on the raised mast, called out "Land, land, ho!"

"The Cove of Harpalos," I said.

CHAPTER SIX

One Link in the Invisible Chain Becomes Visible

The drunken mariner reeled about, goblet in hand. "Fill my goblet!" he cried. "I will tell what I saw!"

"Not again!" moaned a man, nearby, at one of the low, square tables.

"We have heard it!" said another.

"Masters!" wailed the mariner.

"Be off," said a man.

"Go away," said another.

"Cast him out," called a man.

Two of the proprietor's men advanced toward the unsteady figure. I waved the proprietor's men back, and lifted my goblet to the mariner. He stood unsteadily and I had no assurance that he saw clearly. Perhaps he saw more than one of me, and perhaps more than that of the lifted goblet on which his eyes fought to focus.

"Let them cast him into the street," suggested Thurnock.

"He lacks a berth," I said.

"It is easy to see why," said Clitus.

"It is said he was once a captain, that he once had a ship," I said.

"Doubtful," said Clitus. "A copper-tarsk oarsman, at best."

"His name is Sakim," said Thurnock.

The mariner had now stumbled to the table, and I seized his right wrist, to hold it steady, and poured the residue of my goblet into his emptied goblet. "Thank you, Noble Master," he said. He then, head back, greedily downed the last bit of paga, with a single swallow.

"It was twenty paces abeam," he said. "Its head parted the water suddenly like a great rock rising from the sea. Its skin was black and slippery. Five men with arms outstretched could not have embraced its width. It had teeth like shearing blades!"

"Enough, enough," I said. "Your tale is well-known. Tell it another time."

I then pressed a tarsk-bit into his left hand.

"Thank you, Noble Master," he said, and, turning about, clutching the coin, staggered toward the paga vat, to the left of the entrance to the tavern, as one would enter.

"You are patient and merciful, Captain," said Thurnock.

"There are many ways to buy a drink," I said, "the selling of a song, the promise of an address, the waylaying of an enemy, the telling of a story."

"The last three nights we have heard the same story, and others, by others, even thrice told," said Clitus.

"Such stories abound," said Clitus, "particularly as the Ahn grows late and the blood begins to burn with paga."

"Where is the dancer?" I asked.

"The czehar player has not yet entered from the serving corridor," said Thurnock.

"You are out of paga, Captain," noted Clitus.

I lifted the drained goblet. "Paga! Paga!" I called. "Let us have another round," I suggested.

This seemed agreeable to Clitus and Thurnock as they drained their goblets.

"This is the fourth tavern in Sybaris we have visited," said Thurnock, "and we have as yet learned nothing. We hear little now of looted ships and raided villages, not even of wagerings as to when and where the dreaded Bosk of Port Kar will strike next."

"Given such information," I said, "I could enlist the aid of the authorities, even of Cos itself."

"The czehar player has appeared," said Thurnock. "He has now joined the kalika player, the flautists, and a drummer."

"It should be soon now," I said.

"Soon?" said Clitus.

"The dancer," I said.

We had returned to Sybaris, and, particularly, more than once, to this tavern, for it was here we had first learned of the supposedly consummated attack on Nicosia, several days prior to the actual attack.

"Master?" said a woman's voice.

I looked.

She was barefoot.

Her ankles were trim. Her calves were nicely curved. There was little mistaking the loveliness of her legs for she wore a brief Gorean slave tunic. Such tunics do little to conceal, and much to enhance, the beauty of a woman. In such a tunic a woman understands, and others understand, that she is being displayed as what she is, a purchasable object. Beneath the tunic I could see the sweet flare of her hips. She would have an exquisite, inviting love cradle. Her waist was narrow, and her breasts, while not large, were sweetly ample. She would take a belly rope, or belly leash, nicely. It could not be slipped. In Earth measurements, she was five foot three or four. Her neck was the sort which seems made for the collar. Her eyes were brown. Her hair was brown, too, a rich, dark brown. Presumably her master would not permit it to be cut. Long hair is often favored in a slave. There is much that can be done with it, in the furs and elsewhere. She can even be bound with it. Her features were delicate, fine, sensitive, and beautifully, vulnerably feminine. She was the sort of woman whom those women who hated men would despise, begrudging her her attractiveness, an attractiveness they themselves generally lacked. On her former world, I expected that men would have vied earnestly, and expensively, for her favor. On her new world, here, she was owned. Here, they might buy her from her Master. Perhaps some of the women who despised men would consider buying her for themselves, if only to keep her, a natural woman, fittingly the slave of men, from men. It is harrowing for such a slave to be owned by a free woman. They are often punished terribly for their attractiveness to men, an attractiveness often not possessed by their mistress. Slavers select with several criteria in mind, for example, high intelligence, vitality, attractiveness, which is not always the same as beauty, and, at least, latent passion. I admired the taste of the slavers who had acquired her. I wondered why she was not kneeling. If she did not know she was a slave now, I suspected it would soon become clear to her.

"Master?" she repeated.

Women differ considerably amongst themselves. Some women know they are a slave long before their first sight of a coiled rope or a length of chain, long before their slender wrists are pinioned helplessly behind them in slave bracelets, for the clasp of which in their heart they have long yearned.

It takes some women longer, to learn the collar, and themselves.

I looked up at her, and then down, to the table. Her eyes followed mine. The first two fingers of my right hand were bent, and pressed to the table. My thumb and third and fourth fingers were closed and behind the first two fingers.

Instantly she knelt.

Her attitude now was less assured.

Would she be beaten?

Or would her indiscretion be overlooked? But such things are seldom overlooked in the case of a slave.

"First obeisance position," I said.

She put her head to the floor, the palms of her hands down, beside her head. Her hair fell forward, dropping to the sides of her neck. I saw her smaller hair at the back of her neck.

"Why are you permitted to live?" I asked.

"That I may please the free," she said, "instantly, unquestioningly, and in all ways."

"Perhaps you are not pleased to serve?" I said.

"I do not wish to be whipped," she said.

That was understandable. The lesson of the Gorean slave whip is one not likely to be forgotten.

"Perhaps later," I said, "you will desire to serve, will hope to be pleasing, will strive with every bit of your lovely body to serve, will beg to be pleasing, will beg hopefully to be permitted to serve, will live to serve and please."

"As a slave," she said.

"Of course," I said.

She was silent.

"Perhaps you should be sold to a free woman," I said.

She shuddered, keeping her head to the floor. "Please, please, no, Master," she whispered.

This show of genuine emotion pleased me. The female slave is commonly a creature of deep feelings, a creature of profound emotionality.

This makes her vulnerable in a thousand ways.

I supposed she feared that I, displeased, might purchase her, and then sell her to a free woman.

"It seems you have had some interactions with a free woman or women," I said.

"Please do not sell me to one, Master," she said.

"Why not?" I asked.

"They hate us," she said, "for our collars, and tunics, for our not being displeasing to look upon, for our being the properties of men."

"You have not been in your collar long," I speculated.

"No," she said, "I have not been in my collar—long."

"You will grow accustomed to it," I said.

"Yes, Master," she said.

"It looks well on you," I said, "sturdy, attractive, and close-fitting."

"It is locked," she said.

"Of course," I said.

"I cannot remove it," she said.

"Slaves are not to slip in and out of collars as they please," I said.

"I am told I am an animal," she said.

"You are," I said, "you are a slave."

"Thus," she said, "as I am an animal, a collar is appropriate."

"Precisely," I said.

"Yes, Master," she said.

"What is your brand?" I asked.

"Animals are branded, are they not?" she said.

"Yes," I said. "And, pretty animal, what is your brand?"

"The Kef," she said, "the common kef."

"I am not surprised," I said.

"Perhaps she is lying," said Thurnock.

"We shall see," I said. "*Brand*!" I said, sharply.

Instantly, without thought, almost despite herself, as she had been conditioned, she turned to her right, and, half kneeling, half lying, drew up her tunic, exposing her left thigh to the hip.

"I see you need not be lashed," I said. "Resume your former position, hands beside your head, head to the floor."

She complied.

I noted she had failed to say, "Yes, Master."

The use of the expression 'Master' to a free man or 'Mistress' to a free woman is expected of a slave. It is appropriate. She is not free. It marks the chasm that separates her from the free. Its frequent use is recommended. It serves to deepen, confirm, and reinforce the slave's understanding of her status, of what she is. Later, as she thrills to being owned and mastered, and learns the rightfulness of this for her sex, its use is not only gratifying and reassuring, but relished. She now, at last, has a clear, unmistakable identity. She is now something real, at last. As a slave all is clear to her. She now knows how to move, act, and speak, how to be. No longer is she an ambiguity, an uncertainty, a vagueness; no longer is she a nothing. She is now a property, her master's property.

"Master called for paga, did he not?" she asked.

Obviously I had done so.

I continued to regard her.

How beautiful women look in collars.

How desirable they are, as helpless slaves.

Have not thousands of generations bred them to belong to us?

"Master?" she said.

There was no doubt she was beautiful.

On Earth, if she was of Earth, she would have been thought unusually beautiful. Here, on the other hand, on Gor, her beauty was nothing unusual, at least for a slave. I wondered if this dismayed or chagrined her, to be here, in her way, rather average, at least for a slave. Here, on Gor, beauty is nothing special in a slave. It tends to be taken for granted in a slave. Thus, as her beauty is not enough in itself to please, to garner her ease and riches, to assure her of her having her own way, she is well advised to be the best slave she can. To the extent she is unsuccessful, she must expect the whip.

"May I lift my head?" she asked.

"No," I said.

"Yes, Master," she said.

"Were you sold for debt, or taken in war?"

"No," she said.

"What then?" I asked.

She sobbed.

"Master would not understand," she said.

"Speak," I said.

"I am not to speak of it," she said. "I would be beaten."

"Speak," I said.

"I come from far off," she said, "from another world, one called Earth, brought here like a dog or horse, stripped and sold like a pig in a public, open market. But, forgive me. Master does not know those animals."

"I understand the sort of thing you are saying," I said.

"Master is apprised of the Second Knowledge?" she asked.

"Yes," I said.

"Perhaps Master is then of high caste?" she said.

"Perhaps," I said.

"I think the dancer will be soon on the sand," said Clitus.

"Aktis is diligently employed, is he not?" I asked Thurnock.

"Yes," said Thurnock.

"Profitably?" I asked.

"I fear not," said Thurnock. "He has examined several markets, greater and lesser, finding no articles of the sort he seeks."

"The dancer!" said Clitus.

"You may now lift your head and turn about," I said to the kneeling slave. "Observe the dancer and discover how beautiful and exciting a woman can be."

"How shall I kneel?" she asked.

"In the position of the tower slave," I said.

She brought her knees together.

"It seems Master regards me of small interest," she said.

"Beat her," said Thurnock.

"Shall I cross my wrists before my body, as though they might be bound?" she asked.

"Let her be whipped," said Clitus.

"No," I said. "Place your wrists behind you, crossed, as though bound, and kneel up, and well."

"Yes, Master," she said.

"And suck in your gut," said Clitus.

"Yes, Master," she said.

"Nice," said Thurnock.

An ideal tie for a woman is the wrists tied behind the back. In this way she is not only helpless but extremely vulnerable, unable to fend caresses away from the soft terrain of her defenseless beauty. Too, this tie, her arms held back, accentuates several attractions of that very beauty.

"Look," said Thurnock, "Aktis enters the tavern."

Aktis was now within the portal, and was looking about, scanning the tables.

"I see by his expression he has nothing of interest to report," said Clitus.

I lifted my arm, and this caught the eye of Aktis, and he began to make his way toward our table.

Almost at the same moment there was a bright skirl of music and the dancer, in her swirling silks and veils, her ankle bells, and bracelets and necklaces, began to perform.

"Excellent," said Thurnock. "Worthy of Ar or Brundisium."

"Or Port Kar," said Clitus.

"It seems that civilization has come to the Farther Islands," I said.

"I think that dancer is new," said Thurnock. "We have not seen her before."

"Tal," I said to Aktis, who now joined us, cross-legged, at the table.

"What success?" asked Clitus.

"None," said Aktis, dismally.

"The dancer is now making her way amongst the tables," said Thurnock, approvingly.

"Perhaps you will have better fortune in a day or two," I said.

"Perhaps," said Aktis. "But I have searched strenuously and lengthily."

"Perhaps we should try another town," said Clitus.

"But it was here, in Sybaris," I said, "that we heard the report of the destructive raid on Nicosia, days before it actually took place."

"True," said Clitus.

The dancer now, under the dangling lamps, animate, seductive, vital, swaying, negotiating the tables, was but yards away. In most paga taverns the dancer or dancers confine themselves to the square or oval dancing area, normally of polished wood or yellow sand, reminiscent of a camp or caravanserai. The typical reason for this, one supposes, is to isolate the dancer in such a way that she can be well seen and is not likely to have her performance interrupted by grasping hands. I noted that this dancer had, and more than once, eluded hands reaching out for her.

"She approaches," said Thurnock, not in the least displeased.

"Enjoy the dance," I encouraged Aktis. "I doubt that there was anything like this in Nicosia."

Aktis' eyes were dull. He scarcely lifted his eyes from the table.

"She sees the watching, disciplined slave, kneeling at our table, bound by the Master's will," said Clitus. "To amuse herself and the crowd she will ridicule and torment her." There is often a rivalry, implicit or explicit, amongst slaves. A girl who has failed to be pleasing is often an object of derision and scorn. She is likely to be regarded by other slaves as a failed slave, as one inadequate and inferior, as one inept and stupid, as one unworthy of the collar.

The slave who cannot please a man is pathetic indeed.

Then, in a flash of silks and veils, to the sparkle of bells, to the jangle of ornaments, the dancer was at the table, her beauty affronting and taunting the kneeling slave.

"Observe," I said to the kneeling slave, who had stiffened and was trying to draw back, but was careful to keep her wrists, crossed, behind her, lest I have her lashed for "breaking position." "See what a true woman can be."

The dancer's hips rotated; her belly mocked the kneeling slave; her veil fluttered about the kneeling slave sometimes covering her.

There was much laughter amongst the tables.

Clearly the kneeling slave would have wished to brush away the insulting silk but, bound by the Master's will, could not do so.

The dancer, delighted, and triumphant, prepared to swirl away but Aktis, who had scarcely moved and whom she had scarcely noticed, suddenly cried out "There!" and lunged across the table his left hand clutching the belt, sweetly low on her hips, from which dangled rings, cheap, drilled coins, trinkets, and charms.

The dancer cried out, startled.

"Tear it off!" cried a man.

"Drunk as a long-voyaged oarsman!" laughed another.

"Congratulations!" cried another. "You were quicker than I!"

I pulled loose the hand of Aktis. "My apologies to your Master!" I said. "Continue your dance."

"Yes," she said, "handsome Master," and spun away.

"I am sure of it!" said Aktis.

"You noticed nothing," I told him.

"Captain?" said Aktis.

"Slave," I said to the kneeling, humiliated, distraught slave, "you may break position. Rise up, and bring us four pagas."

She rose up, and began to back away.

"Wait," I said. "On the tray, about the stem of my goblet, wind a binding lace."

"Please, no," she said.

"You will learn what it is to be a paga slave," I said.

"Choose another," she begged.

"Must a command be repeated?" I asked.

"No, Master," she said and turned quickly about, to hurry to the paga vat.

Repetition of a command is often cause for discipline. A slave is expected to obey instantly, and unquestioningly.

Aktis leaned across the table. "Captain," he whispered intensely, "I am sure of it!"

"You may be mistaken," I said.

"We must take action," he urged.

"You noticed nothing," I said.

"Captain," he protested.

"We do nothing, we noticed nothing," I said.

"Captain?" he asked.

"We are being watched," I said.

Shortly thereafter the slave returned with the tray. I was pleased to see that she had the sense to kneel when she placed the tray on the table.

As she watched, I slowly unwound the binding lace from the stem of my goblet.

"What, pretty animal, is your name?" I asked.

"Does Master mean the name that has been put on me?" she asked.

"Yes," I said, "your only name."

"'Lais'," she said.

This name, a familiar Cosian slave name, is pronounced, as many such names, in two syllables, in this case, as "Lah-ees."

I continued to regard her.

"—if it pleases Master," she said.

"We are going to drink and converse for a time," I said. "You will wait for us to finish. Lie beside the table, on your belly, your wrists crossed behind you, your ankles crossed, as well, your head turned to the left."

This was the *bara* position.

I then knelt beside her and, with the binding lace, tied her wrists together behind her back.

It is not unusual to make a slave wait, bound helplessly, say, on the couch, or on the floor beside the couch, or on the floor, at its foot. This helps her to understand that she is a slave, is helpless, and is at the mercy of others, who will do with her what they please, at their discretion, when they find time for her. This gives her time to anticipate what will be done with her. She anticipates, she simmers, she imagines. Then, at the least touch, she writhes, ready, begging.

I then rejoined my companions.

"We are in no hurry, my friends," I said. "Be leisurely. We have noticed nothing. We suspect nothing."

"It is interesting, is it not," asked Clitus, "that the dancer wore such a belt, and danced so near our table?"

"Yes," I said, "that is interesting."

"The inquiries of Aktis in the markets may have been noted," said Clitus.

"I am sure they were," I said.

"That was your hope?" asked Clitus.

"Of course," I said.

"Much in Sybaris is interesting," said Thurnock.

"True," I said.

"Even the name of this tavern," he said, "—*The Living Island*."

"Fancy has many flights," I said. "Consider another tavern we visited, *The Sea Hith*."

"Fanciful, indeed," said Thurnock.

The hith, like the ost, is a Gorean serpent. The hith is a gigantic, constricting snake. I had never, personally, seen one. Indeed, I supposed that they were now extinct, or nearly so, having been hunted down and killed over generations. A snake capable of crushing a draft tharlarion does not find it easy to conceal its presence. The ost, on the other hand, tiny, elusive, and venomously deadly, survives.

"Tomorrow, Captain," said Thurnock, "you will be busy?"

"Yes," I said.

"Profitably?" said Clitus.

"That is my hope," I said. "If all goes well, following suitable arrangements, our work, which we alone would be unlikely to bring to a successful consummation, will be done for us."

"By whom?" asked Clitus.

"By those who have a vested interest in its success," I said.

"Who?" asked Thurnock.

"Those who have in charge the safety of the local seas," I said, "the duly appointed authorities on Thera, those reporting to, and responsible to, the throne of Cos itself."

"But they have failed hitherto even to encounter the fleet of the so-called Bosk of Port Kar," said Clitus, "let alone engage and destroy it."

"But one link of the invisible chain has now become visible," I said, "in a tavern in Sybaris."

We then conversed for a time of common things, of skies, currents, and winds, of harbors and ships, of markets and seasons, of the beauty of slaves and the nature of men.

Shortly thereafter we touched our goblets together and placed them, stem-up, on the table.

"Choose now a girl from the girl line at the paga vat, or return to our lodgings," I said. "I will be with you, later."

We wished one another well.

Thurnock left the tavern, and Clitus and Aktis, the latter supplied with a well-earned copper tarsk, left the table to inspect the goods in the vicinity of the paga vat.

I looked down at the prone, tethered slave, on the floor beside the table.

"Stand up, pretty animal," I said.

She regained her feet.

"Head down," I said.

She lowered her head.

Let her understand more keenly that she is a slave. Such behaviors impress the truth of her being on her.

I regarded her.

Did she not understand that the games, jockeyings, ambiguities, tensions, frictions, maneuverings, and competitions of the sexes, so pervasively afflicting her former world, were now over for her? For her those wars were done. She was marked, collared, and owned. Later she would learn that her defeat, total and uncompromising, was her salvation, that her loss, complete and unredeemable, was her victory.

"It seems that Alcove Eleven is unoccupied," I said. "Leading Position."

She bent at the waist, and I put my hand in her hair, to hold her head at my left hip.

We then, I conducting her, made our way amongst the tables to Alcove Eleven.

I paused at the entrance.

"Will you please me?" I asked.

"I do not know," she said.

"I will see that you do," I said.

I then threw her to the furs within.

CHAPTER SEVEN

I Converse with Authorities; I Plead a Case for Action; The Governor's Assurance

"Surely your oarsman is mistaken," said Archelaos, fingering the twin strings of his beard, governor of Thera, his palace on the ridge of Sybaris, overlooking the harbor, crowded with its hundreds of ships.

"It is possible, certainly," I said, "but I deem it unlikely."

"He is of a smitten village, Nicosia, on Chios?" said Nicomachos, dark-haired, and impatient of manner, First Captain of Sybaris, High Officer of Cos, Admiral of the Fleet of the Farther Islands, Thera, Chios, and Daphna, leaning forward, an action which caused the medallion and chain of his office to slide on the surface of the table, inlaid in such a way, with colored glass and stones, as to constitute a map of the Farther Islands and their adjacent waters.

Archelaos frowned.

"Yes," I said.

"Such goods, for trade and such, are plentiful," said Nicomachos. "Their appearance would seem, in itself, largely meaningless."

"Nicosia is on Chios," said Archelaos. "Why did you not bring this matter to the attention of the authorities in Mytilene?"

"It was here in Sybaris, weeks ago," I said, "that I heard a report of the attack on Nicosia days before, as I later ascertained, it actually took place."

"That is interesting, indeed," said Archelaos.

"You heard this in the tavern of *The Living Island*?" asked Nicomachos.

"Yes," I said.

"Why did you venture to Nicosia?" asked Nicomachos.

"To investigate," I said. "To seek clues as to the location of the piratical fleet captained by the notorious Bosk of Port Kar."

"But what concern is this of yours, noble Kenneth Stater-counter?" said Nicomachos. "You are supposedly a merchant of Brundisium."

"I and others hope to trade freely and profitably in these waters," I said.

"And we welcome your efforts and commend you for them, do we not, Admiral Nicomachos?" said Archelaos.

"Certainly," said Nicomachos. "The least bit of real assistance we can garner, even the tiniest genuine clue we can obtain, is immeasurably precious. We have long sought the trail of this mysterious, elusive, merciless corsair, Bosk, of Port Kar." He gestured expansively to the inlaid map on the table. "I have put dozens of scout ships to work. The subtlest of rumors have been investigated. Pertinent waters have been sectioned, apportioned, and examined. Four times the fleet of the Farther Islands itself has put to sea."

"The net has been cast widely, time and time again," said Archelaos, "but, as yet, always with a lack of success."

"How can a raiding, predatory fleet as large as that which I, and doubtless others, have described continue to escape detection?" I asked.

"It sails far away, beyond the waters of the Islands, and waits, and then, when ready, returns to strike again," said Nicomachos.

"And not be seen, arriving or departing?" I said.

"It seems so," said Nicomachos, High Officer of Cos, Admiral of the Fleet of the Farther Islands.

"But, noble officer," I said, "certainly an obvious difficulty attends such an account."

"What is that?" asked Nicomachos.

"Dear Admiral," said Archelaos, governor of Thera, "our friend, the noble Kenneth Statercounter of Brundisium, is no fool."

"Do you imply that I am?" inquired Nicomachos.

"Certainly not, esteemed colleague," said the governor of Thera. "But your desperate attempt to set the noble Statercounter's mind at ease, and perhaps your own, with such an explanation is ill-founded. He is a trader, familiar with winds, currents, and the strength of oarsmen. The numbers of attacks and the times of the attacks preclude an account involving lengthy withdrawals from, and returns to, local waters."

"Then," said Nicomachos, unpleasantly, "we are left with the mystery with which we began."

"Tragically so," said Archelaos.

"Perhaps," said Nicomachos, "you think me remiss in my duties?"

"Not at all, favored Admiral," said Archelaos. "I can think of no one more zealous in their pursuit."

"I do not have the fleet of Cos at my disposal," he said, "only the fleet of the Farther Islands, only twenty heavy ships, and several smaller vessels, all diversely oared."

"That would seem sufficient for locating and engaging some six ships or so," said Archelaos.

"How can I wipe a phantom from the sea?" asked Nicomachos. "How can I draw blood from fog?"

"To do so would be difficult, indeed," said Archelaos.

"I should have been High Admiral of the Cosian navy," he said, suddenly, angrily. "My experience, achievements, records, and honors entitled me to the rank. But they were no match for flatterers and sycophants, for those at the ear of Lurius, for court intrigues, for plotting and patronage. Instead, I am posted to the Farther Islands!"

"Do not resign your commission, dear friend," said Archelaos. "Wherever one finds oneself, one may do one's duty. What true officer could wish for more?"

"There are hundreds of villages on Thera, Chios, and Daphna," said Nicomachos. "How am I to find this Bosk of Port Kar? How am I to know where he will strike next?"

"The seriousness of the challenge is well recognized," said Archelaos. "And I cannot think of anyone other than yourself better able to deal with it."

"Why should so notorious a pirate content himself with villages?" asked Nicomachos. "The loot of isolated, palisaded hamlets is not likely to fill holds with treasure."

"Perhaps," said Archelaos, "it is safer to deal with a hundred vulos than one tarsk boar, with ten verr than one sleen. Perhaps he lacks the resources to molest towns."

"It is strange," said Nicomachos.

"Surely," said Archelaos.

"Would that I had this Bosk of Port Kar within the reach of my sword," said Nicomachos.

"Noble officers, governor and Admiral," I said, "I think that things may not be as hopeless as you fear." I leaned forward, pointing to the map table. I gestured to its width, and complexity. "The map is large," I said. "One part looks much like another. But one looks for tracks. Even the nocturnal, stealthy sleen leaves tracks." I pressed my finger on Sybaris. "I am not speaking of the Farther Islands," I said. "I am not speaking of Thera, I am not speaking of Sybaris. I am speaking of one tavern in one town, a tavern here in Sybaris, *The Living Island*. In that tavern I heard a reference to an attack as completed, which had not yet taken place. Someone was privy to at least that raid. In the same tavern, yesterday night, seeming loot from the raid of Nicosia was glimpsed, strung on a dancer's belt."

"I know the proprietor of *The Living Island*," said Archelaos, "Glaukos, a man of impeccable character."

"He from whom you heard the reference to a raid," said Nicomachos, "was quite possibly a mere patron, with no essential connection to the tavern."

"True," I said.

"And coins, trinkets, baubles, and such often adorn a dancer's belt, as bells her ankles and bangles and bracelets her limbs," said Nicomachos.

"I have come to you, noble officers," I said, "as one concerned with the prospects of trade and the safety of the seas. I offer to you intriguing considerations, bright with portent. It is my hope that you will see fit to act upon them."

"Rumors abound," said Nicomachos.

"I do not speak of rumors," I said.

"I know Glaukos, proprietor of *The Living Island*," said Archelaos. "I play Stones with him. He is beyond reproach."

"The noble Glaukos need not be involved in these matters," said Nicomachos. "We cannot hold him responsible for what a patron may jabber at a table, or for what a dancer may string on her belt. Anyone might be involved, if anyone, at all. What of a paga tender, a floor master, a keeper of a coin box?"

"Noble Statercounter," said Archelaos, "can you recognize he who uttered the remark about an attack on Nicosia?"

"I am not sure," I said. "I paid little attention to him, or to his interlocutor. The table was crowded. I took the remark, as it was said, to be common knowledge, at least in Sybaris. It was only later that I realized it antedated the raid on Nicosia, that it contained an astonishing, illuminating anachronism."

"Of course," said Archelaos.

"What you bring to us is tenuous," said Nicomachos.

"Surely it is grounds for an inquiry," I said.

"Scarcely," said Nicomachos.

"I must disagree, dear Admiral," said Archelaos, fingering the strings of his beard. "Upon reflection, it seems to me that the noble Kenneth Statercounter has brought before us considerations more than ample to initiate an investigation, particularly given the paucity of other avenues of inquiry. Small clues, even seeming clues, are to be preferred to the absence of clues altogether. It is a beginning; it gives us a place to start. Better to follow a road which may lead nowhere than to follow no road. We must avail ourselves of any opportunity which might serve to bring peace to our troubled waters. My duty as governor of Thera, by appointment of glorious Lurius of Jad, Ubar of Cos, demands nothing less."

"Observe *The Living Island*," I said. "Keep it under surveillance. What captains come and go, and what are their ships? Do surprising meetings take place? Do rumors spring into life, and spread? Do some patrons possess coins likely to be beyond their supposed resources? Do strangers appear? Are men recruited for voyages of an undisclosed nature? Be vigilant. Be armed with suspicion. Let the movements and doings of irregular or questionable individuals be monitored. Let dubious patrons be cultivated. Insert spies, posing as brigands searching for fee. Sooner or later, somehow, a word will slip, a contact will be made, a plan will be discovered."

"If there are six or so corsair ships, fully manned, or more than fully manned," said Nicomachos, "one would be dealing with several hundred men. They could hold districts of Sybaris itself. Consider the fighting, from building to building, from room to room. For their apprehension one would require regulars, brought from Cos itself, spearmen, not common oarsmen, not mariners. Tumult would seethe. Fires might start, if only as diversions, and spread. Sybaris might be burned to the ground."

"Learn their plans, their sailing orders, the targets of their raids," I said. "Take them at sea. Heavily then the advantage is on your side. What are six or seven ships against twenty, twenty naval vessels, manned by trained crews, vessels fierce and swift, like hungry sea sleen, armed with snouts of iron?"

"By the Priest-Kings," said Archelaos, enthusiastically, his fist striking the table like a bird of prey, "let us give glad heed to our merchant friend from Brundisium, the noble Kenneth Stater-counter."

"I can almost hear the battle horns," said Nicomachos, drily.

"Away with cavils," said Archelaos. "I myself am now san-guine. The matter is surely possible. Listen with your blood, your fierce, pounding blood, dear Admiral. Is this not what we have been waiting for? Consider the matter. We now know where to look, and what to do. A curtain is drawn back. Secrets are sensed. And secrets must be vulnerable; so rarely are they kept. Cannot plans be learned, or shrewdly conjectured? Let the enemy sense himself safe. Let him not know his lair has been discovered. Let him not know he is stalked, that he is destined for a rendezvous at sea, one as bitter as the waters of churning Thassa herself."

"What does a stranger, an insignificant merchant from Brundi-sium, perhaps a dealer in contraband, know of these things, of espionage and intrigue, of war at sea, of Bosk of Port Kar? Has he been cleared by the harbor authorities in Telnus? Is he authorized to trade in these waters?"

"Patience, dear Nicomachos," said Archelaos. "The Farther Is-lands would be much deprived if all mercantile traffic must first be routed through the corrupt, grasping bureaucracy of Telnus."

"Rumors have it," said Nicomachos, "that some in Sybaris profit from spurious arrangements of local licensing, even issuing documentation purportedly of Telnus."

"At discounted prices, I have heard," I added.

"And I have heard rumors," said Archelaos, unpleasantly, "that even the First Captain of Sybaris, Nicomachos, High Officer of Cos, Admiral of the Fleet of the Farther Islands, has profited from such clandestine emoluments."

"I have paid mooring fees, four times," I said.

"But," said Archelaos, "let us dismiss false rumors as the wretched canards they are, while, in all justice, acknowledging that it is not inappropriate for worthy folk posted far from civili-zation to seek to compensate in some manner, however minimal, for their isolation and remoteness. How is one to occupy one's time? Has not many an administrator, a general, and even an oc-casional Admiral, returned wealthy from the wilderness?"

"There is the matter of *The Living Island*, of piracy, and the safety of the seas, to be dealt with," I said.

"I yield to the governor of Thera," said Nicomachos. "Let him, if he wishes, concern himself with idle inquiries, to assuage the suspicions of an unimportant stranger, a possible merchant from Brundisium. I will have nothing to do with it."

"You need not," said Archelaos. "Investigative subtleties need not concern you. It is your concern, rather, to encounter the enemy and do battle."

"The pirate fleet appears from nowhere," said Nicomachos, "strikes, and vanishes."

"Sadly, true," said Archelaos.

"Find it for me, and I will act."

"We shall hope to do so," said Archelaos. "In the meantime, we must thank the noble Kenneth Statercounter for his concern and assistance."

"It is nothing," I said.

"It is nothing," said Nicomachos.

"Dear Statercounter," said Archelaos, "please ignore the discouragement, the lack of enthusiasm, the disinterest, and even the pessimism, on the part of my esteemed colleague, Admiral Nicomachos. He is a splendid officer, and a fine scion of Cos. But he has had many disappointments in this matter, and he anticipates another. But I, on the other hand, I, Archelaos, governor of Thera, am not only intrigued, but persuaded, and I assure you that I shall personally implement your suggestions. I shall relay your conjectures and recommendations to my friend Glaukos, proprietor of *The Living Island*, soliciting his scrutiny and cooperation. He will prove our most valuable ally. I doubt that *The Living Island* is somehow involved in these dark matters but we shall see. Our investigation will be impartial and thorough."

"I can ask for no more, your excellency," I said, rising.

Archelaos, governor of Thera, and Nicomachos, First Captain of Sybaris, Admiral of the Fleet of the Farther Islands, rose, too, to their feet.

"I wish you well, noble officers," I said.

"And we, too, wish you well," said Archelaos.

I then approached the door, to leave the chamber. It occurred to me that no slaves or servants had been present at our meeting, even to serve a glass of *ka-la-na*, an expected civility. But I supposed that that was just as well, given the nature of the proceedings. I was, of course, disappointed in the lack of responsiveness on the part of the Admiral. Why should my suggestions be ignored? Why should *The Living Island* not be investigated and placed under surveillance? On the other hand, the governor, Archelaos, governor of Thera herself, if his interest was not feigned, would act, and with dispatch. This relieved much anxiety. I had no wish to pit my two ships, with their crews, against an enemy far superior in ships and men. How much better for us that the authorities of Thera, or Cos, whose legal charge it was, utilizing the weapon of the Fleet of the Farther Islands, some twenty ships or so, should locate, engage, and destroy the corsair fleet. Accordingly, I permitted myself to be hopeful.

"Captain," called Archelaos.

I turned back, at the door.

"We must keep you apprised," said Archelaos. "Where are you and your men housed?"

"At the inn of Kahlir," I said.

I then left.

CHAPTER EIGHT

I Receive Notice of an Occurrence in Sybaris; We Will Depart from the Cove of Harpalos

"You have heard, surely," said Clitus, brushing aside the flap of the mottled tent, high and inconspicuous amongst the rocks and ledges below which lay the sheltering Cove of Harpalos, with its small cluster of huts and sheds. Both the *Dorna* and *Tesephone* were beached, prows waterward, near an inlet below, not noticeable from the sea itself. From the height of the camp, one could scan the sea for pasangs around. A watch had been posted. Both ships, even at low tide, shallow drafted, could be brought quickly into the water. The Cove of Harpalos was not heavily trafficked, but it was, in effect, the port by means of which several inland villages, bartering the produce of their gardens and orchards, could reach the sea. Several local families made their living by fishing in the nearby waters, families amongst whom Clitus, master of the trident and net himself, had sought to make friends and cultivate informants. Its wells, too, were known to grateful mariners who would put in for water. The Cove of Harpalos was not a hub of trade nor a metropolis, but its existence was not negligible; it was not likely to be ignored or overlooked. It had been included in the map table in the receiving chamber of Archelaos, governor of Thera.

"What?" I asked.

I was somewhat surprised to note the seeming agitation on the part of my friend. I had supposed, given the observation of the sea, and the occasional coming and going of ships, that I was already likely to be apprised of what slender news might have come recently to the Cove of Harpalos.

"I have this from a caste brother," said Clitus.

"What?" I asked.

"A peasant, from overland, below, returned from marketing olives, brings news heard of Sybaris," said Clitus.

"What news?" I asked.

"It is hearsay," said Clitus. "It may be false."

"Even rumors may be informative," I said. "Why would they start, why would they spread? Even lies can be informative. They have purposes."

"The very night we withdrew from the harbor of Sybaris," said Clitus, "an unconscionable event took place, a riot, a drunken mob, with torches, axes, and clubs, rushed blindly, meaninglessly, pointlessly, inexplicably, upon a large, well-known inn in Sybaris, looting it, tearing it to pieces, putting it to flames, burning it to the ground, robbing its patrons, scattering and beating its clientele."

"The mob was not drunk, nor the event inexplicable," I said.

"I do not understand," said Clitus.

"The inn was that of Kahlir," I said.

"Then you have heard the story," said Clitus.

"Only now," I said.

"How could you know?" asked Clitus.

"I did not know," I said. "I only feared it might be so."

"You took precautions?"

"Of a sort," I said.

"The mob slew no one," said Clitus.

"That is because they could not find those whom they sought," I said.

"Whom did they seek?" asked Clitus, uncertainly.

"I feared this would happen," I said. "That is why we left Sybaris that night."

"Secretly, in the darkness," said Clitus.

"Of course," I said.

"They sought us?" said Clitus.

"Yes," I said.

"We are in danger," said Clitus.

"Extremely so," I said. "A search for us is even now doubtless underway."

"But," said Clitus, grimly, "I think others are now in danger, as well."

"We will make sure of it," I said.

"It seems our cause is advanced," said Clitus.

"A thousandfold," I said. "We now know our foe is centered in Sybaris. We now know that one or the other, or both, of the High Officers of Sybaris, either the governor of Thera or the Admiral of the Fleet of the Farther Islands, or both, command the foe or are high in the command of he who does so. Too, with this advancement, we have now solved the mystery of the vanishing corsair fleet. It is harbored in or near the harbor of Sybaris. It departs the harbor singly, one by one, and groups at sea. When it has done its work, it separates into its component vessels and returns, unremarked, one by one, to the harbor. And all this, if noted, at all, is doubtless ignored or concealed by the harbor authorities, authorities doubtless responsive to the governor or Admiral, or both."

At this point there was a cry from Aktis, who had been set high amongst the rocks, with a glass of the Builders. "Ships, ho!" he cried. "Ships! Ships! I make out four, no, five, no, six!"

"The corsair fleet!" said Clitus. "Four large, two smaller!"

"Likely," I said, rising, and leaving the tent. In a few moments I, followed by Clitus, had clambered up the rocks to join Aktis, who handed me the glass of the Builders.

"The corsairs?" asked Clitus.

"Yes," I said, returning the glass to Aktis.

"We are betrayed," said Clitus.

"I do not think so," I said. "I think the fleet, over the past few days, has been perusing nearby settlements, for it would have been supposed we would not be far from Sybaris. The Cove of Harpalos would be on any list of nearby suspect ports."

"Your orders, Captain," said Clitus.

"Break camp, strike tents, extinguish fires, gather the men, get the *Dorna* and *Tesephone* into the water, masts and sails down. We take our leave, quietly, not easily seen, flat in the water."

Surely it would be unwise to risk being trapped in port, blockaded by superior forces.

Clitus scrambled down the rocky slope, toward the inlet. I could see Thurnock, looking up, standing on the beach below.

"Is there time?" asked Aktis.

"Yes," I said.

"We could flee inland," said Aktis. "I can speak in ways the villages can understand."

"I am counting on that, later, but not now," I said. The caste of Peasants, usually ensconced in remote, isolated settlements, tends to be wary and suspicious of other castes, commonly suspecting them of an impressive variety of ill doings, ranging from subtle deceit to outright chicanery, particularly in the spheres of fraudulent bookkeeping and dishonest weights. I always found this ironic as the average peasant, like the average Tuchuk, is commonly a bargainer whose sense of business shrewdness is not far removed from that of a practiced, marauding pirate. On the other hand, interestingly, a peasant is likely to trust another peasant, even from a remote village. That has something to do with the codes.

"I fear there is little time," said Aktis. "May I hurry to my oar?"

"We will soon be at sea," I said.

"I trust so," said Aktis.

"Are you not curious as to our destination?" I asked.

"If we do not soon depart," said Aktis, "I fear any destination will be unreached."

"Nicosia," I said.

"You have planned that?" said Aktis.

"For days," I said, "should I hear that woe has befallen the inn of Kahlir."

"Why Nicosia?" asked Aktis.

"For four reasons," I said. "First, given its desolation and destruction, I do not think they will look for us there, certainly not soon. This will give us days to plan and prepare. Second, it is far, but not too far. It lies within range of the corsair fleet. Third, I have at hand a guide who knows its land. His name is Aktis. It is easy to conceal oneself within, and strike from, familiar terrain. Fourth, and lastly, I am curious as to an island which seemed to appear from nowhere, shortly after which we came upon a seeming wreck, patent bait in a trap well laid at sea."

"What will we do in Nicosia?" inquired Aktis.

"Mount rams and shearing blades," I said.

"It seems you contemplate war," said Aktis.

"Cover your quiver and keep your bowstring dry," I said.

"I am truly eager to return to my oar," said Aktis.

"Do not permit me to detain you," I said.

Aktis turned about, and began, running, half sliding, to descend the slope.

"Oarsman!" I called after him.

He turned about, wildly, several yards down the slope, slipping.

"Captain?" he cried, catching his balance.

"You did well in sounding the alarm," I said. "Perhaps now you would care to join me, in quaffing a celebratory goblet of paga?"

He howled with misery, turned about, and, half falling, continued to make his way down the slope.

I smiled, and lifted the glass of the Builders. Yes, there was time, but not really, I surmised, enough for a cup of paga.

I must remember to tell Thurnock my joke.

He would think it rich, laughing like thunder, though I was not at all that sure of it myself. But sometimes it is hard to resist such things.

I considered the rhythm of the oars in the corsair fleet. It was steady, but unhurried. Presumably they had been searching for some time. I do not think they had any clear expectation of finding us in the Cove of Harpalos, no more than in any other place, not yet examined.

The *Dorna* and *Tesephone* were already in the water.

CHAPTER NINE

A Conversation Takes Place, Amongst Three Friends

"The raiders," said Thurnock, "have been quiescent."

"They have been active," I said, "but not in the business of looting and death."

I moved aside to let a metal worker pass, coils of chain looped about his shoulder.

"They have been searching for Kenneth Statercounter," said Clitus.

"I had hoped it would be so," I said. "That would give us time to gather further intelligence."

"An endeavor in which we have not been muchly successful," said Thurnock.

"We know much, but not enough," I said.

We passed a stall where a confectioner, a subclass of the Bakers, was vending *tastas*.

"Let them search forever," said Clitus. "Each day they search is a day free of blood and fire."

"I think that they, by now, will be muchly done with their inquiries," I said. "I fear any moment may mark a renewal of depredations."

"Would that they divide their ships, to speed and widen their search," said Clitus.

"I do not think they will do so," I said. "They would lose the advantage of numbers. A single vessel, and perhaps even two, would be unlikely to engage the *Dorna* and *Tesephone*."

"It is crowded today in Sybaris," said Clitus. "Perhaps it is a holiday."

"I do not think so," I said. "I think it is generally like this."

"The nights, too, are busy," said Thurnock.

We continued to press through the crowd, occasionally remaining in place, or going to the side.

"There are hundreds of villages on the Farther Islands," said Thurnock. "How can one know where the raiders will strike next?"

"And," said Clitus, "even if we knew, what could we do?"

"Warn the village," I said.

"It is hopeless," said Thurnock.

"Not as hopeless as it might seem," I said. "The raiders need the sea. It is their avenue of escape and their route to markets. Thus, unwilling to be long separated from their ships, I do not think they would care to venture more than a few pasangs inland. Thus we must think of villages on or near the coast."

"How many such villages are there?" asked Thurnock. "You consult maps."

"Perhaps two hundred," I said. "Much depends on how far the riders are willing to expend resources."

"Many villages," said Clitus, "are situated on or near the coast, or on rivers leading to the coast."

"It is hopeless," said Thurnock.

"Not completely," I said. "Few attacks have taken place on Thera herself. Let us thus, in our speculations, eliminate Thera."

"Too, an attack on Thera might reflect adversely on the governor, Archelaos," said Clitus.

"I think that is highly likely," I said.

"So," said Thurnock, "if we put aside Thera, how many plausible villages are left, on Chios and Daphna?"

"Something like a hundred and twenty," I said.

"It is obviously hopeless," said Thurnock.

"Possibly, but not necessarily," I said. "There is something in the nature of a pattern here. Attacks are less frequent on Thera than on Chios and Daphna, and, for the most part, though there are exceptions, attacks alternate between Chios and Daphna. The last attack was on Nicosia, on Chios. Thus, I would expect the next to be on Daphna."

"That narrows things down muchly," said Thurnock, eyes blazing.

"How many villages do we now speak of?" asked Clitus.

"By my count, given the map, and limiting myself to villages within ten pasangs of the coast," I said, "sixty-three."

"It is more hopeless than ever," groaned Thurnock.

"Hopeless perhaps, but not more hopeless than ever," I said.

"Yet," said Thurnock, "someone here in Sybaris knows where they intend to strike next."

"Perhaps several," I said.

"If I could find one, I could choke it out of him," said Thurnock.

"And the attack would be made elsewhere," I said.

We made our way past a shelf where several women were on sale.

"The matter is hopeless," said Thurnock.

"Not at all," I said.

I was more troubled by the fact that on the voyage from the Cove of Harpalos to the beach of Nicosia we had not encountered the small, dark island originally encountered on the voyage from Nicosia to the Cove of Harpalos. Similarly, on the voyage from Nicosia to Sybaris, after painting the *Tesephone* white and yellow, colors of the Merchants, so that it would stand out, and not be difficult to detect amongst the billows of Thassa, we had again failed to encounter the small, dark island.

"Lands do not move," had said Clitus. "It is small. We passed it, unknowingly."

"That must be it," I had granted him.

"You obtained charts at the Cove of Harpalos," had said Clitus. "Is it not on the charts?"

"No," I said.

"It is not charted," had said Clitus. "It is too small. Many tiny islands fail to appear on the charts."

"You must be right," I had said.

"You do not think the matter is hopeless?" asked Thurnock.

"No," I said.

"It is hopeless," said Thurnock. "How can we know which village, of some sixty-three or so villages, will be attacked?"

"By arranging the matter ourselves," I said. "How else?"

"I do not understand," said Thurnock.

"I have a plan," I said.

CHAPTER TEN

I Return to a Tavern Hitherto Patronized; I Begin to Put my Plan into Effect

"Buy me!" whispered Lais, softly, tensely, that no one would hear. "I beg it, Master! Buy me!"

I had returned, following my plan, to the large tavern, *The Living Island*, whose proprietor, as I understood it, was a man named Glaukos. It was not yet crowded, but it was still early. It was in this establishment that I had first heard of the destruction of Nicosia prior to its actual destruction, and in which Aktis had noted baubles and trinkets on a dancer's belt much like those which had figured in the trade goods of the raiders' advance scout, he posing as an itinerant merchant.

The paga girls who were not yet serving were kneeling in the display area, to the right of the paga vat, each chained by the left ankle to a ring. The chains were some four or five feet in length, and the rings were separated by a pace or so. The length of the individual chains and the spacing of the rings allows the girls to better present themselves for consideration. The chains, holding the girls in place, work out well for both the tavern and the patrons. From the point of view of the tavern the girls cannot rise up and rush about, competing for desirable customers, this arrangement minimizing squabbles and altercations, sometimes resulting in bite wounds, scratch marks, and gouts of lost hair. From the point of view of the patrons, on the other hand, the girls can be examined and assessed, one after another, in a serial, leisurely manner. One picks as one pleases.

I had scarcely arrived at the display area, to peruse the still-available offerings of the tavern, when one of the girls, she, like the others this night, in a brief yellow tunic, slit at the left hip, startled, looking up, hurled herself prone on the floor, squirming forward on her belly, pulling against the chain and manacle, extending her right hand to me, piteously. "Master!" she begged. "Me! Me!"

One or two of the other girls looked at her, annoyed. Such demonstrativeness sometimes brings the lash. Some of the others began to preen, and three others went, too, to their belly.

The most common second-obeisance position is to lie prone with the arms at the side of the head, but one sometimes sees the arms down, stretched back, at the sides of the of the body, commonly palms up. First-obeisance position is more common, where the girl kneels, head down, with her hands, palms down, beside her head.

"Master!" she wept.

"Do not cut your ankle on the manacle," warned the vat master. Carelessness in such matters can be a cause for discipline. Scars can lower a girl's value.

But his admonition did little to reduce the pressure of the manacle, taut on its chain, on her fair, well-formed, slim ankle. Slavers, in assessing goods, take ankles into consideration. In many Earth cultures, ankles are brazenly, conveniently, exhibited. To that extent the slaver's work is facilitated. On Gor, few free women exhibit their ankles. The raider or capturing slaver, of course, always hopes for the best. In the case of many Gorean women their ankles are never really exhibited until they are sold from the block.

"Master, Master!" begged the girl.

"It seems she knows you," said the vat master.

I gave no indication that I recognized her.

"Is she any good?" I asked the vat master.

"She is hot, helpless, and worthless, like any other slave," said the vat master.

"Please, Master!" wept the girl.

"Which one?" asked the vat master.

"That one," I said.

The vat master freed her of the manacle, and I turned and strode away, to an obscure table at the far end of the floor, she hurrying behind me.

"Buy me!" whispered Lais, softly, tensely, that no one would hear. "I beg it, Master! Buy me!"

"Only a slave begs to be bought," I said.

She kept her head down, kneeling at my feet. She shook her head a little, bringing her hair forward, exposing the back of her neck, the tiny hairs. "Master sees," she said, "that my neck is in a collar."

How beautiful is a woman whose neck is in a collar.

"I see," I said, "as you are collared, that you are indeed a slave, an animal, an object, an article of merchandise, which might be bought and sold."

"Yes, Master," she whispered.

"But are you a slave in your mind, your heart, and belly, in every cell of your body, in every drop of your blood?"

"Yes, Master," she said, "since you first bound and touched me, weeks ago."

"I gather then," I said, "that you now understand what you are, and welcome it?"

"Yes, Master," she said.

"You are of Earth, are you not?" I asked.

"Surely Master recalls," she said.

"Need I repeat my question?" I asked.

"I was of that world," she said, "until I was brought here, as I now know was fitting, to be the slave I now am!"

"I gather that your adjustment to legal slavery proceeded expeditiously."

"It takes little time to adjust to legal slavery," she said, "when one is stripped, marked, collared, and whipped."

"On the other hand," I said, "I gather that, in your case, the mark and collar, and such, was no more than a suitable, public acknowledgement of a hitherto concealed inward truth, that you are a natural slave, a rightful slave, a woman who is a slave, and wants to be a slave."

"Yes, Master," she said. "For years I put aside my dreams and fantasies, for years I strenuously denied my most inward and profound reality, as my culture prescribed, but I always knew it, and, after your touch, I accepted it, at last, and gladly. In your arms I could no longer deny it. If one is a slave, why should one not be a slave? Let the free woman be free; let the slave be a slave. Let each find her joy as she can, as she would."

"I think your value, your price, of late, is much improved."

I had gathered that that might be the case from the vat master.

"I am told some of us sell well, indeed, that some of us bring high prices, as much as two silver tarsks," she said.

"And some more," I said.

"Are not the women of my world of interest to Gorean men?" she asked. "Are we not exotic in our way, helpless and different, so needful? Do they not enjoy owning and mastering us, handling us, and treating us, as we deserve, as the properties we are? As a man, perhaps you do not realize how thrilling it is for a woman to be dominated, mastered, and owned."

I did not respond. I supposed that there might be genetic codings having to do with dominance and submission. In any event, these behaviors appeared to be pervasive in the animal kingdom. Could it be that some genetic combinations are selected for, those which lead to survival, health, happiness, and thriving? But such questions are perhaps outside the scope of the codes.

"I now despise the worthlessness, the emptiness of freedom," she whispered. "What is a woman who is not owned?"

"The Gorean free woman," I said, "is glorious and priceless, a jewel of inestimable value."

"I fear free women," she said. "I think they are unhappy, cruel, and filled with hate. What are they really but forlorn, miserable slaves not yet in their collars?"

"You may lift your head," I said.

How beautiful she was, the dark hair, the brief yellow tunic, slit at the hip, kneeling before me.

"I do not think I would be expensive," she said. "Patrons often buy girls off the floor."

It is common for a paga girl, a state slave, a laundry slave, a girl from the mills, to long for a private master. To be the single slave of a beloved Master is a common hope amongst *kajirae*.

"I do not think I am unattractive," she said.

On Gor, beauty amongst slaves is common, and, accordingly, cheap.

"You chose me from the line," she said. "You had me loosed from my chain."

"Perhaps for an evening's sport," I said.

"At first, I did not recognize Master," she said. "The garb? Not of the Merchants? Is he truly of the Mariners, an officer, a helmsman, an oarsman?"

"Do not concern yourself," I said.

"Yet you carry a blade," she said.

"Where one is a stranger, it is well not to go unarmed."

"Many are strangers in Sybaris," she said.

"I am one of them," I said.

"I am helpless," she said. "I can only beg to be bought."

"There are many strong Masters," I said, "capable of treating you as the slave you are."

"And I would be bought by one," she said, "he whom I entreat, he before whom I now kneel."

"I take it," I said, "you are familiar with slave obedience."

"Yes, Master," she said. "A slave is to obey unquestioningly and immediately. I have been taught it by the whip."

"Listen carefully," I said. "I do not think I am recognized here, but I am uncertain of the matter. I came here originally in the guise of a merchant from Brundisium, Kenneth Statercounter. Now, should inquiries be made, I am Eiron, an oarsman from Naxos on Daphna. You know no more. I shall shortly send you for paga. You are to take a goblet from the shelf at random and fill it at the paga vat yourself. I do not want the goblet to be selected by the vat master or filled by the vat master. If this proves impractical, return and inform me. Later, I shall appear drunk. Whatever happens, do not involve yourself."

Her eyes, lifted to mine, were full of fear.

"Do you understand, slave girl?" I asked.

"Yes, Master," she said.

I was standing near the wall of the tavern, far from the entrance, to the right, as one would enter, where few were about.

That seemed appropriate for one who might have a secret to conceal.

"Paga," I said, clearly.

Two fellows at a nearby table looked about, and then returned to their drinking.

"Yes, Master," she said.

CHAPTER ELEVEN

I Meet Glaukos, Proprietor of *The Living Island*; Things Go Smoothly, if Not Altogether Pleasantly

The girl, Lais, had been dismissed.

She was now back on her chain, in the display area.

I thought that that was best for her, safest for her. The vat master, not pleased, had toweled tears from her cheeks. Her hair was damp where she had tried to use it for the same purpose. She must now, in her manacle, on her chain, on her knees, smile, as hitherto, sparkle as she could, and once more present herself well. She is to be attractive to customers. She is a paga girl. It is not pleasant to be cuffed, nor switched, nor feel the kiss of the supple, five-stranded Gorean slave whip, designed to administer admonitions to the female slave who has somehow failed, or is suspected of having failed, to be fully pleasing. A free woman may be as unpleasant and displeasing as she wishes; but the girl who is marked, collared, and tunicked, should the master permit her clothing, may not be so.

The attendant, with belt and coin box, having noted the delivery of paga, the vessel now before me, had arrived at the table.

"Master?" he said.

Paga girls are not permitted to touch coins. Indeed, *kajirae*, as a whole, are seldom permitted to touch coins, save in structured situations, as in shopping, redeeming laundry, or such. In passing it might be noted that, in many cities, it is a capital offense for a *kajira* to touch a weapon.

I pretended sluggishness, even stupor.

"You dismissed the girl," he said. "Perhaps she was unsatisfactory? If so, I will have her beaten."

"Paga, paga," I said, head down, speech slurring. "This is a night to remember. The taverns of beautiful Sybaris, the slaves of Sybaris. No more collar meat, not now. Paga. I want more paga."

"It seems this is not the first tavern Master has visited this evening," said the attendant.

"Paga, more paga," I growled, head down.

"It is before you," said the attendant, and rattled the coin box. "One tarsk-bit."

I raised my head, groggily. "What?" I asked.

"A tarsk-bit," said the attendant.

I reached out, locating the goblet, and, gripping it firmly, determinedly, in two hands, lifted it, and swilled down the contents in one dramatic, cascading drainage.

"A tarsk-bit," the attendant reminded me.

"I have no tarsk-bit," I said.

"What?" said the attendant, eyeing the emptied goblet.

"No tarsk-bit," I said, "no copper. Spent them all."

"Master jests," said the attendant.

"No," I said. "No tarsk-bit, no copper. Spent them all."

The attendant turned about, and signaled, subtly, to two large fellows lounging on a wall-bench behind and to the left of the paga vat, who then, rising, began to approach the table. Their approach was such that I was pleased that I was not without resources.

"Take this, instead," I said.

I reached into my bulging pouch, hung from my belt, and handed the attendant a small, bright disk. Even in the light of the nearby, dangling tharlarion-oil lamp, it was clear that the color of the disk was not copperish.

"This is not a tarsk-bit," he said.

"I know," I said. "I am destitute of tarsk-bits. I am sorry. I hope that will do."

"It is yellow," he said.

"Gold," I said.

"It is not a coin," he said.

"*The Village of Flowing Gold*," I said, "does not mint coins."

"What is *The Village of Flowing Gold*?" he asked.

"Do not concern yourself," I said, warily.

"Is this gold?" he asked.

"Certainly," I said.

"Where is *The Village of Flowing Gold*?" he asked.

"Do not concern yourself," I said. "It does not exist. I misspoke. Doubtless it was the paga. I said nothing."

The attendant bit at the small disk of metal.

"Go, let it be tested," I said.

"I think it is gold," he whispered to the two fellows who were now about him, one on each side.

"One who is of the Merchants, who deals in gold, or one who is of the Metal Workers, who crafts ornaments of gold, or some of those who are of the yellow caste, the Builders, could make the determination," I said. "They have access to the crucible, the heat, the chemicals. The determination can be made in several ways."

"I have not enough money in my coin box to change this," said the attendant.

"Do not concern yourself," I said. "I have plenty more."

The attendant turned to one of the two fellows with him and pressed the disk into his hand. "Laios," he said, "take this to Glaukos."

Glaukos, as I recalled, was the proprietor of *The Living Island*.

The fellow who had been given the small disk sped away.

"I will bring more paga to your table, immediately, noble Master," said the attendant.

"I feel I must be on my way," I said. I reached nervously inside my robe, as if to reassure myself that the rolled parchment there was secure. I trusted that this tiny movement had not escaped the notice of the attendant, whose eyes narrowed at the action.

"Dally," said the attendant. "Ctesippus, here," he added, "will keep you company," indicating the second large fellow. the larger of the two who had approached the table.

"Remain where you are," said Ctesippus.

"Very well," I said.

"I will fetch you some paga," said the attendant, withdrawing.

"He is very kind," I said.

I doubted that the goblet would be filled from the contents of the paga vat.

"Stay where you are," said Ctesippus.

"Why should I not do so?" I asked.

I watched the attendant. He did not stop at the paga vat but carried the empty goblet through the beaded curtain to the side. Shortly thereafter, he re-emerged onto the floor, carrying the goblet, brimming with fluid, and approached my table, now followed by a short, smiling, thick-legged, coarse-featured fellow, in a silken, gold-embroidered house tunic.

The attendant placed the vessel on the table, carefully, turned about, and took his leave.

I looked at the liquid in the paga goblet. It was high, of a quite generous level, but not a drop had been spilled. One would think it had been delivered by a girl, concerned not to be lashed. I could see the light of the nearby tharlarion-oil lamp reflected in the surface of the fluid, the reflection uneasy, from the goblet's recent placement. Then the reflection, after some moments, was still.

"Tal," said the thick-legged, coarsely featured fellow who had followed the attendant.

"Tal," I replied.

The newcomer, with a subtle gesture of his head, motioned that Ctesippus might withdraw.

This conversation, I gathered, was to be private.

"May I join you?" asked the newcomer, settling himself, cross-legged, beside me.

"Please do so," I said.

"I am Glaukos," he said, "master of *The Living Island.*"

I had thought it might be he. I recalled that Archelaos, governor of Thera, had spoken highly of him.

"What is your name?" he asked.

"My name is unimportant," I said. "I am a stranger here, a humble visitor, a lowly oarsman."

"I do not think you are such a stranger as you suppose," said Glaukos, "as you are familiar with the well-known Village of Flowing Gold."

"It does not exist," I said. It is interesting, I thought, how the truth may be told in such a way that it will be taken as a lie.

"Do not concern yourself," said Glaukos. "Hundreds have been there. I myself was once there."

"Oh," I said.

"You may speak freely before me," he said.

"I should be at ease?" I said.

"Certainly," said Glaukos.

"I have had too much to drink," I said, reaching groggily for the paga vessel.

Glaukos' hand rested on my wrist. "Later," he said.

I stared at the paga goblet.

"Your accent," he said, "is not of the Farther Islands, nor, I think, of Cos or Tyros."

I was silent.

"I would guess," he said, "of Torcadino, or of Ti, of the Salerian Confederation."

"How did you know?" I asked, feigning dismay.

"Ti?" he said.

"Yes," I said. I frankly had little sense of my own accent. One seldom does. It is always others who have an accent. My native language was English. My Gorean had been subject to several influences. My first Gorean had been learned in Ko-ro-ba, the Towers of the Morning, in the western, northern latitudes of the vast Gorean continent.

"Ti," he said, "is not a likely origin for an oarsman."

"I left Ti," I said. "And one must make a living."

"You are far from your Home Stone," he said. "What were the circumstances of your departure from Ti?"

"They are not important," I said.

"How is it," he asked, "that you, from far Ti, know of *The Village of Flowing Gold*?"

"Idle talk," I said, "heard in some tavern."

Once again my hand, seemingly nervously, appeared to confirm that some object, perhaps one of interest, might lie within my robe.

"You obviously conceal something within your robe," he said.

"No," I said, pressing my garment closer to my body.

"A parchment," said Glaukos.

"No!" I said.

"It is a map," said Glaukos. "You stole it. That is why you are far from your Home Stone. You are a thief. You fled from Ti."

I made as though I was struggling to rise. "It is late," I said. "I must go. I fear I have drunk too much."

"There is no hurry," said Glaukos. "You are in the tavern of *The Living Island*. You are amongst friends."

"Let me go," I said.

"You have not yet drunk your paga," he said.

"I am not sure I want it," I said.

"Have no fear," he said. "I shall not inform guardsmen. How does it concern us, here in Sybaris, what once was done in Ti?"

"I may trust you?" I asked.

"Certainly," he said.

"You are my friend?" I asked.

"Certainly," he said. "What is your name?"

"Eiron," I said, uncertainly.

"No," he said, "your real name."

"Fenlon," I said.

"A splendid, noble name," he said, "one of a sort of which a large, fine fellow like yourself could well be proud."

"All here are my friends?" I asked.

"Each and every one," he said.

I stood up, unsteadily. "I am generous to my friends," I said, solemnly.

"Of course you are," said Glaukos.

I reached into my pouch and, wavering, began to cast forth its contents.

"What are you doing?" said Glaukos. "Sit down! Sit down!"

"There is more from where this came from, much more," I assured him, casting handfuls of the tiny glittering disks about.

Men looked about, startled, curious, as the bits of metal began to rattle on the floor.

"He is mad!" said one fellow, a few feet away, at one of the low tables.

"Pay no attention," cried Glaukos. "He is drunk, drunk!"

"This is gold!" cried a man, suddenly, who had reached to the side, scooping up one of the disks.

"Gold?" asked another fellow, retrieving a disk.

"Yes, gold!" cried another man, scrambling on his knees to gather in disks.

Chaos then ensued, as patrons, grunting and crying out, rushed to seize up the disks.

"They are gone now!" cried Glaukos to the swarming patrons. "Gone! The pouch is empty! Return to your tables!"

"Gratitude to our benefactor!" cried a man.

"Yes," cried others.

Two fellows were tussling, to the side, presumably disputing the rightful possession of one of the disks.

"Yes," cried Glaukos, "all gratitude to our noble benefactor, my dear friend, Fenlon, come from far Ti, who has so generously manifested his approbation of *The Living Island*, finest of the taverns in Sybaris, and its noble patrons."

This remark was greeted with some acclaim and a pounding of the palms on the left shoulder.

Men then returned to the tables.

"Now you may drink," said Glaukos.

I then sat again at the table. I shook my head, as though to clear it. I stared at the paga goblet, as if uncertain which one I should reach for.

"Drink," said Glaukos, reassuringly.

I knew the paga had been tampered with. Surely it had not been removed from the general paga vat. I was sure the drink would not be lethal. They could not know, for certain, that the parchment within my garment was a map, nor, if it was, that it could be easily read. Certain information might be missing, or even coded. If they knew what they were doing, they would want to keep me alive, in case they might need my help in one particular way or another. Too, as several patrons of the tavern had marked me well, and gratefully, in connection with my calculated distribution of the tiny gold disks, Glaukos might be wary of having me inexplicably disappear from his premises. It would be better for him to have me found unconscious somewhere, presumably sleeping off the effects of a night of prodigious carousing. Presumably I would not be likely to prosecute a vigorous inquiry as to an alleged map that might be missing, particularly as it might be stolen property. If I did prosecute such an inquiry, Glaukos could merely deny knowledge of the map, and even affect a concern that it might be missing. Should our words be set against one another, I recalled that Glaukos was apparently a confidant of Archelaos, the governor of Thera, and, I suspected, thus, a partner, as well, in his possible machinations.

I carefully clutched the goblet in two hands, and lifted it to my lips. I tasted it. As far as I could tell, it was paga, though of an unusually fine character. It reminded me of that of the brewery of Temos.

"This is good," I said.

"It is from my personal, private stock," he said.

Presumably it contained *tassa* powder, or some similar substance, which would be tasteless. *Tassa* powder is sometimes used in the abduction of women for the markets. Depending on the strength, its effects can last from one to several Ahn. In the case of women, it is commonly mixed with a *ka-la-na* wine. The woman, fully clothed, in the robes of concealment, perhaps lifting the glass to her lips, beneath her veil, eyes seductively lustrous over the veil, imbibes the beverage. Later she recovers consciousness, perhaps lying on a stone floor, to find herself stripped and chained, a heated brazier glowing to the side, from which emerges the handle of an iron. If she cries out, though she is still free, she may be cuffed to silence, that she may understand that the kind of woman she is now to be may not speak without permission. The iron then is put to her thigh, high, below the left hip, and a metal collar rudely snapped about her neck. Sometime the slaver or captor, in examining his unconscious catch, realizes that his conjectures as to the value of the catch were overly optimistic. In such a case the woman, her clothing removed and destroyed, is left to regain consciousness in some public place. Not lightly is the brand and collar bestowed. Awakening so, nude, she senses herself a slave, but a failed slave. Often then, unworthy to be so poor a woman, so pathetic and inadequate a female, she will strive, if only secretly, by exercise and diet, by attitude and sensibility, to become worthy of the attention of strong, commanding, lustful, possessive men.

"Laios, Ctesippus," said Glaukos, summoning the two fellows, large, burly fellows, whom I had met earlier, those who had approached the table when it had not been clear that I had the means to pay for paga.

I felt the hand of Glaukos reaching inside the collar of my robe.

Somehow I seemed hardly aware of this.

I decided the drink, after all, had not been drugged. I found this of mild, detached interest.

Then I lost consciousness.

CHAPTER TWELVE

I Obtain News of the Raiders

"This is a lonely area," said Thurnock, looking about, down the long, gently curved beach.

"I chose it so," I said. "There are no known villages within three hundred pasangs."

"Aktis approaches," said Clitus.

"So soon?" I said. "Good. The raiders have acted more expeditiously than I had expected."

We had been camped four days in this spot, some pasangs from the likely landing point of the raiders. In drawing up the false map, which I had arranged to have stolen in *The Living Island*, I had located the spurious Village of Flowing Gold on Daphna, the least populated of the Farther Islands, in a desolate area, where the raiders might be most easily isolated and discomfited, no civilized enclaves at hand from which to obtain support or succor. Though there are some silver mines on Thera, presumably contributing to the wealth of Sybaris, the Farther Islands were not noted for their mineral resources. Certainly they were not noted for their streams glittering with nuggets or mountains and caves bright with veins of gold. To be sure, who knew what undiscovered riches might occur in remote regions? My seemingly reckless, unguarded distribution of the tiny gold disks in the tavern of *The Living Island* was intended to overcome any possible doubts as to the reality of *The Village of Flowing Gold*. Also, of course, the gold need not have been mined or panned. It might have been seized by peasants from shipwrecked vessels, or even cached inland by pirates, possibly generations ago.

"They have landed," said Aktis, hailing us, calling out, his arm lifted, as he trudged through the sand toward us.

A moment later he was before us.

"Hold, catch your breath," I said.

His body was shaking.

Thurnock gave him water from a bota, slung over his shoulder.

"Six ships, many men, as at Nicosia," gasped Aktis.

"Excellent," I said. "I think they will lose little time in being about their business."

"Shall we march?" asked Thurnock.

"No," I said. "Not now. There is time. Let them be well on their way."

On the false map, drawn with care, I had located the mythical Village of Flowing Gold twenty pasangs inland.

That seemed a suitable distance for what I had in mind.

Two days ago, Aktis, who served as our lookout and scout, had followed my instructions, making his way to the supposed location of *The Village of Flowing Gold*, leaving a communication, to be discovered by the raiders.

"What do we do now, Captain?" asked Thurnock.

"We shall dine," I said.

CHAPTER THIRTEEN

We do Business, on a Lonely Beach on Daphna

The fellow's eyes suddenly widened, and he made to spring up, from the shadow of the beached hull, against which he had been reclining.

"Reach for no weapon," I warned him, "or you die."

On the other side of the beached vessel, I heard a cry of alarm.

"Run, run!" cried someone from somewhere.

I heard the quick, heavy impact of an arrow off to my right, presumably into a body, but no cry of pain. I assumed it had been fired by Thurnock, whose aim could seldom be faulted.

As we had reconnoitered, no more than twenty men had been left to guard the ships, so confident of their power and the remoteness of the area were they.

"On your belly," I told the fellow before me, "arms and legs spread." I put the point of my sword to the back of his neck. "Move, and die," I said. I removed the knife from his belt and cast it into the water offshore.

I saw a burst of vulos rising from somewhere, ascending, fluttering, into the air. These small, strong-winged birds are not native to the wilds of the Farther Islands.

Clitus came about the bow of the beached ship. The raiders, so assured of themselves, had not even turned their vessels' bows to the water, from which position the ship can most quickly be brought into action. Clitus' trident was dark with blood. "Four resisted, and are dead," he said.

I heard another cry from somewhere. "Five," said Clitus.

I looked away from the ship, up the beach toward the rimming brush and scrub. I saw three bodies. Several of the raiders had fled, presumably seeking to follow the route which had been taken by the raiders' main force, but they had encountered several of my men. We had drawn the net well. Four of the raiders, disarmed, were now being returned disconsolately, apprehensively, down the beach by several men led by Tab, my cohort, of the Council of Captains of Port Kar. Three of the raiders had attempted to swim away from our attack, but had been unsuccessful. Their bodies had now been washed back on shore. Aktis, with his bow, had accounted for two of these. "For Nicosia!" he had cried, as the bodies, penetrated, had rolled lifeless in the water.

I did not think it would be wise to let Aktis handle prisoners. Peasants do their own slaughtering and think little of the spilling of blood. Too, they do not lightly regard insults to, or threats to, their Home Stones.

"Did any of the raiders escape?" I asked Clitus.

"I do not think so," he said.

"Bring the survivors here," I said.

"That they be bound and slain, each before the other, until the last is done?"

"We shall see," I said.

"Be merciful!" pleaded the prostrate raider, prone on the sand, arms and legs outstretched.

"As you were at Nicosia, and other villages?" I asked.

He groaned.

"You were fools," I said to him, "not to leave more men with the ships, not to mount guards."

"We feared nothing," he said. "What was there to fear?"

"The Friends of Nicosia," I said.

"I do not know of such a band," he said.

"Consider yourself informed," I said.

"Spare us," he said. "There are more than five hundred of us, and they will soon return to the ships. Spare us, and flee while you can."

"This is a desolate area, in which there is little fresh water," I said.

"I do not understand," he said.

"Vulos ascended," I said to Clitus.

"They were released, in a group," said Clitus. "Do not concern yourself. Our attack was swift, and unexpected. There was no time to affix messages to the birds. Their release was a wild, desperate act, the last act of one of the raiders. My trident, cast, saw to it."

"I regret only that I could not affix certain messages to the small, swift carriers," I said.

"When they reach their destination little will be known save that something is terribly amiss," said Clitus.

"Excellent," I said.

Clitus then turned away to gather the survivors amongst the raiders.

"What are you going to do with us?" asked my prisoner, prone, stretched, in the sand.

"What I please," I said. "Perhaps you should be more interested in what you are going to do for us."

"I do not understand," he said.

A bit later Clitus returned with six raiders, their hands bound behind their backs.

"Kneel them there," I said, indicating a place on the sand. I then turned to my prone prisoner. "Join them, on your knees," I said to my prisoner.

The seven were then before us, knelt.

They were surrounded by several of my men.

"Behold, and know this," I said I to them, "we are the avengers, the retaliators, the free men of the Farther Islands, the Friends of Nicosia, and other decimated and razed villages. No longer can you burn, loot, and kill with impunity."

"We will do so no longer," cried one of the prisoners.

"We are changed," cried another.

"What mercy should be shown to you?" I asked. "You are the worthless, lying minions of the nefarious Bosk of hated Port Kar, scourge of gleaming Thassa!"

"No, no!" cried more than one man. "You are wrong! That is not true! We are not adherents of the terrible Bosk of Port Kar! We are not of Port Kar! We are not the men of Bosk, not he of Port Kar! That is a pretense, a sham, a disguise!"

"I do not believe you," I said.

Several of the prisoners wept with misery.

"Now, corsairs, predators of the sea and land," I said, "you urts, enleagued with the shameless, dreaded Bosk of Port Kar, prepare to be slain in accordance with the justice of the great Archelaos, governor of Thera."

"No, merciful Captain," said he who had been my prisoner, he who alone was unbound before me, he who seemed most informed in the group, he who seemed first in the group, "Archelaos is not only cognizant of our doings but organizes and directs them, doubtless on orders from the capital, Jad, on Cos itself."

"You dare malign he who is the worthy governor of Thera itself?" I said.

"It is true, Captain!" he wept. "It is true."

"It is hard to believe," I said.

"It is true," he insisted.

"Yes, yes," said others.

"You would actually have me believe that the noble governor of Thera himself, Archelaos, he of undeniable virtue, is devious and corrupt?" I said, as though I found this hard to believe.

"Yes, noble Captain," said one of the prisoners.

"Next," I said, "you would have me believe ill doings of my friend, Glaukos, proprietor of *The Living Island*."

"Now I know you!" cried he who had been my prisoner. "You are Fenlon of Ti, who was drugged into unconsciousness, and robbed!"

"I had had too much to drink," I said. "Then somehow I found my way outside the tavern, collapsed, and was robbed by some passer-by."

"No," said he who had been my prisoner, "you were drugged and robbed by Glaukos. You were left outside the tavern by his men, Laios and Ctesippus, who even now, with hundreds of others, are trekking to some point inland."

"To *The Village of Flowing Gold*," I said.

"That is it," said he who had been my prisoner. Some of the others exchanged startled glances, from which I gathered, first, that my former prisoner must stand high amongst the raiders, being so privy to their plans, and that the others had thought this no more than another village raid, and would, accordingly, expect no more in the way of booty than what might be garnered from an assault on a typical village.

"What is your name?" I asked.

"Lysis," he said.

"You seem to be well informed," I said.

"We have more than five hundred armed and dangerous men trekking inland," said Lysis. "They will return, laden with treasure, perhaps by nightfall. You cannot hope to meet them in battle. Doubtless you could kill us and flee for your lives. That is true. But then you would receive no share of the unaccountable wealth to be derived from *The Village of Flowing Gold*. A wiser

option on your part, Captain, permit me to say, would be to hold
us as hostages and wait, demanding a goodly share of the riches
for our release."

"You would make this case to your main force?" I asked.

"Yes," he said.

"You are sure that your leaders, say, Laios and Ctesippus,
would negotiate in good faith?"

"Certainly," he said.

I noted that several of his fellows turned white at this prospect. I gathered that they had considerably less confidence in the
practicality of this arrangement than seemed to be professed by
Lysis. Could they really count on their lives being worth more to
their fellows, thieves and murderers, than gold?

"Unbind the prisoners," I said.

They regarded one another, gladly.

"Well done, Captain, noble gesture," said Lysis. "We shall not
attempt to escape."

"You," I said, "resume your former position, prone, down in
the sand, arms and legs outstretched."

"Captain?" said Lysis.

"Now," I said.

I addressed my men. "Take these six prisoners to the ships, six
to each ship, one after the other, and bring all vessels, kegs, barrels, bottles, and such, of potables, all wine, paga, water, anything
drinkable, to this point. If any demur, or attempt to flee, kill them,
instantly."

A half an Ahn later a number of vessels, kegs, crates, and such,
were heaped on the sand before me.

"These are all the supplies?" I asked Clitus.

"Yes," he said.

"You hesitate," I said.

"It is odd," said Clitus, "two of the ships have unusually deco-
rated decks."

"How so?" I asked.

"Bright colors," he said, "wide markings, plain, simple, broad
designs."

"Interesting," I said.

"Why would that be?" asked Clitus.

"I do not know," I said.

"Nor I," said Clitus.

I then returned my attention to the prisoners.

"Now," I said. "Take each of the six prisoners to one of the raiders' ships, have them light brands, and set fire to the ship."

"No!" cried Lysis, prone in the sand beside me.

"If any demur, or attempt to flee, kill them, instantly," I said.

"It will be done, Captain," said Clitus.

"Demur, attempt to flee," urged Aktis, putting an arrow to his bow.

Shortly thereafter six ships were aflame, four fifty-oared, two thirty-oared. Smoke curled into the sky, mingling its fumes with the fresh salt air of Thassa. From where we stood fire raged, loud, hissing, devouring wood and canvas, heated air leaping past us.

I put my sword to the back of Lysis' neck.

"Now," I said, "shatter the vessels, break open the kegs and barrels, empty the contents of all containers. Let the sand be soaked with water, let the ground be drunk with paga and *ka-la-na*."

The six prisoners standing amidst my men, looked wildly at one another.

"Do it!" said Lysis, the tip of my sword bloody at the back of his neck.

Under the weaponry of my men the sand was soon sodden and stained.

"Have no fear," I said. "Your raiders inland will have water, enough for their march and return. Perhaps some will be left when they get back. Perhaps they will share it with you."

"In a day," said Lysis, "it will be gone. They will kill one another for a swallow of water."

"Remember Nicosia," I said.

Lysis squirmed in the sand.

"Bind them all," I said, "hand and foot."

In this way they could not follow us.

"You will be freed when your fellows return," I said. "Then you will be free to share in all the riches brought back from *The Village of Flowing Gold*."

"One cannot drink gold," said Lysis, as he was being bound.

"Nor would it be wise to try," I said.

"Take comfort in the thought of dying rich," said Aktis.

"Sleen, peasant!" hissed Lysis.

"Remember Nicosia," said Aktis.

We were soon withdrawing from the beach. We looked back at the still burning ships. In an Ahn or so I conjectured the main force of the raiders would have reached their destination, that point on the map designated as the location of *The Village of Flowing Gold*.

"We will now return to camp," I said.

"Aktis left a message for the raiders at their march's end," said Thurnock.

"Yes," I said, "on a sign, prominently placed."

"It is all they will find," said Clitus.

"Of course," I said.

"He cannot read," said Thurnock. "Did you tell him what it said?"

"Of course," I said.

"I, too, am of the Peasants," said Thurnock.

An inability to read is common amongst the Peasants, and not that uncommon in the lower castes.

"It said," I said, "'Welcome to *The Village of Flowing Gold*, your ships are burning.'"

CHAPTER FOURTEEN

An Anomaly is Noted, a Day from Daphna

"Ho," called down the lookout, from the ringed platform near the top of the single mast, "land, island, tiny, four points Ror!"

Whereas I, in the interests of intelligibility, have often had recourse to directions apt to my native world, Earth directions, applied to Gor, such as north, south, and so on, Goreans orient their compasses, with its eight major divisions, to the Sardar Mountains, lair of the Priest-Kings, the gods of Gor. Ror is the first of the four divisions left of Ta-Sardar-Var, which, in its orienting role, would be similar to our magnetic north.

Clitus, Thurnock, and I went to the port rail.

We were aboard the *Tesephone*. Earlier, in the vicinity of Nicosia, on Chios, prior to beaching on Daphna, we had mounted shearing blades and rams. The *Dorna*, a formidable ship of war, fifty-oared, capable of a devastating strike, commanded by Tab, was in our lee.

We were a day from Daphna, following our destruction of the raider fleet. I had set our course for the Cove of Harpalos, where resentment of Cos and a judicious gift to the harbor authorities, as before, I conjectured, would do much to give us a relatively secure anchorage. I supposed that the search for us, which we had earlier evaded, it turning up nothing for the raiders, was unlikely to be resumed, at least at that place, no more than at dozens of other inlets and coves which had been examined in vain. Too, if raiders or allies of raiders managed to muster a ship or ships, we might always, well warned by lookouts posted, depart or, if it seemed to our advantage, meet them at sea.

"I did not note that island on our voyage to Daphna," said Thurnock.

"It would be easily missed," I said.

"It is much like the other," said Clitus, "encountered on our course from Chios to the Cove of Harpalos."

"I could not tell the difference," said Thurnock.

"Perhaps it is the same," said Clitus. "It has just moved."

"Beware, Fisherman," growled Thurnock.

"Perhaps there are several such tiny islands, or skerries, in these waters," I said.

We could see some brush, and huts, some drying nets, and some small fishing boats, these beached on the grayish, flattish, featureless surface. One or two men were looking at us. One waved, to which gesture we responded.

"I see no women or children on this one," said Thurnock.

"I think these tiny islets are temporary resting places for fishermen," I said, "transitory camps, scattered locations enlarging their fishing grounds."

"Look," said Thurnock, "there is a spume of gas, or water."

Moisture seemed to rise in the air, several feet, hover, and then dissipate.

"That confirms our guess as to the origin of such islands," I said. "That is a geyser, or an issuance of steam."

"The volcano is still active," said Clitus.

"Clearly," I said.

Our men were not at the benches. We had a fair wind, and, even if it were not so, the lateen-rigged vessel would be little dismayed, as it sails closer to the wind than its square-rigged fellows, commonly found in the north. The lateen-rigged vessel is said to be a brother to the wind.

"I would not care to be on the desolate beaches of Daphna now," said Clitus.

"At *The Village of Flowing Gold*," said Thurnock, "the raiders found neither gold nor water."

"Some," said Clitus, "the most skillful and unscrupulous, will hoard what water there is and kill their way to the nearest village."

"What they take to be the nearest village," I said.

"Captain?" asked Clitus.

"The nearest village," I said, "is some three hundred pasangs away and I neglected to include it on the map. I did include some closer villages on the map, but they exist only on the map."

"Some raiders will construct rafts from the charred timbers of the burned ships, rig sails, and attempt to leave the beach," said Thurnock.

"How far will they get, with little or no water?" asked Clitus.

"Some others, mad with thirst, will wander crazily into the hills, hoping to find streams or wells," said Thurnock. "Others, at last, will rush to the shore, gorge themselves with fluid, and die the hideous salt death."

"In the vast Tahari," I said, "thirsting men have rushed upon the lances of foes, have tried to drink one another's blood."

"How could so fearful a thing be known?" asked Clitus.

"From the bodies," I said, "from the beards and necks."

"We have destroyed the raiders," said Clitus.

"Let us return to Port Kar," said Thurnock.

"What of Glaukos and Archelaos?" I asked.

"Two arrows," said Thurnock, "and they are the feasting of jards."

I looked back, and then looked back, again.

We had left Daphna and were bound for the Cove of Harpalos.

"What is wrong?" asked Thurnock.

"Nothing," I said, "only that it seems odd."

"What?" asked Thurnock.

"Look," I said.

"At what?" he asked.

"The tiny island," I said.

"What about it?" he asked, looking back, shading his eyes.

"Our speed must be greater than it seems," I said.

"How so?" asked Thurnock.

"So soon, that the island is so distant," I said.

CHAPTER FIFTEEN

Disturbing Reports have been Received; Tab Learns of the Fair of the Farther Islands; The *Tesephone* will Depart with the Tide

In my tent, high amidst the crags of the Cove of Harpalos, I angrily thrust aside the reports of several selected men, chosen from the crews of the *Dorna* and *Tesephone*, these acting as informants, frequenting the bazaars, the alleys and streets, the taverns and inns, the wharves and waterfronts, of Sybaris.

"It makes no sense," I said to lean, handsome Tab, excitable, with high cheekbones, fellow captain from Port Kar.

"I have communicated the contents, as directed," said Tab, "to the men. They have, as we, no understanding of how it could come about, no explanation of the business."

"The reports agree," I said. "We cannot dismiss them."

"Perhaps a fleet of round ships was somehow in the vicinity, perhaps blown off course, and responded to beacons of distress."

"I chose the location of the alleged Village of Flowing Gold carefully," I said. "The area is barren, it is not on lines of normal shipping, there was no storm, no evidence of a passing fleet. Surely we saw not the least hint of such."

"Still," said Tab, "the raiders, in their hundreds, are now encamped outside Sybaris."

"Even if the vulos released at the time of our attack, messageless or not, returned to some cot in Sybaris, it would have taken days for ships to reach Daphna, and the raiders, or most of them, would have perished of dehydration."

"Some fortuitous intervention obviously occurred," said Tab.

"Intervention perhaps," I said, "but I suspect little of fortuity in the business."

"It is angering," said Tab. "We thought ourselves rid of the raiders."

"It seems," I said, bitterly, "we were less clever and victorious than we thought."

"No," said Tab. "We did well. Our *kaissa* was flawless. The victory was ours."

"Our victory was barren," I said.

"Not at all," he said. "Our victory was complete. It is merely that the expected consequence of the victory did not materialize."

"Laios and Ctesippus have been seen again in Glaukos' tavern," I said.

"I am not surprised," said Tab.

"Thurnock and Aktis petition to be sent to Sybaris," I said. "They have arrows for Glaukos and Archelaos."

"Will you send them?" asked Tab.

"Not every time is the time to string a bow," I said. "Not every time is the time to draw an arrow from the quiver."

"Raiders may persist," said Tab, "but their ships are gone."

"They are supported in high places," I said, "perhaps even from Jad on far Cos. New ships will be provided, perhaps even from the naval fleet of the Farther Islands. I expect they will soon be active again, a hazard to shipping, a menace to small settlements, proclaiming their ravages to be the work of Bosk of Port Kar."

"We are few," said Tab. "We need allies."

"And they may be found," I said.

"How so?" said Tab.

"Only the armed can be truly free," I said.

"I do not understand," said Tab.

"Have you heard of the Fair of the Farther Islands?" I asked.

"No," said Tab.

"This year," I said, "it is being held at Mytilene on Chios."

"Nicosia was on Chios," said Tab.

"Precisely," I said.

"I do not understand," said Tab.

"On the islands," I said, "there are many stands of *ka-la-na*."

"Wine trees," said Tab.

"The wood is strong, and supple," I said.

"Yes?" said Tab.

"And there are many strong-winged birds, shore birds and sea birds, for example, the sea kite, much like the Vosk gull."

"Granted," said Tab.

"And fibers abound, hemp, linen, and silk, which may be cunningly twisted."

"What has all this to do with?" asked Tab.

"Freedom," I said.

Tab seemed puzzled, but did not pursue the matter.

"I fear it is late," he said.

"Return to the *Dorna*," I said.

"She is restless," he said. "Her ram and shearing blades thirst for blood."

"The larl and sleen are patient," I said. "They bide their time."

"What, for the morrow?" he said.

"The *Tesephone* departs with the tide," I said.

"To what end?" he asked.

"To seek an island," I said.

"What island?" he asked.

"One such that it appears on no chart," I said.

CHAPTER SIXTEEN

The Isle of Seleukos; Cuy; I Depart from the Isle of Seleukos, More Informed than when I Landed

"There!" cried Thurnock, pointing.

We had been three days at sea.

"Good," I said, joining him at the bow.

"At last we have found it," said Thurnock.

"Or one such," I said.

"I do not understand your interest here," said Thurnock. "Why do you want to see such a thing, so empty, so small, so flat, and barren?"

"I am curious," I said.

"Are there not more important matters with which to concern ourselves?" asked Thurnock.

"Possibly," I said.

"Of what interest can such a thing, or things, be?" asked Thurnock.

"Perhaps of considerable interest," I said.

"They have seen us," said Thurnock.

"Approach, at leisure, alarm no one," I called back to Clitus, who communicated this to the helmsmen.

"There are more than some men there," said Thurnock. "There are also some women, festively garbed, young women."

"Bring us alongside," I called back to Clitus.

"Stand off," said Thurnock. "There may be reefs, unseen rocks."

"I do not think so," I said. "I have not thought so, for days."

"Take soundings," said Thurnock.

"Here, so far at sea," I said, "we need not do so."

"You are not so far at sea," said Thurnock. "You are on the brink of land, an island, though one tiny and inauspicious."

"No ordinary island," I said.

"Proceed with care," said Thurnock.

"The inhabitants are few and unarmed," I said.

"I speak not of denizens, of natives, of villagers," said Thurnock. "I speak of rocks, of stones that jut and tear."

The *Tesephone*'s port side rocked gently against a rounded surface which seemed to curve back, and descend, for several feet, and was then lost from sight, under the water. Interestingly, when the *Tesephone* had touched the shore, one sensed, that the shore had drawn back a little, almost imperceptibly, as though reacting to the pressure of the *Tesephone*'s hull.

"Tal," I called to those on shore, my right hand lifted, palm toward the side of my head.

"Tal!" called some of the men, returning the gesture. "You are one of several. We have been waiting for you. Regard the belts of our girls. They are still light. There is still room upon them."

Several of the gaudily clad young women smiled, and laughed, and waved.

"What are they talking about?" asked Thurnock.

"I have no idea," I said.

I noted some of the men in pairs, carrying heavy, drilled stones to the shore.

"Mooring ropes," I said to the port-side oarsmen, who, standing, leaving their benches, had joined Thurnock and myself at the rail.

Ropes from the *Tesephone* were cast ashore and secured to the stones. Others from the shore, fastened to the stones, were cast over the rail of the *Tesephone*, which were then secured on board.

"No!" cried Thurnock.

But I had already vaulted over the rail and, catching my balance, unsteady for a moment, stood upright on the shore.

"Follow me, friend," I called back to him.

"Welcome," said one of the men on shore.

Thurnock eased himself over the rail, had his feet on shore, gained his balance, and was beside me.

"This is not soil, not rock," he said, disbelievingly.

We stood on a gray, coarse surface, the texture of which reminded me of the hide of the common, nine-gilled Gorean shark. But it was hide or skin, which I conjectured might be a foot or more thick. At first, I was much aware that the object on which I stood was not still, not anchored in place, was not like an island, but was responsive to the water, that it rested in the water, that it floated. Shortly thereafter, however, I was no longer attentive to this, nor even cognizant of it. It was more like being afoot on a large vessel, platform, or raft.

"Ai!" cried Thurnock, drawing back.

Several yards away, to my left, where the object narrowed somewhat, a previously submerged portion of the object had suddenly reared upward, shedding water, and, simultaneously, roaring and hissing, there was towering expellation of hot, moist air and water. This phenomenon lasted for ten or fifteen Ihn, creating a towering mist, which then, slowly, dissipated, descending in a cascade of droplets.

We had seen such a thing from far away once, but had misinterpreted what we had seen.

"Ah, Thurnock," I said, "it is not gas, nor fumes, not evidence of volcanic activity."

"Islands cannot breathe," said Thurnock.

"This one does," I said.

There was then a lengthy, auditory intake of breath which lasted several Ihn. It was hard to guess at the volume of oxygen that the creature had drawn within its body, but it must have been considerable.

"How often does the island breathe?" I asked.

"When it wishes," said a villager.

"It can go more than a day," said another.

"It has its breathing door," said another. "It closes the door when it puts its head under water. It does not wish to drown."

"Why does it put its head under water?" I asked.

"It must eat," said a man.

One of the fellows laughed.

"I saw no eyes," I said.

"The eyes are underneath," said a man, "like the paddles, the beak, and tentacles, where it finds its food. I do not know if it could see in air or not."

"I have never seen anything like this before," I said.

"Perhaps you are unfamiliar with these waters," said a fellow.

I did not think it judicious to respond to that speculation.

"They are large," said a man. "There is as much below the water as above the water."

"More, much more," said another.

"Some are larger than others," said a fellow. "It depends on their age."

"This one is somewhere between a hundred and two hundred years old," volunteered another.

"Young," said another man.

"Do you not fear that it will dive, that it will submerge?" I asked.

"We have our boats at hand," said a man.

"There is always warning, a restlessness," said a man.

"They seldom go beneath the surface oftener than every ten or fifteen years," said a man.

"Then to mate," said a short fellow.

"We want our gifts!" wailed one of the women, to the side.

"Fetch them from others," said a man impatiently.

"Yes," cried more than one of the young women, and, released, they hurried away, to mingle eagerly with the crew of the *Tesephone*.

"They have not yet been companioned," said he who had, with a word, released the women. "They wish to enhance their attractiveness by augmenting their dowries."

I scarcely attended to this, as it seemed local business.

"This thing, this living place," I said, "tolerates your presence?"

"I do not think it knows we are here," said a man.

"We are good for it, and it is good for us," said one of the fellows. "It supplies us with a camp, a station, which much enlarges the range of our fishing grounds. On our part, we scrape and clean it, especially the breathing door, fend away predators, and share our catch with it."

"What do you call these things?" I asked.

"Living islands, of course," said he who seemed first amongst those met on shore. "This one is called 'Isle of Seleukos'."

"He who just spoke," said a fellow, "is our headman, Seleukos."

"He is first in our village, the village of Seleukos," said another.

I was much interested in prosecuting certain inquiries but I did not think it politic to make known certain concerns to the men of this transitory fishing camp. I did not know what they knew, or where their allegiances might lie. Accordingly, I would prefer to seek information which might be purveyed more openly, less critically, more innocently.

"I wish you well," I said to the men.

"Enjoy yourself," said Seleukos.

"I trust your pouch bulges with trinkets and baubles," said another.

I turned away, puzzled.

In order that what follows might be more easily grasped, let me give a brief account of certain aspects of the culture of several of the living islands, of which we may take Isle of Seleukos to be typical. The young women of many such islands, villages, or stations, seek the status, security, honor, and pleasures, of the companionship. Thus, they seek to enhance their innate desirability, which is often considerable, by accumulating what is, in effect, a personal dowry. They liberally exchange their favors for coins, pins, badges, beads, medals, brooches, and such, which they commonly hang on their belts. In this way they not only proclaim their interest in, and eligibility for, the companionship, but make clear, given the weight and value of the belt, both their allure and likely prowess.

I made my way carefully amongst fondling couples.

I feared that my quest for a suitable informant, given the general busyness of the afternoon, might come to naught. Then, near the wall of a small shelter, some yards away, a tiny enclosure like a hut of sticks and thatch, I saw a rather plain young woman, one so plain that the plainness itself, regarded carefully, becomes a sort of beauty. She was alone, her dress was unwrinkled and unsoiled. There were tears on her cheeks. There were few adornments attached her belt.

I approached her.

She looked away. "Do not mock me," she said.

"Excuse me," I said, "but you seem unoccupied."

"You are perceptive," she said.

"May I speak to you?" I asked.

"Speak?" she said.

"Yes," I said.

"With me?"

"Yes."

"What is wrong with you?" she asked. "Can you not see? Perhaps the sun is in your eyes."

"The others are occupied," I said.

"And I am not," she said.

"No," I said, "it seems you are not."

"I do not have a face like a hogfish," she said.

"No," I said. "You certainly do not."

"No?" she said.

"No," I said.

"I may look like a hogfish," she said. "But I am good. I cannot help myself. I am hot. I gush and oil."

"I am sure you do," I said.

"He who tries me is never disappointed," she said.

"I am sure of it," I said.

"Try me," she said.

"I have other concerns," I said.

"Then what do you want?" she said.

"To talk," I said.

"Just that?"

"Yes," I said.

"I did not think I was that homely," she said.

"You are not homely," I said. "You have a different kind of beauty."

"I hope not too different," she said.

"I am prepared to pay for your time," I said. "A copper tarsk. You can pierce it, and tie it on your belt."

"Not a tarsk-bit?" she said. "A whole copper tarsk?"

"Yes," I said, "and one not clipped, not trimmed, not even shaved."

"Of what shall we speak?" she asked. "Of love, of fishing, of villages, of men, of Priest-Kings, of the mysteries of the universe? I warn you. I know little of Priest-Kings or the mysteries of the universe."

"Nor do I," I said. "I would speak of living islands, of men, and ships."

"Let me see the copper tarsk," she said.

I drew forth such a coin from my pouch, displayed it, a bit ostentatiously I fear, and then, with great deliberation, replaced it firmly in my pouch. Each phrase of this operation she perused intently.

"What is your name?" I asked.

"Cuy," she said.

This name is pronounced in two syllables. I think it is a village corruption of 'Chloe', which is a familiar name in Cos, Tyros, and the Farther Islands.

"How many living islands are there?" I asked.

"I do not know," she said. "They are rare, but there are several."

"Some are enleagued with ships, are they not?" I asked.

"Of course," she said. "And some are claimed by villages and towns, as is this one."

"On some," I said, "are there kept stores, supplies, tackle, weapons, water, ship gear?"

"I have heard so," she said, "on some of the larger islands."

"Have you heard of the notorious Bosk of Port Kar?" I asked.

"Who has not heard of that dreadful pirate, so elusive and ruthless a corsair?"

"Might his predations, on land and sea, be somehow supported and abetted by living islands?"

"I should hope not," she said.

"Might some not serve as observation sites or posts, enlarging the compass of his intelligence, informing him of passing shipping, and such?"

"I trust that such is not the case," she said.

"But if it were," I said, "would such communication, such an interchange of information, be possible?"

"Easily," she said. "Many message vulos home to particular islands as well as to villages and towns, even to particular ships."

"How could a vulo home to a ship?" I asked.

"If the ship bears its cot," she said. "Like most birds, message vulos have keen eyesight, and the homing circles of a message vulo, searching for its cot, can range over hundreds of pasangs."

I recalled that Clitus had informed me that certain large, simple designs had been painted on the deck of two of the raiders' ships, but I had thought little of it at the time. I had seen no point to the designs at the time, but I now realized that they would be visible from a considerable height.

"Then messages might be sent from a living island to a ship," I said, "and from a ship to a given living island."

"Certainly," she said. "And, in some cases, from ship to ship."

I had, of late, feared such a thing might be possible.

"In the Farther Islands," she said, "vulos have been selected and bred for generations for just such an aptitude."

"I suspect," I said, "living islands, being alive, can move."

"And do," she said. "They swim. How else could they seek food?"

"This island," I said, "seems inert, phlegmatic, immobile, passive."

"So are they all," she said. "How else could they be mistaken for islands? They are a massive life form, which moves little and, after feeding, can sleep for weeks, which two characteristics much diminish its need for food."

"And the men, conveniently accessing new fishing grounds, share their catch with the island," I said.

"Each benefits the other," she said.

"The richest fishing is in shallower water," I said, "where light can nourish plants, and fish come to feed on the plants, and larger fish come to feed on smaller fish."

"Shallower water is not always close to shore," she said. "In many places there are broad, risen plateaus under the water, sometimes several pasangs in width, plateaus which are often no more than twenty or thirty feet under the surface of the water. They make excellent fishing grounds."

"If the islands sleep," I said, "how can they breathe?"

"Easily," she said. "They lift their breathing door from the water, expel used air and inhale fresh air, all this done in their sleep."

"The men told me a living island can go more than a day without breathing," I said.

"That is true," she said. "But usually they do not go so long."

"I have seen brush on at least one living island," I said.

"The men do that," she said. "Some soil, some seeds, some plants. That is done to fool strangers into thinking that the living island is an ordinary island. Too, for those who are familiar with these islands, it makes clear that a given island is spoken for, that it is claimed."

"How long do living islands live?" I asked.

"I do not know," she said. "Some say a thousand years."

"For their feeding," I said, "they must seek fishing grounds."

"When one encounters a living island in the wild," she said, "one may be sure the fishing will be good."

"I do not understand," I said.

"In that way," she said, "they help the men find good fishing."

"In the wild?" I asked.

"But not in the wild," she said, "the men, ranging widely in their boats, can locate fresh fishing grounds. In that way, they can help their living island."

"This is hard to understand," I said.

"The living island is a predator, and territorial," she said. "Their rage and contests are hideous to behold. I have only heard about this, of course. But once, when I was a girl, I swam near the head of the island, which is forbidden. I saw the beak and tentacles, under water. I have never forgotten that. I have never swum there again."

"It is hard to think of a living island, so placid and somnolent, as predacious or territorial," I said.

"Older, stronger islands will drive younger, weaker islands away," she said. "It has to do with what the fishing grounds can support."

"There must be many predators at a fishing ground," I said, "sharks, sea sleen, fanged eels, wide-mouthed grunts, and such."

"The living island is concerned only with its own kind," she said.

"I do not see how men can be of help in such matters," I said.

"They locate fishing grounds and bring their islands to them. In this way the men help the island and the island, in turn, helps the men, giving the men a rich offshore camp or base."

"But such," I said, "would require the living island to be moved, and not only to be moved, but to be moved purposely."

"Of course," she said.

"Is this possible?" I asked.

"Certainly," she said.

Suddenly much seemed to fall into place.

"How is this done?" I asked.

"We have not acted so in months," she said.

"How is it done?" I asked.

"There are various ways," she said. "All animal life withdraws from strong stimuli, perhaps because such stimuli, surprising and unexplained, are often associated with the presence of a danger, such as a predator. The most common way of doing this is to create noise, say, the striking together of chains of pots and pans dangled under the water."

Sound, of course, is amplified under water. A shark, for example, can respond to the thrashing of an injured fish better than two hundred yards away.

"This stimulus is disfavored by the island, and it moves away from the sound. In this way it may be guided in any direction."

"How do men determine the course?" I asked.

"As mariners," she said, "some by compass, others by the sun and stars."

"There are other ways, too, the island may be moved?" I asked.

"By striking on the hide," she said, "with wooden mallets. That does not hurt the island, as far as we can tell, but it does tend to move away from the annoyance. There are cruel ways, too, but we do not practice them on the Isle of Seleukos, for we care for our island, ways such as digging in the hide and striking nerves with pointed sticks, and digging in the hide and applying hot irons to the wound."

"It seems that this would make the island an enemy of men," I said.

"The islands do not even know that men exist," she said.

"You have been more than helpful, Cuy," I said. "I have learned much. I am very grateful."

"I am pleased if you are pleased," she said.

"Perhaps you have your eyes on some young fellow of the village," I said.

"Xanthos and I care for one another," she said. "He does not think I am so ugly."

"You are not ugly," I said.

"How I look is only part of me," she said. "I am more than how I look."

"Certainly," I said.

"Xanthos even likes to talk to me," she said. "We have long talks."

"Good," I said.

"That is unusual for a man, is it not?" she asked.

"Not really," I said.

"But the matter is hopeless," she said.

"How so?" I asked.

"My belt is light," she said. "His father would not permit him to drink the wine of companionship with one so unfit as I."

"A stern father," I said.

"He has his pride," she said. "He must be concerned for his office, his position, his prestige and image."

"Who is his father?" I asked.

"Seleukos," she said, "our headman."

"I promised you," I said, "a copper tarsk for your time."

"And now it will be a tarsk-bit, or less?" she asked, tears appearing in her eyes.

"No," I said, drawing a coin from my pouch, "here, rather, is a silver tarsk."

Many slaves sell for less than a silver tarsk.

"No," she whispered, "no!"

I pressed the coin into her hand, and, with two hands, literally folded her fingers about it, as I feared she could not hold it.

"This will buy a boat, a fine boat, of the workmanship of Naxos, two boats," she said, "one for Xanthos, one for his father."

"You are now, I wager," I said, "the richest girl in your village, and the most desirable girl in your village."

"What is your name?" she asked.

"Kenneth Statercounter, Eiron of Naxos, Fenlon of Ti, or any other name which might appeal to you," I said.

I then turned about and clapped my hands, sharply. "Ho, men!" I cried. "Board, board! The oars are waiting, the canvas is slack. Board! Board! We must be on our way!"

Shortly thereafter, the *Tesephone*, freed of the lines attached to the heavy drilled stones, drifted from the side of the Isle of Seleukos.

Thurnock and I, as we took our departure, oars rising, shedding bright water, like drops of light, looked back to the island.

We waved to the men and they to us. The girls, too, waved, adornments sparkling on many a belt. Among them stood Cuy, smiling and laughing, one hand waving, the other clutched on some small object.

"Do you remember Sakim, the drunken, distraught mariner, he from the tavern of Glaukos, he so mocked, he of the wild stories?" asked Thurnock.

"Surely," I said.

"It seems he was not insane," said Thurnock. "I spoke to men on the island. They, too, have seen the monster."

"The sea hith?" I said.

"Whatever it is," he said.

CHAPTER SEVENTEEN

I Make a Purchase; I Examine my New Property;
I Make Use of my New Property

"Here," said my agent, "is the slave."

Hooded, closely and opaquely, briefly tunicked, bound hand and foot, her wrists tied behind her, the girl was thrown to her belly before me.

Gorean slaves are seldom treated gently.

I could see the collar on her neck, under the hood, locked, closely encircling her throat. I had arranged that she did not know whose collar it was, nor why she had been purchased.

She lay there before me, in the light of the single, dangling tharlarion-oil lamp, prone, helpless, trembling and disoriented, on the dark, polished, wooden floor of my room in an obscure inn, *The Fat Urt*, in Sybaris, near the harbor where the *Tesephone* was inconspicuously at anchor, crowded amongst dozens of similar small ships.

I noted that she was wise enough not to dare to speak.

Though she had not been long on Gor, she, highly intelligent as are most Earth females brought to Gor as slaves, was already well aware of what she might and might not do, what she might and might not be permitted.

That is one of the first things they learn as a slave.

The agent placed his right foot on her back and pressed down, briefly, firmly, for an Ihn or so. Then he removed his foot from her back, and stood to the side. The pressure of his foot on her back had informed her that she was to remain as she had been placed.

But, presumably, of that she would already have been well aware.

The breaking of position on the part of a slave can easily be cause for discipline.

I regarded her for some time, not speaking.

Presumably she knew she was being looked upon.

The tiny, sleeveless tunic she wore, this one of gray, clinging rep cloth, was a typical slave garment. It had no nether closure and was all she wore.

Resources are seldom wasted on slaves.

The daily garmenture of a free woman might clothe a dozen slaves.

Sometimes slaves are clad in mere scraps and rags. Indeed, slaves, as they are animals, need not be clothed, at all. They are often nude before their masters, and, if the master pleases, in public, as well.

I continued to look upon her.

She was a woman from Earth.

Doubtless she was familiar with, accustomed to, and had profited from, the many advantages, preferences, preferments, and privileges, educational, economic, and social, which had been lavished upon her by her society. Perhaps, naturally enough, she had taken them for granted, taken them to be her due, her right. On Earth, as a female, she had been special. She had been important. She had had high status.

"This is a slave," I said. "Why is she clothed?"

The tiny tunic was cut open at the back, from collar to hem, pulled out from under her, and discarded.

"I trust you did not spend much for her," I said.

"Forty copper tarsks," he said, handing me the small sack which would contain my change. "She is a barbarian. She is cheap. Who would want her for anything, save as sleen feed, or to cast her to eels in some garden pool?"

The girl whimpered pathetically but was instantly kicked to silence by a movement of the agent's foot.

I saw she still had to learn something of her collar.

I would be pleased to teach it to her.

Who does not enjoy teaching a woman her collar?

It was interesting that she was cheap, for girls from my native world, Earth, brought to Gor for the collar, often brought good prices, at least on the continent, and on Cos and Tyros, sometimes equaling or even exceeding those of native-born *kajirae*. It seemed, however, that they were less esteemed on the Farther Islands.

To be sure, I was pleased that she had cost so little.

It pleases one to have obtained a good purchase.

In passing, it might be noted that female slaves on Gor are abundant, and, accordingly, tend to be inexpensive, a beauty often going for as little as a silver tarsk. Many a woman whose remarkable loveliness on Earth might have led to the acquisition of considerable advantages in Earth society find themselves, once brought to Gor, the possessions of a fellow with modest, even minimal, means. They find that their silks, diamonds, and furs, so to speak, are exchanged for a rag and collar on Gor.

I looked down at the prostrate, trembling slave.

I knew her, of course, and had made it extremely clear to my agent, by both explicit description, even to tiny marks and blemishes, and current slave name, the particular article I had in mind.

"Regard the slave," I said to my agent. "See the small feet, the slim ankles, the sweet thighs, the delightful, well-formed, fundament, the slender waist, the joys of her figure, the soft shoulders, and the graceful, metal-encircled neck. Surely, you can think of some use for this exquisite object other than feeding it to sleen or eels."

"She is a barbarian," he said.

"Does she juice well?" I asked.

"I have heard so," he said.

I knew, of course, that she juiced well, and beggingly. In an alcove, weeks ago, she had writhed helplessly in her chains.

It is interesting how responsive are female slaves, owned women subject to uncompromising masculine domination.

"I am well pleased," I said. "You have done well. Your fee." I drew five copper tarsks from the sack and placed them, one by one, in his outstretched palm.

"I think I could have found you one who is not a barbarian," he said, "for not much more."

"This one will do very nicely," I said.

He placed the five coins in his pouch.

"Shall I whip her before I leave?" he asked.

"No," I said.

"You have a whip at hand?" he said.

"Of course," I said.

"I wish you well," he said.

"I wish you well," I said.

I watched the agent take his leave.

"May I speak?" she asked.

"No," I said.

Word had reached me at the Cove of Harpalos that the raiders outside Sybaris had broken camp and, as far as my informants could determine, were now scattered about, but proximately, some distributed within Sybaris and others beyond its *pomerium*, in the nearby countryside. I inferred two likelihoods given this information, one encouraging and the other considerably less so. First, and heartening, it seemed that Archelaos recognized the suspicious nature of openly maintaining a large number of armed men in the vicinity of Sybaris, many of a presumably unsavory sort. Would this not elicit curiosity? Might it not seem to require an explanation? Who are these men and what might be their purpose or purposes? This suggested that Archelaos might not be invulnerable in Sybaris. He apparently deemed it prudential, at least at present, to continue to dissociate himself from any possible relationship to the corsairs who had terrorized coastal villages and the local waters. Tyrants thrive where justice sleeps, but what if justice should stir and wake? It behooves the wise tyrant to tread softly and embellish his image as the selfless servant of the people. What tyrant is so stupid as not to do so? Urts and jards take care not to wake the larl on whose kill they feed. Second, and disappointing, the keeping of the raiders at hand clearly signified that Archelaos, despite the recent adventure in connection with the supposed Village of Flowing Gold, had no intention of forsaking his dark enterprises. How soon, then, could he recoup his losses? How soon could new ships be obtained and fitted? What would he do? And where next might he strike? We were few, and knew too little.

I looked down at the girl.

"You may speak," I said.

"I lie before you, prone, stripped, bound, and hooded," she said.

"That is appropriate," I said, "as you are a slave."

"Yes, Master," she said. "Am I bellied before my Master?"

"Yes," I said.

I rose to my feet, went to the side, took the room whip from its hook on the wall, and returned to stand near her.

I then, suddenly, without warning, cracked the whip. Though the blade had not touched her, she had uttered an inadvertent cry of fear.

I saw that she knew the whip and what it could do to her.

"Am I to be whipped?" she asked.

"As is often the case," I said, "that has much to do with the slave."

"I shall try to be pleasing," she said.

I put the whip at my belt, and knelt beside her. I lifted her bound ankles an inch or two and let them drop, and then lifted her bound wrists some three or four inches and let them drop.

"You are well tied," I said.

"Yes, Master," she said.

Even Gorean boys are taught the tying of female slaves, provided by mentors for their practice. It does not take a woman long to learn that she is utterly helpless.

I then loosened and removed the bonds on her ankles and wrists, threw them to the side, and lifted her to her knees.

"Do you know who I am?" I asked. "Do you know my voice?"

"I am not sure," she said. "I think so. I hope so."

I unbuckled the hood at the back of her neck, drew the hood from her, and tossed it, too, to the side.

Her face was red from the hood, and her hair was damp.

It is not pleasant being the prisoner of a hood.

Too, in one, one is very helpless.

"Oh, Master! Master!" she cried with joy, and threw herself to her belly before me. She seized my ankles, and pressed her lips again and again to my feet, covering them with eager, mad kisses, and uttering broken sounds and garbled, incoherent words. "I so hoped," she said. "So hoped! You cannot conceive how helpless is the female slave, how she can do nothing, how she belongs to others, how she cannot help what is done with her, how she has nothing to say or do as to whom she will belong, as to whom she will be traded, sold or given! Oh, Master! Master! I waited for you so long, on my chain. Night after night! But my manacle was removed and I must hurry to serve others! It was always others! Others! I have never forgotten your touch, what it was to be at your feet! Had you forgotten me? Had I been insufficiently pleasing! I hoped, so hoped, again and again, that you would come again to the tavern! Now you are my Master, and I am your slave, your slave!" She was weeping with joy, her damp, dark hair about my feet, her lips pressing more, and more, kisses to my feet.

I seized her hair with my left hand and pulled her up to her knees before me. I removed the whip from my belt and held it to her lips, where, immediately, in tears, she began to lick and kiss it with fervor.

There are many acts and practices on Gor, postures, expressions, and behaviors, which are deeply meaningful and profoundly symbolic. One of these is "kissing the whip," where the slave kisses the very whip to which she is subject. Some Masters require a slave, particularly a new slave, to "kiss the whip" until it is done properly, rightfully, humbly, respectfully, sincerely, authentically, even, eventually, reverently, and gratefully. In the course of this exercise, the slave, if lax or inattentive, or if the least bit reluctant or resistant, may feel the whip, and as often as is deemed necessary, these brief admonitions providing an incentive for her to renew her efforts. By such means, she is encouraged to do better and, eventually, achieve success. A slave is expected to kiss the whip well. By means of this exercise, and several others, she learns her collar. Behavior comes first; understanding and acceptance comes second. One begins by behaving as a slave and then, later, discovers that one is a slave. One realizes, of course, from the very beginning, in one sense, that one is a slave, undeniably, strictly, and in the total fullness of legality. There is no mistaking the brand, the collar, the tunic, the whip. But, then, later, there comes the profound, liberating moment in which one realizes that one is now, in truth, and wholly, a slave.

"You kiss the whip well," I observed.

"What joy," she asked, in her tears, in a whisper I could scarcely hear, "can compare to being the true slave of a true Master?"

I drew the whip away, and sat down, cross-legged, some feet before her.

She was very beautiful in the light of the small, tharlarion-oil lamp.

"Position of the Tower Slave," I said, which position she immediately assumed, back straight, knees together, wrists before her, crossed, as though bound.

A new tear appeared in her eyes. "Do I mean so little to my Master?" she asked.

"Lift your head," I said. In the Tower Position the head may be either bowed or raised. When in doubt the slave bows her head. She is a slave.

"Master?" she asked.

"I would talk with you," I said.

She reached down to the floor beside her, took up the remnants of the tunic which had been cut from her and lifted it before her body.

"Do you dare?" I inquired.

"Forgive me, Master," she said, putting the rent garment to the side, "I thought—"

"You are a barbarian," I said.

"Yes, Master," she said.

"From the world called Earth," I said.

"Yes, Master," she said.

"There is then such a place," I said.

"Yes, Master," she said.

"Do those of Earth know that Gor exists?" I asked.

"Some, I suppose," she said.

"But others, perhaps," I said, "have at least heard of Gor."

"Many," she said, "but they do not think that it exists."

"And you?" I asked. "Had you heard of Gor?"

"Yes, Master," she said.

"Did you think that it existed?"

"No, Master," she said.

"I gather then," I said, "that you did not anticipate that you would one day find yourself in a collar on Gor."

"No, Master," she said.

"Are many women of Earth as beautiful as you?" I asked.

"I am sure, a great many," she said.

"Tell me of the women of Earth," I said.

"They do not know they are women," she said.

"And you?" I asked.

"I now know I am a woman," she said. "I have learned it on Gor. Men have taught me. I am grateful."

"What was your name on Earth?" I asked.

"Whitney," she said, "Whitney Price-Loudon."

"What is your name now?" I asked.

"Lais," she said, "if it pleases Master."

"Anything else?" I asked.

"No, Master," she said. "Just 'Lais'. Only 'Lais'. I am a slave."

"On Earth," I said, "were you well-fixed, say, affluent?"

"Yes, Master," she said, "so much so that I was indifferent to wealth."

"When one has wealth," I said, "it is easy to be indifferent to it."

"I fear so," she said.

"What have you now?" I asked.

"Nothing," she said. "I do not even own my collar. It is now I who am owned."

"Excellent," I said.

"Yes, Master," she said.

"What do you think," I asked, "of the men of your former world?"

"As the women did not know they were women," she said, "so, too, I fear, the men did not know they were men."

"Some?" I said.

"Many," she said.

"But you must have met many men on your former world," I said.

"Males perhaps," she said, "not men. On Earth I did not know there were men such as those of Gor. What can a woman be to such men but a slave, hoping to be found acceptable, hoping desperately to please them, and as the slave she is?"

"I suspect that there is very little difference, if any," I said, "biologically, between the men of Earth and those of Gor. I suspect that the differences are cultural, perhaps entirely so."

"I suspect," she said, "that Master knows more of Earth than he originally led me to believe."

"Perhaps there are some Masters on Earth," I said.

"Perhaps, Master," she said. "I do not know."

"You are not terrified that you are in a collar?" I asked.

"Sometimes I am in terror, for I know what can be done with me. I am not my own. I belong to others. I can be bought and sold, given away, traded, and beaten, but still I would not trade my collar for anything. I belong in it. I want to be in it. In my collar I have come home to myself and am fulfilled. I no longer fight nature. I yield to what I am by nature. Let the free be free; let the slave be slave. Let each find her own joy."

"Do you wish to be whipped," I asked.

"No, Master!" she said quickly.

I saw that she knew the whip, indeed, and what it could do to her.

"You are in the position of the Tower Slave," I said.

"Yes Master," she said. "With my head raised."

"*Nadu!*" I snapped.

Instantly she spread her knees, widely, knelt back on her heels, back straight, palms of her hands down on her thighs.

"Get your head up," I said.

Commonly in *nadu*, the head is lifted. In this way the least expression or movement of the eyes, lips, or face is visible to the Master.

In this position the slave is well-displayed, both with respect to her beauty and her vulnerability.

In this position the slave is in little doubt that she is a slave and what she, being a slave, is for.

The *nadu* position is that of the Pleasure Slave.

Tears of gratitude coursed down the cheeks of the slave.

I noted that she had dared to turn her hands, putting the backs of her hands on her thighs, this exposing the beautiful open softness of her palms, the sensitivity of which tender, concave, living tissue is such that a mere touch can make her cry out in need. It, like the soft bondage knot in the hair, is a way in which the slave may appeal to be noticed, may beg for attention, may mutely make known to her Master the desperation of her need.

"Palms down on your thighs," I said.

"Yes, Master," she whispered, obeying, her voice breaking a little.

I regarded her.

"Does Master not find me pleasing?" she asked.

"What man is not pleased to have a woman before him in *nadu*?" I said.

"Thank you, Master," she whispered. "At one time, I would have blushed scarlet, totally, to be so exhibited before a man. Now it is my hope, a slave's hope, merely to be found pleasing."

"Perhaps," I said, "you would be interested to learn why you were purchased."

"A slave is seldom in little doubt as to that, Master," she said.

"Break position," I said.

"Master?" she asked, startled, puzzled.

I thought it wise to get her out of *nadu*, before I might seize her by the hair or by a wrist or ankle, and put her to swift, vigorous slave use.

"Lie here before me," I said, "on the floor, on your side, facing me."

She, puzzled, assumed the position. I was not sure this was much of an improvement, if any. Her legs were drawn up, curled, and her left hip was high. Surely the terrain between the flared, high hip and the love cradle is one of the most exciting curves in a woman's body, a body in which many such curves vie for a man's attention. It is no wonder that women are hunted, caught, branded, collared, and put in chains. Are they not amongst the most desirable of a man's possessions? I forced myself to look to the side. It is hard for a naked slave not to be beautiful.

"I will speak with you," I said.

"'Speak'?' she said.

"Yes," I said.

"As Master pleases," she said, a small break, again, in her voice.

I waited a bit, hoping that her slave fires might soon burn lower, if not subside, at least for a time. Masters, without regard to the slave, kindle her slave fires, whether she will or no, and, shortly, she becomes the prisoner of her needs. This is usually done before she is brought to the block. Are not her needs the strongest of the bonds that hold her, even more so than the ropes which tie her arms or wrists, than the bands and links of metal which confine her wrists and ankles? Periodically then, she becomes desperately needful, which situation progressively deepens her slavery and increases her market value. This is done for her, for she is a slave. I suspect that free women cannot even begin to understand the slave's sexual experiences, the depth and ferocity of her released needs or the cataclysmic nature of her succession of uncontrollable yieldings. But then, again, perhaps they do suspect, and that is one of the reasons they so hate their helpless, half-naked sisters in their collars.

"Perhaps you have heard," I said, keeping my eyes to the side, "of the notorious pirate, Bosk of Port Kar."

"Much is said of him," she said, "in the tavern, *The Living Island*, and I am told elsewhere, in taverns and brothels, in bazaars and markets, at the wharves and in the streets, everywhere. I fear one hears much of him in beautiful, colorful, crowded, bustling Sybaris."

"You understand him to be ruthless and unconscionable," I said.

"Who is safe at sea?" she asked. "He even attacks and loots small villages, commonly coastal villages or villages near the coast."

"You understand," I said, "that the local authorities have searched for him in vain."

"As of yet, surprisingly, unsuccessfully," she said.

"Perhaps," I said, "I represent an interest which seeks to somehow locate, or at least contact, this Bosk of Port Kar."

"I would think it would fear to do so," she said.

"Risk is sometimes the name of life," I said.

"It wishes to locate him so that it can alert the authorities," she said.

"That is a possibility," I said.

"But," she said, "as I understand it, this Bosk of Port Kar has several hundred men under his command. Thus, local authorities might do well to avoid him. Troops could be brought in from Cos."

"That, too, is a possibility," I said.

"Yet," she said, "in the long months of his predations, they have not been summoned."

"Perhaps they cannot be spared," I said.

"I see now," she said, "why you wish to find, or somehow contact, this dreaded Bosk of Port Kar."

"Speak," I said.

"You represent a party," she said, "doubtless of merchants, or predominantly of merchants."

"That is an interesting speculation," I said.

"You wish then to purchase protection for your party," she said. "You will pay, staters and tarn disks, to have certain ships, your ships, those of your party, exempt from attack, kept immune to predation. You wish your ships and goods to be safe on the seas, while the ships of others remain at hazard or fear to leave port."

"That, too, is a possibility," I said.

"And then trade, and shipping, the wealth of the seas, would accrue to your party."

"It would seem so, would it not?" I said.

"What is to prevent Bosk of Port Kar from accepting your gold, and then attacking your ships, too?"

"The prospect of more gold," I said.

"I do not care for your party," she said.

"These speculations," I said, "are yours, not mine."

"What then," she asked, "is your business with Bosk of Port Kar?"

"Perhaps it is personal," I said.

"The business of blades?" she asked.

"Perhaps," I said.

"Do not seek him," she said.

"Have you heard of Nicosia?" I asked.

"Yes," she said, "it is one of several villages sacked and burned by Bosk of Port Kar."

"There are those who remember Nicosia and other villages," I said.

"Your business then," she said, "is one of great danger, one of vengeance."

"If the state will not act, men must," I said.

"I beg you, Master," she said, "dissuade your party. Do not seek Bosk of Port Kar. Instead, if you wish, send gentle verr to seek the fanged, voracious larl."

"Perhaps you are curious as to why you were purchased," I said.

"Surely for slave use," she said.

"*Nadu!*" I snapped.

Instantly, startled, frightened, she scrambled to *nadu*.

"You are a beautiful slave," I said.

"A slave is pleased if Master is pleased," she said.

"And you are well exhibited in *nadu*," I said.

"Thank you, Master," she said.

"On your former world," I said, "did you ever expect to be as you are now?"

"No, Master," she said, "but I was not then a slave."

"Men often speak freely before a slave, as before other domestic animals," I said, "pet sleen, saddle tharlarion, and such. Slaves are meaningless and, as such, are often taken for granted. Often they come and go, scarcely being noticed. One thinks little of their presence. They may hear things and see things which others might not, without arousing suspicion."

"Master?" she said.

"A slave may frequent locales denied to the free. A slave, putatively on an errand, may tread where a free person would be barred, or perhaps, if admitted, not even permitted to emerge alive. Even if a city falls and the free are put to the sword, the slave, like the kaiila and tharlarion, is spared. Who abandons won booty? Who loots and then discards his loot? Who steals silver, and then casts it into the sea?"

"I fear I begin to understand Master," she said.

"I am recalling men," I said. "I think they have done all they can. I now want them back on the benches. Who knows when a harbor must be cleared, when a foe should be met at sea?"

"Master persists in his madness," she said. "Forgo your dream of revenge. The verr is no match for the larl."

"I want a sense of where the raiders might strike next," I said.

"The raiders have been quiescent," she said.

"They await ships," I said.

"Master needs a spy," she said.

"One subtle, unsuspected, and unnoticed," I said.

"I am Master's slave," she said.

"Though you are a slave," I said, "danger abounds. The foe is clever, guards himself well, and thinks little of killing."

"I understand," she said.

"You will be in great danger," I said. "I would discard this stratagem if I did not deem it necessary. Information is critical. Lives are at stake, on sea and land."

"I am protected by my collar," she said.

"You cannot count on that," I said. "That is why I do not command this of you. I will not do so. Thus, you are fully free to decline this charge. Do so, if you wish. Indeed, I encourage you to do so. This is not your business, not your affair or war. You are a mere slave. You need not concern yourself. And do not be afraid for your future, no more so than any other slave. It would be easy to arrange a small, private sale for you, one in which you could be disposed of safely, with convenient discreetness."

"May I speak?" she asked.

"Assuredly," I said.

"I accept," she said.

"As you are a barbarian," I said, "you may not understand the ways of Gor. Let me give you an illustration. If a free woman should pronounce herself a slave, she is, then, instantly, no longer a free woman but a slave. Pretending, thinking she is lying, mental reservation, and such things, do not enter into the matter. Once the words are spoken she is a slave. Even if she lacks a Master, she is a slave. Do you understand?"

"Yes, Master," she said.

"So, too, it is with the matter in hand," I said. "If you accept, the matter is done. The particle of choice which I gave you is gone. You cannot unchoose. You are then, in respect to this matter, as in all matters in which you are a slave, absolutely helpless, and must obey in all things, instantly and unquestioningly. Do you understand?"

"Yes, Master," she said.

"You may speak," I said.

"I accept," she said.

"It is done," I said.

I stood up and, with my left hand, took her by the hair and pulled her half to her feet, her knees bent. I then with the palm and back of my right hand cuffed her, four times, and then flung her to the floor.

"Master?" she asked, stung and cringing at my feet.

"Now," I said, "you may regret your decision."

"I do not regret my decision," she said.

"And it would not matter in the least," I said, "if you did."

"Yes, Master," she said.

I seized her left ankle and pulled her across the floor to the side, where I deposited her on her belly on the sleeping furs. She looked at me, back, over her right shoulder. Then, seized, she cried, softly, "Ohh!"

"It seems," she said, "I was purchased, at least in part, for slave use."

"I needed a slave for espionage, politics, and war," I said. "That was why the purchase was made. But many girls might suffice for such purposes."

"Then," she said, contentedly, "I was chosen for slave use?"

"Particularly, primarily," I said.

"But might you not, independently, were the world different, have purchased me?" she asked.

"Quite possibly," I said. "You look good on a chain."

"Put me on a chain," she said.

"I do not even know the name of my Master," she said.

"It is on your collar," I said.

"But I do not know what name is on my collar," she said.

"Then," I said, "you do not know the name of your Master."

"I cannot read my collar," she said.

"Others can," I said.

"I am highly intelligent and well educated on my former world," she said. "But here I am an illiterate slave!"

"As many other highly intelligent and well-educated women of your world, now locked nicely, helplessly, in their Gorean collars," I said.

"You approve?" she asked.

"Yes," I said, "it adds a delightful fillip to your ownership."

"On this world," she said, "I am no more than an ignorant, unlettered beast, a vendible domestic animal, a branded, collared animal."

"Yes," I said.

"Yes, Master," she said, pressing against me, curvaceous, warm, and owned.

"Enough," I said. "Do not squirm so."

"Please free my wrists, Master," she begged.

They were locked behind her, in slave bracelets.

In this braceleting a woman is helpless, unable to resist, unable to protect or defend herself, unable to fend off the hands which may now delightfully trace, grasp, and caress her vulnerable, undefended beauty. Too, aesthetically, her wrists pinioned behind her, the wondrous, appealing, exciting curves of her hips, belly, waist, bosom, and shoulders are framed and accentuated.

"Please," she said, thrashing, throwing her head from side to side.

I pressed her soft shoulders to the furs.

"I will speak to you," I said.

A small whimper of dismay escaped her lips.

She looked up at me, and pulled a little, futilely, at the metal that held her hands behind her back. "Of course," she said, "you may do as you wish. You are my Master. I am your slave, and helpless."

"It is true," I said, "that I and my men, in our limited numbers, pose no immediate threat to the raiders."

"The fearful corsairs of Bosk of Port Kar," she said.

"But one hopes and plans," I said.

"Do not seek him," she said. "You might find him."

"Have you heard of the Fair of the Farther Islands?" I asked.

"Yes," she said, "it is being held now, at Mytilene on Chios."

"It is part of my plans," I said.

"This has to do then," she said, "with the corsairs, the raiders."

"Yes," I said. "They may now be without ships, but that is a temporary inconvenience. They will still be active, recruiting cohorts, gathering intelligence, and plotting new enterprises."

"Men attend the fair from all the islands," she said. "And even headmen and high peasants may attend, from dozens of villages, mostly the larger, richer villages."

"This constituting a possible trove of information for the raiders," I said.

"Which harvests were rich, and which not," she said.

"Amongst other things," I said.

"So raiders will be in attendance," she said.

"I expect so," I said. "Some, agents."

"And spies may be spied upon," she said.

"That seems only fair," I said.

"Where are the raiders now?" she asked. "Where do they hide?"

"They are now," I said, "in and about Sybaris."

"Surely not," she said, frightened.

"Sybaris," I said, "is large and crowded. It is in no danger. The raiders strike only when assured of success, on shipping and isolated villages. Too, Sybaris is important to them. It is, in effect, their headquarters and port, their base of operations."

"Should spying then not be better done in Sybaris?" she asked.

"I invite myself to the fair with more in mind than espionage," I said.

"What more?" she asked.

"Curiosity is not becoming in a *kajira*," I said.

"Forgive me, Master," she said.

I then pulled her closer.

"Master?" she asked. She tried to rear up, to see me better, but I thrust her back. "Master?" she asked. Then she said, "Oh, your tongue!"

Moments later she began to gasp and squirm, but my hands were strong upon her. Her small wrists tore against the light, colorful bracelets holding her hands behind her back. Then her hips lifted and she moaned. "Shall I stop?" I inquired. "No," she said, "no! Do not stop, I beg you. Please do not stop. Again! More, yes! Do not stop, Master! Continue! Please, continue! I beg it! Be kind, please be kind to a poor, helpless slave!"

CHAPTER EIGHTEEN

We Approach Mytilene

He stood beside me, at the bow of the *Tesephone*, summoned from the helm deck.

"These are the waters of which you spoke?" I asked.

"Do not enter them," he said. "There are practical, familiar courses to Mytilene."

"I prefer routes less familiar," I said.

"To avoid being sighted?" he said.

"Perhaps," I said.

"There are things worse to encounter than Bosk of Port Kar," he said.

"Many in the taverns," I said, "do not credit your story."

"I have not had a drink in days," he said, "even when others drank."

"And you have not rethought your tale?" I asked.

"I was not always a drunken urt sleeping in alleys," he said, "slinking about the waterfront of Sybaris, pushing into taverns, in rags, unwelcome and mocked, begging, soliciting a goblet of paga. I was a captain, master of a fine round ship of a hundred oars."

"Lost at sea," I said.

"That is the part of the story I did not tell," he said, "the terrible part, the part I would dare not tell, the part I was ashamed to tell."

"If your story is true," I said, "what occurred was no fault of yours."

"I entered the waters," he said, "these waters."

"How could you know?" I asked.

"I did not believe," he said.

"I am sure many ships come and go safely in these waters," I
said.

"These were the waters where it occurred," he said.

"Many do not believe such a thing exists," I said.

"I have seen it," he said.

It had seemed like discarded rubbish, a gray bundle, damp, against
the warehouse's back wall.

I shook it. "Awake," I said. "You have slept long enough."

The fresh, salt smell of Thassa was in the air. Already one could
hear voices from the wharves, loading captains, stevedores, berth-
less mariners at the hiring tables.

"Wake," I said.

It opened its eyes, blinked, twisted to get its back against the
wall. "Who are you?" he asked.

"One who seeks you," I had said.

"I want paga," he said.

"You have not earned it," I said. "And once you have earned it,
I do not think you will want it."

I recalled a tavern faraway, on a steel world concealed amidst
the debris of the asteroid belt, the debris of what might once
have been a green, fertile world, now a wilderness of orbiting
cinders.

"Paga," he said, the sounds slurred.

"I am prepared to turn my back," I said. "I am prepared to
leave you here to die, this month or the next, this year or the next.
What does it matter?"

"What does anything matter?" he asked.

"That is for you to decide," I said.

"Do you know who I am?" he asked.

"Sakim, the mariner," I said.

"Sakim," he said, "the worthless, the failed, the beggar of
paga, the braggart, the liar."

"Are you a liar?" I asked.

"I am thought so," he said.

"These things are not always the same," I said.

"What is this?" he asked, incredulously.

"A gold stater, of Brundisium," I said, pressing it into his hand.
"It is enough to buy you paga for months, or more than enough to
have yourself fed, housed, groomed, clothed, and armed."

"Why are you doing this?" he asked.

"Let us say," I said, "I once knew one such as you, in a far-off place."

"You would save me?" he asked.

"No," I said. "I would offer you the opportunity to save yourself."

"I am a mariner," he said.

"Assuredly," I said.

"I have no berth," he said.

"If you choose, you have one now," I said.

"I would so choose," he said.

"Be warned," I said. "I chart my course in dangerous waters. If you sign with me, you may die."

"Better to die at sea, in the open air," he said, "on treacherous, beautiful, mighty Thassa than in an alley in Sybaris."

"I would think so," I said.

"What is your ship?" he asked.

"The *Tesephone*," I had said.

Many regard the monstrous hith, even on the continent, as a myth. Surely I had never, personally, seen one, nor had conversed with anyone claiming to have seen one. I did know, however, that such things, or things much like them, once existed. That was not controversial. That was not a matter of myth, at least to those possessed of the Second Knowledge, but of distant, remote fact, fact dating back to what must have been fearful times. I myself had seen, once, dug out of sand in the Vosk basin, the petrifaction of a titanic, fanged, serpentine skull, and once, washed free of collapsed strata in the Voltai, petrifications of the knobs of a spine far longer than those of any known form of tharlarion. Putting together what we think we know of the hith, from stories, legend, and evidence, it was an immense, constricting serpent, over a hundred feet in length with a girth the diameter of which would have been something like eight to ten feet. It seems to have ranged widely on the continent, from the latitudes of the Voltai to the jungles of the Ua. As it was not herbivorous, one supposes it preyed on animals as small as the tabuk and as large as tharlarion, even carnivorous tharlarion, the encounters with which must have produced epic battles. It is possible that the land hith still exists on Gor, doubtless in remote areas, but it seems more likely that that form of hith is extinct. The tiny, elusive, venomous ost survives while, it seems, the enormous hith perishes. The pebble is unnoticed; the mountain announces itself to the sky. Interestingly, it seems likely, as such things have often occurred, that large animals, megafauna, are commonly brought to extinction by a smaller, seemingly unlikely foe. It seems probable that, long ago, thousands of years ago, the nemesis of the hith was less the carnivorous tharlarion with which it thought to dispute its world, but an unexpected adversary, smaller and weaker, more vulnerable and fragile, but less forgiving and tolerant, more determined and tenacious, a miniscule foe, one scarcely noticed, but a foe that could plan and would not forget, an unanticipated usurper determined to set itself on nature's throne, the human. But nature is not without its resources; amongst thousands of changes in form and behavior, small and otherwise, some favor the replication of genes and others do not. A paw becomes a hand; a cell sensitive to light becomes an eye; the enlargement of a knot on a spinal cord becomes a brain. And, one supposes, it might be, that some members of a species subject to extermination on land might, in diverse behaviors, in withdrawing from strong stimuli, in fleeing, in avoiding discovery, discover that the same muscles which allow it to move on land permit it to move in water.

"I am sure many ships come and go safely in these waters," I had said.

"These were the waters where it occurred," had said the mariner, Sakim.

"Many do not believe such a thing exists," I said.

"I have seen it," Sakim had said.

"I recall your story," I said.

"My account," he said.

"It came up, like a great rock rising from the sea," I said.

"Its skin was black and slippery," he said. "Several men could not get their arms around it."

"It had teeth like shearing blades?" I said.

"I saw it," he said.

"You saw something," I said, "perhaps in the fumes of paga, in a dream, in an aberration of the mind."

"I lost my ship," he said.

"Ships are sometimes lost," I said. "There are collisions, rocks that tear the hull, corsairs that strike, loot, and burn."

"No," he said. "No, Captain."

"There are storms in which waves rise up black and swirling, and might be seen as anything," I said.

"The sea was calm," he said, "almost."

"'Almost'?" I said.

"There was a stirring," he said.

"Currents, tides," I said.

"You do not believe me," he said.

"Thurnock, second to me on the *Tesephone*," I said, "heard speak of a sighting of a hith, that from men on the Isle of Seleukos."

"There must then be another," he said, "and, if so, then others."

"Perhaps," I said. "But these things are the things of legend. The men of the Isle of Seleukos may be mistaken, as well. Men sometimes see what they want to see, or what they fear to see."

Sakim looked out over the bow rail, smiled, and shrugged.

"Surely you admit sightings are few, if any," I said.

"Surely few," he said.

"How did the hith attack your ship?" I asked.

"In coils," he said, "encircling it, and crushing it, like straw."

"You survived," I said.

"I clung to a plank," he said. "I was picked up the next day by a ten-oared fishing boat."

"A small boat, a light boat," I said.

"Yes," he said.

"Why would the hith attack your ship?" I asked.

"I do not know," he said.

I wondered if the hith, if it existed, was territorial. Territoriality is biologically valuable to large animals. It distributes members of a species, thus expanding access to food. Too, in many species, the female will seek a male with a desirable territory. In this way, too, then, having a territory is favorable to gene replication. Perhaps a hith, then, I thought, if territorial, might react aggressively to any large object it might deem an intruder.

"Mytilene," he said, "has a fine harbor."

"I do not intend to berth at Mytilene," I said, "not in the harbor."

"You are afraid the *Tesephone* might be recognized?" he said.

"It is possible," I said.

"I shall not inquire into your business," he said.

"That is wise," I said.

"Thus I could not reveal secrets," he said, "even under torture."

"I have no intention," I said, "of jeopardizing you more than is
inevitable. Often the less you know the safer you are."

"I would be one of your men," he said.

"I think you will be," I said.

We continued to stand at the rail, regarding Thassa.

"Have you been to a Fair of the Farther Islands?" he asked.

"No," I said.

"One is held each year," he said, "and they alternate amongst
the major islands, and amongst the larger towns on the islands.
Last year it was on Thera, at Sybaris, the year before on Daphna,
at Pylos. You will enjoy the fair. There are many festivities and exhibitions, dozens of markets and sales. You can see prize verr and
tarsks. There are always acrobats, fire eaters, jugglers, and rope
dancers. Merchants, with their goods, come from as faraway as Cos
and Tyros, even from Brundisium on the continent."

"Surely all this cannot take place within the walls of a town,"
I said.

"No," said Sakim, "mostly in the fields, outside the walls, and,
if the town has no walls, like Pylos, and Naxos, outside the *pomerium*. It is like a city of tents, with its own streets, water tanks and
dumps, a city often larger than its host city."

"And then," I said, "in a few days, it has vanished."

"Leaving tracks of mud, refuse, and debris," said Sakim.

"These fairs are well-attended," I said.

"Thousands come, in hundreds of crowded ships and small
boats, from throughout the islands," said Sakim, "and then they
are gone."

At the great Sardar Fairs on the continent, associated with the
solstices and equinoxes, there are many permanent structures and
no lack of amenities, such as fountains, inns, and paved streets.
Indeed, a tiny population remains in place all year.

"I expect that you will enjoy the fair," said Sakim, "and that
your men will enjoy it, as well, even if they are not interested in
prize verr and tarsks. One can always peruse slaves in the markets,
and there is no dearth of brothel and tavern tents."

"Are there official delegations?" I asked.

"Not really," said Sakim. "But there are informal delegations,
and there are always visitors from Cos."

"Spies?" I asked.

"Secret guardsmen," said Sakim. "It is said that Cos is the loving mother of the islands."

"Interesting," I said.

"This year," said Sakim, "Nicomachos, Admiral of the Fleet of the Farther Islands, is expected to be in attendance."

I must have somehow reacted to this observation.

"What is wrong?" asked Sakim.

"Nothing," I said. "Perhaps he is representing Archelaos, governor of Thera?"

"I do not think so," said Sakim. "I think it is in connection with his office as Admiral, assigned by Cos to guard the seas of the Farther Islands. Presumably he seeks clues as to the whereabouts of the feared corsair, Bosk of Port Kar, who has so plundered the coast and ravaged the local waters."

"He will have ships with him?" I asked.

"Some," said Sakim. "Enough to be deployed in the hunt for Bosk of Port Kar, enough, should his whereabouts be determined, to engage him at sea."

"But not the whole fleet?" I said.

"I do not think so," said Sakim.

I much doubted that the Admiral was interested in Bosk of Port Kar. I found it far more likely that his absence from Sybaris had more to do with the schemes of Archelaos. Perhaps his presence in Mytilene was to absent himself from Thera, to open the very harbor at Sybaris to attack. Perhaps it was to permit the unchallenged, uninvestigated delivery of new ships to the corsairs in Sybaris. Perhaps his ships were being used to land corsairs on some coast, from which, following a raid or raids, they might be conveyed back to safety. This would be feasible while they still lacked their own ships. Who knew? Perhaps his own ships might turn to piracy themselves, seizing riches and even ships which might later be refitted as corsairs themselves. Crews of such prizes might be recruited or exterminated.

At the sound of a woman's cry, startled, and laughing, from the rowing deck, Sakim and I turned back from the bow. "No, no, Master!" she laughed from between the benches. "Water, only water!" She then handed the leather bota to an oarsman, who, head back, drank, and then passed the container to his fellows.

"She is pretty," said Sakim.

"I call her 'Lais'," I said.

"I have seen her," said Sakim, "when not working, wandering about the ship. When she is not working, why do you not chain her at the foot of the steps to the stem deck?"

There was a ring there, which might well serve such a purpose, as well as one aft, at the foot of the steps to the stern deck.

"I do not think she will leap overboard," I said.

"Are you taking her to Mytilene to sell her?" asked Sakim.

"What do you think she would bring?" I asked.

"A silver tarsk, easily," said Sakim.

"She is a barbarian," I said.

"Then not so much," said Sakim.

There is a superstition shared by many Gorean mariners, that it is unlucky to have a free woman aboard ship, particularly if there is only one. As with many superstitions, it may have its origin in forgotten or neglected realities. For example, many Goreans will give up, or postpone, a journey which begins with a misstep, or stumble. This view may be less pointless than it seems. If one recognizes, perhaps only subconsciously, that a journey is likely to be ill-advised, or ill-fated, such a little thing as a stumble may constitute a warning to be well-heeded. In the case of the free woman, mysterious, exalted, lofty, veiled, possibly beautiful, and inaccessible, particularly in a long voyage, as tensions rise, one has something analogous to fresh, raw meat cast before hungry sleen, or, say, a banquet placed before starving men. Add to this the normal penchant of a woman to affect men and the very natural, human pleasure she is likely to derive from stimulating masculine desire, even without satisfying it, one has a concoction which well may prove inflammatory. Many such women who begin a journey as a free woman complete it in the chains of a slave. She is, after all, a female. A female slave, on the other hand, despite her obvious attractions, does not excite similar apprehensions. She is owned; she is property; she is collared chattel; she is in her natural place, and is, in theory, havable, even if not had; she is accessible, not inaccessible; she is possessable, even if not your particular possession. She is exhibited and displayed, openly presented before one, for one's delectation, consideration, and appraisal. She is vendible, even if not, at the moment, vended. She is a delight to have aboard; she is soothing to the eyes, and a promise as to what may be waiting for one in the next port.

Lais continued to dispense the contents of the heavy bota.

I turned back to the rail.

Sakim was white, grasping the rail. "Do you feel it?" he asked.

"Yes," I said. Something was different.

"Oars inboard!" I called. Those mighty levers were drawn back, inward through the thole ports. "Lower the yard," I said. Down came the yard, the canvas folding and crumpling. The *Tesephone* rocked, quiet in the waves. "Be silent," I said. "No noise. Be easy, fellows, be easy, do not move! We are not here. We are not here!"

"There," whispered Sakim, pointing.

To the left, from the bow, some points to port, I saw a heaving and roiling in the water, several yards in length, and then it seemed as though there was a slow, swelling, rising of water, and it was as if a long, low, broad river of water had risen from the surface, and then, as suddenly and inexplicably, it sank back and disappeared.

Other than this phenomenon I saw nothing.

"What now, Captain?" asked Sakim, his hands clenched on the rail.

"We shall wait a bit," I said. "Then we shall resume our course to Mytilene."

"Perhaps we should rely on the sail," he said.

"In these waters," I said, "I think that is an excellent idea."

CHAPTER NINETEEN

We Attend the Fair at Mytilene

Clitus had cast his net expertly, it enveloping and settling about the opponent like a swift, soft, corded rain. Another turn and twist and the opponent's feet were drawn from under him, and Clitus stood over him, his trident poised at the opponent's throat.

"A kill," announced the umpire.

"Nicely done," said several of the spectators.

A judge awarded Clitus the copper tarsk.

The opponent disentangled himself from the net, carefully, folded it, and returned it to Clitus. "Well done," he said.

Few blades in the islands can divide a loose, falling, unresisting net. I had seen one or two which could do so at the World's End. I was not sure whether the opponent had thought to cut through the net or simply lift it, or brush it, aside. Whatever might have been his intention, it had been unsuccessful. In dealing with the net and trident, it is desirable, if possible, which it seldom is, to have seen the fishermen earlier, in other matches. Many fishermen have habits, techniques, or tricks which tend to characterize their play, an over-the-head cast, a side cast, a certain movement of the feet before the cast, and so on. Clitus varied such things from match to match, which made it difficult to anticipate, and thus compensate for, his moves. Some fishermen sometimes feign an awkwardness or loss of balance to lure the opponent within range. Sometimes I had seen Clitus use the net as a distraction, preparing for a thrust of the trident. No rule determines whether the net or trident is to have priority. The common foe of the fisherman is a swordsman or spearman, but sometimes it is another fisherman. Who says that fishermen cannot have disagreements with one another, who is to cast first and where, over women, and

so on? It is common for a swordsman or spearman to underestimate the fisherman as a foe. He does not seem an armed warrior.
He is different. Can the net and trident be taken seriously as weapons? Are they not rather, merely, the tools of a trade, not weapons
but the equipment of a way of life, like the peasant's sickle and
plow? Needless to say, in war, such an error of judgment is likely
to be made only once. Each net, of course, has a diameter and a
likely range of flight. Such things can be important. Few fishermen will risk a long cast for two reasons, first, the extra bit of an
Ihn that the net is in the air gives the opponent that much more
time to avoid the net, and, second, the net, if avoided, may be
lost. Without the net the fisherman is little more than a lightly
armed spearman, the bearer of a javelin. My recommendation for
the foe in these matters is movement and patience, maintaining a
constant change of place while staying outside the range of the
net as much as possible. One tries to make oneself a difficult target
while searching for opportunities. If the net is being spun it can
be spun only so long before the arm tires and weakens. When the
arm lowers or the arm draws back for a cast, that is an opportunity. Sometimes one can roll under the net before it settles, and
then spring up, blade ready, between the net and the fisherman.

"We have been at the fair four days," said Thurnock, "and we
know no more now than when we came."

"Some days are left," I said.

"New ships, with merchants and their goods, still arrive each
Ahn," said Clitus.

Lais came up beside us, knelt, looked up, and smiled. "Master," she said.

"You seem pleased," I said.

"I am," she said. "I have learned the name of my Master."

Thurnock and Clitus reacted, exchanging quick, apprehensive
glances.

"It is on my collar," she said, "as you said. I found a slave to
read it to me. I gave her the candy you gave me yesterday. I saved
it for such a purpose."

"If the slave could read," said Clitus, "she was probably once
of high caste." Clitus, like many Goreans, could not read. Many
Goreans deemed it sufficient that Scribes could read. Reading was
for Scribes.

"Even if she was once of high caste," sniffed Lais, "she is now
no more than me, only another slave."

"I am surprised she read it for you," said Thurnock, "you, a barbarian."

"I do not think she knew I was a barbarian," said Lais.

"Who could not know that?" said Thurnock, of the Peasants.

"My Gorean is improving," she said. "Besides, she wanted the candy."

"But she did not take the candy and then strike you afterwards?" asked Thurnock.

"No, Master," she said.

"Perhaps your Gorean is improving," granted Thurnock.

"There are many accents on Gor," she said. "What is another, particularly in a slave, who might be from anywhere?"

"How do you know that she read the collar correctly?" asked Thurnock. "Perhaps she knew you were a barbarian and lied. Perhaps she could not read but pretended to read, to get the candy."

Lais suddenly looked dismayed.

"What did she tell you the collar said?" I asked.

"It said," she said, "'I am Lais. I am the slave of Eiron of Brundisium.'"

"That is correct," I said.

The girl smiled; her anxieties melted away like a spoonful of snow in a bowl of steaming black wine.

"I had thought," she said, "in the tavern, long ago, you were Kenneth Statercounter, of Brundisium. Then you told me to speak of you as Eiron of Naxos. Then you were Fenlon of Ti."

"Names are like caps," I said. "One may put them on and take them off."

It is one thing, and a useful thing, to tell a slave to speak of me to others as Eiron of Naxos when in a tavern on Thera. People would think little of that. That would not arouse suspicion. It is quite another thing, however, given the accents involved, to try to pass oneself off as an Eiron of Naxos when one's accent is not only not that of Naxos, a town on Daphna, but would be unusual in the Farther Islands themselves, where accents tended to be much like those of Cos and Tyros. Therefore, as I had had little difficulty in passing myself off as Kenneth Statercounter of Brundisium, a far port and one of many accents, I deemed 'Eiron of Brundisium' a plausible alias. Given the looting and burning of the Inn of Kahlir in Sybaris, it did not seem wise for me to retain the Statercounter name, at least publicly.

"It seems," said Lais, "that you put them on and take them off frequently."

"Have you been whipped recently?" I asked.

"No, Master," she said. "Forgive me, Master."

We stopped speaking, for three palanquins, one after the other, with drawn curtains, moved past. They were borne, I noted, not by slaves, but free men who had more the look of mercenaries than bearers. Swords were at their belts. These palanquins, too, were accompanied by armed guards, two to a palanquin.

"Free women," said Thurnock.

Lais shuddered, and shrank down a little.

"Possibly of high caste," said Clitus.

"At least rich," said Thurnock.

When the palanquins had passed, Lais was noticeably relieved.

"The curtains were drawn," I said. "They did not even see you."

"Why do they hate us so?" she asked.

"Perhaps you should ask one," I said.

Lais turned white.

"I will not order you to do so," I said.

She smiled, gratefully.

She looked very beautiful, kneeling at my feet. One of the joys of a slave is kneeling before her Master, being at his feet. How right that seems to her, in her collar. That is where she belongs, and where she wants to be. Free women, too, I have heard, from several slaves who were once free women, often feel the inclination, the impulse, the desire, the temptation, to kneel before a suitable male. How troubling and tormenting must this be for the regal free woman! Is she, despite her robes and veils, a slave? And some do so kneel, freely, scorning the pressure of prescribed resistance, putting themselves at the feet of such a male, in effect, offering themselves to be his slave.

"In the four days we have been here," I said, "I have received six offers for you."

"I did not know," she said, uneasily.

"One does not discuss such things with a tarsk, a verr, a slave."

"What were the offers?" she asked.

"What a vain she-tarsk," said Thurnock.

"A slave is curious about such things, Master," she said.

"All of them," I said, "were for far more than you are worth."

"You are a barbarian," Thurnock reminded her.

"Please," she said, lifting her head to me, her eyes suddenly bright with tears, "do not sell me, Master."

"Some men," said Thurnock, "grow rich, speculating in slaves, buying and selling them."

"I am not one of them," I said.

"May I speak, Master?" she asked.

"No," I said.

The control of her speech is one of the mightiest and most effective of controls to which a woman may find herself subject. Women are marvelous speakers, bright, charming, gifted, and loquacious, nimble-tongued, perceptive, and quick-witted. What a joy to hear them speak! Her words are much to her, and important to her; they are her offense and defense, her shields and her weapons. With her words she can startle and soothe, delight and amaze, humiliate and lash, stab and cut, mock or encourage, bolster or humiliate, exalt or diminish. Take from her her words and she finds herself disarmed and helpless. Let us suppose that she wishes to speak, and is not permitted to do so. Few things can so convince her that she is a slave. And, chafing under this restriction, suffering from this frustration, she has the exquisite pleasure of realizing that she is where she wants to be, at the feet of her Master.

The long street, dusty and bordered by stalls and tents, was crowded. Most of the visitors to the fair were men, but many women were present, as well. Most of the women were free, but some slaves were also in evidence, approximately one slave to every fifteen or twenty free women. The slaves took care to avoid the free women, often crossing to the other side of the street, and keeping their heads down. Much of the garmenture in the crowd, in cuts, lengths, and folds, in brightness, richness and texture, was festive, as Fair Days are holidays. Whereas the main colors about were the peasant browns, in their variations, brightened with pins, ribbons and sashes, the colors of several other castes were visible, as well. The slaves were easy to recognize, with their bare arms and legs, their brief tunics, the collars on their necks.

A fellow with a stick was herding an immense tarsk past. That you would not have seen at a Sardar Fair.

"What a splendid animal," marveled Thurnock.

I motioned that Lais should rise.

"Watch where you step," I said.

"Guardsmen," whispered Clitus.

I did not turn about. "Guardsmen of the fair?" I asked.

"I think not," said Clitus.

"Then of Mytilene," I said.

"I do not know the uniform," said Clitus.

I turned about. "Those are the uniforms of regulars," I said, "of Cos."

"The laws of Cos march with the spears of Cos," said Thurnock. It was a saying.

"What are they doing?" I asked.

"They are making inquiries," said Thurnock.

"Let us take our leave," said Clitus.

"Why are soldiers of Cos at the fair?" asked Thurnock.

"They may not be soldiers of Cos," I said.

"Let us be on our way," said Clitus.

"Hold," said one of the two men in uniform.

We turned about.

"How may we be of assistance?" I asked.

"We search for a forbidden weapon," said he who seemed first of the two, he who seemed most in authority.

"It has been reported at the fair," said the second man.

"In the possession of a man named Aktis," said the first.

"What weapon?" I asked.

"The terrible bow," he said, "from which fly the birds of death."

"It is not like the glorious spear, or the noble sword," said the second man.

"It is an unfair weapon," said the other. "It can kill at more than a hundred paces."

"Dreadful," I said.

"Farther than the spear can be cast, far beyond the reach of the sword," said the second.

"Terrifying," I said.

"It is a weapon of cowards," said the first, "who dare not face a real weapon."

"I did not know that," I said.

"Its use, if permitted to any, should be restricted to those who are entitled to its use," said the second.

"The servants of the state?" I said.

"Obviously," he said.

We knew that the bow had been prohibited to the Peasantry of the islands by Cosian law. Accordingly, Thurnock did not carry his bow at the fair. As far as I knew Aktis did not either. Certainly he was aware of the law, and doubtless more so than we.

"The citizenry must be kept safe, they must be protected from one another," said the first.

"The banning of the bow is thus for their own good," said the second.

"I see," I said.

"From whence are you?" asked the first.

"Brundisium," I said.

"A great port," he said.

"Thank you," I said.

"The man we seek, Aktis, he who is the alleged bearer of the bow," said the leader, "is a peasant, we think, of Nicosia. Have you heard of him, or do you know of him?"

"No," I said.

"We shall then detain you no longer," he said. "I wish you well."

"And I you," I said, hoping it would not be necessary, later, to kill him.

We looked after the two uniformed men, who were now accosting another visitor to the fair, this time in the gray of the metal workers.

"Soldiers of Cos are far from Cos," said Thurnock.

"I do not think they are soldiers of Cos," I said. "The laws are the laws of Cos, but the enforcers of the law need not be Cosians."

"Who then?" asked Thurnock.

"Who would most wish the villages and towns of the Farther Islands to be defenseless?" I asked.

"Raiders," said Thurnock.

"I would think so," I said.

"Aktis must walk with care," said Clitus.

"I hope that he is wise enough to do so," I said.

"I have not seen him in three days," said Thurnock. "Where is he, what has he been doing?"

"Contacting peasants, from many villages," I said, "and particularly, as far as possible, headmen, pleading for an end to apathy, for an awareness of the threat they face, particularly the coastal villages."

"Suppose he is successful," said Clitus. "Then what?"

"That is the secret of the long tent," I said, "to the north of the fairgrounds."

"I have not heard of these things," said Clitus.

"Peasants," I said, "have their codes, like other castes. Commonly they do not inform on one another."

"But the guardsmen, or soldiers, were seeking Aktis," said Clitus. "Someone must have reported him, betrayed him, informed upon him, called him to the attention of others."

"Sometimes," I said, "an ost is found even within the walls of a city."

"It is unfortunate," said Thurnock, "that Nicomachos, Admiral of the Farther Islands, contrary to announcements and expectations, is not in attendance at the fair."

"Yes," I said. "I had hoped to meet him, in the absence of the governor."

"To kill him?" asked Clitus.

"If necessary," I said.

"Master," asked Lais, "may I speak?"

"No," I said.

"I would really like very much to speak," she said.

"No," I said.

"Very well," she said.

"You seem content," I said.

"I am," she said.

"Do you wish to be beaten?" I asked.

"Not at all," she said.

"Very well," I said, "you may speak."

"Admiral Nicomachos," she said, "is in attendance at the fair, but secretly, not officially, not publicly."

"Are you sure of this?" I asked.

"Yes, Master," she said.

"You know his location, his visitors, his guards?"

"Of course," she said.

"How could you know these things?" I asked.

"Slaves talk," she said, "—when permitted."

CHAPTER TWENTY

The Meeting in the Long Tent

"Dear friends," said Aktis, "caste brothers, members of the first and greatest of castes, members of the mightiest of castes, members of the caste upon which the Home Stone rests, be welcome."

The long tent, save for a long, central aisle, was crowded, so crowded that all stood. Clitus, Thurnock, and I were to one side, our backs to the canvas. There must have been five or six hundred men in the tent, but that number, as large as it was, would scarcely be missed from the population of the fair.

It was night.

Torches illuminated the interior of the tent.

"I have met many of you personally," said Aktis, "and have urged the case of solidarity and manliness."

"Of jeopardy and absurdity," cried a fellow near the front.

"What entitles you to call this meeting?" asked another. "Have you cleared this meeting with the Mayors of the fair?"

"We are not on the grounds of the fair," said Aktis, "nor are we within the *pomerium* of Mytilene."

"I think there is lawlessness here," said another man.

"Speak," called another fellow.

"What right has he to speak?" called another.

"The Right of the Shared Hearth," said a man.

"We wait," called more than one man. "Speak, speak!"

"Sedition and treason, criminality and treachery, have no right to be heard," said a fellow.

"It is no sedition to survive," said Aktis. "It is not treason to be true to oneself. It is not criminal to be ready to defend oneself. It is not treachery to cling to honor!"

"Beat him and cast him forth," called a man.

"Bind him and let him grunt and swill with his fellow tarsks," said another.

I noted, uneasily, two or three men slipping from the tent.

I had little doubt as to what their departure betokened.

"You think you are in no danger," said Aktis, "because you see no danger. You think there are no sleen because you have not yet felt their teeth. You think you are safe until the larl claws at your gate. Are we truly ignorant, naive, simple, thoughtless fools, just as the other castes think we are?"

"Beware!" cried several men.

Many castes do tend to look down upon the Peasantry, particularly in the larger cities. On the other hand, this was not a fault for which I could honestly blame myself. I had always entertained a high opinion of the Peasants, their wisdom, foresight, and astuteness, their understandings of seasons and weathers, their stalwart copings with winds and rains, droughts and floods, their somehow making fields rich and bountiful, their somehow bringing forth the harvests which enabled the high cities to touch the sky, which produced a world in which the glories of art and civilization were possible.

"My name is Aktis," said Aktis.

"The Aktis for whom guardsmen search?" asked a man.

"It is so," said Aktis.

"Seize him!" called a man. "Deliver him to the law!"

"Hear me, oh my caste brothers!" called Aktis.

"Let him speak," said a man. "He has the Right of the Shared Hearth."

"It is true I am Aktis, he for whom your enemies seek."

"Our friends!" called a man.

"I am of Nicosia," said Aktis, "of which village some of you have heard."

"It no longer exists," said a man.

"It was set upon by raiders proclaiming themselves to be of Port Kar," said Aktis. "It became the scene of burning and looting, of slaughter."

"It is gone, it is no more," said a man.

"Its Home Stone, hidden, survives," said Aktis.

Interest, like a swift rivulet, coursed amongst those present. Men exchanged wild, insightful glances.

"Yes," said Aktis, "Nicosia lives, but it is bloodied, emptied, and scarred. Harvests and treasures, small as they might be, are gone. The palisade is burned, the *pomerium* violated."

"So, too, with other villages," said a man.

"I know of one," said a man.

"I have heard of two," said another.

I myself supposed that there must have been at least a dozen such onslaughts, but it was not surprising to me that many in the room knew little, or nothing, about such incidents. Much of the news in the Farther Islands is carried afoot, in the packs of peddlers, so to speak. Probably those of Sybaris, or even of far Telnus and Jad, on Cos, knew more of such things than small isolated communities within a hundred pasangs of the actual occurrences.

"Next," cried Aktis, "will it be you who hears axes on the gate? Will it be your fields which will smoke to the sky, your homes which will be consumed in flame, your blood upon the hearth?"

"Summon guardsmen!" cried a man. "He has been seen with a forbidden weapon!"

"Yes!" cried Aktis, "and so see me once more!" He seized up a long package, tore aside the wrappings, and lifted, displayed, and brandished his bow.

Some men drew back.

"That is a forbidden weapon!" cried a man.

"It has been forbidden to us," said a man.

"That is to keep us safe," said another.

"And who has forbidden it to you?" asked Aktis. "Cos, hated Cos! That not you but that it will be safe, that it may do what it wants with you, and to you. That you will be defenseless and at her mercy! Every tyranny wishes to deprive the tyrannized of the means to resist! What tyranny would not seek to do so, what tyranny would not struggle to bring about a situation so much to its advantage? And meanwhile, the docile verr, so proud and jealous of their weakness, so enamored of their impotence, find themselves not only at the mercy of the tyranny but at the mercy of outlaws, rogues and raiders! My brothers, my caste brothers, put aside the timidity of the urt. Seize up the stealth and cunning of the sleen, the courage of the mighty larl. Arm yourselves! Arm yourselves!"

At that point, from outside the tent, there was a shouting and a clanging on shields. A moment later swords were slashing through the walls of the tent.

Consternation ensued.

"Do not move!" cried a commanding voice. "Stay where you are!"

Uniformed, armed men had thrust through the rents in the canvas, pushing men closer together, until, in a moment, there was no longer an aisle in the tent.

"Remain where you are," said the fellow with the commanding voice. "Do not attempt to leave the tent." He looked about, and men dared not meet his gaze. He then called out, "We seek a villain wanted on Chios, and elsewhere, a spreader of sedition, a fomenter of discontent, the harborer of a forbidden weapon, an Aktis, once from that nest of osts, Nicosia."

"I am he," said Aktis, from toward the front of the tent.

I noted that he had now strung his bow, and had an arrow fitted to the string.

"Put down your weapon!" ordered the fellow with the commanding voice, leader of the uniformed men.

"Put down yours," said Aktis.

"Do so," roared the leader of the newcomers.

"No," responded Aktis.

"That is a forbidden weapon," said the leader of those who had cut their way into the long tent.

"Not to me," said Aktis. "I permit it to myself."

"Disarm yourself, now, in the name of Lurius of Jad, Ubar of Cos," roared the leader.

The hearing of the name of Lurius visibly dismayed several of those in attendance.

"I decline," said Aktis, "in the name of the Home Stone of Nicosia."

"Do you wish us to fall upon all here," said the leader, "putting every man to the sword?"

"I would not do so," said Aktis, in a voice which touched my spine with ice.

"Seize him, bind him!" said the leader to the crowd, but even those who had disputed, or objected to, the words of Aktis did not stir.

"I am authorized by great Lurius to apply decimation," said the leader.

In decimation men are randomly aligned and, beginning with a man randomly selected, every tenth man is slain. It is commonly used with troops which have behaved in a cowardly or dishonorable fashion, failed to engage under orders, fled the field of battle, and so on.

"Dear caste brothers," said Aktis, "it is late. You must be tired. Feel free to seat yourselves." They soon, then, group by group, settled on the dirt floor, sitting cross-legged in the fashion common to Gorean men.

It was undoubtedly clear then to the leader, and his men, that a field of fire had been cleared between them and the arrows of Aktis.

"Rush him, seize him!" cried the leader to his men.

But his men did not move.

Given the seated crowd and the inevitable impediments imposed on movement, I speculated that Aktis could discharge four, and perhaps five, arrows before anyone could reach him. Thurnock, on the other hand, I thought could improve on that somewhat. He was, of course, more familiar with the weapon.

I could not blame the intruders for not wishing to be the first, or the second, and so on, to respond to their leader's order.

"Lurius of Jad, tyrant of Cos, grows fat in his palace," said Aktis. "He knows little, and cares less, about the Farther Islands, save what he can tax and what his officers can steal for him."

The crowd, startled, reacted. But I heard a muttered 'Yes' from more than one man. Could such words have been spoken? Should they not have been spoken long ago? As I may have suggested, Cos is little loved by many in the Islands. The ambivalent attitudes of the harbor authorities at the Cove of Harpalos were not untypical.

"Slander! Treason!" cried the leader of the uniformed men.

I should mention that 'tyrannos' in Gorean is a much more neutral term than 'tyrant' in English. It signifies little more than rule by one, rule by a given individual. Accordingly, in Gorean, it does not carry the inevitable negative connotations associated with the English term. In Gorean it would not be a contradiction in terms, or such, to speak of a public-spirited tyrannos, a good tyrannos, and so on. On the other hand, such an office obviously carries its temptations, to which it is not unknown for some men to succumb. Consequently, I have no reservations with respect to using the word 'tyrant' in English, with its familiar English connotations, when referring to Lurius of Jad.

"You have no authorization from Lurius of Cos, to apply decimation, even to intrude in this place," said Aktis. "He is faraway, and knows nothing of your actions."

"I have a warrant for the arrest of Aktis of Nicosia," said the leader of the uniformed men, slapping his hand on his wallet.

"If so, display it, now," said Aktis. "There are many here who can read!"

I doubted that. Few of the brown caste can read.

"Surrender!" shouted the leader.

"To soldiers of Cos?" asked Aktis.

"Yes!" bellowed the leader.

"Regulars of Cos?" said Aktis.

"Yes!" roared the leader.

"Produce them!" said Aktis.

"You are at the point of their swords," said he who was the leader of the uniformed men.

"Regulars of Cos are spearmen," said Aktis, "veterans of the defense and attack of two spears, long spears and casting spears, masters of the fence of death, stalwarts whose lines of braced spears deter even tharlarion. I see no spears, long spears, or casting spears. How can these be regulars of Cos? Have they overlooked or forgotten their primary weapons? And consider the variety of swords carried by these men, variously hilted, variously edged, single and double, with diverse reaches. And sheaths are not uniform. The cuts and hems of tunics differ. At best you are militia, at worse impostors."

I was pleased that Aktis had noticed these things. To be sure, he had seen Cosian regulars in Sybaris, posted there presumably to remind Therans of the presence, and power, of Cos.

"Now," said Aktis, "I call your attention to this bow. It is of the sort called the great bow, or the peasant bow. Behold. I now draw it. Not every man could do so. Those unfamiliar with the bow have little understanding of the force it imparts to the string, and the released string to the freed arrow. It can be fired accurately and rapidly over considerable distances. At this range it could sink several inches into the trunk of a full-grown Tur tree. If I were to release the string, I doubt that even you, my fraudulent, unwelcome, intrusive friend, could follow the flight of the arrow to your heart."

At this point the leader of the uniformed men cried out, turned about, and fled through the slashed canvas, while his men took their exits similarly.

Aktis then bent and unstrung the weapon, and the crowd in the tent, uneasily, and looking at one another, rose to their feet.

"It is a forbidden weapon," said a man.

"We do not wish to anger Cos," said another.

"You will get us all killed," said another. "Our villages will be burned."

"Without the bow," said Aktis, "it is far more likely your villages will be burned."

"Flee," a man advised Aktis.

"Contact me, at Nicosia," said Aktis. "Bows have been smuggled in from Sybaris, dozens. I and certain others can supply them. Learn them. Use them as models for others. All this can be done in secrecy."

But the men turned away, and, one by one, looking about as if they expected to find a Cosian soldier at their elbow, left the tent.

Then only Aktis, Thurnock, Clitus, and I were left in the tent.

"You did well," I said to Aktis.

"I have failed," said Aktis.

"You did well," I said. "The failure is theirs, not yours."

"It is easier to plow around a stump," said Aktis, "than remove it."

"Yet, one spring," said Thurnock, "the stump, inch by inch, is drawn from the soil."

I looked about, at the shredded walls of the long tent, now so barren, now so empty.

The rent canvas moved a little, responding to a soft wind, coming in from the harbor.

"Let us suppose," I said, "that this meeting never took place."

"It never took place," said Thurnock.

We then, each one of us, took one of the torches which illuminated the interior of the long tent and set fire to the rent canvas.

Then, the flaming tent behind us, bright in the darkness, we made our way across the fields to our camp, where the *Tesephone* was beached.

CHAPTER TWENTY-ONE

I Visit with Nicomachos, Admiral of the Fleet of the Farther Islands.

"I know you," said Nicomachos, Admiral of the Fleet of the Farther Islands, rising, angrily.

"We have met," I said.

"Access to this enclave is denied," said Nicomachos.

"Not to those who intimate they have information pertaining to Bosk of Port Kar," I said.

"How could you know that?" he asked.

"Let us say it was judiciously surmised," I said. Surely one needed not disclose one's sources, particularly if they were collared and subject to discipline. Slaves, as noted, love to speak. And who does not wish to be thought important, and to be privy to knowledges unavailable to others, but which might, at sufficient urging, be shared with others? The slave often delights in intriguing other slaves, even tormenting them, with mysterious hints, and then delights in revealing their hitherto concealed information. What pleasure it is to share confidences, even secrets, which must now be guarded, of course, ever more closely than before. How important they then become in the eyes of their sister slaves. It is little wonder that Masters often strive to keep much from their slaves. A casual remark at a private supper may become common knowledge by the next day. Along these lines, the trysts, liaisons, and affairs of free women may not be secrets as well kept as the free women are likely to believe. Much bubbles about at the laundry troughs.

"You are not one of my spies, one of my agents," said Nicomachos.

"I do not have that honor," I acknowledged.

"What is it you carry?" he asked.

"Samples," I said. "I am a merchant of wines."

"How did you know I was at the fair?" he asked.

"I am sure many know," I said. "How is one to conceal the presence of a giant, how overlook the blazing of a star, how not notice the sun in the sky?"

"My presence here is to be unremarked," he said.

"Your secret is safe with me," I said.

"I do not think you are here to tell me of Bosk of Port Kar," he said.

"No," I said.

"I do not think you are a simple merchant," he said. "I did not think so, even in Sybaris, in the audience chamber of the governor."

"Yes," I said. "Let me now expand on the hint I gave you in the chamber of Archelaos. I represent a consortium of merchants in Brundisium, concerned with the safety of the seas between Cos and the Farther Islands."

"I supposed as much," said the Admiral.

"As I thought you would," I said. "I fear the governor is less quick than the Admiral of the Fleet of the Farther Islands."

"He is a larcenous bureaucrat, crude and without subtlety," said Nicomachos, "well posted to the Farther Islands."

"'Larcenous'?" I asked.

"Yes," said Nicomachos.

"Rumors suggest," I said, "that even you, Admiral of the Fleet of the Farther Islands, sometimes accrue profits in wily ways."

"When money lies about," he said, "one is not to be blamed for picking it up."

"I have heard that governors often return from remote posts, the provinces, and such, far richer than when they took office, that they bleed their jurisdictions," I said.

"Sacrifices, virtual exile, and such," he said, "deserve compensation."

"In Sybaris," I said, "I was amazed to discover that one such as you, one of your intelligence, family, experience, and talent, indeed, the famous Nicomachos of Cos, was on Thera."

"You have looked into such things?" he said.

"Yes," I said, "in Brundisium."

"I am known in Brundisium?" he asked.

"Yes," I said. "Your reputation shines even in Brundisium."

"I am feared in the court at Jad," he said. "I have enemies. Others have the ear of the glorious Lurius, who can do only so much. He is distracted by the affairs of the ubarate. He must delegate authority. His self-seeking minions manage much. Vulos are preferred to tarns, urts to larls. Preferments are wheedled. Rank is for sale. Offices are auctioned off. And I find myself on Thera."

"Tragic," I said.

"But," he said, "if I could achieve a master stroke, if I could ignite a blaze of glory visible across the seas, even to the towers of Cos, I could no longer be ignored. I would be summoned to Cos. They would send a hundred-oared ship for me, decked with flowers, to bring me to the harbor of Jad. Lurius himself, with a retinue of a thousand, would greet me at the dock."

"If," I said, "you could encounter and destroy the fleet of the notorious pirate, Bosk of Port Kar."

"Yes!" he said, striking his right fist savagely into the palm of his left hand.

"I suspect your presence at the fair is pertinent to that end," I said.

"Precisely," he said. "I am sure that the pirate, Bosk of Port Kar, or his spies, will be at the fair, to assess the wealth of villages, to note the cargos of what ships are bound where, and so on. It is here that I hope to obtain information which will allow me to meet his fleet and wipe it from the sea. But what is your purpose here, noble Statercounter?"

"Much the same," I said, "hoping, of course, to convey my findings to the proper authorities."

"Deal with me directly," said Nicomachos. "It will save time."

"You do not trust the governor?" I asked.

"He is slow and inefficient, venal and grasping," said Nicomachos. "I trust that you have your own spies at the fair."

"Of course," I said.

It seemed clear to me that Nicomachos did not think highly of the governor. That much seemed to me authentic. On the other hand, I thought it likely that he, in his hostility, far underestimated the shrewdness, the subtlety, the depth, mind, and energy, of the governor. What captain does not wish to be underestimated by the enemy? It seemed likely to me, of course, that he and the governor were enleagued, and that both profited from the depredations of the false Bosk of Port Kar. Did not the fleet of the Farther Islands seem inert much of the time, and had not its searches for the raiders proved invariably futile? Few thieves arrest themselves. Surely Nicomachos and Archelaos were colleagues in crime.

"In Sybaris," I said, "I urged the surveillance of the tavern, *The Living Island*, the proprietor of which is a man named Glaukos. I gather that nothing came of your investigations in that quarter."

"Nothing came of them, as I expected," said Nicomachos.

"Unfortunate," I said. Certainly I did not find this outcome surprising. What other result is expected when guilty parties investigate themselves?

"The Inn of Kahlir," I said, "was attacked, looted, and burned the very night I met you and the governor in Sybaris."

"An interesting coincidence," he said. "You were staying there, as I recall."

"I was absent at the time," I said.

"That is fortunate," he said.

"I think so," I said.

"Should you be successful in acquiring information pertaining to Bosk of Port Kar or his fleet, I trust that you will relay it to me as amply and quickly as possible."

"You may depend on it," I said.

"Rumors fly about," he said, "and we must guard against being misled by contrived intelligence, supplied by the corsairs themselves, to confuse and baffle us, to lead us astray, to trick us into expending our resources fruitlessly."

"Certainly," I said.

"I must know when information arrives from a reliable source," he said. "Each of my spies has a secret device, a signal, a reference, a code phrase, a password, that sort of thing."

"That is very wise," I said. "Let mine be 'Falarian'."

"The wine of myth and legend?" he said.

"I am sure that it once existed," I said. "Much evidence suggests that. I suspect that some still exists, somewhere, only that it is often hidden."

"To keep thieves and murderers from killing for it?" asked the Admiral.

"Presumably," I said.

"Very well," he said, "let your token be 'Falarian'."

"I take it we are cohorts," I said.

"Be it so," he said.

"Shall we drink upon it?" I asked.

"Rika!" he called.

"No," I said. "I have wine and slaves babble."

"Of course," he said, "you are a wine merchant, of great Brundisium, and no more need be explained to slaves than to other animals."

"Master?" inquired a blonde, briefly tunicked, entering the inner tent. Such a hair color is unusual in the Farther Islands.

"Bring two goblets," said Nicomachos, "place them on the table, and then leave us."

"Yes, Master," she said, softly, backing gracefully away. I suspected she had received her training on the continent. I had no idea what she would cost in the Islands, but in Brundisium or Ar I would suppose as much as two silver tarsks. Shortly thereafter the two goblets were on the table and the slave had retired.

I reached into the package I had brought with me.

I placed one of the two bottles received from the three female decoys we had encountered earlier at sea, supposedly waiting to be rescued from the seeming wreckage on which they stood, to which they pathetically clung.

The bottle was subtly and quaintly marked. I did not think there would be any mistaking the bottle. Sips from the contents of one of the bottles, I was sure, would have killed those who drank on the *Tesephone*, and sips from the other, I was sure, would have killed those who drank on the *Dorna*. Maneuverability and armament are not the only ways to win a battle at sea.

"This bottle is oddly marked," he said.

"Clearly," I said.

I watched Nicomachos closely. I detected no sudden cast of apprehension in his eyes, no tiny drawing back of a body, no trembling of a hand.

"It was touted to me as Falarian," I said, "by three lovely, carelessly veiled free women."

"You did not believe them, I hope," he said.

"No," I said.

"If it was Falarian," he said, "you should be accompanied by a hundred guards."

"True," I said.

"The women," he said, "should have been immediately stripped, branded, collared, thrown to their bellies, and whipped."

"It is true," I said, "they are playing a dangerous game."

"I gather it was inconvenient at the time," he said, "to inform them that their behavior was not acceptable."

"I fear so," I said.

I undid the stopper and poured a bit into each of the goblets.

"Could it be," I wondered, "that Nicomachos does not recognize the danger? Is he a master actor, worthy of the stage in Ar? But perhaps the poisoned wine was not known to him. Perhaps it was known only to others, say, Glaukos of *The Living Island*, Archelaos, governor of Thera, the captains of certain ships, the decoy women, or such?"

Would he insist that I drink first?

He lifted his goblet.

Would he now deliberately spill the wine, as though accidentally? Would he pretend to put the wine to his lips, and then reject it, for some defect of coloration or bouquet?

Perhaps he would pretend to sip the wine, and then wait for me to drink?

But he brought the goblet to his lips.

I feared he was going to drink.

My hand touched his wrist. "Hold, noble officer," I said. "Forgive me. I am chagrined. I am dishonored by my parsimony. Blame it on the thrift of my caste, the desire to save a tarsk-bit wherever possible. I am shamed. This wine is unworthy to celebrate our understanding. Too, could I really suppose that the Admiral of the Fleet of the Farther Islands, the First Captain of Sybaris, High Officer of Cos, could not tell the difference between a decent wine and a *ka-la-na* worthy at best to fortify common *kal-da*?"

I then took both goblets and emptied them into the dirt floor of the tent, outside the rugs on which we sat.

"Save the rest," suggested Nicomachos, "we can give it to the slaves."

"I would not give this even to tarsks," I said, pouring the bottle out, its contents following their predecessors into the now-soaked dirt.

It had been a close thing. Nicomachos, I was sure, for better or for worse, would have died a terrible death. I still had one bottle of poison left, back on the *Tesephone*. It was dangerous to have it about. I must consider its disposition.

"It had an interesting bouquet," said Nicomachos.

"Nonetheless," I said.

I did not doubt but what the poison's taste, if it had a taste, would have been well masked, intentionally concealed by attractive additives.

I then reached into my container of samples and produced another bottle. With a cloth I wiped the goblets free of any residue of what they had recently contained. I then unstoppered the new bottle and put a large amount of fluid into each of the goblets.

"You are generous," said Nicomachos.

"I must retrieve my honor," I said.

I trusted he would find the beverage acceptable. It had cost me a silver stater in Brundisium.

"Excellent," he said sampling the beverage. "It reminds me of home."

"It should," I said, "it is from the Ta grapes of lovely, terraced Cos."

"Central Cos," he said.

"Of course," I said.

After we had drunk and wished one another well, I paused in the doorway of the inner tent.

"Falarian," I said.

"Falarian," he said.

I then walked out, into the night. Surely Nicomachos was a confederate of Archelaos, the governor of Thera, and Glaukos, proprietor of *The Living Island*, both deeply involved with the corsairs. How could it be otherwise? But I was not sure.

CHAPTER TWENTY-TWO

Intelligence is Gathered; I Form a Plan

"I feared it might be," I said. "It has been three days since we have seen him. Where did you find him?"

"Outside *The Tent of Flaming Paga*, where he had been thrown," said Thurnock. He and Clitus lowered the large, inert, blanketed form, groaning and soaked with paga, to the sand beside the beached *Tesephone*, in our camp a pasang or so away from the harbor at Mytilene, near which the teeming streets of the fair were still lit by hundreds of torches.

"He should not have touched it again," I said.

"One finds a thousand excuses," said Thurnock.

"When one lives at the edge of a cliff," said Clitus, "one should watch where one steps. Even a small step can lead to a long fall."

"Paga loosens the tongue," said Thurnock. "Who knows where he has been and what he has said."

The vast sprawling fair, its perimeters changing day by day, as new tents were pitched and stakes drawn on older ones, like cells in a body, was like a transient canvas behemoth, its body breathing, expanding and contracting. This monstrous creature had appeared as though from nothing, and, in a few days, it would vanish as quickly, leaving behind little more than torn, trampled grass, memories, bleakness, and desolation. In this city of canvas what could be bought and sold was bought and sold; copper met silver and silver met gold, and often enough, gold once more met copper; here, amidst concessions, exhibits, and emporiums, mingled with stalls, pens, brothels, taverns, markets, gambling tents, and theaters, friends met and enemies clashed, rumors were credited and truths ignored, fortunes were made and fortunes lost, and information was gathered and plans were made.

"Have they gone?" asked Sakim, sitting up.

"Yes," I said.

"Good," he said. "I would first speak to you alone."

"Are you not drunk, wasted, helpless, and inert?" I asked.

"Not at the moment," he said.

"I thought that you had succumbed, that you had betrayed yourself, that you had once more surrendered to paga."

"I hoped to convey that impression," he said. "I have made my way about for three days, to dozens of paga tents."

"You must have drained buckets of paga," I said.

"It is one thing to buy paga," he said, "but another to drink it."

"You reek of paga," I said.

"When one spits paga, and drains paga, into one's garments, soaking them with paga, that result is only to be expected," he said. "Do not fear, nor abandon camp. I will shortly burn my robes and blanket and wash in Thassa."

"I do not understand the purpose of your absence," I said. "You explained nothing."

"Had I explained my purpose," he said, "I feared you would have forbidden its pursuit."

"Quite possibly," I said.

"When men drink they become less aware of their surroundings," he said. "Too, they commonly speak freely to one another when no one is about, or no one they need take seriously, such as the stupidly and blindly drunk, the somnolent and unconscious."

"Granted," I said.

"Ctesippus and Laios, henchmen of Glaukos, proprietor of *The Living Island* in Sybaris, are at the fair."

I looked at him, narrowly.

How much did he know?

"Of what interest could this be to me?" I asked.

"Of great interest, I suspect," he said.

"Continue," I said.

"Dear Captain," he said, "I, too, was once a captain. I am not a fool. You have told me little but I have gathered much. You muchly conceal your vessels. You chart unusual courses. Your crews are not common oarsmen and mariners, but fighting men, well armed. Your larger ship, the *Dorna*, is no round ship. Nor is the *Tesephone*. They are knife ships, fighting ships. Indeed, I gather from an overheard conversation that the *Dorna*, recently lying near to the ruins of Nicosia, has a ram mounted, and shearing blades. A word is dropped here and there, and connections are made. Even in Sybaris I heard tell of *The Village of Flowing Gold*, and the discomfiture of the fleet of Bosk of Port Kar."

"You know much," I said.

"Ctesippus and Laios, as you doubtless know, are involved with the corsairs," he said. "That became clear with the evacuation of the corsairs from their debacle on Daphna, that of *The Village of Flowing Gold*."

"Many would not have noted the connection," I said.

"I did," he said.

"Interesting," I said.

"Perhaps you should not have taken me aboard," he said.

"If I were unwilling for you to know certain things," I said, "you would not be with us. I feared to explain all at first as I was not sure of you, of you and paga."

"You are not the corsairs," he said, "nor are you enleagued with them."

"True," I said.

"You would foil them and destroy them," he said.

"Perhaps," I said.

"Thus I thought you would be interested to learn of the presence of Ctesippus and Laios at the fair," he said.

"I am interested," I said.

"I have learned more of interest," he said.

"Speak," I said.

"Seven ships, warships, each a fifty-oared ship, have come to the harbor of Mytilene," he said.

"Vessels of the Fleet of the Farther Islands?" I said.

"No," he said. "Ships out of Telnus on Cos."

This was dire news indeed. I had no doubt these were replacement vessels for the corsair ships I had burned on Daphna. The destroyed corsair fleet had possessed four ships of fifty-oars and two of thirty-oars. Now there were seven enemy ships, each of fifty-oars, a far more formidable fleet than the one we had managed to destroy by trickery. Moreover, if the ships were out of Telnus, the greatest of the harbors on Cos, it seemed clear that Lurius of Jad himself, the Ubar of Cos, had invested resources in replacing the corsair fleet. It seemed incredible that he would attend to such seemingly trivial matters as abetting corsairs afflicting the Farther Islands. There must be a great deal more in this, I supposed, than was apparent, at least to me. Why would Lurius interest himself in such unimportant, distant matters? The winnings of the corsair fleet, with its plundering of small villages, and the sacking and sinking of an occasional merchant-man, could bring no more than tarsk-bits, so to speak, into the treasury of Cos.

"I fear," I said, "the corsair fleet, and a more formidable one this time, is now at Mytilene."

"I think so," said Sakim, "and I think it may soon weigh anchor."

"How is that," I asked.

"I, hooded and reeling, followed Ctesippus and Laios to the paga tent of *The Drunken Sleen*," he said. "There they met with seven captains."

"What transpired?" I asked.

"They spoke softly," said Sakim. "I could not risk approaching more closely, particularly as Ctesippus and Laios might recognize me from Sybaris."

"Leaving the fair," I said, "the corsairs will seek prey at sea. But in the harbor at Mytilene there are more than two hundred ships, and most will not raise their sails and depart until the closing of the fair. And, from such a rich, departing swarm, pirates could intercept few more than one or two ships."

Indeed, that was why a common departure was to take place.

"But," said Sakim, "what if three ships, round ships of Brundisium, splendid ships with rich cargos, leave the harbor unexpectedly early, to elude pirates. Indeed, they might travel together for protection."

"Three round ships, together or not, would be easy prey for seven knife ships," I said.

"I heard about the three ships independently, earlier," said Sakim. "Drunken mariners talk, and are proud of their cleverness, how by an early departure they can outwit pirates."

"Perhaps Ctesippus, Laios, and their confreres were discussing just that small fleet," I said.

"It is possible," said Sakim, "but I do not know. There will be many ships, and rich cargos, after the fair."

"What if," I said, "one could seize the early departures, and return in time to cast a new net?"

"There may be other early departures," said Sakim, "motivated by similar considerations."

"Surely," I said. "Have you heard other news of possible interest?"

"There was a meeting of peasants outside the fairgrounds," said Sakim, "which was disrupted and ended by guardsmen."

"That is true, in a way," I said.

"And our Aktis, one of our oarsmen, is the subject of a search by guardsmen," said Sakim, "that having to do with the possession of a forbidden weapon."

"They will not find Aktis at the fair," I said. "We are keeping him here, at the camp. He is in hiding."

"Good," said Sakim.

"Later we are to join the *Dorna*, near Nicosia," I said. "Peasants who seek some word from Aktis, or wish to obtain samples of the great bow, are to contact him there."

"I gather that it would not to do to carry such bows about at the fair," smiled Sakim.

"I think not," I said. "You have done well. Is there any other news you might wish to impart?"

"There are always strange things, puzzles, anomalies, little things to wonder about," said Sakim, "but I think there is nothing else of much interest."

"Strange things have causes," I said, "much like familiar things."

"You have heard of *The Gambling Tent of the Golden Urt*?" he asked.

"Yes," I said, "it is connected with *The House of the Golden Urt* in Sybaris."

"Managed by the Three Ubaras," said Sakim.

"They are not Ubaras," I said.

"They claim to be exiled Ubaras, from three cities," he said.

"Perhaps some will believe that," I said.

"It is merely an advertising image, a merchandising persona," he said.

"I care little for such frauds," I said, "even when obvious and droll."

"You know the reputation of *The House of the Golden Urt* in Sybaris?" said Sakim.

"Its reputation is unsavory," I said. "There is much suspicion, of tampering, of chicanery, of dishonest gaming."

"It is even worse here, in *The Gambling Tent of the Golden Urt*," said Sakim.

"Crowds at the fair are often happy and gullible," I said. "And thousands here are of the Peasants, many of whom are new to colored placards, cupped dice, and whirling wheels, let alone marked placards, weighted dice, and manipulable whirling wheels."

"Trickery, even when palpable, even when the scent is strong," said Sakim, "is difficult to prove."

"Why do you mention these things?" I asked.

"The 'Three Ubaras' are here at the fair," he said.

I recalled the three closed palanquins, with their bearers and guards, noted some days ago, when Lais, kneeling beside us, had been so alarmed. *Kajirae* much fear free women.

"Oh?" I said.

"In *The Gambling Tent of the Golden Urt*," said Sakim, "business flourished for them, pouches and wallets of coins were lavished on the games."

"It is one way to become rich," I said.

"But yesterday," he said, "the tent was closed, despite cascades of copper tarsks."

"And why would our 'Three Ubaras' seal their tent, turning their presumably lovely backs on such a rain of wealth?"

"I do not know," said Sakim.

"Silver is to be preferred to copper, and gold to silver," I said.

"I do not understand," said Sakim.

"Where now," I asked, "are our 'Three Ubaras'?"

"No one knows," he said.

"They will need a day's start," I said.

"Captain?" asked Sakim.

"It is nothing you would know about," I said. "But tomorrow, I wager, a valuable cargo will leave the fair early, perhaps that of the three ships bound for Brundisium of which you spoke earlier."

"I do not know when they will leave," said Sakim.

"Someone will know," I said. "And then, the next day, seven knife ships will depart the harbor."

"They would overtake the merchantmen at sea," said Sakim.

"Easily," I said, "unless delayed."

"How could they be delayed?" asked Sakim.

"First," I said, "I must encourage the merchantmen not to respond to signals of distress, not to be solicitous of stranded survivors, the pathetic victims of a casualty at sea."

"I do not understand this," said Sakim.

"You have just succeeded in saving several lives, three ships, and three holds filled with goods," I said.

"I do not understand," said Sakim.

"Do you know what you must do now?" I asked.

"No," he said.

"Burn your clothing and wash your body," I said. "Gleaming Thassa awaits."

I was not discontent.

There are few things which may not be purchased somewhere in that city of tents which constituted the vast, transitory metropolis of a Fair of the Farther Islands.

CHAPTER TWENTY-THREE

We Entertain a Visitor, Near the Ruins of Nicosia

"Few have come here to the ashes and cinders of Nicosia," said Clitus.

"We have done what we could," said Aktis, fletching an arrow with the feathers of the sea kite.

"Cos lulls the villages into a false sense of security," said Thurnock.

"In the towns," said Clitus, "more is known from refugees than in the isolated villages themselves. Two have been sacked and burned since the closing of the fair at Mytilene."

We had posted agents, in guises such as that of peddlers and itinerant workers, in several of the larger towns of the Farther Islands. In this way, though news traveled slowly to us, we were probably better informed, on the whole, than any single town in the Islands, including Sybaris, or Sybaris not counting the precincts of *The Living Island*.

"At least," said Sakim, "we have managed to discomfit and annoy the enemy."

"Largely thanks to you," I said.

"I did little," he said.

"You did much," I said.

"I wished I could have seen our 'Three Ubaras', in their contrived gowns, carefully soiled and rent, their ankles in water, apparently piteous and needful, waiting to be rescued, and not being rescued, their signals ignored," said Clitus. "They must have been adrift, alone, for three or four days."

"A little frustration will be good for them," I said.

"Besides being hungry and thirsty," said Clitus, "they must eventually have been dismayed and frightened, fearing that something was askew, that they might have been overlooked, ignored, forgotten, or abandoned. Doubtless they feared they might have been, inadvertently or not, left to die on the decoy platform."

"The delay," said Thurnock, "gave the merchantmen an unrecoverable lead, one which not even the swiftest knife ship could overcome."

I will briefly explain the nature of the "delay." Gorean mariners, as is often the case with mariners, have a very special sense of their ships. The landsman may think of a ship as an object or artifact, little different, in essence, save in size and purpose, from a cabinet or chair, a wall or flight of stairs. The mariner, on the other hand, who entrusts his life to his ship, commonly views it differently, more deeply and closely, more personally. It braves storms; it protects him from the terrors of the deep. It carries him from port to port. It shelters him and he cares for it. From its decks he sees vast skies and the glory of the sea. Sometimes, small and wondering, he can become for a moment an aspect of immensity. As the ship becomes one with the sea, so he becomes one with the ship. He knows a world the landsman knows not. But beyond such things the Gorean mariner, like many of the mariners of the ancient world of Earth, has a deeper, odder, more mystical view of a ship. It is, for him, in its way, alive. The horseman has his horse, the tarnsman his tarn, the mariner his ship. It is common with Gorean ships to have eyes painted on each side of the bow. Most mariners will not serve on a ship without eyes. How could it see its way? Indeed, the last thing the shipwright does, whether in the arsenal at Port Kar or in a hundred shipyards elsewhere, is to paint eyes on the ship. It is then that it can see. It is then that it comes alive.

On the morning the corsair fleet, with its seven ships, was to depart the harbor at Mytilene in pursuit of the three Brundisium merchantmen, superstitious terror gripped savage crews. Consternation reigned. Who would risk their lives on a blind ship? Who would be so foolish as to take such a ship to sea? The eyes of the seven ships were blackened over with paint, presumably administered from small boats in the night, possibly by means of paint-soaked rags or sponges fastened to poles. In any event, however this may have happened, the seven ships would remain in port while paint must be scraped away, wood sanded, smoothed, sealed, and refinished, and new eyes carefully painted.

"Someone comes," said Clitus, rising, trident in hand, loosening the strands of his net.

"He wears peasant brown," said Sakim.

"Anyone may do so," said Aktis.

Thurnock turned to me. "Do you know him?" he asked.

"No," I said.

He strung his bow.

The stranger, approaching, climbing the trail, raised his right hand, palm facing the body, in Gorean greeting.

I returned the gesture.

"He seems unarmed," said Clitus.

"He is a fool," said Thurnock.

"Perhaps," I said, "he wishes to make it clear that he comes in peace."

The stranger was a tall, blond-haired, young man.

"Tal," he said.

"Tal," I responded.

"I seek one called Aktis," he said, "who, I understand, spoke of unsettling matters at the Fair of the Farther Islands."

"I am Aktis," said Aktis, rising.

"I would speak with you," said the stranger.

"You are welcome here," I said to the stranger. "But speak before all, and freely."

"I am Xanthos," he said, "the son of Seleukos, headman of the village of Seleukos, on Thera."

"We have heard of the village, and your father," I said.

We had heard of such things, and others, while on the living island, the Isle of Seleukos.

"It is a village well known on Thera," he said.

"We have also heard of the Isle of Seleukos," I said, "the living island."

"That is far less known," he said.

"You appear dusty and weary," I said. "Perhaps you are hungry. May we offer you food?"

"I hunger," said the stranger, "but not for food."

"I take it," said Aktis "that you were at the fair at Mytilene."

"No," said Xanthos.

"How is it then that you have heard of Aktis?" asked Aktis.

"From those who would not listen to him," said Xanthos, "from those who mocked and scorned him."

"Then from some who had heard him at the fair," I said.

"Yes," said Xanthos.

"Thera is far," I said. "But you are come to Nicosia on Chios."

"I have a small, fine boat," said Xanthos. "It can make such a journey."

"Why have you come here?" I asked.

"Before the Fair of the Farther Islands," said Xanthos, "the village of Seleukos was amongst the richest villages on Thera."

"But not now?" said Thurnock.

"It was burned and looted," said Xanthos, "presumably by the minions of Bosk of Port Kar. Such, in any event, was to be gathered from the signs left behind by the bandits."

"It is unusual, as I understand it," said Clitus, "for attacks to take place on Thera."

"Possibly," I said, "the bandits, at that time, lacked ships."

"A child, herding verr," said Xanthos, "noted the approach of the bandits, in their long lines, and alerted the village. We took to our fishing boats and fled to the Isle of Seleukos, the living island of which you seem to know, with little more than the clothing on our backs."

"And thus a small shepherd became a great man," said Thurnock.

I thought I saw now what it was for which our young friend was hungry.

"What can we do for you?" I asked.

"Teach me the bow," he said.

CHAPTER TWENTY-FOUR

The Vote of Two Urns

"We had best leave Nicosia," I said. "There has been enough time to arm and train hundreds but only four gave answer to the call of Aktis at the fair. It has already been a week since young Xanthos, of the village of Seleukos, departed with a dozen bows."

"It is hard to move Peasants," said Clitus. "They are inert and unstirring, like mountains."

"But should a mountain choose to move," said Thurnock, "who will stand against it?"

"Of what value are a dozen bows?" asked Clitus.

"A dozen bows may turn into a thousand," said Thurnock.

"What shall we do, Captain?" asked Aktis. "Where shall we go?"

"The Peasantry will not rise," said Clitus. "The corsairs have a more formidable fleet than ever. They may now have fifteen hundred men, mariners and brigands. We have but two hundred and fifty."

"How can several hundred men, perhaps now fifteen hundred, be sustained by the looting of villages, most of them small and poor?" I said.

"Clearly they are subsidized," said Sakim.

"But why?" I asked.

"One does not know," said Sakim. "It is strange."

"I fear," said Clitus, "there is nothing to do but return to Port Kar."

"And leave brigands free to ravage in the name of the captain?" said Thurnock.

"Given the scouring of the seas," said Clitus, "we may not even be able to return to Port Kar."

"Would you, dear Clitus," I asked, "return to Port Kar?"

"I fear there is nothing else to do," he said.

"You are doubtless correct," I said. "But what would you do?"

"I would stay," said Clitus. "My trident is angry and thirsty. It has not yet tasted blood."

"This is a deep matter," I said, "not one for a captain to decide. All shall decide, each man. Tonight we shall take a vote, the vote of two urns."

I tried not to look into the firelight. "Have the pebbles been placed?" I asked.

"Yes," said Thurnock.

Each of our men had filed, one at a time, behind the blanket raised and stretched on poles, on the other side of the fire.

It was late, near the nineteenth Ahn.

The men now sat, cross-legged, in rows, facing the fire. Rising and turning, I could see the firelight reflected on their faces.

Our camp was situated in the open space which had been the clearing at the center of the village of Nicosia. The somber ruins of huts were visible in the light of the two moons in the sky. Farther away were the remains of the blackened, burned palings which had constituted the village's palisade.

The *Dorna* and the *Tesephone* were beached nearby. The ship guards, like the camp guards, had taken turns voting, that a constant guard be maintained.

Commonly Gorean votes are taken on marked ostraca deposited in urns. As ostraca, usually fragments of broken pottery, were less than practical in our present circumstances, we had resorted to the vote of two urns. In such a vote an ordinary pebble is placed in one of two urns, or containers, both of which are concealed from view. In this way the vote is kept secret.

Thurnock walked about the fire, to the blanket stretched on its poles, and tore it away.

Revealed then were two urns.

One urn was for withdrawal to Port Kar, the other was for war.

"Let the pebbles be counted," I said.

Thurnock bent down and lifted one urn. It was heavy. He shook it and pebbles rattled within it, crowded and weighty, like hail on a metal buckler. He then lifted the other urn, and turned it upside down. He shook it vigorously. It was empty. Not a pebble fell.

"The decision," said Thurnock, "is for war."

CHAPTER TWENTY-FIVE

I Conduct an Inquiry, in the Vicinity of Mytilene

I looked about. The fairgrounds were now barren. One could see the walls and harbor of Mytilene in the distance. In the harbor there were several small boats, but only a single large vessel, a ship-of-war, one of fifty oars.

"It is different now," said Thurnock.

Large patches and tracks of grass were gone, patches where tents had been pitched, tracks where streets had been formed.

A wrapper, lifted by the wind, fluttered past.

I could see beyond the fairgrounds, to the west, the place where the long tent had been pitched, and later burned, the house of a meeting which, we had agreed, had never taken place.

I then returned my attention to the empty fairgrounds.

They were vast, desolate, and lonely.

A land breeze was moving toward Thassa.

In the distance a child was hunting through the grass, probably for a lost bauble or tarsk-bit.

"Next year," I said, "the fair is to be at Pylos on Daphna."

"Why have we come here?" asked Thurnock.

After the vote of the two urns I had withdrawn from Nicosia. To my disappointment, the islands' Peasantry had not responded, stirred by Aktis' pleadings, flooding to the ruins of Nicosia to organize for a common, redoubtable defense of their lives, property, and land. Only four had come, including the last, Xanthos, of the village of Seleukos. I had dispatched the *Dorna* to the Cove of Harpalos, which location was to be favored because of its congenial harbor authorities, no friends of Cos; its proximity to Sybaris, the apparent headquarters of the corsairs; and its precincts having been previously, fruitlessly, searched by the corsairs. I hoped that they would not return, and, should they return, it seemed their approach, as before, given the terrain, could be detected in time to clear the harbor. I had left two men at Nicosia to receive reports from our dispersed spies, and redirect their future reports to the Cove of Harpalos.

"I have come here," I said, "thinking about the corsair fleet. Will it be here? If not, where is it? Did it return here after an unsuccessful pursuit of the three merchantmen of Brundisium, or go elsewhere? Is it still at sea? Might it not return here? Might not this be its new base?"

"The first fleet, disguised as merchantmen, lay to in the harbor at Sybaris," said Thurnock.

"It is one thing," I said, "for four fifty-oared ships and two thirty-oared ships to separate, assuming the appearance of innocent merchantmen, and lose themselves in the harbor at Sybaris, but it seems that seven knife ships, new and armed, might be an entirely different story."

"True," said Thurnock.

"At least," I said, "we have determined that the corsair fleet is not at Mytilene."

"Or not all of it," said Thurnock.

"Thurnock?" I asked.

"Would not the enemy assume that some such inquiry as yours would be made?" asked Thurnock.

"Quite possibly," I said.

"And act accordingly?"

"Perhaps," I said. "Why?"

"Because," said Thurnock, "that knife ship, even now, is leaving the harbor."

CHAPTER TWENTY-SIX

The Flight from Mytilene

"Keep the beat, lads, keep the beat!" I called down from the stern deck.

The beat is regulated by the *keleustes*, commonly on a drum or bar, but sometimes by voice. Occasionally this is done, particularly on large, ornate, slow-moving vessels, by a flute. This is not as strange as it might seem, for on Gor, as in the ancient world on Earth, flute music was often used to time and regulate repetitive tasks and physical labor. Indeed, in many cities military exercises are timed and regulated by the flute. Pyrrhic dances are also known in which individuals or groups simulate combat. Such dances often involve intricate footwork and swift, if rhythmic, bodily movements. Sometimes, too, particularly when silence is important, the *keleustes* times the beat by means of a flag, cloth or wand; at night a shielded lantern, opened and closed, may be used. As the rowers face the stern, they have a full view of the *keleustes* at all times. A smooth beat, however it is timed, is important, particularly in battle, as an awkwardness or mixing of oars can lead to an impairment of maneuverability. It is a rare captain who is not particular in his choice of a *keleustes*.

I clutched the rail of the stern deck, looking upward, uneasily tracing the long, graceful, looping arc of the fire-streaming projectile launched from the ship in our wake. It fell into the water, with a great splash, hissing and steaming, some two or three yards abeam.

"Easy, lads, smoothly, lads," I said.

Water from the splash had drenched several of the oarsmen.

"Be steady," I called, "be steady."

Under such conditions, the oarsmen, facing the stern, unable to see behind them, must resist the almost irresistible impulse to look behind them, even to leap from the bench. It is a horrible death to be struck by, almost enveloped by, a descending, barrel-sized, clinging ball of burning pitch.

"You know your course, do you not?" asked Sakim, next to me on the stern deck.

"Yes," I said.

This was the same course, reversed, by means of which I had first approached Mytilene, at the time of the opening of the fair.

"The *Tesephone* is light, swift, and shallow-drafted," said Sakim. "You hope that it will not be noticed?"

"That is my hope," I said.

"I fear they are finding the range," said Sakim.

"Helms left, four points," I called to the helmsmen.

Most Gorean vessels are lateen-rigged and double ruddered. Commonly then they have two helmsmen. The double rudder adds an increment of water resistance, or drag, to the vessel's passage, but this is regarded as a negligible disadvantage which is more than compensated for by the gain in maneuverability. The double rudder allows quicker, sharper turns. The dragonships of Torvaldsland, far to the north, are square-rigged and single-ruddered, the rudder, or 'steering board', usually on the right side, presumably because most human beings are right-handed. 'Starboard', referring to the right side of a ship, is presumably a contraction of 'steering board'. If a ship has a steering board on the right side, it is most convenient to disembark cargo from the left side of a ship, and thus the left side of the ship becomes the 'port side' of the ship. The reader may have noted that I am occasionally reluctant to use the expressions 'port' and 'starboard' in referring to one or another side of a ship. That is because I usually associate 'port' and 'starboard' with side-ruddered vessels.

Had I kept a straight course I was reasonably confident that the next projectile, or its successor, would strike the *Tesephone*, perhaps crashing through the main deck, perhaps destroying a section of a rowing frame, in either case setting the ship afire.

"Helms right, two points," I called.

It is important to make evasive action as unpredictable as possible. The catapult master conjectures and the prey conjectures. Each, in a sense, tries to anticipate the other. A duel of wits takes place. A game ensues, a guessing game, with possibly mortal consequences. Some catapult masters have an almost uncanny sense of a prey's next move, but I trusted that the corsairs, being the hired brigands they were, would not be likely to have the services of a seasoned, skillful catapult master at their disposal. Indeed, I had not expected a naval catapult in their arsenal.

"Steady, helms," I said, "two points more!"

"The corsair gains," said Sakim.

That was to be expected. In deviating from a straight line one sacrifices distance for position.

"Sakim," I said, "bring me, quickly, a marked gambling stone."

"Captain?" he said.

"Now!" I said. "Clitus is fond of the stones. Bring me one, hurry!"

The human being is a pattern-seeking animal. Out of this springs rationality, learning, science, and usually survival.

"Left, two points!" I cried.

Another projectile, hissing and flaming, plunged into the water, not four yards astern.

I shook my head, and wiped my eyes with the sleeve of my jacket, which was drenched.

The catapult master was seeking pattern, my pattern. What will seem right or appropriate to the prey, for whatever mysterious, perhaps unconscious, reasons, may be sensed by the predator. The prey may vary his pattern but might not the variations, too, have their pattern?

The marked stone was pressed into my hand.

"Even numbers, whatever they may be," I said, "are right. Odd numbers, whatever they may be, are left."

"Captain?" said Sakim.

I shook the stone in my right hand and slapped it into the palm of my left hand.

It was 'six'.

"Helms right," I called, "two points."

Next it was 'four'.

"Helms right," I called, "two points."

Then it was 'four', again.

"Right," I called, "two points."

At that point, another projectile struck the water, but some ten yards to the left.

"I thought," said Sakim, "you would call to the left."

"So, too," I said, "did the catapult master."

I could impose no pattern on the marked stone. It lay as it would. We could surely have been struck by a projectile, but, if so, it could then be no more than a matter of coincidence, or happenstance. It is difficult to anticipate an individual's pattern if the individual has no pattern.

I kept the points to two or three, to keep the stern to the enemy. In that way, the ship presents a narrower target.

After a quarter of an Ahn, and some six or seven more projectiles, the catapult on the enemy ship was quiescent. By now the enemy ship was uncomfortably close, so close one could see faces at the enemy's rail, but it was not close enough to bring either its ram or shearing blades into play.

"They are out of ammunition," said Sakim.

"We do not know that," I said.

Again I applied the stone.

"Helms left, two points," I called.

An Ihn or two later a projectile hissed into the water much where we would have been had I maintained my former course.

Hair rose on the back of my neck.

I was shaken.

"The impact," said Sakim, "would have been square and devastating."

"We were fortunate," I said.

"The enemy," said Sakim, "guessed wrong."

"He could not outguess the stone," I said.

After a time the enemy ship was falling behind.

"We are out of range," said Sakim.

"I think so," I said.

"It was a fast ship," said Sakim. "It is fortunate we were not cut off by another."

"We will seem to set a course for Pylos on Daphna," I said. "Then, after the fall of night, we will raise the mast and yard, resting our fellows, making our way back to Thera and the Cove of Harpalos."

"I shall inform Thurnock and the others," said Sakim.

"Please do so," I said.

In passing, one might note that the ship catapult, one of several such devices, can rotate, this altering its direction of fire. It can fire aft as well as forward and to the side. It might also be mentioned that the ship catapult is, as would be expected, much smaller and lighter than the common siege catapult whose projectiles, commonly large boulders, are designed to crash through stone walls. Another point of interest, though perhaps one too obvious to mention, has to do with the platform and target of fire. The land catapult is commonly stationary and commonly has a stationary target. It is seldom used, for example, against infantry. The naval catapult, on the other hand, is mounted on a moving ship and its target is usually in motion as well.

"Captain," said Sakim.

"Yes?" I said.

"You know the waters you have just plied?" said Sakim.

"Yes," I said.

"You chose a bold route of flight," he said.

"I was hoping we might deprive the enemy of one of their seven ships," I said.

"I thought so," he said.

"Do you think it was unwise?" I asked.

"It was surely a course fraught with danger," he said.

"We traversed these waters safely when first we sought to attend the fair," I said.

"Given the lightness of the *Tesephone*," he said.

"Presumably," I said.

"Its quick passage, like a shadow on the water?" he said.

"In war, one counts on such things," I said.

"But you did not count on a catapult," he said.

"Not on a corsair ship," I said.

"Perhaps it was not a corsair ship," he said.

"It was a ship of corsairs," I said, "even if it was not a corsair ship." I thought of Nicomachos. "It did not attempt to contact us. There was no hailing, no signaling, no flags, no horns. It did not identify itself or demand that we identify ourselves."

"But your plan failed," he said.

"Clearly," I said.

"You would have lured the enemy into a trap, having him follow you, having him pursue you, possibly to his doom, into the waters of the powerful, gigantic, territorial, aggressive hith."

"That was my hope," I said. "But there was no hith."

"It does exist," said Sakim.

"Or did exist," I said. "It may have perished, or gone elsewhere."

"I once saw it," he said.

"Or once," I said, "in the midst of travail, confusion, terror, and shipwreck, you wanted to see it, to explain a debacle to yourself, a breaking, shattering ship, and thought you saw it."

"I did see it," said Sakim.

"Many mariners, and others, have claimed to see strange things at sea, serpents, monsters, and such," I said.

"Tricks of light, configurations of waves, surfacing sea sleen, tricks of the atmosphere, shapes detected in fog?" said Sakim.

"That sort of thing," I said.

"In any event," said Sakim, "certain waters, feared waters, waters often avoided and seldom crossed, are now behind us."

CHAPTER TWENTY-SEVEN

The Gambling House of the Golden Urt; What Occurred Therein

"It is like a circle of fire," said Aktis.

The colored wheel spun madly.

Men were calling out numbers, clutching colored, marked ostraca.

"And it can burn you," I said.

Soon the wheel spun more slowly, and then its pointer stopped.

"Red, fifteen," said the wheel master.

Red stood for day and black for night. The numbers stood for the twenty Ahn in the Gorean day.

"I have won!" cried Aktis, clutching his ostracon. "My ostracon cost me but a single tarsk-bit and I have won ten tarsk-bits!"

"Well done," granted Thurnock.

"Patrons must lose more than they win," I said, "or the house will cease to exist."

"And in this house, *The House of the Golden Urt*," said Clitus, "there is little danger of that."

The Gambling House of the Golden Urt, managed by the 'Three Ubaras', was on Garland Street in Sybaris. Its reputation, as I noted earlier, was unsavory. There was much suspicion of fraudulent play. We had determined, at the time of the fair, at least to our satisfaction, that the 'Three Ubaras' were also utilized by the corsairs as decoy women, the supposed survivors of shipwrecks or piratical attacks, three pathetic free women seemingly in desperate need of rescue.

"I merely chose a color and number," marveled Aktis, "and I now have ten tarsk-bits."

"Congratulations," said Thurnock.

"And you could choose a color and a number, and lose your tarsk-bit," said Clitus.

"Cash in your winnings and be pleased," I suggested.

"Surely not," said Aktis.

"Do you not think the wheel master has some sense of what is wagered?" I asked. "Do you think he cannot read the signals from the cashier, particularly when more valuable ostraca are purchased? Have you not noticed that sometimes the wheel spins differently than at other times, that it occasionally slows earlier and so stops sooner?"

"When I wager anew," said Aktis, "I shall have another ten tarsk-bits."

"Or one less tarsk-bit," said Clitus.

"Had I bought a notched copper-tarsk ostracon," said Aktis, "I could have won ten copper tarsks."

"True," said Thurnock.

"Had I bought a silver-edged ostracon," said Aktis, "I would now have ten silver tarsks."

"And," said Clitus, "had you purchased a gold-edged ostracon, as might be wagered once or twice in an evening's play, you would have ten gold tarn disks."

"Yes," said Aktis.

"—if you won," said Clitus.

"Of course," said Aktis.

"It is common to award winnings to small bets," said Clitus, "that others may be encouraged to play and larger sums be wagered."

"I feel lucky," said Aktis.

"Wheels are skilled at changing such feelings," said Clitus.

"I shall wager again," said Aktis, "but, as I am sensible and realize I might lose, no more than a copper tarsk."

"A whole copper tarsk?" said Thurnock.

"Certainly," said Aktis.

"May fortune smile upon your madness," said Thurnock.

"Come to the side," I said to Thurnock and Clitus. "Leave Aktis to learn the lessons of life, the mathematics of chance, even should the wheel be honest."

"Sometimes," said Thurnock, "one gambles successfully, again and again."

"Until it comes to the attention of probability," I said, "or to that of the house."

"Intermittent victories," said Clitus, "encourage the dismissal of countless defeats."

Outside it was night, and there were crowds in the torch-lit streets of Sybaris.

"It seems likely," I said, "that the three free women who own or manage this place, the 'Three Ubaras', as they will have it, are in league with the corsairs. Too, our men posted in Sybaris report that Archelaos, the implicated governor of Thera, is a frequent guest not only of Glaukos, in the tavern of *The Living Island*, but of our 'Three Ubaras'."

"He might easily pose as a patron of either establishment," said Clitus.

"What we need," said Thurnock, "is some clue as to where the corsairs will strike next, that we might intervene, or, at least, alert the potential victims."

"Another ruse, like that of *The Village of Flowing Gold*," said Clitus, "seems impractical."

"I fear so," I said.

"How naive we were," said Thurnock, "thinking that the victory was ours."

"Not really," said Clitus. "We had every right to suppose that the victory was ours. We had burned the corsair fleet and left the corsairs themselves to perish, stranded in what may well be Daphna's most inhospitable region."

"We did not anticipate," said Thurnock, "that the corsairs would be somehow evacuated, nor that their destroyed fleet would be replaced by one even more formidable."

"Consider the expense," said Clitus.

"Why should Cos support corsairs who ravage the Farther Islands, from which tax revenues are derived?" asked Clitus.

"It is odd," I said. "But in the large picture, there is little damage and small loss. Only villages and ships at sea are preyed upon."

"By Bosk of Port Kar," said Thurnock.

"So it seems," I said.

"It is still unclear to me how the corsairs could have been evacuated from Daphna," said Thurnock.

"Happenstance," said Clitus, "a passing fleet."

"Or a single living island controlled by corsairs," I said, "a single living island reacting to the arrival of dozens of message vulos, message vulos surprisingly returning messageless to their cot, a single living island much as that we saw at sea, in departing from Daphna."

"Could it be?" asked Thurnock.

"Of course!" said Clitus.

"I think so," I said.

I looked about. The lamp-lit premises were large. In the crowded room there were more than two dozen tables devoted to various games of chance. Many dealt with colored placards or marked stones. There are several such games. Two tables were devoted to the 'Which-Cup?' game, in which one guesses beneath which of three cups a tarsk-bit may be found. Once the tarsk-bit is placed, the cups are rapidly shifted about, making it difficult to determine beneath which cup the tarsk-bit now resides. A skilled game master can, by sleight of hand, should he be so minded, remove the tarsk-bit from the cup and, if challenged, seem to retrieve it from beneath a different cup. There were also 'Urn Games', playable for different amounts. In these games, one generally draws marked ostraca from an urn, with one result or another. In one 'Urn Game', even numbers of red and black ostraca are placed in an empty urn. One chooses a color and then, if one draws two ostraca of that color from the urn, one doubles one's money. In such an arrangement the odds are clearly unfavorable to the player who, mathematically, has only one chance in four of winning. But such considerations are often unlikely to deter the zealous gambler. In gambling, more seems to be involved than mathematics, probability, and rationality. Who would not be pleased to receive two tarsk-bits for one tarsk-bit, or two gold staters for one gold stater?

"There seems no clue here," said Thurnock, "as to where the corsairs will strike next."

"It seems not," I said.

At one wall, to the left as one would enter, there were low tables, and, nearby, behind them, a counter at which light foods, paga, and *ka-la-na* might be obtained. At gambling houses, unlike taverns, free women, if escorted, were welcome. Might not they be parted from their money as well as their male counterparts? There is little economic point in neglecting possible sources of revenue. At the opposite wall, there were some curtained thresholds behind which slaves might be kept. These were not permitted on the floor during business hours, in deference to free women. It is a rare gambling house on Gor which does not contain certain aspects of the restaurant, tavern, and brothel. I did note three free women, unescorted, presumably the 'Three Ubaras', mingling with the customers, doubtless listening and chatting, making fellows feel at home, putting them at ease, calling attention to the house's amenities, and, one supposes, encouraging play.

"Yet I suspect some here know," said Clitus.

"I am sure you are right," I said.

"We are told Archelaos is a patron of this establishment," said Clitus.

"I do not think he is here tonight," I said.

"Might not the 'Three Ubaras' be confidants of the governor?" asked Clitus.

"I think that is likely," I said.

We had earlier determined that the names of the 'Three Ubaras' were Melete, Iantha, and Philomena. Melete was thought to be first amongst them.

"They would be accomplices, clearly," said Thurnock.

"I think they may be more than that," I said.

"Women are famed for their curiosity," said Clitus. "They often wish to know more than they need to know. They press and wheedle well. And many men, to please them, to appear important, and such, will let slip a sly sentence or so, with respect to what is in the offing."

"Do you think the three women, the decoy women, our 'Three Ubaras', know the next strike of the corsairs?" asked Thurnock.

"I do not know," I said.

"They might," he said.

"I think it possible," I said.

There was then a scuffle, or altercation, near the front of the room. Two men in the same livery as that of the fellows who had borne or guarded the three palanquins we had noted several days ago at the fair had seized a now-struggling figure, which they then pummeled and threw into the street.

"That is not Aktis, is it?" asked Thurnock.

"No," I said.

"Greetings, handsome fellow," purred a woman's voice. The lightness of her veil left no doubt as to the loveliness of her features.

My face, I thought, might be interesting, or coarse, or strong, but it was scarcely what I would call handsome.

"You are not playing," she said.

"I am not here for the games," I said.

"I understand," she said, smiling, and, with a small movement of her head, gestured toward a curtained threshold. "We have women the way you men want them, half naked and collared. If any of them fail to give you complete satisfaction, they will be well lashed."

"I understand," I said.

"Let it not be said that *The House of the Golden Urt* is not hospitable," she said.

"I have not come here for slave sport," I said.

"I do not understand," she said.

"Do you not recognize me?" I asked.

"You look familiar," she said. "I am sure I have seen you somewhere. But I do not recall you."

"I am Glycon, captain of the *Hermione*," I said.

"Of course," she said.

I had invented this identity just then.

"The *Hermione*," I said, "—of the fleet of the corsairs."

"Of the corsairs!" she said.

"That," I said.

"I shall inform guardsmen!" she said.

"That is unlikely," I said.

"What are you doing here?" she said. "How dare you be here?"

"Are you Melete?" I asked.

"No, Iantha," she said.

"Summon your colleagues," I said.

"What is this about?" she asked.

"I come from Archelaos," I said. "There is little time. Make haste."

At the mention of the name 'Archelaos', she sped away.

"What are you doing?" asked Thurnock. He and Clitus were standing back in the shadows.

"I am trying to find out where the corsairs will strike next," I said.

"She may not know," said Clitus.

"I am not prepared to see Archelaos and ask him personally," I said.

Very shortly Iantha returned with two other women. I was pleased to see, given the contrived texture of the veiling, both were equal to her, if not superior to her, in beauty. Archelaos, I supposed, had an eye for such things.

"I am Melete," said one of them. "What is this about?"

"Tomorrow," I said, "with the first tide, a round ship of Anango, fat and slow, heavy with riches, departs the harbor."

"What is that to us?" asked Melete.

"The pretended wreckage, your platform of deception, has already been towed into place."

"I do not understand what you are talking about," said Melete.

"We can find others to take your place," I said.

"The last time," said Melete, angrily, "the quarry ship did not respond to our signal. It passed safely, untrapped, unpursued. Our friends were late. They had been delayed. We drifted for four days. We had food and water for only three days. I told Ctesippus he could hereafter find others for such work."

"We were clear on that point," said the other woman, whom I took to be Philomena.

"The delay was inevitable," I said. "The fleet was vandalized, injured, and defiled, unbelievable so, and could not immediately leave port. Archelaos himself begs your forgiveness, and assures you that such a situation will not arise again."

"It is dangerous work," she said.

"And should be compensated accordingly," I said. I had no idea, of course, of what fees might have been in place.

"'Compensated'?" said Melete. She and the other two exchanged glances.

I suddenly realized that some emolument other than a transfer of coin, per transaction, must be involved.

"A gold coin each, a gold stater of Brundisium," I said.

"We shall consider the matter," said Melete.

"Do so," I said, "and, if you do not accept, Archelaos will find three others, three new 'Ubaras', if you like, and transfer *The House of the Golden Urt* to them."

"He would not!" exclaimed Melete.

That told me what I wanted to know.

"He has told me so," I said. "He said, for all he cares, you can eat garbage and sleep in the street. And I suspect you know the common fate of street waifs, the brand and collar."

"I will look into this," said Melete. "I will speak with the governor directly."

"There is no time," I said. "The pretended wreckage is in place. You must be conveyed to it immediately. The round ship of Anango, a most valuable prize, leaves earlier than we had anticipated, tomorrow, with the first tide."

I removed from my pouch three gold staters, each struck from the molds of the coin house of Brundisium, and pressed one into the small right palm of each of the women.

"We must hasten," I said.

"Have I not seen you before?" asked Melete. "You seem familiar."

"Perhaps at the palace of the governor," I said.

"We shall be with you shortly," said Melete.

The three women then hurried from the floor.

I turned to Thurnock and Clitus. "Proceed me to the *Tesephone*," I said. "Ready her for departure. Also, take some planks and boards and nail them together, about the size of a large door, such that they may serve as a small raft."

Thurnock nodded.

"Collect Aktis on your way out," I said.

"He approaches," said Clitus.

"I have lost fifteen copper tarsks," he informed us, gloomily.

"Be pleased it is not more," I said.

"Could you afford that loss?" asked Clitus.

"Not really," said Aktis.

"Then," said Clitus, "I trust that you have now learned your lesson."

"I have," said Aktis. "Had I played differently, more carefully, more astutely, had I chosen different colors and numbers, I would have won."

"Accompany us," said Clitus. "We are returning to the *Tesephone*."

"You saw," said Aktis, "that for a single tarsk-bit I won ten tarsk-bits."

"Let us be on our way," said Thurnock.

CHAPTER TWENTY-EIGHT

Intelligence is Gathered at Sea

I stood upon the stem deck of the *Tesephone*, looking about. The three women, the so-called 'Three Ubaras', Melete, Iantha, and Philomena, were with me. They were well robed and heavily and discreetly veiled, for they were at sea with strong, hardy men.

Thassa was in one of her quiet, pleasant moods. The sky was blue, the clouds a congenial white, the waters gentle and calm from horizon to horizon.

"This place," I said, "will do nicely. It is remote and far from traversed shipping lanes."

"I take it," said Melete, "the Anango round ship, fearing pirates, has chosen an out-of-the-way course home."

"These waters are seldom frequented," I said.

"Where is our platform," asked Melete, "that designed to resemble wreckage, stocked with food and water, and the materials used for signaling passing ships?"

"I do not know where it is," I said. "We will make do with a substitute."

"I take it, Captain Glycon," said Melete, "that your ship, the *Hermione*, and the others of the corsair fleet, are properly positioned."

"I take it otherwise," I said. "As far as I know, there is no Captain Glycon and no ship, *Hermione*, and the corsair fleet, I would suppose, presumably disguised as merchantmen, is in the harbor at Sybaris."

"I do not understand," said Melete.

I signaled to Thurnock and Clitus and they heaved the tiny, improvised raft, nailed together from some planks and boards, overboard.

"Fellows," I called to some oarsmen, "our guests are ready to disembark."

"No!" screamed Melete.

"Stop! No!" cried Iantha and Philomena, as they, with Melete, were seized by oarsmen.

"Release us, unhand us, you misbegotten boors, villains, rogues, bumpkins!" screamed Melete.

The small improvised raft was at the side of the *Tesephone*, rocking, when Philomena was lowered to its surface. She lost her balance and she fell to its surface, her knees in the water. The small raft began to drift from the hull and when Iantha was held over the side and released, she fell half across the planks, her belly and legs half in the water. It took her only a moment to climb, terrified, on the planks.

"One more," I called to the oarsmen, "another fine, splendid, noble lady. Cast her well!"

"Unhand me!" screamed Melete.

"Unhand her," I said.

The oarsmen, with a great laugh, flung Melete high over the rail and, with a great splash, she struck the water, and, struggling, thrashing about, encumbered by her robes, she reached out, clutching wildly at the raft. Iantha and Philomena tipping the raft, reached to her, and drew her to its surface. As it was precarious to stand on the raft, unsteady as it was, they were all on their knees, knees in water, looking wildly back, up at the rail.

"Let us trust that the splash does not attract sharks," I said. "They can note such things, even from quite some distance away."

"Take us back aboard!" screamed Melete, rising to her feet, struggling to keep her balance, steadied by her fellows.

"What are you doing?" cried Philomena.

"Why are you doing this?" cried Iantha.

"Out oars," I called.

"Do not leave us!" wept Iantha.

"We are free! Show us mercy!" wept Philomena.

"We are truly helpless!" said Iantha.

"Perhaps a ship will pass by," I said.

"We have no way to signal a ship!" cried Iantha, "no whistling, climbing, streaming flares, visible for pasangs."

"Perhaps, in this lost desert of water, a ship will come close enough for you to call out and wave your veils," said an oarsman.

"If your modesty will permit it," said another.

The men at the rail laughed, but the humor, it seems, was lost on the women.

"This is a cruel joke, surely!" said Iantha.

"They will search for us!" cried Philomena.

"Where?" I asked.

"Let them search every hovel and palace in Sybaris," said Clitus.

"You are all rogues, criminals, villains!" said Melete.

"Show us mercy!" begged Philomena.

"Why?" I asked.

"We are free women, noble and free!" cried Philomena.

"How many ships have responded to your signals of distress?" I asked. "How many ships have you lured to their doom? How many captains and crews have you distracted and held in place while corsairs closed in upon them?"

"You cannot leave us here," said Melete.

"You are mistaken," I said.

"We did only what we were paid to do," said Melete.

"You should be more judicious as to the fees you accept," I said.

"Tarsk, sleen!" cried Melete.

"Mercy, mercy!" begged Philomena.

"Look upon me, carefully," I said. "You wondered if you had seen me before. You had. Think back. Think of yourselves, below, on seeming wreckage, looking up at me and others, we above you, at the rail."

"You were not destroyed by the corsairs?" said Melete, disbelievingly.

"We escaped," I said. "And we lived to remember."

Iantha shuddered and Philomena put down her head, moaning.

"You cannot frighten us," said Melete.

"Whether you are frightened or not is immaterial," I said. "What does it matter?"

"Mercy!" cried Philomena, looking up, her eyes filled with tears.

"Do the others ask for mercy?" I asked.

"No!" said Melete.

"I do!" cried Iantha.

"Oars ready," I called.

The oarsmen returned to the benches and the great levers dipped into the water, ready for the first stroke.

"I, also!" screamed Melete. "I, too! I, too, beg for mercy!"

She, too, I now saw, was on her knees.

"Aktis," I said, "bring a loaf of bread, a bota of water."

When these were brought, I tossed them to the kneeling women, on the tiny platform, their knees in water.

"Thus," I said, "you are shown mercy."

I then turned to the benches, my right hand lifted.

"Wait! Wait!" screamed Melete. "You are enemies of the corsairs. I am sure of it! Who can forget the hoax of *The Village of Flowing Gold*? We know much! We are privy to their secrets. We are confidants of the governor himself! Yes, he is implicated in these things. Let us reveal to you their plans!"

I doubted that they were as informed as they claimed, but it seemed reasonable to suppose that they might possess some information pertaining to at least the corsairs' more obvious and immediate intentions.

"Where do the corsairs strike next?" I asked.

"The village of Zeuxis on Daphna!" she cried.

"When?" I asked.

"I do not know," she said, "but soon! Soon!"

"You will be in our power," I said. "Thus I trust that your statement is true."

"It is true!" cried Melete.

"Your recent experiences have been unpleasant," I said. "You have been, if not wholly immersed, much drenched in the waves and spray of Thassa. You are soaked. As a consequence, your robes and veils cling muchly to your bodies and features. Thus it is hinted that you, beneath all, though free women, are females. Accordingly, I suggest that you readjust your veils and pull your garments away from your bodies. I think you can understand the reason for this. There are men aboard."

Glancing at one another, the three women swiftly, apprehensively, complied with my suggestion.

"Good," I said.

"And now, Captain?" asked Thurnock.

"Now," I said, "take them aboard."

CHAPTER TWENTY-NINE

An Account of What Occurred, Following a Supper at the Cove of Harpalos

"Master," said Lais, kneeling, her head down, submissively, between her extended arms, lifting the goblet of paga to me.

"Disgusting," said Melete.

"You may withdraw," I informed Lais.

She rose, gracefully, backed away some feet, head down, and then turned, and hurried from the room.

"At least," said Melete, "you could put her in some clothes."

"She is clothed," I said. "She is in a slave tunic."

"She might as well be naked," said Melete.

"Were no free women present," I said, "she might well so serve."

"The collar is pretty on her neck," said Iantha.

"They are designed to be lovely," I said, "and secure."

"Some women, low women, worthless women," said Melete, "belong in collars."

"And find themselves in them," said Captain Tab, currently assigned the captainship of the *Dorna*, fifty-oared, larger and more formidable than the light, swift *Tesephone*, sped by twenty oars. The *Dorna*, in my view, was the match for any of the seven ships in the corsair fleet.

We were at table, a benched table, in the common room of the harbor authority of the Cove of Harpalos, kindly made available to us by the harbor master and his deputies. Several, aside from the 'Three Ubaras', were present, primarily ships' officers, and others associated in one way or another with our enterprise amongst the Farther Islands. We had now finished a simple, pleasant supper, served by Lais.

"Captain Glycon, if I may use the name," said Melete, "we are grateful for the courtesy and honor with which we have been treated."

I nodded.

I had even managed, given the sorry condition of their original clothing, following their experiences at sea, to supply them with a fresh, ample wardrobe, footwear, robes and veils, purchased locally.

"It is our due, of course," she said, "as we are free women."

"Certainly," I said.

She was seated with Iantha on her right and Philomena on her left. Given their robes and veils, I could see little but the eyes of the three. In the manner of free women with strangers present they would lift the veil with their left hand and eat and drink discreetly behind the veil.

"You have even allowed us, properly supervised, of course, the liberty of this small, lovely port."

"My pleasure," I said.

"On what island is it," she asked, "and what is its name?"

"It is a location suitable for my purposes," I said. "You need know no more."

"I understand," she said. "But, as we have been open and forthcoming, even generous, with respect to your inquiries, I trust that we, given our assistance and your gratitude, will shortly be freed and returned to Sybaris."

"I can understand your interest in the matter," I said, "but before one could think of such a thing, returning you to Sybaris, there is the matter of Zeuxis, on Daphna, which would need to be confirmed."

"We understand," she said.

"But," said Iantha, "that will soon take place."

"It is clear your ships, even now, are readied to leave port," said Philomena.

"That is true," I said. "We will raise our masts tomorrow."

"As I suspected," said Melete, "this supper, then, in this special place, in this special chamber, is one of special moment. It looks forward to your departure, your setting forth to Daphna."

"That is so," I said.

"You are foolish, Captain," said Philomena. "Best free us now, that we may plea with the governor to spare your life."

"Your concern is appreciated," I said.

"It is no happy, brave adventure you contemplate," said Iantha. "You will sail into the jaws of a seven-headed monster, the seven ships of the corsair fleet."

"Do not go," said Philomena. "You will have no chance. You will be destroyed, every ship, every man."

"Be quiet!" snapped Melete. "Let these brave and noble men not be deterred from their worthy, noble task."

"We appreciate your support, noble lady," I said. "We are heartened. Too, we appreciate the data supplied to us pertaining to Archelaos and the plans of the corsairs. Your assistance, that of all three of you, has been invaluable. We appreciate the names and ranks of enemies, their numbers and weaponry, their supplies and stores. Therefore, let us close this pleasant evening with a grateful toast to you, all three of you, our gracious guests, the 'Three Ubaras', Mistresses of *The House of the Golden Urt*, the noble, and perhaps lovely, ladies Melete, Iantha, and Philomena."

This suggestion was welcomed by those present.

"Be it so," said Tab.

"Be it so," said Thurnock.

"Be it so," said Clitus.

"Be it so," said others.

Men lightly struck their left shoulders with their right hand in polite Gorean applause.

I clapped my hands, twice, sharply. "Wine," I called. "Wine!"

A moment later Lais entered, holding a bottle wrapped in white linen.

Lais looked to me, uncertain as to how to proceed. In the tavern of *The Living Island*, she had never served free women. Free women were not allowed in the tavern. In some cities a free woman foolish enough to enter the precincts of a tavern is arrested, stripped, branded, collared, and sold.

"Surely, slave," said I, "you know enough to serve free women first."

"Yes, Master," she said. "Forgive me, Master."

"I wonder what it is, to call a man 'Master'," said Melete.

"I must do so, Mistress," said Lais, softly. "As I am a slave, I must call all free men 'Master' and all free women 'Mistress'."

Slaves are expected to speak clearly, softly, and with abject deference, to free persons. They must never raise their voice to a free person. That can be cause for swift and savage discipline. Goreans treat slaves as the slaves they are.

"That is fitting for you, half-naked, meaningless, worthless, collared slut, slave," said Melete.

"Yes, Mistress," said Lais.

She poured a bit of wine into the goblets of the three free women, and then poured a similar, small amount into my goblet.

"That will do for now," I said.

I gestured that she should leave the bottle at my place.

I lifted my goblet. "Shall we drink?" I asked.

The three free women lifted their goblets.

As they did so I, as though inadvertently, with a casual gesture, slipped the wrapper of white linen down, away from the bottle.

Melete sprang to her feet, screaming in horror, hurling the goblet away from her. Iantha thrust the goblet from her, spilling the contents on the table. Philomena shook her head in terror, and, shaking, pushed her goblet from the table, to the floor.

"Ladies," I said, "you have spilled your wine."

At a gesture from me, Lais, frightened, restored order, replacing the goblets before the three women and pouring a small amount of wine into each goblet.

"What is wrong?" I asked the three women. "Do you suspect that the wine is inferior? Are you perplexed, or curious, as to the quaint markings on the bottle?"

"Do not make us drink," said Melete, shuddering, struggling to appear calm, now once more seated, as were Iantha and Philomena.

"This wine may not be Falarian," I said, "but Falarian, if it exists, is quite rare. Perhaps, if you had access to the cellar of a Ubar, you might find a bottle."

"Do not make us drink," said Melete.

"It would be easy enough to do so," I said. "One binds the woman, kneels her down, holds her head back, pours the liquid into her mouth, and pinches her nostrils shut. Then, when she must breathe, the liquid goes down her throat."

Lais shuddered. Doubtless slave wine, which prevents conception, had been administered to her in such a way. The breeding of slaves, of course, as with other animals, is at the discretion of their owners.

"But," I said, "as you and your colleagues are free women, and are entitled to the privileges of your status, we are willing in your case to refrain from the embarrassing unpleasantries of vulgar coercion. Rather, we accord to you the privilege of drinking of your own free will, of drinking with honor, with stately dignity, which you may now do."

"No!" cried Melete.

"Then you leave us no alternative," I said.

"Wait! Wait!" said Melete. "Are we worth nothing? Have we no value?"

"Free women are priceless," I said. "Thus they have no value."

"But slaves have value!" said Melete.

"Of course," I said, "a greater or lesser value. They can be bought and sold."

"And ridding yourself of a slave," she said, "would be foolish, like casting money into the sea."

"That is true," I said.

"No free man would do that," she said.

"I would not think so," I said.

"Then!" cried Melete.

"But what relevance have such considerations to the present case?" I asked.

"I have often felt acute uneasiness in the presence of men," she said. "I do not know what is going on in my body when I am near them. I feel small, weak, and needful. I have wanted to obey them, to be commanded by them. I have felt the impulse to kneel before them, abjectly, and kiss their feet, hoping to please them, being ready to feel their whip if I did not. I fought these feelings resolutely and savagely. How unworthy they were of a free woman! Yet they were my feelings, and though I denounced them, I could not deny them!"

"I, too!" cried Iantha. "My body felt like fire and I wanted to throw off my clothes, and put myself before them, on my belly, vulnerable, begging, and naked!"

"I, as well!" wept Philomena. "I have long wanted a Master, and, naked, to feel his chains on my limbs!"

"I fear what they might speak," said Thurnock. "Be quick! Bind shut their mouths before they can speak and then cut their throats."

"I pronounce myself slave," cried Melete. "I am a slave!"

"I am a slave!" cried Iantha.

"I am a slave!" cried Philomena.

Thurnock's great fist smote the table in frustration.

Melete laughed, abruptly, an uncontrollable exclamation. There were tears in her eyes. Iantha and Philomena sobbed in relief.

"On your knees, slaves," I said. "How dare you be sitting in the presence of free persons?"

Swiftly the three slaves knelt.

"Unveil yourselves," I said. The faces of slaves are to be kept naked. They are to be looked upon as the animals they are. Too, their features bared, their least expression can be read. They cannot hide. This makes it easier to master and control them. One reason Gorean men, apprised of the Second Knowledge, commonly regard the females of Earth as slaves is the thought-lessness with which they commonly bare their features. Are they trying to present themselves for the perusal of Masters? Do they not know how stimulating and exciting their features are to men?

The three slaves lowered the veils they had worn as free women.

"Excellent," said more than one man at the table.

The women shuddered, viewed as the properties, the meat, they now were.

I rose to my feet and regarded the slaves.

"It seems," I said, "that you are no longer the 'Three Ubaras'."

"That was a feint of advertising," said Melete, "a joke, a way of calling attention to ourselves, an image designed to amuse the wise and impress the unthinking and ignorant, those few who were stupid enough to take it seriously."

"By now," I said, "I would suppose that there are three new 'Ubaras' in Sybaris, managing *The House of the Golden Urt*."

The slaves looked at one another.

Even were they freed what would there be to which they might go back? And they had been prisoners of the enemy and had doubtless revealed secret information, confidences, and plans.

"What are you now?" I asked.

"Three slaves," said Melete.

I regarded her.

"Three slaves—Master," she said.

"Master," said Iantha.

"Master," said Philomena.

I gestured to the table.

"Masters," said the three.

"It may be difficult for you, in the beginning," I said, "to use words such as 'Master' and 'Masters', 'Mistress' and 'Mistresses', but soon you will use them easily and aptly, thoughtlessly and naturally, thinking nothing of it, for there is a great difference between the owned and the unowned, the collared and the uncollared, and you are the owned and collared."

Too, of course, using expressions such as 'Master' and 'Mistress' to the free is not only appropriate, but deepens, confirms, and reinforces the slave's sense of herself as slave, which she now is. Later, as the slave learns her collar, she comes to accept, welcome, celebrate, and treasure her subservience and submission, her new and exciting way of being, her new reality. Owned and dominated, possessed and commanded, now a mere property, subject to purchase, bargaining, and sale, she finds herself as she should be, and wants to be.

I then went to the three goblets left on the table, each of which had been before one of the three women, each of which contained the small measure of fluid which had been poured into it by Lais. I poured the contents of these three goblets into my own goblet, and added more from the bottle, the sight of which had so dismayed our three guests. I then, calmly, drained the goblet.

The three slaves looked up me, aghast.

"I decided, some days ago," I said, "after a certain incident at the Fair of the Farther Islands, that it was dangerous to keep the original contents of such a bottle about. They might have been imbibed inadvertently, or thoughtlessly, or possibly unknowingly, by someone unaware of their nature, perhaps even a thief, soon to discover that what he stole was no more than his own death. Accordingly I disposed of the original contents, had the bottle thrice cleansed, and filled it with an innocent, modest *ka-la-na*."

"You tricked us!" hissed Melete.

I regarded her.

"You tricked us, Master," she whispered.

"Clitus," I said, "thong the wrists of these slaves behind them, and then put them on a single rope, with three loops, each loop circled and knotted about the neck of one of them, Melete first, then Iantha, and then Philomena. Then take them to our camp. Irons are already heating and collars have been prepared."

Clitus kept the slaves on their knees while securing them according to my instructions. In this way a frightened slave is less likely to leap up and try to run.

"On your feet, worthless slaves," said Clitus.

The three slaves rose to their feet.

"Shall I strip them?" asked Clitus.

The slaves exchanged sudden glances of dismay and terror.

"No," I said, "that can come later."

Melete threw me a look of anger. She would soon learn that that indulgence can be a cause for discipline. Slaves are not free women.

"Hold," I said. "Are not names such as 'Melete', 'Iantha', and 'Philomena' too fine for slaves?"

"Surely," said a man.

"Then," said I, pointing to Melete, "you are now 'Margot'." I then pointed to Iantha. "You are now 'Millicent'," I said. I then indicated Philomena. "And you," I said, "are now 'Courtney'."

"What sort of names are those?" asked the man.

"Earth-girl names," I said.

"Slave names," said the man.

"Please do not name us so," said Margot.

"It is done," I said.

On Gor, Earth-girl names are regarded as slave names, much as Earth girls are regarded as actual or potential slaves. The slave, of course, being an animal, has no name in her own right. Her name is at the discretion of the Master. Sometimes a natively Gorean slave girl is given an Earth-girl name to further reduce and demean her. Sometimes it is done as a punishment. Giving our three new slaves Earth-girl names, I thought, would let them know how we regarded them, and help them to understand all the more quickly that they were no longer free women. A slave, incidentally, is almost always given a new name. This helps her to understand that her life has changed radically and completely, and that she is no longer who, and what, she was. She is now a slave, only a slave.

"Back on your knees," I said.

They then knelt again before me, thonged and neck-roped.

It is on their knees that slaves commonly acknowledge their new names.

"What is your name?" I asked Margot.

"'Margot', Master," she said.

"What is your name?" I asked Millicent.

"'Millicent', Master," she said.

"What is your name?" I asked Courtney.

"'Courtney', Master," she said, tears in her eye.

"You may now take these slaves to our camp," I said, "where they will be stripped, branded, and collared."

"Yes, Captain," said Clitus. He then shook the rope, startling the slaves. "Get up, two-legged tarsks, meaningless sluts, chain garbage," he said.

The slaves struggled to their feet.

"Hold," I called to Clitus, as he was leading the slaves from the room.

"Hold," said Clitus to his small coffle.

"Margot, Millicent, and Courtney," I said, "you are lovely little beasts."

"Thank you, Master," said Margot, uncertainly.

"And I am sure," I said, "you will appear even lovelier when the impediments of garmenture no longer obscure our perusal."

The women trembled. Well they knew that slaves, as animals, had no right to clothing.

"And if not," I said, "diet and exercise will quickly remedy the situation."

Slaves, of course, may be fed and exercised, trimmed and trained, as other animals. They are seldom brought to the block, for example, if not in prime condition. Gorean buyers tend to be particular about such matters.

"Before your clothing is removed," I said, "and before you keep your appointment with the searing iron, and before your new collars are locked on your necks, I would like to express my appreciation for your concern for my welfare, and that of my crews, expressed earlier, after supper. It is true that our two ships, one of merely twenty oars, are grossly overmatched by the seven ships of the corsair fleet. *Ela*, we cannot help that. What are the odds of survival? Slim, surely. Yes, certainly you are well aware of the perils and hazards we face. Indeed, it seems highly likely, thinking of the matter from a wagering standpoint, that our ships will be boarded or rammed, or burned and sunk, and that we may perish to a man, disappearing without a trace. Yet, too, you acknowledged the glory, if futile glory, of our endeavor, our 'worthy, noble task', as one of you put it. Such admiration, even encouragement, touches us deeply."

"Master?" asked Margot, uncertainly.

"But be of good cheer, lovely cargo," I said. "Do not think that we would be so tragically unfair and grossly remiss as not to permit you some share in our splendid endeavor. You shall not be left behind. You will accompany us on our brave, if unwise, foolish, and ill-fared course."

"No, no!" screamed Margot.

"Sell us!" begged Millicent. "Do not take us with you!"

"Mercy, Masters!" begged Courtney. "Leave us here!"

"I have had a sturdy slave ring fixed in the main deck of the *Tesephone*," I said. "To that, exposed to the sun and weather, the three of you, naked, as befits slaves, will be chained."

"No!" screamed Margot.

"What if the ship burns?" wept Millicent.

"Then," I said, "you will burn with the ship."

"What if the ship sinks?" asked Courtney.

"Then," I said, "chained, you will go down with the ship."

"Mercy!" wept Margot.

"Think on those ships, and mariners, you lured into traps," I said.

"Mercy, mercy!" wept the slaves.

"Think, too, of this from the point of the crew," I said, "men weary from the oar and starved for the sluts of the taverns. Think how pleasant it will be for them to look upon you, shapely, well-curved collar meat, chained helplessly, close at hand, delectable and convenient, ready for use."

The slaves tried to throw themselves to their knees, pleading, a common placatory behavior for slaves, but Clitus, rudely, by means of their neck-rope, kept them on their feet.

"Take them away," I said.

They looked wildly behind them, distraught, Margot, Millicent, and Courtney, three slaves, as they were led away.

CHAPTER THIRTY

We Observe the Enemy

I motioned down, with the flat of my hand, from the crest of the hill to which I had crawled, where I lay on my belly.

Thurnock, Clitus, and Aktis crouched down, and then joined me, prone, just below the crest.

"Seven ships," I said.

"The whole fleet," said Aktis.

"Offshore," said Thurnock.

"I see they have learned something," said Clitus. "No more beached ships, inadequately guarded."

"How do you make the numbers?" I asked Thurnock.

"Some twelve hundred ashore," said Thurnock.

"Then some three hundred or so aboard," I said.

Our best estimates of the enemy's strength, given the increase in ships, and the manning of the earlier fleet, was in the neighborhood of fifteen hundred. This conjecture seemed plausibly corroborated by remarks overheard in Sybaris by the former Melete, Iantha, and Philomena, which remarks, fearing for their lives, they were kind enough to share with us. We, on the other hand, had brought two hundred and fifty men from Port Kar, most of whom were with us, saving some posted as spies in Sybaris; some left at the ruins of Nicosia, in the hope that, following the fair, more peasants would seek arms and direction; and some at the Cove of Harpalos, our *de facto* headquarters. These latter men would receive the reports of spies, and, should the Cove of Harpalos be seized by the enemy, signal us from high crags before we returned to port, possibly proceeding into a trap.

"With that many men," said Clitus, "they might attack a town, say Mytilene, Naxos, or Pylos. They might threaten even Sybaris."

"We are far outnumbered," said Thurnock.

"But," I said, "they do not know that."

"They will learn it soon enough," said Thurnock, "in open battle."

"Thus," I said, "there will be no open battle."

"What then?" said Thurnock.

"Harassments, divisions, pretended flights, traps, ambushes, raids," I said. "Smaller forces, under special circumstances, can rout larger forces."

"Luring them into treacherous terrain," said Thurnock, "as in the debacle of Ar in the Vosk's Delta?"

"Or leading them into the Tahari, where water is precious and scarce, or into canyoned areas where passes are narrow, easily blocked, and can be fired on from cover," said Clitus.

"Such things," I said. "But, too, in many instances a smaller force, cleverly applied, can outnumber a larger force. Suppose the smaller force applied one hundred men where the enemy has applied, or can apply, only fifty. In that special situation or selected incident, the smaller force outnumbers the larger force two to one. Consider then the multiplication of such situations or incidents."

"Consider, too," said Thurnock, "the rate of fire. The great bow can fire several arrows in the time the crossbow can fire one or two. Thus, one man with the great bow could outmatch four or five with the crossbow."

"Our advantage at the moment," I said, "is that the enemy does not know our strength."

"And might fear it to be greater than it is," said Thurnock.

"Yes," I said, "and there are various techniques for concealing our numbers and making them seem larger than they are in actuality."

"A number of bowmen changing their places of fire," said Thurnock, "the enemy being likely to assume, naturally enough, that each place of fire means a bowman still at that place."

"I have in mind, too," I said, "an interesting tactic used more than once, though faraway."

"What is that?" asked Thurnock.

"That of terrifying the enemy by actually showing them our forces," I said.

"It seems that would hearten them," said Thurnock.

"That is the last thing we should do," said Clitus.

"We shall see," I said. "But, my friends, we must first convince the enemy that we exist. Thus, I suggest that we think about making our way now to the vicinity of the fine village of Zeuxis."

"Aktis," said Clitus, "you have made it clear, I trust, to the villagers that Zeuxis must be sacrificed."

"Many do not believe they are in danger," said Aktis. "But, as a precaution, Zeuxis has been evacuated and its Home Stone concealed."

"They would not believe even Xanthos, from the village of Seleukos, which was last burned by the corsairs?" asked Clitus.

"No," said Aktis.

"A woeful pity," said Thurnock.

After we had left the Cove of Harpalos, we had visited the ruins of the village of Seleukos, where we had taken Xanthos, the son of the headman Seleukos, and some twenty of his fellows aboard, to whom he had introduced the great bow.

We had hoped that Peasants would listen to Peasants.

"They are preparing for their march," said Clitus, beside me, peering over the crest of the hill.

"Then," I said, "to Zeuxis."

CHAPTER THIRTY-ONE

What Occurred in the Vicinity of the Village of Zeuxis

One supposes that the quiet of the village of Zeuxis, on Daphna, must have been disconcerting to the enemy. They had approached it, this group, some four hundred we conjectured, cautiously, as inconspicuously as possible, and had then, say, a hundred yards from the gate, crouching down in the grass, waited for the signal of attack, and then the rushing forward, the shouting, and the brandishing of weapons. The gate, with its two leaves, was open, but this was not unusual, given the time of day, about noon, the tenth Ahn. What was unusual was the lack of activity in, and around, the enclosure.

"Soon," I said. "Soon."

"One fellow removes his helmet, straps it to his side, and puts on some sort of wig," said Aktis.

"What color is it?" asked Clitus.

"An outrageous reddish color," said Aktis.

"I do not care for that," I said.

"It does not even look real," said Aktis.

"It is not real," said Thurnock.

"It is bright, loud, and grotesque," said Aktis.

"I am not pleased," I said.

"Be calm, Captain," said Thurnock.

"They would never have seen the real hair of Bosk of Port Kar," said Clitus.

"I trust that my hair, before I dyed it, was not so," I said. Often, particularly in my childhood, I had had to reprove peers for critical, even uncomplimentary, remarks on my hair. These aesthetic discussions had often resulted in bruises and bloody noses.

"Not at all," said Clitus.

"Or not so blatantly," said Thurnock.

"So that is our Bosk of Port Kar?" said Clitus.

"Their Bosk of Port Kar," said Thurnock.

At that point there was a quick, shrill, piercing blast on a whistle and the corsairs, shouting, leapt up from the grass and, led by the figure in the red wig, stormed toward the opened gate.

Shortly thereafter they had entered the palisade, where they found not an armed resistance nor startled, terrified villagers, intimidated villagers, but nothing, only crowded, dry empty huts, stripped even of pots and pans. Within we heard consternation, cries of disappointment, bewilderment, and rage.

I stood up and called to my men, hidden in the grass. "Close the gate! Brush! Flames! Fire arrows!"

Some twenty fellows rushed to the gate and pulled it shut, tying the two, in-swinging leaves together, and another twenty hurried to the closed gate with thick bundles of brush, grass, and straw which they piled before the tethered gate. At the same time, small fires were lit in clay pans and arrows, the heads of which were wrapped in oil-soaked cloth, were ignited and fired into the village, which shortly thereafter roared with flames, the heat of which jarred the air and carried even to our positions surrounding the village. Not a moment after the gate had been tied shut and the first arrows fell looping down into the thatched roofs of the huts, the corsairs were hacking at the ropes binding the gates closed. But no sooner had they freed the leaves of the gate and swung them inward than the brush, dried grass and straw which had been heaped up in the threshold was fiercely burning, creating a wall of fire behind which we could scarcely mark dark, moving figures. As the village had been carefully emptied of water before its evacuation the corsairs began to scoop up dirt in their helmets and cast it on the fire. Through the flames into the village flew arrows, several of which found targets in the figures trying to extinguish the flames. Within the village we could hear screams of rage, terror, and pain. I had placed archers about the village, and some corsairs, trying to climb over the palisade to escape the flames, were detained by arrows and soon several bodies were wedged lifelessly between the pointed palings, and some lay outside the palisade, inert, bristling with feathered shafts. A few Ehn later the flames at the gate, from the bundles of brush, grass, and straw, had lessened. One could now wade plunging through the smoke and diminished flames. "Be ready!" I called to a platoon of archers now stationed before the gate, and two groups of swordsmen, one group to the right of the opening and the other to the left of the opening. I conjectured that the first to flee through the gate would meet arrows, and that the corsairs would then draw back, if typically commanded, and arrange a sudden assault *en masse* to close the gap between themselves and the archers. This meant they would rush forth. It was then that the swordsmen on each side of the gate, waiting, were to strike into the unsuspecting, unprotected flanks of the enemy. Within a few Ihn, the corsairs, met with arrows from the front and swords from the sides, withdrew into the village and swung shut the seared leaves of the gate, closing themselves inside, where the blackened huts had now mostly collapsed and the flames were subsiding. Bodies of corsairs littered the open space within and outside the gate.

"What now, Captain?" inquired Thurnock, unstringing his bow.

"We will leave a token force here," I said, "to convince the enemy it is besieged. I doubt that he will dare the night, being unacquainted with our numbers. His cohorts near the beach, not hearing from him, will presumably investigate in the morning. He is thus well advised to await relief."

"While growing ever more hungry and thirsty," said Thurnock.

"They called for no terms and you proposed none," said Clitus.

"Neither action would be in order," I said. "For their part, they expect prompt succor. For my part, I prefer to keep the nature of their enemy as secret and mysterious as possible."

"I do not think that they expected resistance," said Clitus.

"Yet, in their numbers, they were prepared for it," I said.

"I was impressed by Xanthos and the fellows from the village of Seleukos," said Clitus. "Xanthos himself slew four of the enemy with his arrows."

"He is new to the bow," said Thurnock. "His marksmanship will improve."

"What of Aktis?" I asked.

"Six," said Thurnock. "But he lost some time with the fire arrows."

Thurnock, I gathered, was pleased with his protégé.

"And what of Thurnock?" asked Clitus.

"I was not counting," said Thurnock.

"We will now withdraw the bulk of our forces, make four camps, have a good supper, and get a good night's sleep," I said.

"I do not think the enemy within the palisade will sleep well," said Thurnock.

"Will they be attacked? Will the gate be forced? Will the palisade be scaled?" said Clitus.

"Fear dresses itself in shadows," said Thurnock.

"I think it probable that the enemy's main force, or most of it, will march on Zeuxis in the morning," I said.

"It seems then," said Thurnock, "that we shall have a busy day tomorrow."

"That is possible," I said.

"It is only some four pasangs between the beach and Zeuxis," said Clitus. "That is a short march."

"Under certain conditions," I said, "short marches may no longer seem short."

"How so?" asked Clitus.

"Between the beach and Zeuxis," I said, "there is much tall grass."

CHAPTER THIRTY-TWO

The Battle of the Road

"They are coming now," said Thurnock.

"I see them," I said.

A small contingent of the corsairs, some ten men, was advancing before the larger column, consisting, we supposed, of some eight hundred men. The column, extending far behind, was separated by some two hundred yards from the advance group. This small advance group, I supposed, was intended to constitute something in the nature of a scouting or reconnoitering party. It stayed on the road. This suggested that there were few, if any, of the scarlet caste amongst the corsairs. Had there been I would have expected a point with flankers to the side, proceeding through the grass, each of whom would be in contact, by sound or visual signal, with the column itself. Perhaps, however, the corsairs, puzzled as they might have been by the lack of contact with the village raiders, now pinned within the palisade of the burned village, did not believe anything might be seriously amiss. Perhaps the village raiders were occupied, gathering loot, drinking home-brewed paga, abusing captives, pursuing fugitives, or such. In any event the advance party, which we would let pass, remained on the road and was out of touch with the main group. Given this arrangement, the advanced party might not even be aware, at least immediately, that the main group was under attack. Needless to say, the advance party's narrow adherence to the road allowed our archers to be in a position to fire at almost point-blank range. Moreover, as our archers were on both sides of the road, the shields of our targets, which could face but one way at a time, would be largely ineffective. I expected the enemy, at least initially, to be unwilling to enter a locale in which it could scarcely see its way, given the high, mazelike grasses. Some might even try to retreat to the beach, accepting the perils of the gauntlet they must then run. I did not expect much discipline amongst the raiders. Thus, one might hope that the surprise following a sudden, unexpected attack might burst into panic, which, ideally, would be soon transmitted to their as-yet uninvolved cohorts. Had the enemy been disciplined, and had I assumed command following the attack, and I did not know the nature or numbers of the enemy, I would have ordered the retreat of the double-shield wall, that to reach the beach, my supplies, and additional support. In this retreat both sides of a moving column are covered by shields, one side changing the shield arm. What I did expect to take place, and what did take place, with various disorganized groups of the raiders, other than simple, precipitate flight, was either forming shield rings, circles of shields, which, in effect, immobilizes the group, or counterattacks in which the beleaguered group rushes into the grass, on one or both sides, shields forward, to close with the archers. In this situation the archers withdraw, usually in such a manner as to encourage the now-confident enemy to follow them into a trap, where swordsmen are waiting for them, swordsmen in groups likely to outnumber the pursuers.

"Xanthos," I said.

The son of Seleukos, headman of the village of Seleukos, recently pillaged and burned, with two of his village cohorts, crouching down in the grass, were within whispering range.

"Captain?" he said.

"Recall your instructions," I said.

"Be steady and focused," he said. "Do not rush. Pick your targets with care, and change your place frequently."

"And what are your targets?" I asked.

"First," said he, "ideally, those who seem to be first, who appear to give commands, who seem to be obeyed, who seem to be leaders. Second, ideally, those who seem to accept the orders, and obey them promptly. And, lastly, the confused and bewildered, the stunned, the paralyzed, the immobile, the hiding, the running."

"I wish you well," I said.

"I, too, wish you well," he said.

It requires patience, but patience is important. There is a time to wait, and a time to act. It was not now the time to act. What hunter is so foolish as to spring a trap prematurely, what fisherman so foolish as to draw his net too soon?

Thurnock's knuckles seemed white, grasping his strung bow.

The advance party was now well down the road. If all went well, they might fail to be aware of what was to occur behind them. They might even reach Zeuxis, bearing news of an impending relief, before learning of an attack on the column. Then, one might hope that the supposedly besieged corsairs, hungry and thirsting, rejoicing in their putative delivery, might rush from the protection of the palisade to join the supposedly relieving column.

Thurnock looked at me.

I shook my head, "No."

From where we knelt or crouched in the grass, but yards from the road, we could hear the voices of the men in the column, conversing, cursing, bantering, complaining. Carts should have been brought for their shields; the paga ration last night had been meager and of poor quality; the porridge this morning had been no better than slave gruel; yesterday's column had spent a comfortable night in the village, carousing and sleeping, not in blankets between rowing benches; the best loot had already been seized and hidden, and so on.

I had distributed our men carefully.

Given our numbers, we could not begin to expose the entire column to a simultaneous attack. I hoped to cut the column in two, attacking its centrality. In this way, the enemy would be divided, and, for a time, both the first third of the column and the last third of the column, perhaps confused and uncertain, would not be engaged. Few men, undisciplined and disorganized, without competent leaders, are going to act promptly and resolutely. What brigand cares to rush into a possible danger the nature of which is not even clear to him, particularly if he observes his fellows routed and fleeing, desperately seeking their own safety?

Thurnock looked again at me.

I nodded.

He fitted a signal arrow to his bow, an artifact whose nature and use I had learned from the high warriors of the Pani, the men of two swords, at the World's End.

Thurnock was an enormously large and strong man and his bow was mighty, one which few men could draw.

The arrow, with its shrill whistle, sped upward, farther and farther. My men were instructed to hold their fire until the sound lessened, stopped at the height of its missile's long arc, and then began again, shrill again, in its plummeting descent.

I counted, successfully as it happened, on two things. First, the column would not understand the likely meaning of the arrow, and, accordingly, would not come to arms at its first note, and, second, the men of the column, detecting the arrow, would be likely, in fascination, to follow it in its flight, however apprehensively. That being that case, their heads lifted and their attention directed upward, they should constitute easy, close, stationary targets for the first volley of arrows from my men, rising from the grass and firing.

Well before the signal arrow had begun its descent, Thurnock had set a fresh arrow to his string and no sooner had the missile begun its descent than one of the corsairs, one in a crested helmet, knelt in the road, perhaps unclear as to what had occurred, and then collapsed. Then another corsair spun about, turned by the blow of an arrow. Xanthos, too, and his fellows, launched shafts.

There was much scrambling about and cries of rage and horror from the road. Archers sprang up, loosed shafts, and disappeared again, in the grass, only to rise again, to release another shaft, often from a different position. Few of the corsairs dared to plunge into the grass, and those who did, pursuing archers, were led, as by phantoms, into places where swordsmen rose behind them, before them, and about them. The center of the column was shattered and, in moments, as corsairs fled, the road was empty save for dust, bodies, and loot bags. Interestingly, neither the first third of the column nor the last third of the column came to the relief of their beleaguered fellows. The last third of the column and some remnants of the broken center hurried back to the beach, where the corsair fleet lay to, some forty or so yards offshore. I later learned from some of my men who followed them, keeping apprised of their movements, that their plea to be taken aboard the fleet's ships was refused. Subsequently they dug, largely with their helmets, a semicircular trench with the sea at their backs. This trench was walled toward the land by the dislodged sand and surmounted by a shield wall. The openness of the broad beach would deny cover to archers and we would not choose to attack in force as that would risk our men unduly, storming a fortified position, and might well reveal the paucity of our numbers. That the corsairs were not aware of our numbers, or even who we were, were factors, however limited, in our favor. We had, at Zeuxis, and on the road, profited enormously from the element of surprise, but the chances of repeating such a stroke were now minimal. The enemy was now alerted and wary.

"Do not pursue the fugitives," I had said. "Such might betray our numbers. Rather, let them, bewildered and in consternation, sow the seeds of panic amongst their fellows."

"What of the beginning of the column, and the men from within the palisade?" asked Thurnock.

"Close the road," I said. "I do not think they will care to traverse it. Should any enter the grass, give way before them, and lead them to the waiting swords. If others, avoiding the road, decline engagement, follow them and harass them. See that few reach the beach. But I expect that most, learning the danger of the road, will withdraw into the palisade."

"It will be most crowded," said Thurnock.

"I think I know such men," I said. "I think soon they will kill for a mouthful of water, should any be found."

"There will be none to be found," said Thurnock. "The villagers, in their evacuation, saw to that."

"Captain," said Xanthos, "they will surely, in one or two days, become desperate and rush forth, shields forward, in numbers we will be unable to resist or turn back."

"They do not know that," I said. "What could they have to hope for but a swift and bloody death, pitting themselves against our vast numbers."

"'Our vast numbers'?" said Xanthos.

"In their mind," I said.

"What do you expect them to do?" asked Thurnock.

"First," I said, "attempt to ascertain our numbers."

"And when they cannot do so?" asked Thurnock.

"What do you think they will do, hungry, thirsting, and frightened," I asked, "before risking all on a final, desperate rush to freedom, losing themselves, perhaps to a man, against possibly insurmountable odds."

"Parley," said Thurnock.

"Precisely," I said.

CHAPTER THIRTY-THREE

The Parley

"You are, I take it," I said, "the dreaded Bosk of Port Kar, come from that port known to many as the Scourge of Thassa, that Bosk of Port Kar come to mercilessly pillage and plunder the innocent, peace-loving Farther Islands of Thassa, Thera, Chios, and Daphna?"

"I am indeed he, Bosk, of Port Kar," said the fellow in the absurd wig, "but I am come not to disturb the gentleness of peace, dear to us as well as you, but rather to wage dire war upon aggressive, threatening Cos, our mutual and perennial enemy."

"How then," I asked, "is it that you would attack the small village, Zeuxis?"

"It is a nest of Cosian spies and sympathizers," he said. "Unfortunately, knowing their wickedness and our resolve, they fled before we could punish them. I trust that you are not of the village of Zeuxis."

"No," I said.

"Notice," he said, uneasily, looking about, "we bear the green flag of parley."

"That has not escaped my attention," I said.

"I have emerged from the palisade," he said, "under conditions of parley."

"I understand," I said.

"But I see no flag of parley borne by one of your followers," he said.

"That is because we did not bring one," I said. "We of the Peasantry do not always see things as you of the cities see them."

"We came unarmed to this meeting outside the gate," he said.

"That was one of my conditions," I said.

"But you and your followers are armed," he said.

"I set the conditions as I please," I said.

"Is that just?" he asked.

"What is justice?" I asked. "Is it just that we roast captives on spits, that we bait our hooks with the flesh of prisoners, that we feed our enemies, bound and screaming, to starving tarsks?"

My interlocutor turned white.

I trusted that Thurnock and Aktis were not paying close attention.

"I have brought twenty of my followers, unarmed, and of diverse ranks and importance," he said.

"Another of my conditions," I reminded him. I had made this a condition because I wanted the outcome of this parley, or, better, some version of it, to be widely disseminated amongst the corsairs, preferably by rumors, innuendoes, and exaggerations. I wanted the least of the brigands to have some idea, and, ideally, a terrifyingly inaccurate idea, as to what took place.

"Yet," he said, "you have, surely, better than two hundred men with you."

"My personal bodyguard," I said.

"So many?" he asked

"Yes," I said.

"Who are you?" he asked.

"Eiron, of the Fields of Chios," I said, "commander of the Peasant Army."

"There is no Peasant Army," he said.

"It is true," I said, "that it consists of only five thousand now, but the number grows each day."

"I do not think there is such an army," he said.

"The Peasantry rises," I said. "The Islands are weary of the depredations of pirates, the oppressions, economic and military, legal and illegal, of violent, savage Cos. We think of liberty. It is in the air, like the wind of Se'Kara or the scent of the sea. The wooden shoe, tied to the lance point, is even now being carried from village to village."

"Show me this army," he said.

"Return to the palisade," I said. "Eat cinders and drink ashes. In two or three days you will thirst to death. It matters not to us. It saves us time and arrows. Even now you are hungry and weak. Shortly you will not be able to carry a shield or hold a sword. Do you truly think that you, even now, in your present condition, could fight your way, outnumbered ten to one, to the beach, to join your fellows? If so, withdraw, consult with your high officers, and then, within the Ahn, charge bravely forth, and die, by the end of the same Ahn."

I turned about.

"Wait, noble Eiron, he of the Fields of Chios," he called.

I faced him, once more.

"It is true we are in straits," he said.

"That is why you called for this parley," I said.

"As we are both lovers of peace," he said, "and both lack amity with Cos, resenting its exploitations and villainies, we should be friends, and allies, not foes."

"Speak further," I said.

"The rogues of Zeuxis did not merely sympathize with Cos, but spied on its behalf, betraying other villages, thus making themselves partisans," he said.

"I did not know that," I said.

"Surely then you do not hold it against us that we hoped to dissuade those of Zeuxis from their Cosian sympathies," he said.

"How could one do that?" I asked.

"And we would not have harmed so much as a hair on the head of one of the villagers," he said.

"That was not clear to me," I said.

"And I, Bosk of Port Kar," he said, "am powerful in Port Kar. I can abet your aims and hopes. I can sway the Council of Captains, that body sovereign in Port Kar, to enleague themselves with your faction. Consider the value of a mighty alliance between you, the Peasantry of the Farther Islands, and the sea-scouring navies of Port Kar, the Jewel of Gleaming Thassa."

"Such a vista," I said, "I had dared not contemplate."

"Free us, let us go to the beach and our ships, uncontested, and it is within your grasp," he said.

"I shall do so!" I said.

"Surely not, Commander!" cried Thurnock.

"No, Commander!" cried Clitus.

"You cannot do so," said Sakim.

"Do not trust them," begged Aktis.

"The decision is made," I said.

He who claimed to be Bosk of Port Kar, and those of his oddly assorted retinue, men high and low, exchanged swift glances of relief and gladness.

"Who is Commander?" I demanded of those about me.

"You, Commander," said Thurnock, in seeming disappointment.

One or two of the others added their acquiescence, as well, seemingly grudgingly.

I was pleased. I thought that my fellows handled it all pretty well.

"However," I said, "in your safe, uncontested passage to the sea, generously allowed to you, you may bear no arms, either offensive or defensive, no swords, no spears, no knives or axes, no shields, no helmets, no bucklers, or such."

"Impossible!" he cried.

"It is quite possible," I said, "easily managed."

"Never!" he said.

"The choice is yours," I said. "Time is short. I recommend that you gather your forces, wish one another farewell, and rush forth. It should all be over within an Ahn. Your fellows at the beach will be proud of you, that you died so well."

"We would be vulnerable, helpless, we could be slaughtered to a man," he said.

"That is true," I said.

"How can we trust you?" he asked.

"I suppose you cannot," I said. "Certainly we admit that it would be difficult."

"It would be dishonorable to lure us forth, trusting and unarmed," he said, "and then fall upon us, butchering us like defenseless verr."

"Yes," I said, "quite dishonorable."

"But you will not do so," he averred.

"That is a risk you must take," I said.

"I trust that you are honorable," he said.

"And you may gamble that your trust is not misplaced," I said.

"Surely you can understand my misgivings, my apprehensions," he said, "were you in my place."

"I think so," I said. "I am glad, incidentally, that I am not in your place."

"Your terms are harrowing and cruel," he said.

"But attractive and lenient," I said.

"We count upon your honor," he said.

"Strange that you, Bosk of Port Kar, should speak of honor," I said. "Is Bosk of Port Kar not a rogue, a pirate and villain, a fellow

perfidious and merciless, a cad and scoundrel, one both treacherous and dishonorable?"

"No," he said. "I am a good fellow, pleasant, trustworthy and
honorable, honorable to the core."

"I am glad to hear it," I said.

"Enemies speak falsely of me, they lie about me," he said,
"they besmirch my name."

"I am sorry to hear it," I said.

"We will arrange," he said, "to leave immediately."

"One more thing," I said, "your passage, while safe and uncontested, is not free. Each man must pay for his passage, by all the
coins and valuables in his possession."

"That is theft," he said.

"Why should a thief not have his plunder stolen?" I asked.
"What entitles a cut-purse to complain when his own purse is
missing? What right has a looter to object to being looted?"

"It is still theft," he said.

"It is more in the nature of a toll," I said.

"You leave us no choice," he said.

"None that is pleasant," I agreed.

A few Ehn later, less than a quarter of an Ahn later, the corsairs, the advance party, those who had been in the first portion of
the column, and those who had been trapped within the palisade,
in twos and threes, some hurrying, some hobbling, some assisted
by others, all unarmed, and bereft of valuables, were on the road,
moving toward the beach.

"There are enough there," said Thurnock, "to wipe us out."

"If armed," said Aktis.

"If knowledgeable," said Clitus.

"If well led," said Sakim.

"Only if in broad, open battle," I said.

"I do not think," said Thurnock, "that they believe we are
truly numerous, that there is a Peasant Army."

"But they do not know," I said.

"True," said Thurnock.

"But we must change their belief," I said.

"And how can we do that?" asked Thurnock.

"Easily," I said.

"How?" asked Thurnock.

"By showing them the army," I said.

CHAPTER THIRTY-FOUR

What was Observed, from a Hill on Daphna

"They are still in place," said Thurnock.

"They are unclear as to how to proceed," I said.

As once before, when scrutinizing the enemy, I, Thurnock, and some others, lay at the crest of a hill overlooking the beach and the seven ships of the corsair fleet. The scene was much the same as before, except for a number of newly pitched tents and the semicircular, defensive ditch, with its heaped sand and shield wall, its back to the sea, by means of which a number of corsairs, those denied boarding on the ships, had cordoned off a portion of the beach.

"It seems," said Thurnock, "the fleet is still reluctant to take its raiders aboard and depart."

This seemed clear from the newly pitched tents on the beach.

"I think they are considering a new march inland," I said, "one cautious, but in force."

"I would have liked to hear the reports of the corsairs, given the recent incidents, and how they were received by the fleet's high command," said Clitus.

"I expect the exchanges were lively," I said.

"Many," said Clitus, "would be the exaggerations, excuses, recriminations, denunciations, and challenges."

"I would be curious as to the high command of the fleet," said Thurnock, "who is in charge of the corsairs, and who leads them."

"I, too," I said. "It must be a lieutenant of Archelaos."

"And to whom is Archelaos lieutenant?" asked Clitus.

"That, I think," I said, "is clear."

A provincial governor might well be corrupt, even to the extent of supporting and protecting raiders, but the elaborate hoax of identifying the raiders as the minions of a foe from faraway, of whom many in the Farther Islands might well have never heard suggested a darker, higher politics.

"Surely the leader of the corsairs, or one of their high leaders," said Aktis, "is the false Bosk of Port Kar."

"I do not think so," I said.

"He is a figurehead," said Clitus, "a buffoon, possibly even an actor, one whom they tell to lead, or pretend to lead, one expendable and easily replaceable."

"Who then is first amongst the corsairs?" asked Aktis.

"That we do not know," I said, "perhaps it is Nicomachos, First Captain of Sybaris, a High Officer of Cos, Admiral of the Fleet of the Farther Islands."

"That would make sense," said Clitus.

"Let them not march inland," said Sakim. "They would be wary, and we would be far outnumbered."

"We could fall back, disappearing, like water into sand," said Clitus, "or even, as possible, hang about their flanks, reappearing and then fading away again, selecting occasional targets."

"In either case," I said, "they would be better informed as to our numbers, and might then depart, far more emboldened. The mighty trident-horned kailiauk of the plains goes about its business, ignoring the tiny zarlit fly."

"I fear," said Sakim, "that they will choose to march inland in force."

"I do not think they will," I said.

"Why not?" asked Sakim.

"Be patient," I said.

"I am troubled," said Thurnock.

"How so?" I asked.

"In your recent parley with the false Bosk of Port Kar," said Thurnock, "before permitting him and his men, weaponless and shorn of valuables, to return to the beach, you claimed you had a Peasant Army of some five thousand men at your disposal, indeed, one being augmented daily."

"I recall having said something like that," I said.

"I can understand the motivation for some such fabrication," said Thurnock, "but, objectively, such a claim is preposterous. Consider the corsairs relaying that claim to their fleet. It will not be believed. Such a claim will be met with derision and scorn. Even the false Bosk of Port Kar, hungry, thirsting, and terrified, was skeptical."

"It is clear," said Aktis, "that the claim was not believed. Behold the beach. Even now a new column is being marshaled."

"But not as well equipped," said Thurnock. "We saw to that."

"There is not so much of a lack there as we might hope," said Clitus. "It seems armament and weaponry are in evidence, presumably supplied from the crews and arsenals of the ships."

"That was to be expected," I said.

"We had best withdraw," said Thurnock, "vanishing into the high grass, being as though we never existed."

"You suspect, dear Thurnock," I said, "that the corsairs doubt the strength of our numbers, doubt that we number in the thousands?"

"If they believed that," said Thurnock, "the beach would be clear and the ships under sail."

"How could we convince them?" I asked.

"I do not know," he said.

"It is not so difficult," I said.

"How?" he asked.

"Consider the gap, the declivity between those two hills," I said, "where the beach rises to the road."

"So?" said Thurnock.

"That is the most likely approach to the beach," I said. "Surely it, and other paths, given the battle of the road, the fighting near Zeuxis, and such, would be under surveillance."

"Certainly," said Thurnock, "lest an attack be made on the beach."

"And under surveillance," I said, "not only from the camp, but, one supposes, also from the ships, by means of the glass of the Builders."

"One supposes so," said Thurnock.

"Keep your eye on that point," I said.

"I see some of our fellows filing by," he said, "in rows of four or perhaps five. It is hard to tell at the distance."

"In the brown of the Peasantry," I said.

"Yes," he said. "Shortly they will be gone."

"Keep looking," I said.

"They are still filing by," he said, after a time.

"What would convince the enemy that we are numerous?" I asked.

"The evidence of his own senses," he said, "what he sees with his own eyes."

"Keep looking," I said.

"I do not understand this," said Thurnock.

"Recall our conversation after the parley at Zeuxis," I said. "Should the enemy doubt that we have an army it is easy to convince him that he is wrong. One need only show him the army."

"They are still filing by," said Thurnock.

"Keep looking," I said.

"And still," said Thurnock.

"Keep looking," I said.

"The sun descends from the meridian," said Clitus.

"This is madness," said Thurnock.

"On the beach they are striking the tents," said Aktis. "The column is disassembling. The shield wall is being dismantled. Longboats are coming ashore to convey the corsairs to the ships. Masts are being raised, and sails drop from the yards. Ships come about. Oars are outboard."

"They are still filing by," said Thurnock.

"But not for much longer," I said. "I think that some five thousand in our army will do, at least for now."

"The fleet departs," said Aktis.

"We, too, must soon make our departure," I said. "Our work here is done."

CHAPTER THIRTY-FIVE

A Discussion Ensues in the Command Tent; Blood May Rest Upon the Blade of Honor

"How could one fall for so obvious a ruse?" asked Thurnock.

"By not understanding it is a ruse," I said.

"There is risk in adopting such a tactic," said Clitus.

"In war there is always risk," I said. "Yet, had it been ineffective, we would not have been much worse off."

"The paucity of our numbers would have been understood," said Aktis.

"Most likely," I said. "It was suspected, in any event."

"And would surely have been determined had the corsairs marched inland," said Sakim.

"But," said Thurnock, "the tactic was effective."

"It has been used on another world," I said, "successfully, and more than once."

"What world?" asked Aktis.

"Earth, or Terra," I said.

"It exists?" asked Aktis.

"It," I said, "and doubtless others, as well."

"Such things are clear in the Second Knowledge," said Sakim, who had once been a captain.

"Knowledge is knowledge," said Aktis. "How can there be a Second Knowledge?"

"Many who are limited to the First Knowledge," said Sakim, "do not even know there is a Second Knowledge."

"And it is said," said Clitus, "that there is a Third Knowledge, known only to Priest-Kings."

We were conferring in the command tent, hidden high amongst the crags overlooking the harbor of the Cove of Harpalos.

The tactic mentioned was, in essence, simple, like surprise, diversion, screening, posting agents and spies, cutting lines of communication and supply, planting false information, and such, but was in execution subtle. In this case, visually, there is little difference between seeing one hundred soldiers and seeing one soldier a hundred times. I had had our some two hundred and fifty men, march in a closed loop, visible only at a certain point, as between two cliffs, or, in our case, between two hills. Every part of the moving loop would be, in its turn, seen and then unseen, and then seen again, over and over, for, as some marchers were seen, other marchers would be circling back through a concealed ditch. In this way, one receives the impression of a continuous, unbroken column of men. After the success of this tactic, I had had the ditch refilled, lest its existence excite curiosity, and seem to call for an explanation.

"Our spies in Sybaris," said Sakim, "report widescale defection amongst the corsairs. Many have fled Thera. Panic is rampant. It seems village raids have been discontinued. Rumors abound. Tales of a merciless Peasant army, one spread amongst the islands, circulate in the taverns. Recruitment of pirates, save for crews, lags, or is nonexistent. Brigands do not seek to pit themselves against insurmountable odds. Brigands look for loot, not death."

"The villages are safe," said Clitus.

"For a time," said Aktis.

"They must be kept safe," I said.

"Thanks to Xanthos, and his fellows," said Aktis, "emissaries are contacting and enleaguing villages, carrying messages of pride and resolution, urging vigilance, preparedness, and a common defense."

"It seems," said Clitus, "the Peasants are rising, if only belatedly."

"Word has spread," said Aktis. "Dozens of my caste brothers, from as many villages, recalling the fair at Mytilene, have come to Nicosia, for instruction in the making of bows. They no longer choose to put themselves, even if laws prescribe it, at the mercy of thieves and killers. They will now dare to protect themselves, their children, their companions, their possessions and lands."

"Too," said Thurnock, "watch towers are built, and signals, by day and night, have been devised."

"Cos will not be pleased," said Sakim.

"Cos may crush any village," I said, "but it would not be wise to do so. Communication obtains. Unity waxes. If one village is attacked a hundred may retaliate. If the islands rise, Cos would be swept from their shores. It would be her best policy to overlook certain modest infractions of her self-seeking laws, such as denying the means of effective self-defense to subject populations to better rule them, and keep peace in the islands. It well known that war impedes the collection of taxes. Indeed, it has even been known, upon occasion, to topple tyrants."

"Making way for new tyrants," said Clitus.

"Frequently," I said.

"I have been in touch with Seleukos, here on Thera, as you requested," said Sakim. "The village of Seleukos is being rebuilt, and the living island, the Isle of Seleukos, moves amongst living islands which have spied for the raiders or abetted them in some way."

I recalled the likelihood that, long ago, one such island had transmitted our position to the corsairs.

"To what effect?" I asked.

"Much effect," he said. "The cooperation of such islands with the corsairs, surely enemies, had always been founded on fear, that if they refused to cooperate, their villages would be destroyed. They are now muchly freed of that fear. Currently corsairs are reluctant to strike villages, and, soon, even should they lose their apprehension of a lurking Peasant army, they would, with the likelihood of only modest loot, be likely to face warned, dangerous fighters, recruited perhaps from several adjacent villages. That is a prospect unappealing to corsairs."

"Too," I said, "those on the living islands could always simply neglect reporting sightings, and such."

"Not so easy," said Sakim. "Many islands were posted with a partisan of the pirates."

"And what of such partisans?" I asked.

"Their foreheads were branded, on the recommendation of Seleukos," said Sakim, "and they were subsequently put ashore."

"It seems then," I said, "that the living islands need no longer supply services to corsairs."

"Most never did," said Sakim.

"I expect," I said, "that bows will sooner or later reach the living islands."

"In many cases," said Sakim, "they have already done so."

"If a living island was threatened," I said, "its population, too, could board their vessels, fishing and otherwise, and abandon the island."

"That is true," said Sakim.

"Yet you seem troubled," I said.

"One living island," he said, "is not associated with a village. It is possessed by, and manned by, brigands, villains clearly imbanded with corsairs. It was that island which evacuated the corsairs stranded on Daphna, after the quest for *The Village of Flowing Gold*."

"I think I know the island," I said. "We saw it, Thurnock, Clitus, and I, and others, when we had been a day or more away from the coast of Daphna, where we had supposedly left corsairs to an unpleasant fate. I recall thinking that our speed must be unusually swift, measuring it against a presumably stationary island. Now I understand that that was an illusion, for the island was moving, too, indeed, moving in the other direction."

"Not only moving, but, I gather, moving rapidly," said Sakim.

"I think so," I said.

"The islands are commonly guided by, and moved by, gentle means," said Sakim, "say, noise, which it finds aversive, light taps on its body, a soft thrusting against its bulk, and such."

"But the movement produced," I said, "tends to be gradual."

"It can take a day to move a living island a pasang," said Sakim.

"How then could the brigand island, if that is what it is, an island manned by brigands, move so quickly?"

"By the application of means less gentle," said Sakim, "gouging, wounding, exacerbating wounds, applying hot irons, torches, and such."

"I anger," I said.

"Remember," said Clitus, "it is not a kaiila, a verr, a bounding hurt, even a vulo. It is a living island, gigantic and sluggish."

"Still," I said.

"Such things have a dull, inactive physiology," said Clitus. "They lack irritability. They are inert, insensitive."

"Yet," I said, "they respond to stimuli, benign or intense, and the hot iron, a fierce, fiery goad, elicits more response than pans clanking under water or the pressing of a paddle or oar."

"The living island cannot feel pain," said Clitus.

"You do not know that," I said.

"That is true," said Clitus, thoughtfully. "I do not know that."

"Men camp upon them, even live upon them," said Aktis.

"Each life form, in its own way, can be good for the other," I said.

"It is unlikely that the living island even knows it is inhabited," said Clitus.

"That could be," I said.

"Perhaps they can feel discomfort," said Clitus, "but not pain."

"Who knows?" said Aktis. "Perhaps there is a point."

"A threshold might be reached," I said.

"They cannot feel pain," said Clitus.

"You cannot know that," I reminded him.

"I do not think they can feel pain," said Clitus.

"Perhaps," said Aktis, "they remember, and are patient."

"Let us not discuss things we cannot know," I said. "We do know, or at least believe firmly, that that living island, the Brigand Island, if you like, rescued stranded corsairs, and conveyed them to safety, possibly even to the vicinity of Sybaris, following their ill-fated adventure on Daphna, seeking *The Village of Flowing Gold*."

"That seems clear," said Sakim.

"But the debacle of *The Village of Flowing Gold*," I said, "could not have been anticipated. Yet the Brigand Island was available, ready to be brought into play. The reason for its existence then, or its justification, must be independent of its possible utility in such an incident."

"May I speculate?" asked Sakim.

"Do so," I said.

"I think," said Sakim, "its utility is best seen as fourfold. First, it is fully enleagued with the corsairs, unlike other living islands. Thus it could police and threaten other islands, ensuring their cooperation. Second, it could give the corsair ships a port at sea, out from Sybaris, a depot where they could obtain water, food, and other supplies, and even, if necessary, repairs. In this way the corsair ships could remain longer at sea. It could also serve as a warehouse for bulky or unusually valuable loot, not easily disposed of at a given time in Sybaris. Thirdly, it could support the corsair fleet in action, interfering with attacked vessels, impeding movements, blocking escapes, even delivering reinforcements to the corsairs in the way of boarders equipped with grappling irons and scaling ladders."

"You spoke of its utility as fourfold," I said.

"I am uneasy with respect to the fourth utility," he said. "I hesitate to speak of it. It is terrible, and it has never been, as yet, enacted."

"You are amongst friends, and fellows," I said.

"We have speculated on the oddity of the corsairs' concern with villages, even prosperous villages," he said, "so large an expenditure of effort for so little gain."

"And the apparent subsidizing of the corsairs," I said.

"I think that ambition looks higher, and further," he said.

"The possible fourth utility?" I said.

"It is based," he said, "on something I heard long ago in Sybaris, when I lay in a half stupor in the tavern, *The Living Island*. A mariner spoke, whom I now realize must have been a corsair. He was telling of something he himself had overheard."

"Proceed," I said.

"What can this be but hearsay based on hearsay?" he asked.

"Sometimes," I said, "nothing is something, and a little may be much."

"There was thinking going about, following what was heard," he said, "that it might be possible to attack, loot, and raze not a village but a town."

"Most towns have walls," I said.

"Yes," he said.

"I do not think that Lurius of Jad, our dear Ubar of Cos, would be likely to approve of a town being attacked. Towns mean revenue."

"This had nothing to do with the Ubar," said Sakim.

"It seems that Archelaos, governor of Thera, grows ambitious," I said.

"The town would not be on Thera," said Sakim.

"Presumably it would have to be a small town," I said, "but one prosperous—and perhaps one expected to be soon enriched?"

"As by a fair," said Sakim.

"Mytilene," I said.

"I fear so," said Sakim.

"Mytilene has walls," I said.

"That," said Sakim, "is where the Brigand Island, as we have spoken of it, becomes relevant. Consider the corsair fleet, in its

full strength, seven ships with crews, supplemented with mercenaries, accompanied by the Brigand Island, itself not only a
transport for additional mercenaries, but conveying an arsenal of
supplies and siege equipment."

"Mytilene is on Chios," I said. "The Peasantry is perhaps most
organized on Chios, from the fair, and from the role of our men at
Nicosia, on Chios, in spurring on resistance, and in distributing
bows and demonstrating the subtleties of their making."

"Do not look to the Peasantry," said Thurnock. "There has
long been tension and suspicion between the towns and the fields.
The towns despise the fields and look down upon them, while the
fields scorn the towns and think little of them. They do not share
Home Stones or interests."

"There are surely markets," I said.

"Local markets," said Aktis, "but most villages are remote from
towns and are substantially independent."

"I had hoped," I said, "that with communication and cooperation amongst the villages, the building and manning of watch
towers, the arming of peasants with an effective weapon, that the
land would be closed to the raiders, this protecting both villages
and towns."

"Would that it were so," said Clitus.

"And that the attention of the raiders," I said, "would then be
directed to shipping."

"And that we might meet them at sea," said Thurnock.

"That was our hope," I said.

"A forlorn hope," said Thurnock. "The Dorna returned to port
yesterday, after a third hunt, once more with her game bag empty."

"I would match Tab and the Dorna against any single ship of
the corsair fleet," I said.

"But there are no isolated ships of the corsair fleet," said
Thurnock.

"It moves as a unit," said Aktis. "It is unassailable, impregnable. No single ship, or pair of ships, could match it at sea."

"They sacrifice intelligence for security," said Thurnock.
"They cast a narrow net when seven ships move as one."

"Many ships must elude them," said Clitus.

"They would lose prizes," said Sakim.

"Why would they accept that?" I asked.

"They are afraid," said Aktis.

"Of what?" I asked.

"Of something they do not understand," said Thurnock. "I do not think they know their foe."

"But perhaps," said Clitus, "they suspect."

"Which will make them far more cautious and dangerous than otherwise," said Thurnock.

"In their discontent they may kill every man, woman, and child in Mytilene," said Clitus.

"What are we to do, Captain?" asked Aktis.

"Do you think that Mytilene is in danger?" I asked Sakim.

"I fear so," said Sakim.

"We are too few to lift a siege," said Thurnock.

"That is true," I said. "Let us hope that Mytilene is not threatened."

"And if it is?" asked Thurnock.

"Then," I said, "I suppose there are worse places to die than Mytilene."

"You will free the men?" asked Clitus.

"The decision will be theirs," I said.

"You know what their decision will be, do you not?" asked Clitus.

"I think so," I said.

"This has to do with honor, does it not?" asked Clitus.

"Yes," I said.

CHAPTER THIRTY-SIX

One Converses with Three Slaves

"Here are the three slaves, Master," said Lais, "Margot, Millicent, and Courtney."

There was a rustle of chain.

"Kneel them before me," I said, "head to the floor."

"Be so," said Lais.

The three slaves knelt, head to the floor.

They were chained together by the neck, and their hands were fastened behind them in slave bracelets.

I let them remain that way for a time.

They did not know why they had been permitted into my presence.

They were apprehensive.

"Kneel up," I said.

They then knelt straightly, but kept their heads bowed.

"State your collars," I said.

"I am Margot," said the first. "I am the slave of Fenlon of Ti."

"I am Millicent," said the second. "I am the slave of Fenlon of Ti."

"I am Courtney," said the third. "I am the slave of Fenlon of Ti."

"You are untrained, lowly slaves, pointless and meaningless," I said. "What good could you be to anyone? Perhaps you should be fed to harbor sharks."

These were small sharks, most less than a foot in length, but they often traveled in groups. In an Ehn or so, thrashing in the water, they could eat a full-grown tarsk to the bones.

The slaves trembled.

"Yet," I said, "you are not without interest, slave interest."

Margot moaned.

"Did I not know better," I said, "that sound might be taken for the sound of a needful slave girl."

She half raised her head, pleadingly, but then, swiftly, lowered it again.

"You are all nicely featured, and well figured," I said. "You look well in your collars."

"Thank you, Master," said Courtney.

"Collars in which you belong," I said.

"Yes, Master," said Courtney.

The morning following the stripping, marking, and collaring of the slaves, we had set forth for Zeuxis on Daphna. The three slaves, as I had informed them they would be, had been taken with us, exposed to the elements, chained naked to a deck ring on the *Tesephone*. Thus, they were bared to glare and heat, changes of temperature, wind and rain, even spray, and the waves that occasionally washed across the deck, flinging and rolling them to one side or the other of the ring, to the ends of their ankle chains. Such experiences, like their brands and collars, like close chaining and the whip, help new slaves to understand what they now are. One can deny an obvious truth only so long. Fortunately for the slaves, neither the *Tesephone* nor the *Dorna* saw action on the voyage to Daphna.

"Do you know the outcome of our concerns on Daphna?" I asked.

"A little, Master," said Margot. "We heard men speak. When we dared to ask questions, we were cuffed to silence."

"The business was largely successful," I said. "The raid on Zeuxis proved fruitless for your former colleagues. They lost several men, and withdrew. It seems that raids on villages will be suspended, at least for a time."

"It seems," said Margot, "that it was a great and costly defeat for the corsairs."

"It could not have been achieved," I said, "had you not revealed their plans."

The slaves were silent.

"And that," I said, "is likely to be obvious to the corsairs, given your disappearance from Sybaris and your presumed capture."

"Surely not, Master!" said Margot, alarmed.

"I do not think you would care to fall into their power," I said.

"No, Master!" said Margot. "No, Master!" exclaimed Millicent and Courtney.

"I understand, from Lais, your first girl," I said, "that on the very first day of our return from Daphna, you, perhaps not yet fully understanding your collars, doubtless conspiring, thought to shirk your tasks and were hesitant to obey commands instantly."

"Forgive us, Master," said Margot. "We were close chained and whipped. We then begged to be full and perfect slaves!"

"Yes, Master!" said Millicent.

"Yes, Master!" wept Courtney.

"And you now know that you are slaves, and only slaves?" I asked.

"Yes, Master," wept the slaves.

"Spread your knees," I said.

They did so.

"More," I said.

They complied.

"I have heard better reports on you of late," I said.

"Thank you, Master," they whispered.

"I am even thinking," I said, "of allowing you slave tunics."

"Yes, Master! Please, Master!" cried Margot.

"A bit of clothing, a bit of cloth," wept Millicent, "please, please, Master!"

"Yes, yes, Master, please, Master!" wept Courtney.

"Perhaps you are aware of subtle changes in your bodies," I said.

"We have been fed carefully, and, as it seemed appropriate, judiciously exercised," said Margot.

"That is common with domestic animals," I said.

"Yes, Master," said Margot.

"I had in mind," I said, "other sorts of changes, changes not only in your body, but in your feelings and emotions."

The slaves were silent.

Then Millicent said, suddenly, openly, "We cannot help ourselves!"

"That comes with the collar," I said.

"We are helpless," said Courtney. "We no longer own ourselves!"

"When we are chained to our stake on the beach," said Millicent, "we whimper and beg!"

"What have you done to us?" said Margot, distraught.

"The strongest bonds of a slave," I said, "are not ropes and chains."

"How I, when a free woman," said Margot, "despised slaves for their needs!"

"Now they are your needs, as well," I said, "as you are now also a slave."

"I was proud," she said. "I was arrogant. I held myself superior to such things!"

"The collar releases the female, which you are," I said.

"The feelings, the needs!" wept Margot.

"They will grow fiercer with time," I said. "Shortly, you will crawl on your belly to a male, begging him for his touch."

"You gave us no choice!" said Margot.

"No," I said. "You are slaves."

"I want to be in my collar!" blurted Courtney.

"What are you saying?" cried Margot.

"I want to be what I am," blurted Courtney, "a meaningless slave!"

"I, too!" wept Millicent, "I want to be a property, owned, a possession, a meaningless slave!"

"No, no!" cried Margot. "Speak not so! Be shamed, shamed!"

"I am not shamed!" said Millicent. "I am proud! I am now myself! I have never felt more free, I have never been more free!"

"Slaves!" exclaimed Margot.

"Yes!" said Millicent.

"Yes!" said Courtney.

"Life is rich and deep, and real," said Millicent. "Live on its periphery, if you wish."

"Let conventions, prescriptions, rules, conformities, and fears be your Master," said Courtney. "I prefer one of flesh and blood, of pride and strength, who sees me as, and treats me as, the slave I am."

"Lais," I said, "Millicent and Courtney are now permitted slave tunics."

"I will find tunics for them," said Lais.

"Thank you, Master!" said Millicent.

"Thank you, Master!" breathed Courtney.

"What of me?" begged Margot.

"Surely you do not wish a slave tunic," I said.

"I want one," she said.

"Why?" I asked.

"I belong in one," she said. "I have known that since puberty."

Millicent and Courtney laughed.

"Margot is permitted a slave tunic," I said.

"Yes, Master," said Lais.

"Thank you, Master," whispered Margot.

"Slaves," I said.

"Yes, Master?" they said.

"Why do you think you were brought here?" I asked.

"We were not told," said Millicent.

"They tell us little," said Courtney. "We are slaves."

"Let me then," I said, "as I have reports, tell you a little. *The House of the Golden Urt* in Sybaris has reopened. There are a new 'Three Ubaras'. Its games are reportedly as dishonest and unfair as before. Both Archelaos, governor of Thera, and Nicomachos, Admiral of the Fleet of the Farther Islands, are patrons. Interestingly, their luck at the tables, and such, seems surprisingly good. These two notables also patronize the tavern, *The Living Island*, managed by one of whom you have doubtless heard, Glaukos of Sybaris. That tavern, as you know, is intimately involved with corsairs, particularly in the past, with their organization and recruitment. Following the withdrawal of the corsair fleet from Daphna, after the Daphna incident, many mercenaries left the corsair fleet, and few enlisted to take their places. Indeed, the attention of the raiders seemed then to depart from the land and turn to the sea, far from the arrows of a watchful Peasantry. On the other hand, of late, recruitment has begun again. Mercenaries are again taking fee for participating in dark enterprises. Do you not find this of interest?"

None of the slaves spoke.

"If these mercenaries are not mariners and are not intended to be risked against villages, one wonders as to the purpose of their recruitment," I said.

The slaves remained silent.

"You are all well acquainted with the governor and the Admiral, Archelaos and Nicomachos," I said, "and men often speak pridefully and loosely in the presence of attentive, beautiful women, especially if lifted upon the gentle wings of paga or *kala-na*."

"We have told you all we know, Master," said Margot, fearfully.

"We spoke of Zeuxis, of ships, supplies, equipment, organization, arrangements," said Millicent.

"Search your memories, deeply," I said.

"There is no more, Master," said Courtney.

"Contemplate harbor sharks," I suggested, "schools of small harbor sharks, like clouds in the water, clouds with teeth."

"We told you everything!" said Margot.

"I am thinking of selling you," I said.

"You may do with us as you wish," said Margot. "We are slaves."

"In Sybaris," I said.

"Not in Sybaris!" cried Margot.

"No!" cried Millicent.

"Anywhere but there, Master!" begged Courtney.

"Perhaps the new 'Three Ubaras' could use you to tenant the side rooms in *The House of the Golden Urt*," I said. "Perhaps Glaukos could find a place for you amongst the paga girls of *The Living Island*. Perhaps you might simply be vended from a public shelf in downtown Sybaris. To be sure, it would be easy to circulate a rumor that you were once more in the port, and now available for rent or sale."

"We have been prisoners," said Margot. "We have told much. This will be suspected by corsairs. Do not let them acquire us. Their displeasure would be deep, their tortures grievous, our deaths mercilessly prolonged."

"You have heard, I assume," I said, "of the hoax of *The Village of Flowing Gold*, the burning of corsair ships, and the near extermination of an entire force of raiders in a waterless, inhospitable region of Daphna."

"Yes, Master," said Margot.

"Do you know the name of he who perpetrated that hoax, who wrought that trap, who nearly, at a stroke, brought about the end of the corsairs?"

"No, Master," said Margot.

"Fenlon of Ti," I said.

Margot's hands, behind her, jerked against the confining slave bracelets. Her eyes widened in terror. "No!" she whispered.

"No, no!" cried Millicent.

Courtney's hands struggled against the slave bracelets. She lifted her head and shook it, and turned it from side to side, wildly, as though she could somehow, by such an absurd means, free herself of the collar. "Take it off!" she begged. "Take it off! Any collar but this! Let it be a high collar, a weight collar, a punishment collar! Let it have inside spikes, anything! But let it not be this collar, not a collar which identifies me as the slave of Fenlon of Ti. Do you not know what would be done to us if we should come into the power of the corsairs?" Again, futilely, she shook her head, and turned it, wildly, in helpless frustration.

"Do not be stupid," said Margot. "Even if we were not brace-leted, even if we could tear at our collars with our hands, we could not begin to remove them. We are slaves. We are in them. They are on us. They are locked on our necks."

Courtney's body shook with sobs.

"Please be merciful to poor, helpless slaves, Master," begged Millicent.

"And," I said, "as you must understand, it would be easy enough for it to be arranged that you should all come into the power of corsairs, into the power of Archelaos, into the power of Glaukos, perhaps into the power of Nicomachos."

"Do not do so," begged Margot.

"Do not let it happen!" said Millicent.

"We beg you!" said Courtney.

"We know no more," said Margot. "In your interrogation, you were thorough. We were terrified and helpless. We could not re-sist. You questioned us for Ahn, for days. You drained us of infor-mation. You left us dry of fact. You took from us every particle of clandestine intelligence we had to give."

"We told you all," wept Millicent.

"We could give you no more," wept Courtney.

"Be merciful," said Margot.

"I suspect there is something else," I said.

"There is nothing else," said Margot.

"Something," I said, "which is small. Something which you did not think important. Something which you did not recall at the time."

"Master?" asked Margot.

"Mytilene," I said.

"That is a town on Chios," said Margot, "where this year's Fair of the Farther Islands was held."

"We were there," said Millicent.

"What of Mytilene?" asked Margot. "We know no more of Mytilene than thousands of others."

"Think back," I said, "long before the fair, something alluded to, perhaps in passing, say, in *The House of the Golden Urt*, over cups, a remark overheard, a sentence begun and then, obviously, not finished."

A sudden look of recognition, as of recalling a bird in flight, dating past a window, a little thing scarcely noticed, flickered across the countenance of Margot.

"It was only a thought," she said.

"But heard long before the fair," I said.

"It was not important," she said. "Nothing came of it."

"What was it?" I asked.

"That Mytilene would host the fair, and might thereby prosper," she said.

"What else?" I asked.

"One said," she said, "that Mytilene had walls, and another said that walls could be breached."

"What else?" I asked.

"Nothing," she said. "It was only a mere thought."

"It may no longer be a mere thought," I said.

I then rose to my feet.

I had gathered that a raid on Mytilene had been considered, even from long before the fair. The remark about breaching walls suggested the use of siege equipment. This sort of thing meshed with Sakim's speculations. It seemed reasonably clear that an attack on Mytilene was in the offing. And, I suspected, given the currently limited success of the unified corsair fleet, which could no more scour the seas for victims than could a single ship, and the risks of now attacking villages, that it might be soon. That mercenaries were now being recruited afresh in Sybaris also suggested the likely prospect of such an action.

"Lais," I said, "conduct these slaves to the beach. There, chain them by the left ankle to the pleasure stake, and then remove their other bonds, the neck chain and their slave bracelets. After the crews are done with them, wash and feed them, and then put them in their cages."

"Yes, Master," said Lais.

"In the morning," I said, "before their work assignments, give them slave tunics."

"Thank you, Master," said the slaves, gratefully.

"They will look attractive in slave tunics," I said.

"What woman does not?" asked Lais. "To be sure, the men might prefer them without tunics."

"The tunic," I said, "conceals little and suggests much. It proclaims the woman an article of property, a purchasable slave. That in itself is exciting. It is also a garment which is easily removed."

"Get up, slaves," said Lais. "We are going to the beach where you will be put to man-use."

I watched the slaves being conducted from the tent.

I must see that they have new collars. The Fenlon-of-Ti collars had served their purpose, dismaying and terrifying them, presumably advantaging me in my interrogation. Then, should things go badly at Mytilene or elsewhere, and they be seized as slave loot, it was less likely that they would be associated with he who had engineered the hoax of *The Village of Flowing Gold*. One could always hope, too, that the corsairs, if victorious, might not recognize them as those who had once been the 'Three Ubaras', those of the gambling house, *The House of the Golden Urt*.

CHAPTER THIRTY-SEVEN

What Cannot Speak May Say Much

The salt scent of Thassa, borne inland over the piers, was bright in our nostrils.

"Some of these piers are guarded," said Thurnock.

"Few," I said.

"I wonder why they are guarded," said Clitus.

"Who knows what arrives and departs from Sybaris?" I said.

"Some ships at closed piers may be corsair ships," said Clitus.

"I think that is likely," I said.

"They depart singly and then join at sea," said Thurnock.

"Presumably," I said.

"There to mount rams and shearing blades," said Clitus.

"Or perhaps at some landing nearby," I said.

"And thus a merchantman becomes a corsair," said Thurnock.

It was early, but work on Gor commonly follows the sun's day, not the conventions of clocks, whether of turning gears, ribbons of falling sand, or draining water. Longshoremen trundled carts over the planking, rattling over the wood. Men called to one another. Some fellows, bearing sacks of Sa'Tarna, climbed gangplanks, to deposit their loads according to the directions of cargo officers. One could smell frying sausage.

"Would that I had my trident and net," said Clitus.

"Let us be inconspicuous," I said. I myself had left my sword on the *Tesephone*. Thurnock would not carry his bow, of course, as Sybaris was a stronghold of Cos on Thera, and the weapon laws of Cos forbade bows to any but authorized personnel, guardsmen, guards of officials, and such.

Our guise was that of common workmen, supposedly making our way about the hiring tables, looking for fee.

Some ships, crowded together, sterns to the dock, protected themselves from other ships with thick coils of cushioning rope dangling over their gunwales. Others, at higher-priced wharfage, had their hulls parallel to the pier. Their mooring ropes, fastened to shore cleats at stem and stern, with their conical or disklike urt guards, would, as they lifted and tightened, shed water in a rain of sunlit droplets, and then, again, relaxing, would loop downward, settling again into the water.

"Give way, give way!" cried a voice, and we stepped aside, making way for a railed cart piled with baskets of larmas, a fruit well to have aboard on long voyages.

"What are we here for?" asked Thurnock.

"To learn what we do not know," I said, "to understand what we do not understand."

"The possible attack on Mytilene?" asked Thurnock.

"The almost certain attack on Mytilene," I said.

"Well," said Thurnock, "I do not think that many of these fellows about, even the rough, coarse fellows who may be corsairs or mercenaries, are likely to tell you what you want to know, whether, or when, Mytilene is to be attacked."

"I suspect that there are few corsairs or mercenaries on the piers," I said.

"And if there are," said Clitus, "they might know no more about it than we. Detailed plans are seldom shared with minions."

"Then, again," said Thurnock, "what are we doing here?"

"Sometimes," I said, "things which cannot speak say a great deal."

"I do not understand," said Thurnock.

"We are scouting cargo," I said.

"Such as siege equipment?" said Clitus.

"That would certainly do very nicely," I said.

"But items that large, that bulky and distinctive," said Clitus, "would be easily noticed, and difficult to explain."

"Too," I said, "they would be difficult, if not impossible, to conceal."

"We are wasting our time here," growled Thurnock.

"Ho, fellows," called a man. "You are large and strong. Are you looking for fee?"

"Not now," I said. "Perhaps later."

He then turned sway, to accost others.

I did not care to abandon our scrutiny of the piers.

"Why does he not set up a hiring table?" asked Thurnock.

"Perhaps he did," said Clitus.

"If so, unsuccessfully, it seems," said Clitus.

There are two harbors at the port of Sybaris, the great harbor, serving the city, and much of Thera, and the smaller harbor, the naval harbor, base of the vessels of the Fleet of the Farther Islands.

From where we were, we could look across the harbor and see the low wall behind which several ships of the Fleet of the Farther Islands lay at anchor.

"I fear our visit is fruitless," I said.

From where we stood we could hear the water lapping against the pilings supporting the pier.

Ships, mostly small craft, would come and go.

I saw the water break once as a small, slender, spined thar-larion surfaced, and then dove again. Such eschew deeper waters and live on tiny fish and garbage. Its heavy scales doubtless afford it some protection against local predators. On the other hand, its spine is venomous, and it would presumably be the last meal of almost any predator luckless enough to attack it, let alone eat it. Interestingly, the small harbor sharks do not bother it. They apparently find its appearance, for some reason, aversive. One supposes that harbor sharks, perhaps in the far past, which did not find its appearance aversive, might have attacked it and, statistically, would have died and thus failed to replicate their genes. On the other hand, those harbor sharks which, for whatever reason, found its appearance aversive, would leave it alone, and go about their business, including replicating their genes.

"We have been here for two Ahn," said Thurnock.

"I think three," I said.

I think we had lost track of the bars, and half bars.

"I am hungry," said Thurnock.

"There are venders' carts about, cooking carts," I said. "What of some hot bread, eggs, and sausage?"

"And a mug of *kal-da*," said Clitus.

"Why not?" I said.

Soon we sat side by side on a bench near a vendor's cooking cart.

"Enjoy your meal," said Thurnock.

"We have made no progress," I said.

"The vulo eggs are good," he said.

I did not doubt it. He had had several.

"The *kal-da* is now drinkable," said Clitus, following a careful sip. We had set the three mugs beside us on the bench, waiting for them to cool. I had had my first cup of *kal-da* in far Tharna, long ago.

"The bread is good," I said. I wished it had come with some cheese.

"Yes, very good," said Thurnock, finishing his fourth triangle. Gorean bread is commonly baked in flat, round loafs, sliced either in fourths or eighths. Also, it is usually eaten on the same day it is baked.

"Why," I asked, "was a fellow going about, trying to recruit laborers? Why would he not set up a hiring table and wait for them to appear?"

"I would guess that he had done so, and had had little success," said Clitus.

"I have seen fellows at other hiring tables," I said. "There seems no shortage of fellows looking for work."

"Perhaps they were not enthusiastic about the work he was offering," said Clitus.

"Why?" I asked.

"I suspect," said Clitus, "it was too onerous."

"I suspect that you are right," I said.

"That was good," said Thurnock, putting his wrapper aside and wiping his large hands on his tunic. "What shall we do now?"

"I think," I said, "we will look for work."

"Are you lazy, Thurnock?" I asked.

"Not lazy," said Thurnock, "sane."

"If the loading is complete by the Sixteenth Ahn," said the fellow, "there will be an extra tarsk-bit in it for each of you."

"It is scarcely possible to comprehend such generosity," said Thurnock.

"Do not complain," said Clitus, "lift."

Thurnock was on one side of the block and Clitus and I on the other.

"There is no way we can get this done by the Sixteenth Ahn," said Thurnock.

"That is why the bonus is offered," said Clitus, "lift."

Backs aching, tunics soaked with sweat, and hands bleeding, we raised the block and set it on the low, sturdy, ten-wheeled cart. Thurnock then slipped the harness about his body and set himself to draw the cart up the iron-reinforced loading planks and

onto the nearly square deck of the barge. Clitus and I thrust from
the back. Once on the wide, flat barge we moved the cart to the
stacked layers of blocks which arrangement was now ten blocks in
depth and, in most places, three blocks high. It was not practical
without steps, a ramp, a crane structure, pulleys, and counter-
weights, or such, to add a fourth layer. It was easy to see from the
first moment why our solicitous, cheerful fee-giver had left his
hiring table, which was abandoned on the pier near the barge, in
favor of sallying forth on his venture of personal recruitment. Less
grievous employments at better rates abounded.

"Be careful lads," advised the fee-giver.

We managed to get the block off the cart and place it on the
growing third tier.

"Well done," said the fee giver. "Only a few more rows to go."
He then turned about, left the barge, and went to the bench at his
canopied hiring table. He did share the water he kept there with
us. Indeed, he even allowed us, from time to time, to rest with him
in the shade. An advantage to being a free laborer is that one can
simply walk off the job. This is a possibility seldom overlooked by
an attentive employer.

Thurnock, standing beside the cart on the deck of the barge,
wiped his forehead with the sleeve of his tunic. "We are mad to
work for these wages," he said, "two tarsk-bits an Ahn! I have
seen fellows whom I suspect turned down this work. They walk
by, sneer, and laugh. They must think we are naive bumpkins."

"Or Peasants," said Clitus.

"Beware," said Thurnock.

"Dear Thurnock," I said, "we are not working for tarsk-bits.
We are working for something far more valuable."

"What?" asked Thurnock.

"Information," I said.

"Is loading stone informative?" asked Thurnock.

"I think it may be," I said.

"Two tarsk-bits an Ahn is not enough," said Thurnock.

"But apiece," said Clitus.

"Still not enough," said Thurnock, "by far."

"I am sure he is an agent," I said. "He is presumably pocketing
the difference between what he is authorized to pay and what he
actually pays."

"The sleen," said Thurnock.

"But a pleasant, affable sleen," I said. "Let us engage him

in conversation. If he is truly an agent, uninformed as to the designs of his principal, his speech is likely to be frank and unguarded."

"Welcome, fellows," said our fee-giver, rising and smiling, shortly thereafter. "Join me in the shade. Rest, and drink all the water you want, before returning promptly to work."

The bota was passed about.

"The day is hot, the work heavy," I said.

"It is the time of year," he said. "I wish I could pay more."

"I, too," said Thurnock.

"From whence is this stone?" I asked.

"From the quarries near Pylos," he said.

"Not from Thera," I said.

"No," he said.

Pylos was on Daphna.

"Why not stone from Thera?" I asked.

"I do not know," he said. "Perhaps it is too expensive."

"Some town," I said, "is investing in a wall?"

"Raiders are about," he said. "The dreadful Bosk of Port Kar."

"I have heard of him," I said.

"One who makes the seas unsafe," said the fellow. "And a ravager of villages."

"What town is thinking of building a wall?" I asked.

"I do not know," he said.

"There is a great deal of stone on the barge," I said.

"A few more blocks and it will founder," said Thurnock.

"But not enough to build a wall," I said.

"The barge comes and goes," he said. "This is not its first cargo. Each trip it gets more and more difficult to recruit good fellows to unload the stone from Pylos and reload it here in Sybaris."

"The word gets around," said Thurnock.

"How often," I asked, "does the barge here in Sybaris load?"

"Every three days," he said. He retrieved the bota and thrust the stopper into the nozzle. "I have enjoyed talking with you fellows, but we are all rested now, and I think it is time for us to get back to work. We must keep those tarsk-bits coming."

Later, on the deck of the barge, now low in the water, Thurnock, Clitus, and I paused, the ten-wheeled cart at our feet.

"That was the bar for the Seventeenth Ahn," said Thurnock.

"It seems," said Clitus, "as we did not finish by the Sixteenth

Ahn, that we will not garner that extra tarsk-bit each."

Torches, here and there, provided light on some of the piers.

"With some luck," I said, "we may finish by the Nineteenth Ahn."

"Has this not been an arduous, wasted day?" asked Thurnock.

"Not at all," I said. "We have learned a great deal. Why is this stone brought in from Pylos on Daphna when there is quarry stone conveniently available on Thera? Surely not because the stone is cheaper on Daphna. Even if it were somewhat less expensive on Daphna, one would have to think about the loss of time getting it to Sybaris and the shipping costs. Therefore, the point of bringing it in from Daphna, to a common pier in Sybaris, is to make the entire operation less obvious. Who notes, or would be interested in, the transport of rude cargo in and out of Sybaris? Legitimacy has no need of secrecy. It is miscreants who strive to be unnoted."

"Corsairs," said Clitus.

"The barge is slow," I said. "Yet it returns every third day."

"It cannot go far then," said Thurnock. "Not to Chios or Daphna."

"It must transfer its cargo to another carrier," I said, "one large, one capable of many loads, and waiting."

"A living island," said Clitus.

"I fear so," I said.

"The Brigand Island," said Thurnock.

"Almost certainly," I said.

"It could kill the island," said Thurnock.

"Eventually," said Clitus.

"I do not think that concerns the corsairs," I said.

"The agent hires us," said Thurnock. "Who hires the agent?"

"Ultimately Archelaos," I said, "but to distance himself from sensitive matters, one supposes such details would be handled through the tavern, *The Living Island*, which, as we know, is much involved in these matters."

"Presumably the contact would be Glaukos, the proprietor?" said Clitus.

"Or one of his men," I said, "say, Ctesippus or Laios."

"Perhaps," said Thurnock, "we were better paid than I thought."

"We have also learned," I said, "the attack on Mytilene is clearly intended, and that it will occur soon, but that it is not imminent."

"How do you know these things?" asked Thurnock.

"We know the attack is planned from the stone," I said. "We know that it will occur soon, in the relatively near future, from the preparations already underway, and we know that it is not imminent from the modest fees paid for loading stone. If time were crucial, workers might be getting as much as a copper tarsk per Ahn."

"The agent may not be paying what his principal would be willing to pay, to hasten the work," said Thurnock.

"I would not be surprised if the agent is keeping some of the hiring fees, as well as his own fee," I said, "but I suspect that the discrepancy is within reason."

"Why do you think that?" asked Thurnock.

"Because the agent is still alive," I said.

"You said," said Thurnock, "that we know the attack is planned from the stone. How is that so?"

"Consider the stone," I said.

"I have been doing so, much of the day," said Thurnock, unpleasantly.

"It seems the sort of stone from which one might build a wall, does it not?" I asked.

"Certainly," said Thurnock.

"Yet," I said, "several of the blocks are not well cut."

"I have noticed that," said Thurnock.

"And Mytilene," I said, "has a wall."

"So what would be the point of taking these blocks to Mytilene?" asked Thurnock.

"Stones such as these," I said, "can make walls."

"And," said Thurnock, "break walls."

"They are ammunition," I said.

"It is getting late, fellows," called the agent from below on the pier. "Let us finish up. If you finish before the Twentieth Ahn, you will each get an additional tarsk-bit, even though you did not finish before the Sixteenth Ahn."

"Our thanks," I called down to him.

"How can one refuse such an offer?" muttered Thurnock.

"Let us get to work," I said.

"We now know what we came for," said Thurnock. "Let us now take our leave."

"No," I said.

"Why not?" asked Thurnock.

"That would arouse suspicion," I said.

"True," he said.

"Besides," I said, "I want my pay."

CHAPTER THIRTY-EIGHT

A Plank in the Sea

"If one has no ship," I said, "one will seize at a plank in the sea."

"There is no plank in this sea," said Thurnock.

"The Admiral," I said, "is disgruntled. He longs for reinstatement in Cos. He deems himself wrongfully denied the High Admiralty of Cos, the post of High Admiral of the Cosian naval forces. Here he is only the commander of the Fleet of the Farther Islands, of only some twenty heavy vessels, and a miscellany of minor vessels. He objects to flattery, favoritism, bribery, and corruption, these rampant, it seems, at the court of Cos in Jad. He deems his experience, qualifications, and skills overlooked. He deems himself removed from Cos by jealous sycophants, feeble save in intrigue, by mediocre, untested opponents, enemies who have the ear of Lurius of Jad, Ubar of Cos. He deems himself, in effect, sentenced to an unwarranted exile."

"I do not know if it is unwarranted or not," said Thurnock, "but to despise so high a post on Thera, the Admiral of a Fleet, suggests a mighty vanity and an ambition that might fly with tarns."

"He does not fit in well with the conventions and protocols of a luxurious court," I said. "He would be more at home, I would think, on the bridge of a knife ship."

"Some at court," said Clitus, "do not know when to smile and when to frown. They, though courtiers and servitors, are unskilled at bending the knee and bowing the head. They may not laugh when it is judicious, and they may laugh when it is not wise to do so."

"True," said Thurnock.

"Poor, noble fools," said Clitus.

"It is easy to see," I said, "why the robes of a courtier might not hang well on the body of a Nicomachos of Cos. He is short-tempered, rude, outspoken, and impatient. He despises mediocrity. Its triumph over him, accordingly, is particularly galling. I would suppose he lacks diplomatic skills. I would guess he fails to pretend to admire those whom he despises, and is reluctant, as many, to coat his tongue with the oil of lies."

"How then could he stand as high on Thera as he does?" asked Thurnock.

"He doubtless comes from one of the high families of Cos," I said. "Such families wield influence and have great power."

"Too," said Clitus, "even those who hate and fear him must recognize the accouterments of what they hate and fear, his force and probity, his records and accomplishments."

"He has allied himself with Archelaos," said Thurnock. "How could he search so long for the corsair fleet and somehow never find it? He does not want to find it. His searches are for show. Can he really not suspect that it anchors before him in the harbor of Sybaris? Is he not a patron of the tavern of Glaukos, *The Living Island*? Does he not game, and suspiciously successfully, as does Archelaos, at *The House of the Golden Urt*? Does he not profit, as does his colleague, Archelaos, from multiple taxes, from arbitrary levies, from demanded licenses, from various schemes, and frauds, in Sybaris?"

"He has ships and we have not," I said, "only two."

"He is in league with Archelaos," said Thurnock.

"Yes," I said, "but how and to what extent?"

"It is absurd to try to enlist him in our cause," said Thurnock.

"If one has no ship," I said, "one will seize at a plank in the sea."

"But," said Thurnock, "there is no plank in this sea."

"We do not know that," I said.

"It is not there," said Thurnock.

"That we must learn," I said.

"It is not there," reiterated Thurnock.

"Tomorrow," I said, "we will reach it."

CHAPTER THIRTY-NINE

I Fail to Contact Nicomachos, Admiral of the Fleet of the Farther Islands

"Away, be off, both of you," said the officer of the guard.

"I am Kenneth Statercounter," I said, "envoy to Sybaris from Brundisium. I am known to the Admiral. I come on urgent business."

"The Admiral is on patrol," said the guard. "He will not return for several days."

We were at the high, heavily barred gate to the Cosian naval base on Thera, the base of the Fleet of the Farther Islands. Thurnock was with me, and we were both in merchant robes, white and gold. Behind the officer of the guard there were another four guards. Interestingly, they, as the officer of the guard himself, were not in the habiliments of Cosian marines or in those of the city guard of Sybaris. Rather, they were in a livery which I recognized as that of the guards of the palace of Archelaos, governor of Thera.

"I petition then," I said, "an immediate interview with he who is highest in the administration of the base, or, if need be, a lesser officer, even one of the base harbor officers."

"In the absence of the Admiral," said the officer of the guard, "all messages, communications, inquiries, and such, must be directed to Archelaos, governor of Thera."

"I see," I said.

"If what you have to communicate is truly urgent," said the guard, "hasten now to his palace. You will find him welcoming, and cooperative."

"Excellent," I said.

"He will be zealous to be of assistance," said the officer.

"I am sure of it," I said.

I turned away from the gate, followed by Thurnock.

"Those were men of Archelaos," said Thurnock, "were they not?"

"Yes," I said.

"You could tell by the livery," he said.

"Yes," I said.

"What better evidence of the collusion between the governor and the Admiral?" asked Thurnock. "So much for your 'plank in the sea'."

"Things do not look well," I said.

"Do you think Nicomachos is in Sybaris?" asked Thurnock.

"I do not think so," I said. "The Admiral's Port Flag is not flying."

"Surely you do not think that he, an Admiral, would be out on patrol," said Thurnock.

"It is not impossible," I said. "Occasionally such things are done. Occasionally an Admiral wants to see things for himself."

"I suspect," said Thurnock, "he is out on the business of the corsairs."

"That is highly likely," I said.

"Mytilene is in danger," said Thurnock.

"More so each day," I said. "The canopied hiring table on the barge pier has been taken down."

"They have enough stone then?" said Thurnock.

"More than enough, I would guess," I said.

"Then," said Thurnock, "we may expect seven ships, singly, over the next few days, to depart the great harbor."

"To join nearby," I said.

"For all we know," said Thurnock, "the mercenaries are already at the rendezvous point."

"If I were a corsair," I said, "that is the way I would arrange it. If I were concerned to ship quarry stone as inconspicuously as possible, I would certainly be even more concerned over the public embarking of large numbers of mercenary troops."

"We do not know the schedule of the corsairs," said Thurnock. "Let us leave as soon as possible, join Tab and the *Dorna* at the Cove of Harpalos, and make our way to Mytilene. We can clear the great harbor by noon."

"He who travels swiftest does not always travel surest," I said.

"Even the swiftest kaiila," said Thurnock, "cannot outpace the soaring tarn."

"We must dally a day, possibly two days, in Sybaris," I said, "and at least a day at the Cove of Harpalos."

"He who wastes moves in *kaissa*," said Thurnock, "asks for the loss of his Home Stone."

"And he who moves without care might as well leave the pieces in the box," I said.

"The *Dorna*, at the Cove of Harpalos," said Thurnock, "can cast her moorings within an Ahn of the *Tesephone*'s arrival."

"But would not be well advised to do so," I said.

"How so?" asked Thurnock.

"Consider the *Tesephone*," I said, "disguised now as a merchant's vessel, painted in white and gold. How she would stand out. What a liability she would be to the *Dorna*. Why not blow trumpets in your stealth, or carry torches to offend a needed blanket of darkness?"

"All right," said Thurnock, "we will paint her green, the green of Thassa, green as night is to the sleen, green as high, tawny grass is to the larl."

The *Dorna*, of course, was already painted green, a color often favored by pirates, as it is difficult to detect at a distance.

"Let her not be seen," I said, "or not seen until too late."

"Still," said Thurnock, "time is lost."

"The corsair fleet," I said, "if it remains united, can move no faster than its slowest ship."

"You are not thinking of engaging the corsair fleet at sea, are you?" said Thurnock.

"No," I said, "that would be madness. But I would hope to reach Mytilene undetected."

"That Mytilene be warned," said Thurnock.

"Certainly," I said.

"That the town might be evacuated?" asked Thurnock.

"Presumably," I said. "I do not see how it could be long defended."

"What if they refuse to leave?" asked Thurnock.

"They must leave," I said. "The alternative is unthinkable. Recall when the corsairs had a free hand with villages."

"In the fields, outside their walls," said Thurnock, "the townsfolk might perish, starving and thirsting, dying of exposure and beasts, driven away from palisades, forced into the wilderness, by hostile peasants, jealous of their lands and resources, their crops, animals, and stores. Those of my caste look not benignly on crowds of dangerous, hungry refugees."

"We can do no more than we can," I said. "But let us do at least that."

"It will be terrible," said Thurnock.

"I fear so," I said.

"But why, Captain," asked Thurnock, "given the threat of each day, each Ahn, do we remain today, and perhaps tomorrow, in Sybaris?"

"And perhaps another day, as well," I said.

"But why, Captain?" asked Thurnock.

"I would still like to get a message through to Nicomachos," I said.

"That 'plank at sea'," said Thurnock.

"Yes," I said.

"He is in league with Archelaos, Glaukos, and the corsairs," said Thurnock.

"I fear you are right," I said.

"And he is absent from the city," said Thurnock, "presumably at sea, presumably for days."

"I think that is true," I said.

"Archelaos controls Sybaris," said Thurnock. "It seems he even controls access to the naval harbor. How can you possibly get a message through to the Admiral, even if he were here to receive it?"

"There is a possibility," I said.

"What is that?" asked Thurnock.

"Finding the right messenger," I said.

CHAPTER FORTY

Mytilene

"Why should I believe you?" asked Thrasymedes, portly administrator of Mytilene. "What evidence do you have?"

"What we have seen and heard," I said.

"We do not know you and have no reason to believe you," said
Thrasymedes. "It is absurd. You must think me a fool. Corsairs
do not have the numbers or strength to challenge towns or cities.
They raid villages. So I should evacuate Mytilene, gather supplies
and water, and turn out our good citizens, having them escape
into the fields, so that you might loot our town with impunity?"

"Better that than slaughter," I said. "If the town is abandoned
it may not be burned. Who knows what gold might be hidden in
walls or under floors? Corsairs, with time, unhurried, can look for
such things. Why should they risk the loss of possible wealth?
Take what you can of value with you, away from the town. I do
not think the corsairs will follow you far inland, away from their
ships. Also, I think they may now fear the Peasantry."

"Why should they fear doltish Peasants?" asked Thrasymedes.
"It is rare that one can find one who can read. Many have never
seen a coin larger than a copper tarsk."

"Give heed to our warnings," I said.

"I think," said Thrasymedes, "you may be of the corsairs yourselves, or of their ilk. You would trick us from our walls to have
an open, vulnerable town at your disposal. If you are truly of the
Merchants, where is your ship?"

"Our ships are elsewhere," I said. "I did not wish to risk having them trapped in the harbor."

"Rather," said a council member. "that it not be noted that
they are painted green, the color of piracy."

"They are painted green," I said.

"Pirates!" exclaimed a council member.

"No," I said. "We are not pirates, but we may meet them at sea, and would prefer to do so with similar advantages."

"You are not in the habiliments of Cos," said Thrasymedes. "I do not think your crews are of the Fleet of the Farther Islands."

"They are not," I said. "We are independent."

"Merchant warriors?" asked a man, scornfully.

"I think time is short," I said. "I bid you act, and expeditiously."

"You are of the corsairs," sneered a man.

"If I were of the corsairs," I said, "I would not be here, trying to convince you of your danger."

"Then you are of the breed of corsairs," said a man, "wanting us to flee from a shadow, an invented foe, a larl that does not exist, so that you might despoil Mytilene at your leisure."

"We are not such that we might be so easily fooled," said another member of the council. "We are not ignorant Peasants. Foist no lies upon us. Struggle to market your shoddy goods to gullible beasts, behind the poles of some flimsy palisade."

"If what you say is true," said Thrasymedes, Administrator of Mytilene, "why are you here? You would put yourself in peril."

"My reasons are my own," I said.

"Arrest him," said a council member.

"And what of more than two hundred of his men, waiting outside our gates?" asked Thrasymedes. "Will you ask them to disarm themselves and submit to chains?"

"Impale their leader and they will flee in terror," said a man.

"And if they do not?" asked Thrasymedes. "Will you pit our ten guardsmen against two hundred brigands? Vengeful thieves and murderers might lurk about our walls for days. With steel and fire they might close the harbor for months."

"Heed me," I said, "and save yourselves."

"You are a lying knave," said a man.

My hand went to the hilt of my sword, and then, angered, I withdrew it.

This swift, inadvertent act had not been unnoted by Thrasymedes.

"I do not know your game or purpose," said Thrasymedes, "but I must ask you, unless you have honest business here, to withdraw, with your men, from Mytilene."

"My business here is honest," I said, "but, it seems, without profit."

"Even if what you say is true," said Thrasymedes, "it would be absurd to abandon the town and risk the fields. We would be better advised to stay where we are. Mytilene has walls of stone. Our walls and stout gates will keep us safe. No rabble of corsairs or brigands could do more than scratch at our defenses."

"If you are determined to remain in the city," I said, "prepare its defenses. Gather stones which may be hurled downward from the walls. Bring vessels of oil to the walls which may be ignited and poured on the enemy. With stone, timber, and sand, be ready to reinforce your gates. Within the walls guard your wells. Gather stores of supplies and food from which the townsmen, supervised, may draw. Consider monitored rationing. Impose martial law. There will be theft and hoarding. Be vigilant. There may be defection and betrayal. Gold has opened more gates than the stroke of the battering ram."

"He is mad," laughed a council member.

"We hosted the fair this year," said another.

"And in all the fair," said another, "there was no rumor of such an attack, no rumor of hostility or even envy."

"None would seek to harm Mytilene," said another. "We are loved."

"And rich from the fair," I said. "Beware."

"We have walls," said Thrasymedes. "We fear no handful of brigands."

"These are not the corsairs of villages," I said. "This is a formidable force of perhaps two thousand men, mercenaries, supported by seven ships. This force has siege equipment and plenitudes of ammunition. It will be capable of investing a town like Mytilene and breaking through its walls."

"Preposterous," said a council member.

"Your ruse of luring us from our homes, so that you can rob them as you wish, without fear, has failed," said another man.

"Get out," said another.

"I fear I must ask you to leave," said Thrasymedes.

"What can I say that might convince you of your danger?" I asked.

"Nothing," said Thrasymedes.

"The matter is final?" I asked.

"Final," said Thrasymedes.

"I wish you well," I said.

"I wish you well," said Thrasymedes.

At that point an alarm bar somewhere in the town began to ring, repeatedly, frenziedly.

Thrasymedes rushed to the exit of the council chamber. "What is going on?" he demanded.

"I do not know," said someone.

Steps, running steps, sounded in the hall outside. Then, shortly thereafter, a fellow in the garb of a guardsman, gasping for breath, stood outside the chamber, clinging to one side of the portal.

"What is going on?" asked Thrasymedes.

"Seven ships, unidentified, flying no flags," said the guardsman, "approach the harbor."

CHAPTER FORTY-ONE

Besieged

It shattered sharp loud startling sudden debris leaping blossoming out and down then the gray waterfall of stone the narrow cascade of loosened rocks the width and weight of it the avalanche the tumbling and rolling of rock and then dust like dry rain choking hard to breathe hard to see get the grit out of your eyes wipe face cough out dirt.

"Where are your robes of white and gold?" had asked a man, eyes widening.

Sometimes, if one is on the wall, and it is still light, one sees it coming, like a large slow bird rising, and then descending, approaching, growing larger and larger.

"Stone!" one cries, and points to the likely point of impact, to which spearmen rush, that the breach not be exploited.

Yet, of late, there was little danger of that. Several times in the early days of the siege, the enemy had attempted to apply a tactic brilliant in the manuals but hazardous in the field. The tactic is for contingents of the invasive force, in the "box formation," shield walls to the sides and a shield roof or ceiling overhead, to protect against arrow fire and cast stones, to approach under artillery fire so as to be able to enter a new breach almost instantly, before defenders can reach the point in sufficient numbers to repel would-be entrants and repair the breach. This tactic, plausible and attractive in theory, had proved costly in practice. The quarried stone from Pylos, serving as ammunitions for the three catapults of the enemy, each block being of approximately the same size and weight, was theoretically ideal for the use of this tactic. Indeed, it seemed likely to me that the blocks, which were larger and heavier than the blocks commonly used in constructing walls, to the annoyance of Thurnock, Clitus, and myself in Sybaris, had been designed with three characteristics in mind. First, as they could easily pass as wall blocks, attention was diverted from their true purpose. Second, they were of an ideal size and weight, if not shape, for use with heavy siege engines. Thirdly, their conformities standardized them for ammunition, which makes it easier for the catapult engineers to calculate and adjust parameters of angle and force. Wherein then did theory encounter fact to its disappointment? The tactic in question works best with well-constructed, well-tested equipment, utilized by experienced, muchly practiced engineers, or "gunners," in conjunction with skilled, well-trained, well-disciplined troops. None of these prerequisites seemed satisfied in the present case. The machinery had most likely been put together somewhere on the Farther Islands. Cos and Tyros are essentially naval powers, and, traditionally, rely on continental mercenaries when faced with warfare in the field. Thus, I suspect that the machinery put together by the corsairs was muscular but unsubtle. It was certainly capable of lofting great weights but perhaps it was less capable, less precise, when it came to meeting certain challenges of adjustment, those pertaining, for example, to distance and targeting. Secondly, catapult engineers, "gunners," and such, are rare and highly paid. If one is looking for the best representatives of that profession, one would not be well advised to go to Thera, Daphna, or Chios, but to Ar or Turia. Lastly, the enemy were hastily recruited mercenaries, not intensively trained troops, not disciplined troops, perhaps having the same Home Stone, troops familiar to one another, troops having confidence in themselves and their officers. In short, after several mishaps or mistakes, such as great stones falling short, falling amidst advancing mercenaries, or mercenaries arriving too early at the wall and being afflicted with their own fire, or mercenary contingents lagging or holding back to avoid such fates, thus subverting the whole point of the supposedly coordinated attack, the enemy generalship apparently decided to leave the tactic in question in the manuals, where its peril was considerably minimized.

"You are no Merchant," had said a man, startled.

"I think he be not Kenneth Statercounter," had said a council member, then in a begrimed tunic, bearing a basket of rocks to be carried to the parapet.

We had had, in the fifteenth and sixteenth day of the siege, heavy rain. This was beneficial to Mytilene. Catapult cordage, heavy with water, rendered their engines, of which, as noted, there were three, inoperative. One gathers that the "artillery men," so little versed in the technology they were attempting to exploit, had not anticipated the effect of rain and moisture on the efficiency of their machines. In such a situation, experienced cata-pult engineers would have removed exposed cordage and placed it in waterproof bags. Commonly, too, extra cordage, in containers sealed against moisture, would be on hand, to be emplaced when the time was opportune. Similarly, had they been more practiced in the craft to which they were addressing themselves, they might have availed themselves of more costly cordage, woven from, say, women's hair, which is stronger, more resilient, and more weather resistant than common cordage. In the sieges of tower cities on continental Gor, it is not unknown for free women to shear their hair, offering it for use in the defense of their city. In passing, it might also be mentioned that the heavy blocks used as ammuni-tion, striking at the walls, or falling within the walls, particularly given their size and shape, were useful, in filling and repairing breaches. Carts were used to move them, and inclined planes and levers, to fit and place them. As of now, the twentieth day of the siege, no major assault, with a massed infantry, had been made on the walls. It seemed to be the enemy's belief that their artil-lery would so reduce the effectiveness of the walls at so many points that it would be pointless to risk the hazards of a scaling attack, in which the advantages would be so clearly on the side of the defenders. One also supposes that the enemy, which largely consisted of mercenaries, knew enough of the facts of warfare to be disinclined to participate in so perilous an endeavor. Such men prefer situations in which there is minimum risk and the prospect of maximum gain. The generalship of such troops must always, in their decisions, weigh the possibility not only of noncompliance but of mutiny.

On the eleventh day of the siege, on a gouged street, near the rubble of houses, Thrasymedes, seeing the startled faces of others, had spun about. "What garb is that?" he had asked.

"You know it," I said.

"I deem it not the rich cloth of the Merchants," he had said.

"It is the plainer cloth of a different caste," I said.

"The color!" said a man.

"Scarlet," said another.

"The scarlet of the Warriors," whispered another.

That color was seldom seen on the Farther Islands.

"I am assuming command," I said.

"By what authority?" said a man.

"By that of the sword," I said.

"You cannot do this," said a man.

"This says I can," I said, drawing my sword.

"You are mad!" exclaimed a council member.

"If so," I said, "it is the madness which is your only hope, the madness which stands between you and death, between you and the end of Mytilene, between you and the destruction of your Home Stone."

"We shall consider the matter," said a council member.

"It has already been considered," I said. "I have considered it."

"We shall vote," said another council member.

"The vote is in," I said. "Steel has won."

"He has men," had said a man.

"Who will dispute this?" had asked Thrasymedes.

Men regarded one another. There was silence.

"You are in command," had said Thrasymedes.

It is now, as mentioned, the twentieth day of the siege.

Let me recount, with brevity, certain recent events. On what we might call the first day of the siege, the seven ships of the corsair fleet closed the harbor at Mytilene. On the same day, several hundred mercenaries, who had been landed earlier somewhere north of the harbor, moving overland, invested Mytilene. On the second day, the ships in the harbor, large and small round ships, fishing boats, coasters, and sundry small vessels, were attacked, looted, and burned. Surviving harbor personnel and the fleeing survivors of the attacked ships were funneled between contingents of the investing forces into Mytilene. The purpose of this was to place additional stresses on the supplies and stores of Mytilene. Following the entrance of these refugees into the town, the investing lines closed and Mytilene was encircled. Predictably, Mytilene was encouraged to open its gates, with given assurances of lenience and mercy to the population. This overture was refused by Thrasymedes and his council, apparently on two grounds, first, their terror of the supposed Bosk of Port Kar and their awareness of the merciless depredations inflicted in his name on several villages, such as Nicosia on Chios itself, and, second, the accounts of the harbor refugees of the unconstrained savagery and blood-thirstiness of the pillagers in the harbor. On the fourth day of the siege, Thrasymedes and the council attempted to negotiate a withdrawal of the corsairs, offering them fifty stone of gold for their departure and a pledge never to return, and then, later, a hundred stone of gold for their simple departure. The corsairs found this offer, generous as it might be, unsatisfactory. They reasoned, one supposes, that where there might be a hundred stone of gold there might be more than a hundred stone of gold. The heads of the council's small negotiating party were catapulted over the wall of Mytilene. This act, if it was intended to dismay or terrify the citizenry of Mytilene, failed of its purpose, as it produced in most, but not all, a hardening of a general intention to resist. Next, the corsairs, as if regretting their grisly act, or perhaps, more likely, as if regretting its unforeseen consequence, its general stiffening of a will to resist amongst the besieged, offered an uncontested exit from the city to adult males. Why only adult males? The ulterior motivation of this proposal was presumably to reduce the number of able-bodied defenders within the city. Accordingly, dissent abounded. One council member, however, benign Tarchon, skilled with the lyre, advocated its acceptance on two grounds. First, its acceptance would reduce the strain on stores of food and water within the walls. Second, the town had no right to deny individual citizens the right in such a matter to choose for themselves. As I later learned, not having been permitted to attend or address the council, the view of Tarchon was accepted. The next morning some four hundred male citizens of Mytilene abandoned the town of their Home Stone and, rejoicing at their deliverance from danger, and encouraging others to follow their example, exited the great gate. Shortly thereafter they were shackled and put to work, with mercenaries, on the first and, later, the second, of two siege ditches, by which the town was then twice encircled. On the eighteenth day of the siege, the work done, within sight of the walls, they were decapitated.

It was toward noon, the tenth Ahn, on the twentieth day of the siege, a bright, windy day, that Thrasymedes joined Thurnock, Clitus, and myself on a ragged, uneven portion of rebuilt wall, now, at this point, only some fifteen feet in height. Our footing

was on a broad, wooden scaffolding, formed from timbers of demolished houses.

We were looking toward the many tents of the main encamp-
ment of the mercenaries, some two hundred yards behind the second of the two siege ditches. From our location we could see that
all three of the enemy's siege engines had now, for only the third
time, been brought together, almost side by side.

"Is there no end of the great stones?" asked Thrasymedes.

"There are many, but there is an end to them," I said.

"The engines have been quiet for two days," said Thurnock.

"They are stockpiling ammunition," said Clitus.

"For a great attack?" said Thrasymedes.

"Possibly," I said.

"How could so many stones, so much weight, in so short a
time, have been obtained locally?" asked Thrasymedes.

"It was not," I said. "It was imported from quarries near Pylos,
and perhaps elsewhere, and shipped through Sybaris."

"Surely not," said Thrasymedes. "To transport it would require a dozen round ships."

"I think," I said, "it was barged to a living island, then near
Sybaris, one I have thought of as the Brigand Island."

"It would destroy such an island," said Thrasymedes.

"It may have," I said.

"Desertions are few, happily," said Thrasymedes, "even before
the digging of the double ditch."

In such cases, an individual would anchor a rope to the ramparts
and lower himself over the wall. As the town was invested, one
supposed that few such attempts at escape had proved successful.
Indeed, sometimes the individual was killed at the foot of the wall.

"Glory to the Home Stone of Mytilene," I said.

"Your men have stayed with you," said Thrasymedes. "They
are as loyal as sleen."

"As sleen with love, as sleen with honor," I said.

"One fled," said Thurnock, angrily. "One sought to save his
skin, and may have been successful in doing so. One sought to
flee, thus reducing defenders and imperiling his fellows the more,
a Peasant, one of my own caste, Aktis of Nicosia."

"I cannot hate him," I said, "I cannot despise him. Do not do
so either."

"He was my friend, I trusted him," said Thurnock. "We drank
from the same bottle, we shared the same watch."

"Blame him not," I said. "His Home Stone is not ours. It is that of Nicosia. What hold have we on one whose Home Stone is not our own?"

"The hold of the sword brotherhood, the hold of fellowship," said Thurnock.

"Sometimes," I said, "it is not clear what honor prescribes."

"It can be hard to keep the codes," said Clitus.

"He will find no forgiveness in my heart," said Thurnock. "He has betrayed our caste."

"Be cheered," said Clitus. "Perhaps he will survive."

"But at a cost I would not pay," said Thurnock.

We were then silent, and looked over the wall, past the double ditch and the now-quiescent engines of war, the three mighty catapults, to the many tents of the enemy, plentiful in the distance, like scattered, disorganized litter.

"It is near the end," said Thrasymedes.

"Do not despair," I said.

"I love Mytilene," he said.

"It is the place of your Home Stone," I said.

"You and your men have wrought much on our behalf," he said. "Yet you are not of Mytilene. It is not the place of your Home Stone. I do not even think you are of the Farther Islands. Why have you done so? Why have you stood with us on the wall and in the breaches?"

"Accept that we have done so," I said, "and do not enquire further."

"It has to do with codes?" he asked.

"That, and such things," I said.

"We cannot hold out much longer," said Thrasymedes.

"In the great rains, recently," said Thurnock, "much water was gathered from stretched sail canvas and entered into many containers, dozens of barrels and kegs."

This canvas had been obtained from naval stores held in Mytilene, supplies on which the harbor would normally draw.

"Eight of Mytilene's wells, now closely guarded, still have water," said Clitus.

"Very little," said Thurnock.

"I still do not understand," said Thrasymedes. "How could three wells have been fouled?"

"As the saying has it," I said, "there is an ost within the walls."

"We grow short on food," said Thrasymedes.

"In some sieges," said Clitus, "straws are drawn. He who draws the short straw is quickly and mercifully put to death, that his fellows may feed."

"Better," I said, "to finish remaining stores at once, with a great feast, and then, in the morning, hardy and nourished, in the sunlight and open air, scorning the enemy, singing, go forth to die in battle."

"The codes?" said Thrasymedes.

"Of course," I said.

"I think then," said Thrasymedes, "that that time is not far away. We cannot hold out much longer."

"The enemy also requires food and water," I said.

"But," said Thrasymedes, "they need only go out and find it."

"That may not be as easy as you think," I said.

"They have still not mounted a massive attack with scaling ladders," said Thurnock.

"They are not eager to do so," I said. "It requires great courage to cling to a ladder with one hand and try to defend oneself with the other, against burning pitch, axes, jabbing blades, cast stones, and such. Most such assaults are turned back with a great loss of life. That is one reason towns and cities have walls."

"That is a great advantage of siege towers," said Clitus. "They can conceal and protect men, be wheeled to walls, overtop walls, and, when they suddenly drop their gates, permit besiegers bearing shields to rush downward with great force upon defenders."

"They have no siege towers," I said. "Nor do they have thousands of men."

"This is not a war between great cities with enormous resources," said Thurnock.

"And even so," I said, "siege towers can be at but one place at one time and, at that place, and time, can be faced."

"The combination of siege towers with massive scaling is difficult to deal with," said Clitus.

"That is true," I said. "If one masses defenders to confront the siege tower, one commonly thins defenses elsewhere on the walls."

"I think," said Clitus, "by now, the enemy should have grown impatient."

"Let us hope so," I said.

"The enemy," said Thrasymedes, "has brought his three siege engines together."

"Closely together," I said.

In this way, fire can be concentrated.

"I am not skilled in the ways of war," said Thrasymedes, "but does not this massing of engines suggest an imminent assault, a barrage of stones, softening resistance, to be followed by a massive attack, presumably with an attempt to scale walls?"

"It certainly suggests that," I said. "And I think that is exactly what it is intended to suggest."

"I do not understand," said Thrasymedes.

"I do not think the enemy wants a prolonged siege," I said, "one that, as far as it knows, might last months."

"Presumably not," said Thrasymedes.

"On the other hand," I said, "I do not think, either, that he is eager to risk ordering paid troops, with no loyalty to anything but loot, to subject themselves to the obvious peril of a general assault on a still stoutly defended town."

"What is your thinking?" asked Thrasymedes.

"I think," I said, "he would prefer to pour his troops into Mytilene through an opened gate."

"The gates are guarded from within," said Thrasymedes. "It would require several men to overcome the guards and open a gate."

"What if there were several men?" I asked.

"I do not think there are so many traitors or spies in Mytilene," said Thrasymedes.

"I do not, either," I said.

"Then how could it be done?" asked Thrasymedes.

"Easily," I said.

"I do not understand," said Thrasymedes.

"First," I said, "how numerous is the enemy ashore?"

"We do not know," he said. "But, as you know, several, with the Builder's Glass, have counted the tents as being in the neighborhood of five hundred."

"Suppose, then," I said, "there were five men to a tent."

"There may be more," said Thrasymedes.

"Granted," I said. "But if five?"

"Then twenty-five hundred," said Thrasymedes.

"That would be the largest corsair force we have faced," said Thurnock.

"And there might be more," said Thrasymedes.

"But still too few, in my opinion," I said, "for the classical assault I have in mind."

"What is that?" asked Thrasymedes.

"Mining," I said.

"Digging?" he said.

"Yes," I said. "Classically, ideally, one digs beneath the walls at many points, say, twenty to fifty. The wall is then supported from beneath by timbers. At a given signal, the blasting of trumpets, the clashing of cymbals, the whistling of smoke arrows, the beating of drums, or such, the timbers are removed by ropes or blows, not fire, as fire is unpredictable and slow. When this is done successfully, the walls collapse at several points simultaneously, opening the town or city to the enemy."

"You fear such an assault?" asked Thrasymedes, anxiously.

"The enemy," I said, "outnumbers our men several to one, but their numbers are not sufficient to mount such a general assault."

"But surely they might collapse the wall at one point or another," said Thrasymedes.

"To be sure," I said, "but the siege engines might do as much."

"And one could rush our men to the limited point or points of danger," said Clitus.

"Hopefully," I said.

"Then you think we need not fear so general an assault?" said Thrasymedes.

"I think not," I said. "Too, we are dealing with mercenaries, not disciplined troops, used to labor, as in building ditched and palisaded fortress camps, as well as fighting. Just consider the nature of the enemy's tenting. There is no serious suggestion there of organization, discipline, or control. I cannot conceive of our friends on the other side of the wall delighting in the arduous, unpleasant, and dangerous work of digging several tunnels."

"Then there is nothing to fear?" said Thrasymedes.

"What if there were but one tunnel?" I said.

"Then," said Thrasymedes, "the collapsed wall at that point would be as easy to defend and repair, as in the familiar case of a blow resulting from the strike of one of the great engines."

"But what if the tunnel emerged within the walls, in the town itself?" I asked.

"We could deal with it even more easily," said Thrasymedes.

"Not if it were not seen," I said.

"Then," said Thurnock, "several men could be brought within the walls, enough to overcome the guards at, say, the great gate, and then open the gate to the enemy."

"Precisely," I said.

"I am afraid," said Thrasymedes.

"The stones of the enemy have fallen heavily and plentifully into Mytilene," I said. "Consider the broken roofs, the shattered houses."

"Ruin is rampant," said Thrasymedes.

"Notice now," I said, "something odd." I pointed to an area within the walls, south and west of the great gate, not one hundred yards from that massive portal.

"What am I to notice?" asked Thrasymedes. "I see nothing wrong."

"That is what you are to notice," I said, "that where I point there is nothing wrong."

"Some buildings are fortunate," he said. "They have not been damaged."

"Why?" I asked.

"They have been missed by the great stones," said Thrasymedes.

"I find that of interest," I said.

"It is a coincidence," said Thrasymedes.

"Possibly," I said.

"What is that sound?" asked Thurnock.

"It is the sound of a lyre," said Thrasymedes. "Tarchon, of the Council, is skilled with the instrument, and, when not engaged in defensive duties, often plays it."

"That is his house?" I asked.

"Yes," said Thrasymedes, "that house, the large one amongst the unharmed buildings."

"Is he on duty tonight," I asked, "patrolling the wall, watching in the streets, guarding wells?"

"No," said Thrasymedes. "No member of the council is on duty tonight."

CHAPTER FORTY-TWO

What Occurred One Night Within the Walls of Mytilene

"Be quiet, fellows," I said. "Stand back, to the sides. Let it seem the gate is undefended."

Those on the wall, above the gate, readied the unlit lamps and cords.

The night was unusually dark.

No moon was visible in the sky, and the light of the stars, many of which I might have recognized from Earth, could not be seen, their fires concealed by a tent of clouds.

"They are coming, filing forth," I said. "Let them reach the gate, that they may be pinned against it."

I surmised, from the stealthy, furtive darknesses within the darkness, figures scarcely discernible, that there might be something like fifty in the party issuing forth from the domicile of benign Tarchon, amiable and respected member of the council of Mytilene. Surely that was considerably more than would be needed to overcome the handful of men commonly posted to guard the gate. In the vicinity, awaiting my signal, were some three hundred men, mostly citizens of Mytilene, armed with pikes, knives, spears, stones, axes, hammers, chains, and clubs.

I sensed some surprise, some consternation, at the gate. Where were the guards?

"Question not!" said a voice near the gate. "The fools suspect nothing. They do not even have the sense to watch their own gate."

"It is too easy," said another voice.

"Get the gate open," said the first voice. "Our troops are waiting. When the gate is open, they will rush forward, from the near ditch."

This was to have been expected, of course, that enemy troops would have been marshaled in, and concealed within, the closest of the two ditches encircling Mytilene. In this way, as soon as the gate was open, they would presumably clamber forth in a thick column matched to the width of the opened portal, and hurry into the city. The ditch in question was some fifty yards from the great gate. This distance and the likely width of the advancing column were both of interest.

"The beams are heavy," said a voice.

"To reinforce the gate against the pounding ram," said the first voice.

"None defend the gate," said a man.

"Gratitude to the fools of Mytilene," said a man. "They serve us well. They make our business easy."

"Now, we need not the ram," said a man, pleased.

"It is unpleasant to use it under fire," said another voice.

"How stupid are those of Mytilene," said another man.

"Talk not," said the first voice. "Move the beams, both! Now!"

The enemy was uneasy, milling near the gate, while some four or five men addressed themselves to the first beam.

Each beam, in its brackets, stretched across the portal and was anchored, on each side, within a brick-lined bracing, part of the wall itself.

I waited until the first beam, in its brackets, was thrust aside, fully to the right, deep into its brick-lined bracing.

When the second beam was moved to the left, fully within its own bracing, the portal would be cleared, and the two heavy leaves of the gate could be swung inward.

When I heard the second beam begin to move, slowly, and heavily, in its brackets, I called, "Lamps!"

At this point a dozen men on the wall above the gate thrust the wicks of tharlarion-oil lamps into the flames of their then unshuttered dark lanterns, and lowered the lamps, on their cords to a height of some eight or ten feet above the ground.

This illuminated the gate area.

"Vengeance for Mytilene!" hissed better, I conjecture, than two hundred voices.

Corsairs turned about, startled, dismayed, terrified.

They impeded one another, pressed back, trapped against the wall and gate. Many, crowded together, could not wield their weapons. The irate, half-starved citizens of Mytilene fell upon them, slaughtering them like penned verr.

In their hearts there was no mercy.

"No cries of gladness or triumph," I called. "Emulate the sleen. Kill in silence. Do not alarm the herd!"

Men lost their footing in the red mud at the gate.

I thrust my blade into the side of a corsair who sought, half mad with fear, to brush past me.

Thurnock picked three targets, which then moved no more.

Behind our men torches were lit, by means of which any who might break our lines and attempt to escape, say, into the town, might be dealt with. A dozen men, at my cry "Lamps!" had simultaneously invaded the house of Tarchon, to seize him, if he were there, and prevent any fugitives from retreating through the tunnel.

"Clear the portal," I called.

Bodies, many of which had been struck repeatedly, were dragged to the sides.

"It is victory," said Thrasymedes, breathing heavily, two hands grasping the long handle of a double-bladed ax, one blow of which might have split the common shield or cleaved a helmet to the chest, "victory, quick and terrible."

"It is not victory," I said, "until the sword's work is done."

"Tonight it may sleep easily in its sheath," said Thrasymedes.

"As in *kaissa*," I said, "momentum is to be exploited."

"I do not understand," he said.

"In war," I said, "there is much confusion. Corsairs waiting in the ditch, to climb forth and hurry through an opened gate, know little of what has occurred. They know there was resistance, and little else. Should the gate be opened, what would they think?"

"That their fellows have been successful," said Thrasymedes.

"Remove the second beam," I said. "Extinguish the lamps and torches, and prepare, on my signal, to light them again."

The second beam was slid to the left, deep into its brick-lined housing, this clearing the portal.

"By the gate, listen!" I called. "When I order the gate opened, open it to the width of four men. When I cry out, 'There is danger, stop, go back', or such, close the gate."

"Surely we will not open the gate," said Thrasymedes.

"Briefly and narrowly," I said. "Enough to admit numbers we can deal with easily, enough to mass confused others before the soon shut gate, where, crowded together, they will be vulnerable to stones cast down from the wall over the gate."

"Still?" asked Thrasymedes.

"The corsairs do not know what has occurred," I said. "When they see the gate opened, they will assume that all is well, that their fellows have secured the gate and that the town is at their mercy. Then they will discover otherwise. Confusion will reign, inside and outside the gate."

"And all is in darkness," said Thrasymedes.

"And darkness," I said, "is the house of terror."

"Until the lamps and torches are lit," said Thrasymedes.

"At that point those trapped inside the gate will discover that their terror was well founded, and those outside the gate, still in darkness, will withdraw in disarray, fleeing a rain of stones."

"I see," said Thrasymedes.

"Surely your ax is still thirsty," I said.

"It is," said Thrasymedes. "But I suspect that there is more in your plan than the shedding of more blood."

"Yes," I said. "One desires to confuse and unsettle the enemy, so that he will not know what is going on, will not know what to expect, or when; one wishes to reduce his confidence, to make him suspect the competence of his leaders, to make him doubt the value of his cause or the likely success of his efforts. Let him understand that things are not going according to plan, and not know why this is so."

"Ah," said Thrasymedes.

"Much of war," I said, "is fought in the mind. Why else the drums and trumpets? Why else the songs and chants? Why else the Pyrrhic dances? The very name of a Marlenus of Ar can rouse a city to revolt. Is not the reputation of a Dietrich of Tarnburg worth a thousand troops? Whose hand does not shake on the pieces if, across the *kaissa* board, he sees a Centius of Cos, a Scormus of Ar? An army believing itself doomed does not hurry to the field. What soldier does not fight well, bravely and gallantly, for a commander he deems invincible?"

"Proceed," said Thrasymedes.

"Open the gate," I called, softly, "but open it carefully, and slowly, as though it was done with stealth, and open it so that only a column of four can enter."

This was done, the sound of the hinges of the leaves of the great gate almost inaudible.

"The gate is open," I heard someone say, a hushed voice, outside in the darkness.

"Convey the word," said another voice, one farther off.

"Back, fellows," I said. "Let the enemy not encounter immediate resistance. Let the net first be full; then draw its cords. Be quiet, be patient, be ready."

I counted Ihn to myself. I had little doubt that, by now, corsairs had begun to climb from the ditch.

I took it that traversing the distance between the ditch and the partially opened gate, given the darkness and the danger of footing, might take something over an Ehn. Too, the first of the visitors would be likely to enter cautiously and attempt to make contact with their fellows, presumed to be inside, with the gate secured.

It was not a long time, but it seemed long.

I sensed Thrasymedes and others beside me.

I heard a voice, whispering, from the darkness, from the vicinity of the gate.

"Publius?" it said, "Publius?"

"Enter," I whispered. "Be silent! Be cautious!"

I heard soft sounds, the shuffling of high-laced marching sandals.

I counted ten Ihn.

I sensed bodies were before me, within perhaps three or four yards.

"Stop!" I cried, suddenly. "Danger!"

The progress of the visitors was abruptly arrested. There was a cry of alarm. The two leaves of the great gate, slowly, began to close. Visitors sensing the huge, slow, heavy movement of the gate, scrambled wildly, crying out, to be inside or outside the leaves, anything to avoid being caught between them. There was, also, almost immediately, cries of anguish as limbs or bodies were crushed between the leaves. "What is going on?" cried a voice from somewhere near the gate. I heard pounding on the gate, both from outside and within. There was a sound as of crushed fruit and breaking wood and a miserable cry was cut short. I then heard the sound of the two heavy gate beams slid through their brackets, one from the right, one from the left.

"Publius! Publius?" cried a voice.

"Light!" I called. "Lamps!"

Even before the lamps were lit, and dangling on their cords, the men of Mytilene, with cries of rage, rushed toward the gate, brandishing their miscellany of weapons, including those taken from the fallen mercenaries slain in our earlier action, stabbing and striking.

Outside the gate I could hear, too, cries of consternation, as our men on the wall, those above the gate, hurled heavy stones down upon the startled mercenaries, crowded together outside the gate.

What occurred within the gate was much what had occurred before. It was a butchery of men crowded together, who could scarcely lift their weapons to defend themselves.

Three mercenaries had been trapped between the leaves of the great gate. One arm was thrust through from the outside. There was a scream from the other side as Thrasymedes, with a single blow of his double-edged ax, cut it off. "No! No!" cried another mercenary, on his belly, looking up, much of whose body lay within the gate, his foot caught between the leaves. "Yes," said Thrasymedes. "Yes, for Mytilene." He then struck the foot off. He then stood there with the bloody ax, looking down, breathing heavily, watching, watching. "It is enough," I said to him. "Let your weapon rest. It has done its work." "He is not yet dead," said Thrasymedes. "He is," I said. "Look, he is still. He does not move." "How can he be dead?" asked Thrasymedes. "He has bled to death," I said.

Another body had been caught between the leaves of the closing gate. It was muchly compressed. The head and torso dangled on our side of the gate, suspended by a rope or ribbon of muscle and tissue.

I stepped to the side, and back, past another body.

"Publius?" it said.

"I am not Publius," I said.

Then it was still.

Thrasymedes joined me then, some yards back from the gate. "Victory, again," he said.

"Momentum is to be exploited," I said.

"I do not understand," he said.

"*Kaissa*," I said. "The *kaissa* of blood."

"Surely not," said Thrasymedes. "Not now. Our steel no longer thirsts. Even my ax has drunk its fill."

"The leadership of the enemy," I said, "will not yet be fully apprised as to what has occurred. If what I contemplate now comes to fruition, I think he will have no choice but, if he wishes to bring this business to a quick conclusion, to mount a scaling attack on the walls which, I suspect, will prove costly to him and, given the unruly and reluctant nature of his troops would not be likely to be repeated."

"What is your plan," he asked.

"I have selected thirty men," I said, "three groups of ten each; I shall command one group, Thurnock another, and Clitus the last. Each group will have dark lanterns, axes, and quantities of tharlarion oil."

"Unusual supplies," said Thrasymedes.

"Not for what I have in mind," I said.

"And what do you have in mind?" asked Thrasymedes.

"Paying our friends a surprise visit," I said.

"We are vastly outnumbered," said Thrasymedes. "Do not do so. The clouds thin. The yellow moon will soon be in the sky. It will soon be morning. You would be noted as soon as you left the gate."

"We will not leave by the gate," I said. "Our friends have left us a fine road, their own road, whereby we may approach them unseen and emerge in their midst."

"The tunnel," said Thrasymedes.

"Has the noble Tarchon," I asked, "been taken into custody?"

"No," said Thrasymedes, "but he is surely somewhere within the town."

"Hiding," I said.

"You suspect he is involved in this, that he was aware of the tunnel, which was opened within his domicile?" asked Thrasymedes.

"Certainly," I said. "See the metal rod which he sank in his floor, used to convey sound into the earth, to mark the point where the tunnel might be safely opened."

"We will seek him," said Thrasymedes.

"Do so," I said.

"You are serious about your plan, about going visiting?" asked Thrasymedes.

"Of course," I said.

CHAPTER FORTY-THREE

How the Remainder of a Busy Night Was Spent

"I do not care for this," said Thurnock, a yard or so behind me, crouched down.

"It was not dug for fellows of your size," I said, lifting the now-unshuttered dark lantern a little. Its light was dim, but extended some feet ahead, illuminating the tunnel.

"My back hurts," he said.

"I would not care to meet the enemy in these confines," said Clitus, behind Thurnock.

"Nor they us," I said.

"What does the enemy know of what occurred?" asked Clitus.

"I suspect," I said, moving ahead, "very little. Their informants will be confused, distraught mercenaries, fled back in the darkness from the closed gate of Mytilene. What they know will be little more than the fact that something, as they see it, had gone terribly wrong."

"Will they send more men through the tunnel?" asked Clitus.

"Not immediately," I said. "They will wish to gather intelligence."

"The opening of the tunnel in the corsair camp will be guarded," said Thurnock.

"It should be," I said, "but it might not be. We are dealing here with raiders, with looters, cutthroats, and killers, not trained, disciplined troops."

I brushed aside a handful of dirt, fallen from the roof of the tunnel.

"There should be more reinforcement, more bracing, more timbers," said Thurnock, uneasily.

"We are not mining silver here, as in Tharna or Argentum," I said. "This is not intended for the work of several men over an indefinite period of time. This was doubtless expected to be used but once, to allow a small force to access a single point."

"We must be past the first ditch by now," said Thurnock.

"I think so," I said.

"Where will the opening be?" asked Clitus.

"Think carefully, my friend," I said.

"One supposes," said he, "between the inner ditch and the camp, close to the inner ditch, to shorten the tunnel."

"It must be farther away," said Thurnock. "From the walls of Mytilene we saw no evidence of digging."

"There you have the matter, my friends," I said. "What would satisfy the desiderata of concealment and the shortest tunnel?"

"The inner ditch," said Thurnock, "where digging and the removal of dirt might take place unseen."

"I think so," I said. "Too, the inner ditch is a more secure location, more so than the outer ditch, one easier to defend, lest an excursion take place from within the walls of Mytilene."

"True," said Thurnock.

"In any event," I said, "we shall soon know."

"Shutter the dark lanterns," I whispered.

I slid shut the panel on my own lamp, and this action was copied, one by one, for several lanterns behind me, the tunnel progressively growing darker and darker. There are beasts, such as the sleen, which can see in situations in which a human being could see nothing, situations in which a human being would find itself in pitch blackness. On the other hand, if there is no light whatsoever, then, of course, as in certain caves, even the sleen would be unable to see.

"Be silent," I whispered. "Ahead, there are voices."

I proceeded in great stealth, and the voices, though soft, became louder and louder. In a few moments I saw the edging of the tunnel, that rimmed in a dim light, apparently that of a small tharlarion-oil lamp outside, and to the right. I arrested my progress and those behind me did the same. Beyond the opening of the tunnel I could see what seemed a wide trench.

From the voices I did not think there were more than two or three men in the vicinity of the tunnel opening.

I coughed, softly.

"I heard something," said one of the voices.

I coughed, again.

"It is our fellows," said one of the men, "returned from Myt-ilene."

I stood back a bit in the tunnel, in the shadows.

"How are things in Mytilene?" asked one of the men.

"Splendid," I said.

"Excellent," he said.

"What have you heard?" I asked.

"Reports differ," he said. "One hears, on the one hand, from one fellow lost from his unit, that the city is taken and the towns-folk are being put to the sword, man, woman, and child, and, from another, similarly somehow separated from his fellows, that something is amiss, possibly muchly so."

"I am ready to come forth," I said. "I am ready to be chal-lenged."

"What are you talking about?" one of three men asked, for there were three.

"Surely I am expected to give the watchword for the night," I said.

"There is no watchword," said a second man.

"Does it not seem as if there should be?" I said.

"What is a watchword?" asked the first man.

"A password," I said, "a sign, a countersign, that sort of thing."

"None is needed," said a man. "We know our fellows."

"You know us?" I asked.

"Of course," said the first man.

"How do you know we are not of Mytilene itself?" I asked.

"You are in the tunnel, you left through the tunnel, you return through the tunnel," said the third man.

I handed my dark lantern to Thurnock, who was behind me, slightly to my left.

"If things are splendid in Mytilene," I asked, "why should we return through the tunnel?"

"I do not know," said one of the men. "Why?"

"What are you doing here?" I asked.

"Keeping independent looters from the tunnel, who might hope to sneak into Mytilene and seize wealth prior to the general gathering and division of the spoils."

"And have you done so?" I asked.

"Yes," said the first man.

"Well done," I said.

"Were you given a watchword?" asked the first man.

"I give you one now," I said.

"What is that?" asked the second man.

"Trust no one," I said, easing my sword silently from its sheath, emerging from the tunnel, and thrusting the blade to his heart. The first man I caught by the ankle as he tried to climb from the ditch, pulled him back down, and cut him across the back of the neck, swiftly and cleanly, no deeper than necessary, a warrior's stroke. At the same time I was peripherally aware that the third man had drawn his sword and was rushing toward me. I had expected him to run, which would have been his best option, in which case I would pursue him for a pace or two and launch my sword with an overhand hilt cast, hoping, if all went well, to penetrate his back below the left shoulder blade, after which one would hope to draw out the sword, turn the body, and plunge it in again. As it was, my blade, so lightly engaged in my earlier stroke, leapt up and easily parried the savage downward stroke of the mercenary's blade, a fierce, heavy, frenzied stroke which might have cut away the head of a saddle tharlarion. He then backed away, eyes wide. I suspected he knew what was soon to ensue.

"You had your stroke," I said. "You should have run."

"Who are you?" he asked.

"Bosk," I told him. "Bosk, of Port Kar."

He drew back his arm to strike again, a blow he did not live to deliver.

Thurnock, Clitus and the others emerged, one by one, from the shadows, through the tunnel's narrow opening.

Thurnock and Clitus then stood close to me, partly illuminated in the light of the small tharlarion-oil lamp which rested to the right of the tunnel as one might exit the tunnel.

"You know what you are to do," I said.

"It is clear," said Thurnock and Clitus.

"My lamp," I said. "See that you have yours."

"They are with our men," said Thurnock.

I took the dark lamp from Thurnock.

"The clouds part," said Clitus. "The Yellow Moon has risen."

"We must act swiftly," I said.

"We shall do so," said Thurnock.

"I wish you well," I said.

"We wish you well," they said.

* * *

I climbed from the inner ditch, followed by my ten selected men, four swordsmen, four archers, and two men bearing vessels of tharlarion oil and axes, not war axes, but woodsmen's axes. To my right, Thurnock, with his men, was climbing from the ditch, and, to his right, I trusted, so, too, was Clitus, followed by his men.

The three catapults, mighty war engines, were aligned several yards behind the inner ditch, between the ditch and the camp of the mercenaries, a hundred or so yards beyond.

"Ho! Stop!" called a guard.

I had not before realized the size of the catapults, which, with their mounting on heavy wheeled carts, were something like three stories high.

"We come from Mytilene," I announced.

"How goes it at Mytilene?" inquired the guard.

"Well," I said.

"Good," said the guard.

"First slaughter, then gold," said another guard.

"I wish that I were there," said another guard.

"But you are not," I said.

He made no sound when he fell.

Simultaneously my swordsmen attacked the other guards, only two of which managed to clear their weapons from the sheath.

Yet the flashing ring of struck steel was bright under the moon and surely that sound would carry well beyond the catapults, even were it not noticed amongst the distant tents. I heard steel sound, too, to my right, and then farther to my right.

I then began to count, aloud, to eighty Ihn.

My four archers drew, and ignited, from the flaming wicks of unshuttered dark lanterns, one by one, five arrows, each tufted with oil-soaked, shredded cloth, which fiery missiles they launched toward the distant tents. Meanwhile my last two fellows drenched the catapult and its cordage with tharlarion oil, following which they wound back the casting basket and, once it was secured, cut it to pieces.

"Seventy-eight Ihn," I counted, "seventy-nine Ihn, eighty Ihn." Then I said, "Set fire to the catapult." I could already see, far to my right, that the third catapult was afire. "Hurry," I thought to myself, "hurry, Thurnock, get it done." Then I said to my men, "Back to the ditch, back to the tunnel, back to Mytilene!"

I moved away from the catapult at hand, as it seemed, foot by foot, to be painted with fire.

The area about was illuminated. I could hear men crying out near the mercenary camp. Four tents there were already, visibly, afire.

"Go!" I ordered my men, for it seemed they were reluctant to leave without me.

I was about to turn, and make my way to the second catapult, that which had been assigned to Thurnock, when I saw it spring, almost in an instant, into flame.

"Well done, mighty fellow," I thought. Clitus, I supposed, must be at the ditch by now.

"Go!" I ordered my men again, angrily.

They then hurried away.

Three catapults were burning.

I looked up.

The Yellow Moon was now well in the sky.

In the distance, now, several tents were afire. Silhouetted against the light I could make out numbers of small figures rushing about, striking tents, carrying water.

Mercenaries, it seemed, as I had expected, were more interested in preserving their goods than in rushing off, possibly at the risk of their lives, to investigate what might be amiss with ponderous siege equipment.

I stood, for a time, looking back across the field, at the many burning tents.

I hoped my stratagem would prove fruitful, that of bringing about a scaling attack on Mytilene, which presumably would be unsuccessful and inflict heavy losses on the enemy, losses which mercenaries would be unlikely to accept with equanimity. Their leadership's recourse to siege engines, that walls might be demolished, and mining, that the town might be taken from within, both suggested that scaling, which in many cases, at least where larger numbers were involved, would have been a commander's first choice, was here an undesired alternative, something more in the nature of a last resort. Yet, assuming the unwillingness of the enemy's leadership to maintain a lengthy siege, it seemed he would have little choice now but to order a scaling attack, despite the risks involved. Certainly he would not wish to lose time and expend resources indefinitely at Mytilene when his efforts might be more lucratively applied elsewhere. It had doubtless been his hope to take the town by surprise and sack it within two or three days at most, which hope, one notes, had been disappointed.

I then turned about and made my way back to the ditch and tunnel, to return to Mytilene.

CHAPTER FORTY-FOUR

Attacks Diminish; Unrest in the Enemy Camp; The Most Dangerous Enemy

I, with two others, with the long, stout forked stick, caught an upright of the ladder and thrust it back, several feet, where it wavered, and then tipped backward, and men, crying out, leapt free or fell backward.

When an attacker climbs a ladder, he is, in a sense, not only precariously vulnerable, with narrow footing, clinging to the ladder, and managing a weapon, or shield, but alone. If the wall were high, there might be fifteen or twenty men behind him on the ladder, but he would still be alone, at the top of the ladder. The first man on the ladder is always alone. The walls of Mytilene, a town on Chios, were far from the high, thick walls of an Ar or Turia, but the dangers and principles of this form of warfare were quite similar. The defenders not only have height and can strike both downward and horizontally, and are protected by the wall, but they can fight side by side. The climber may be frustrated by one defender alone, but, commonly, will encounter two or three. In this way, a single defender, or two or three, is a match for as many as the besiegers can place on a single ladder. It is similar to defending a bridge or narrow pass, in which a single man, or a handful of men, may slow or stop the advance of far greater numbers, save that the defender of the wall has the additional advantage of, so to speak, a higher ground. Walls reduce the advantage of numbers. Let us suppose the besiegers outnumber the defenders ten to one. Let us suppose the besiegers have ten men on each of ten ladders. At the top of the ladder, one attacker, at a considerable disadvantage, given his position, might encounter, say, one defender. In this way, one attacker, at one time, would meet one defender, with the attacker, given his position, at a serious disadvantage. Thus, the advantages of what might prove to be overwhelming numbers in the field are likely to be nullified at the wall. Indeed, if one had two defenders to one attacker hoping to scale the wall, at one time, the defenders would at that point, the point of military interest, outnumber the attackers two to one. These simple facts were lost on no one, particularly mercenaries. It is no wonder that towns and cities are seldom overcome, save by treachery, subornation, or subterfuge.

The trident of Clitus darted forth, one prong entering a throat. His target, arterial blood bursting forth, tried to hold to the ladder, but, a moment later, lost its grip, and fell, forcing two others, looking up, then half blinded with blood, from the ladder.

Arrows, too, might be fired, largely with impunity, given the crenellations of the parapet, picking targets as they might present themselves, often mercenaries trying to advance ladders to the walls. In this way many ladders never reached the walls, sometimes because enough of their bearers were killed or wounded, or, more often, because many men, after a time, declined to bear the ladders forward. Twice, from the wall, we saw a mercenary slain by an officer, presumably in connection with some such reluctance or noncompliance, and twice we saw the officer die; in one case, men gathered about him, closer and closer, despite his protests, and, later, when the men dispersed, the officer's bloodied body lay behind, crumpled and inert; in the other case, the officer was simply cut down from behind by one man, while others looked on.

Far to the right I heard a wild, eerie scream where a large bucket of flaming pitch, by means of its socketed rods, was tipped over the parapet.

Near me, Thurnock fitted another arrow to his string.

"The wall holds," I said.

"It is like shooting penned verr," he said.

"Yet," I said, "I would have more skilled archers, such as you and your caste brother and friend, Aktis."

"He is not here," said Thurnock.

"Do not think ill of him," I said. "His Home Stone is not that of Mytilene."

"Nor is yours or mine," said Thurnock.

I was silent.

"He fled," said Thurnock.

"'Withdrew'," I suggested.

A citizen passed us on the narrow parapet, carrying a basket filled with chips of wood, minor kindling, fuel for braziers set intermittently along the parapet, from which protruded the handles of irons. These irons, red-hot, were used in repulsing attackers. These irons, more commonly used for driving animals and criminals onto the sands of arenas in large cities, such as Ar, were formidable defensive weapons, thrust into the faces, eyes, and bodies of men trying to climb over the wall onto the parapet. These devices, together with war torches, torches mounted in the sockets of thrusting poles, proved their worth in battle. War torches, for example, last night, not only engaged climbers but illuminated targets. Too, the sight of war torches and irons, particularly at night, the torches blazing and the irons bristling with heat, glowing in the darkness, have little difficulty in convincing an enemy of possible dangers likely to attend his proposed assault, the memories of which will persist later, indefinitely, even in daylight. Fear of a weapon, as it is said, sharpens its edge.

"Attention subsides," said Thurnock.

"For a time," I said. "Waves come and waves go."

"I think the tide is going out," said Thurnock.

"It may return," I said.

"Were it water, yes," said Thurnock, "as blood, I think not."

"I expect one last attack," I said.

"I do not think it will be whole-hearted," said Thurnock. "Men will kill for gold, but few will die for it."

"Recall the meeting before the tents," I said.

"Exactly," said Thurnock.

I suspect that the ruses of 'pretended traitors' and 'seeming weaknesses' had done much to dishearten the mercenaries. Doubtless an account of such episodes had reached even to the command tents of the enemy, and even to the command cabins of the corsair fleet. As most mercenaries fight for loot and pay, their allegiance is likely to be less to the cause of their lord than to his purse. Similarly, they prefer to enter a town or city, whenever possible, by means of a surreptitiously opened gate or a deliberately abandoned parapet than by a storming of stoutly defended walls and a fighting of their way across ditches filled with their fallen fellows. Such things being the case, and their conviction, at least initially, that they were dealing with foes which need

not be taken seriously, not formidable foes, but only with unpre-
pared and naive townsfolk, led them to make mistakes which they
would be unlikely to have committed at the walls and gates of
cities. A supposed defender casts messages down from the wall
at night, offering treason for sale, willing to arrange the opening
of a gate, if a dangling basket will be filled with gold. The gold is
provided and the gate, as anticipated, is opened but, as was not
made clear in the arrangement, is swiftly closed, as well, trapping
intruders within. Those who buy treason may not understand the
treason they have purchased, treason to the defenders or treason
to the attackers. Similarly, it is not always wise to avail oneself of
ladders of rope surreptitiously lowered from walls. Such conve-
niences may not be the gift of traitors. A parapet flooring at that
point may be contrived to collapse, dropping visitors to the rubble below where townsfolk are waiting with their clubs and axes.
Too, the enemy soon became wary of 'seeming weaknesses' as too
often, in such locations, defenders proved to be the most numerous and best prepared. As a consequence of such lethal hoaxes
the enemy's audacity was soon diminished, with the result that
he sometimes failed to exploit opportunities that might have been
much to his advantage. One must number, as is well known, deceit
and misinformation amongst the tools of war.

"Behold," said Thurnock, "Thrasymedes approaches."

"Tal," said Thrasymedes, in a work tunic, his double-bladed
ax slung across his back.

"Tal," we responded.

"Do not stand quietly before the crenellation," said Thurnock.
"Quarrels carry easily from the first ditch."

Thrasymedes stepped back from the opening.

At the edge of the opening was a short, diagonal gouge in the
stone, bright and stark against the otherwise well-weathered surface.

"How stands Mytilene?" I asked.

"We must ration supplies more closely," said Thrasymedes.
"How holds the wall?"

"Attacks grow infrequent," said Thurnock. "I fear the enemy
grows weary of dying."

"I expect one last attack," I said.

"Why just one last attack?" asked Thrasymedes.

"This morning, in the Builder's Glass," I said, "we saw a large
number of mercenaries congregated about the high tents in the
distance. The large number suggests unrest."

"It is a delegation, of sorts?" asked Thrasymedes.

"If so," I said, "in no normal sense. It does not appear organized; it seems no small, appointed group conveying an entreaty or petition to leaders, at least to those on shore, but something more spontaneous and popular in nature."

"Mutiny?" asked Thrasymedes.

"Would that it were," I said. "But I think that unlikely."

"We saw no burning tents, no stormed redoubts, no impaled officers," said Thurnock.

"Nor is it likely we will," I said.

"How so?" asked Thurnock.

"View the harbor," I said. "What do you see?"

"Nothing," said Thurnock. "Only the remains of the ships, scuttled and burned, when the corsairs first attacked."

"And that is why," I said, "a mutiny is unlikely."

"How so?" asked Thurnock.

"The seven ships of the corsairs left the harbor last night, and are now some distance offshore."

"So?" asked Thurnock.

"Clearly," I said, "a mutiny was feared. Thus, supplies and transport, removed from the harbor, could not be seized by the mercenaries. Moreover, should a mutiny be mounted, the corsair ships need only withdraw, leaving the mercenaries stranded on Chios."

"And some of their own officers," said Thurnock.

"I do not think that would be of great concern to Archelaos," I said.

"But surely the minions of Archelaos are unwilling to return to Sybaris empty handed," said Thurnock.

"I would not envy them, did they dare to do so," I said.

"I would we had a spy in the enemy camp," said Thrasymedes.

"But we do not," said Thurnock.

"In a sense, we do," I said, "the glass of the Builders. We noted that violence did not ensue upon the visit to the tents of the corsairs' land command. Thus, mutiny is not in the immediate offing. Second, the meeting did not take long. That suggests that some sort of obvious compromise was reached. The most obvious compromise would be one in which the command would manage to save face, seeming to have preserved power and surrendered nothing, while the mercenaries would, in effect, achieve their own aim, the aim of the most loot with the least possible risk."

"What then ensues?" asked Thrasymedes.

"A token attack," I said, "a nominal attack, with much beating of drums, a great blasting of war horns, and a bold brandishing of gleaming standards."

"But we must be ready," said Thrasymedes, "should the attack be massive, vigorous, and desperate."

"Of course," I said. "An enemy which appears reluctant, dispirited, and weary may not, no more than a clever swordsman, be so."

"I shall return to my post," said Thrasymedes.

"Hold the wall," I said.

"Hold the wall," he said.

"Thrasymedes," I said.

"Yes?" said he, turning about.

"The enemy is patient," I said, "and can be supplied by sea."

"I know," he said.

"If the attacks cease," I said, "you know what then begins."

"The end," he said.

"Did not the end begin with the first day of the siege?" asked Thurnock.

"Forgo despondency," I said. "One beginning is not another beginning; one end is not another end."

"I see no hope," said Thrasymedes. "Supplies are short, the town is twice invested; already we have endured several days of siege; how many more can we stand?"

"Do not feed too eagerly on the bitterness of despair," I said. "Leave that indulgence to the enemy."

"I see no alternative," said Thrasymedes.

"Then look further," I said.

"Surely we can speak honestly amongst ourselves," said Thrasymedes.

"Do not be your own foe," I said. "What more dangerous enemy could you face? Who but yourself could be your most dangerous enemy? He who will defeat himself does not deserve a sword."

"Mine is not the scarlet caste," he said. "My codes do not oblige me to courage, or its semblance."

"He who defeats himself," I said, "regardless of caste, dishonors his Home Stone, and he who dishonors his Home Stone has no Home Stone."

"We will, of course, fight to the end," he said.

"Or the beginning," I said.

"I wish you well," said Thrasymedes.

"I have not heard that Tarchon, the lutist, and traitor, has been found," I said.

"He has not been found," said Thrasymedes. "I do not think he is any longer within our walls."

"I do not see how he could have escaped," I said.

"An urt could not squeeze free of this place," said Thurnock. "An ost could not do so."

"He has not been found," said Thrasymedes.

"I wish you well," I said.

We then watched Thrasymedes withdraw, move along the parapet, and make his way down a ladder, ax strapped across his back, to the rubble-strewn ground.

"You spoke bravely," said Thurnock.

"Would you have done otherwise?" I asked.

"No," he said.

CHAPTER FORTY-FIVE

The Attack in the Night; A Spy Escapes;
We Take Stock of our Stores; We Confirm Plans;
We Reflect on the Nature of Historiography

I lay alone in the commander's quarters.

It was in one of the houses near that of Tarchon, the lutist, which, like his, perhaps because of its nearness to his, had been spared in the bombardment of heavy blocks of stone. I lay to one side, near a wall, on the ground, in a blanket, my sword within reach. More in the center of the room, rather toward the door, on the bed, I had placed some sacking and bundles of rolled cloth over which I had arranged a blanket. I trusted that, at least in the darkness, it might constitute a plausible semblance of a sleeping figure.

I was having trouble sleeping.

I think this was less from hunger than from something discovered this afternoon. Some small depredations had been made on one of our three storage areas. This diminishment, which was not large, presumably would not have been noticed earlier when supplies had been more plentiful. Thus, it may not have been the first such reduction. Neither Thrasymedes nor I had imposed a punishment for theft as yet, if only because we had not expected to encounter such a problem, not amongst the citizens of Mytilene. A common punishment in such cases is to bind and hood the thief and then beat him to death. It must be a sad thing, I thought, to die for so little as a biscuit or a peeling of sul.

The last attack on the walls of Mytilene had taken place ten days ago. As we had anticipated, the attack had been brief and

light. It seemed to have been more for show than anything. Many
ladders had not even been placed against the walls. Significantly,
the battle horns, pounding drums, and flourishing standards, so
prominent in their thunderous sound and bold array, were not
advanced beyond the outer ditch. War cries, concerned to inspirit
the assailant and intimidate the enemy, were half-hearted, rare,
and isolated. Purpose and aggression seemed feigned.

"They are acting, playing at war," had laughed Thurnock. "I
think they are tired of dying."

"Surely they must know that they are under the eye of their
commanders, behind the inner ditch, equipped with the glass of
the Builders," said a defender, his beard not cut in days, not ten
feet from me.

"Why are their brave commanders not leading them?" asked
Thurnock.

Many of the mercenaries who had passed the outer ditch remained in its vicinity, crouched down, covering themselves with
their large, round shields of leather, rimmed and bossed with
bronze.

"Had we hundreds of spare arrows to flight," said Thurnock,
"they would soon rush back, seeking the cover of the ditch."

"I have never seen warriors so reluctant to engage the enemy,"
I said.

"They are not warriors," said Thurnock. "They are the dregs
of hirelings. They came to feast with impunity, and found a lean,
inhospitable table. They came to seize gold and found iron. They
came to slaughter verr and encountered men."

"The men of Mytilene," I said.

Clearly the mercenaries did not fear decimation. Decimation
is a harsh military punishment, one usually inflicted on troops
which have failed to follow orders, have exhibited cowardice in
the face of the enemy, and such. It can be imposed in a variety
of ways. The troops deemed guilty of insubordination, cowardice, or such are divided into groups, commonly of ten, but sometimes less or more. Most commonly a gambling takes place, with
cards, marked stones, a drawing of straws, and such. The man
who loses in the gambling is then put to death by his fellows.
Commonly this is done with stones or clubs, so that the observing
troops, better armed, can enforce the killing, and kill the entire
group, should the 'guilty group' be recalcitrant or reluctant to
carry out the decimation, which reluctance, incidentally, seldom

occurs. Commonly the majority of the group, say, nine out of ten, rejoicing in their survival are only too happy to finish the matter and return to duty. There is some point to decimation, hideous as it may seem. It is generally regarded as good for discipline. Also, troops which have followed orders and risked their lives in battle are unlikely to view with tolerance or equanimity those who have shirked their duty and thus, quite possibly, put their fellows in greater peril. In some manuals it is recommended that troops should fear their own officers more than the enemy. I have never, personally, found this crude recommendation persuasive. If something is to be feared more than the enemy, I think it should be that one might, in a moment of terror or self-betrayal, fail to do one's duty. Honor, of course, is involved in such matters. The good officer, I think, should be such that, first, men would follow him gladly into a den of larls, and, second, one who, to the best of his ability, makes certain that he never, if it can be avoided, leads his men into a den of larls. The mercenaries, obviously, given the nature of their last 'attack', did not fear decimation. I suspect that their commanders, their paymasters, feared that the attempt to impose so terrifying a stringency on such troops, hireling troops, might have provoked a mutiny.

As we had feared, of course, the failure of their assaults on the town did not result in their withdrawal but rather, in their reconciliation to the possibility of a lengthy siege. We in Mytilene, of course, realized, as the enemy presumably did not, that the siege could not be too lengthy. That was guaranteed by the dwindling supply of our rations.

I was then reminded that some evidence of theft had been discovered this very afternoon. I supposed then that either I or Thrasymedes, or both, should decide upon, and publicize, a sanction pertaining to such behavior. Perhaps, I hoped, it had been a regretted lapse, which would not occur again.

In any event, we had placed a guard on that particular storage area. If supplies should seem to be missing from the other two areas, we could place a guard there as well, but we preferred to keep men free for the walls and gate. Already we were keeping a guard at our end of the tunnel leading to the enemy camp, a guard with a bell which might be sounded at the first hint of an approach through the tunnel.

My senses suddenly became alert, extremely alert.

The sound was tiny, and had perhaps only been imagined.

Had it been the lifting of a latch, a latch I had deliberately left unsecured?

Had I imagined this?

I slipped the blanket to the side.

Had I heard anything?

For moments I thought not.

In war there is a time for audacity and a time for patience, a time to move and a time to remain still.

"It is nothing," I thought.

I considered replacing the blanket.

Instead I reached for my sword, unsheathed, lying beside me.

This time I had detected sounds, soft, tiny encroachments on the silence, cautious, careful, almost inaudible sounds. I smiled to myself. He with whom I was now alone in the room was clearly untrained. The sounds were resultant from the movement of sandals on the wooden floor. Even a novice, climbing the third of the nine steps of blood, aspiring to membership in the Black Caste, would not wear sandals in such a business, but would go barefoot or wrap his feet in rags, his sandals tied about his neck or to his belt.

"Die!" I heard, a fierce whisper, and then there was the sound of a frenzied stabbing and cutting into the materials arranged on the bed, followed almost immediately by an expostulation of rage, frustration, disappointment, and fear as the assailant realized his error and possible jeopardy.

I sprang up. "Hold!" I cried.

There was a sound of abrupt movement, of a falling, a rising, and a dashing toward the door.

"Hold!" I cried again, making my way to the door.

I did not rush through the door, wary as to the possible skill or intelligence of the assailant. He might be just outside the portal, stopped, his flight arrested, waiting for me to rush through, reckless in pursuit, into the blade of his waiting knife.

I remained within the portal. I called out, "Waken! To arms! Intruder! Intruder!"

Within moments I saw the approach of torches and roused, hurrying men.

"Commander?" said a man.

"An attack on my life failed," I said. "The attacker fled. Look about. Seize any who flee or hide. Let every man encountered give a satisfactory account of himself. Bring any who fail to do so before me."

Men turned about.

More torches were brought.

Shouting was heard, and instructions were conveyed to others.

I returned to my room and lit a tharlarion-oil lamp. I lifted the lamp and noted the shredded bedclothes and slashed straw mattress. I then put the lamp on a shelf near the portal, and sat down on the bed, shaken, breathing heavily. I would have preferred to be in action, joining in the hunt for the fugitive, as movement is calming, but I deemed it more important to remain where I was, located so as to coordinate matters and receive reports should they be forthcoming.

Soon I rose up and went to the portal.

I could smell smoke.

The time of the cooking fires was over.

I heard a cry, "Fire!"

Then, from elsewhere, again I hear a cry, "Fire! Fire!"

I left the portal, racing to the gate. It was secure, sealed with its two beams. Men were rushing about in the darkness. There were shouts. I heard no bars ringing from the wall. "Hold your position!" I shouted to a citizen, descending a ladder. He turned about, climbing, returning to the parapet. "Where is the commander?" I heard. "I am here!" I shouted. "By the gate!"

Reports soon began to fly to the gate. I listened, and sometimes I accompanied observers, inspecting points to which I was led. I needed issue no orders, nor would have another, for, in some situations, men respond instantly and appropriately, a time in which there is no time in which to seek instruction or guidance, but only time to act, if that. Thrasymedes and I had distributed Mytilene's common supplies amongst three well-separated storage areas, three lest one or two areas become accessible to enemies during street fighting, should the walls be successfully breached. These three areas, moving from west to east, were what we referred to as the 'Grain Room', the 'Central Room', and the 'Harbor Room'. The 'Grain Room' was farthest from the gate. It was less a room than what had been the basement of a private house, now ceilinged and reinforced with timbers. The 'Central Room' was what was left of the antechamber of the Council Room where I had first addressed Thrasymedes and other members of the Council of Mytilene. It was the 'Central Room' from which had been noted the absence of certain supplies earlier in the day, and at which Thrasymedes and I had, in consequence, reluctantly, placed a guard. The 'Harbor

Room' was a storage area in one of the four warehouses nearest the harbor.

The reports I received were ugly, various, and disconcerting. I shall not report the order in which I received the reports, but rather the nature of the five acts, or attempted acts, reported in what would seem to be the order, or near order, in which they took place. It seemed likely that all the acts, or attempted acts, were the result of the activities of a single individual. The first act was the surprise of, and murder of, the tunnel guard whom Thrasymedes and I had posted at our end of the tunnel, that tunnel which had been opened in the house of Tarchon, that through which mercenaries had sought to steal into the camp and overcome the gate guard, opening the gate to their waiting cohorts, and through which, shortly afterward, I and others had managed to reach the enemy camp and destroy his three monstrous catapults. The accomplishment of this act was a necessary prelude to the other acts, assuming the perpetrator wished to effect an escape. The second and third acts, though the order was unclear, were the placement of a carpet of straw and a candle in both the 'Grain Room' and the 'Harbor Room'. The candles were lit and would soon burn down to the straw, which, when ignited, would set everything within reach afire. The fourth act, an act which failed, was the attempt to treat the 'Central Room' similarly. In this case, however, the would-be arsonist, doubtless to his dismay, was challenged by the guard whom Thrasymedes and I had posted, having earlier in the afternoon become aware of some missing stores. Challenged, the would-be arsonist had feigned confusion in the darkness, pacified the guard, and withdrawn. Later straw and an unlit candle were discovered in the external corridor. At that point, the stranger in the darkness, in his intended fifth act, had made his way to my quarters, where, in fury and terror, he soon realized he had spent his attack not on a living body but on rolls of bundled cloth. We later discovered the body of the slain tunnel guard and the evidence of the killer's exit through the tunnel, within feet of the sunken metal rod, by tapping on which Tarchon had identified the point at which the tunnel might be safely opened.

"It was Tarchon," said Thrasymedes. "He was still within our walls. He was here. He has escaped."

"I take it so," I said.

"The tunnel guard was surprised," said Thrasymedes.

"He did not expect it," I said. "The attack came from an unexpected quarter."

"The killer will inform the enemy of our straits, our shortage of food," said Thrasymedes.

"Doubtless," I said.

"This will hearten the enemy," said Thrasymedes. "He no longer need fear a long siege."

"Nor we a long defense," I said.

"Supplies were already quartered," said Thrasymedes. "And little could be saved from the Grain Room and the Harbor Room."

"You have solicited estimates," I said.

"Night falls," said Thrasymedes. "The vise tightens."

"Twenty days?" I asked.

"Perhaps," said Thrasymedes. "And then little to do but lie still, and hope to sleep, little to hope for other than the strength to climb one last time to the parapet, the strength to once more unsheathe a sword, to lift an ax."

"Let us suppose," I said, "such estimates seem plausible to the enemy, as well."

"I am sure they will seem so," said Thrasymedes, "given the information which will be supplied to them by the killer and arsonist."

"Tarchon," I said.

"Undoubtedly," said Thrasymedes.

"Which information they now have at their disposal," I said.

"I fear so," said Thrasymedes.

"Our plans remain as before," I said.

"We shall not wait until the end," said Thrasymedes, "but, shortly before the end, we shall feast, and then, the next day, go forth in good cheer, go forth, singing, with a strong heart."

"It is better to die as a well-fed larl than a starving verr," I said.

"I am not sure I look forward to that feast," said Thrasymedes.

"Have no fear," I said. "You will be hungry enough then to look forward to a crust of bread at the foot of an impaling pole."

"So let it be," said Thrasymedes, "the feast—then, the following morning, the opening of the gate and the issuing forth."

"Singing?" I asked.

"Why not?" said Thrasymedes.

"When all is lost," I said, "the least one can do is to put a good end to things."

"It would be well to finish with a final, noble gesture," said Thrasymedes. "Such is not alone for the scarlet caste. What Merchant, what Metal Worker, what Peasant, would have it otherwise?"

"Let us do our best," I said, "all of us, to give a good last account of ourselves."

"How will it be represented?" asked Thrasymedes.

"One does not know," I said.

"Our moment of glory," said Thrasymedes, "will never be forgotten; it will be recorded in the annals of war; it will be told in a thousand camps, sung in a thousand taverns, as long as fire burns and men drink."

"Unlikely," I said.

"How so?" he asked.

"Those last to leave the field are those who tell the tales," I said. "It is they who will speak, as they wish, say what they want, or not speak, at all. History is doubtless replete with acts of self-sacrifice and heroism, with last stands and doomed charges, with gestures, valiant, gracious, and noble, of which none have heard or will ever hear."

"But we will know," said Thrasymedes.

"And that is enough," I said.

"Yes," said Thrasymedes, "that is enough."

CHAPTER FORTY-SIX

The Feast; We Reflect Upon Societies; I Will Check the Watch; An Anomaly is Brought to my Attention

"Be careful," I warned Clitus. "Make do with the paga, not spill it on the table."

"The cup moved when I reached for it," said Clitus.

"Only in the last Ahn," I said.

"More meat and cheese, gravy and coarse bread," said Thurnock, reaching across the long table, sweeping bowls and plates toward himself.

"I have not had such a meal in weeks," said Thrasymedes.

"It is at least large," I said. "I doubt that it would meet with the approval of the master chefs of Ar or Turia, or Jad or Telnus."

The great hall of Mytilene, where indoor markets, public meetings, and expositions were often held, had lost a wall and a portion of its roof, but the loose plaster, stone, wood, timbers, rafters, boards, and paneling had all been swept, or carried, aside and five long tables, two of them improvised, were laden with what, compared to the sparse rations of recent date, constituted a banquet, in quantity at least, fit for a Ubar, though, frankly, one of a somewhat modest wealth.

"The goblet moved again," said Clitus.

"Perhaps we could nail it to the table," I suggested.

"But then it would be difficult to drink from," said Clitus.

"It was only a thought," I said. "Tomorrow morning I am sure it will be content to stay where you put it."

"Now there are three goblets," said Clitus.

"Reach for the one in the middle," I said.

Given the nature of this feast, and the grim prospect of the morrow, no women or children were present. The share of the feast allotted to women and children was distributed amongst some four dwellings which had been less damaged in the bombardment of the great catapults. This was not a time amongst men, the time of this banquet, for tenderness, but a time for distraction, for forgetfulness, not a time for regrets and sorrows, but a time for thrusting such things to the side, not a time for farewells and tears but a time for laughing and drinking, for the pounding of tables, the telling of stories, the singing of paga songs, boisterous songs fit for the taverns, in which no free woman may enter. In the morning, surely, there would be time enough for the weeping of women and the uneasy puzzlement of children, understanding little or nothing.

"I think," said Thrasymedes, shaking his head, presumably to clear his vision, "we should not issue forth too early."

"I do not think we would be in a condition to do otherwise," I said.

"Why should verr hasten to the slaughter?" asked Thrasymedes.

"I can think of no good reason," I said.

"We are not verr," said Clitus.

"True," I said.

"Let the butchers beware," said Thurnock, "lest, in their carelessness, it be they who are butchered."

"The wall and gate guards must be soon relieved," I said. "They must have their share of the feast."

"I trust that the new watch can climb the ladders to the parapets," said Clitus slowly, considering his words carefully.

"They will manage," I said, "given perseverance and determination."

"What if the enemy should attack?" asked Thurnock.

"Terror and alarm conduce to sobriety," I reassured hm.

"Tospits!" called Clitus, hailing a nearby table. Shortly thereafter an obliging citizen staggered to our table, and placed a basket of dried tospits before us.

"Thank you," I said.

The bounding urt is fond of dried tospits, men less so.

Still a feast is a feast, or nearly so.

I feared I had had too much to drink.

"A splendid feast," said Clitus, helping himself to a handful of tospits, his behavior forcing me, reluctantly, to reconsider my views of tospits and human beings. The tospit is a yellowish white, bitter fruit. It looks something like a peach, but is usually about the size of a plum. Some people, I knew, liked the bitter taste. Apparently Clitus was one of them. My thoughts drifted back to what some called the Plains of Turia, others the Lands of the Wagon Peoples, faraway and long ago, in the southern hemisphere. Most tospits, I knew, commonly had an uneven number of seeds, except the long-stemmed tospit which commonly has an even number of seeds.

"Yes," said Thurnock, reaching for a pair of tospits, "a splendid feast, though somewhat plain."

I reminded myself that Clitus was of the Fishermen and Thurnock of the Peasants. What do Fishermen and Peasants know of tospits?

"We are missing one thing, surely," said a man.

"Slaves," said another.

"What is a man feast without slaves?" said Thurnock.

It was true that the beauty of slaves, even when scarcely noticed, contributed much to the ambience of a feast.

What true man does not enjoy being humbly served by a beautiful woman, his property, his to do with as he pleases?

"Slaves are worthless," said a man.

"Yes," said another, "but what is more desirable, and precious, than a worthless slave?"

"The women of the towns," said Thurnock, "are richly garmented, arrogant, proud, and spoiled. They look down on those of my caste. We are muchly pleased then when, in one way or another, they fall into our hands. Their soft, easy life is then done. We strip, brand, and collar them. We put them to work in the fields; they hoe and dig; they bear sacks and carry water; they weed and clear land; they scratch out stumps; we turn them into draft beasts, harnessing them to our carts, yoking them to our plows."

"Do you not use them for pleasure?" inquired a citizen.

"Certainly," said Thurnock, "in our blankets and furs, in their kennels, in the mud of tarsk pens, in the furrows of the field, and they will soon beg for our touch."

"Exempt the women of Mytilene," I said. "These women are our allies."

"Of course," said Thurnock.

"Are not the victory feasts of generals, commanders, and Ubars," said a man, "served by the women of the enemy, stripped, branded, and collared, terrified that they might not be found pleasing?"

"It is common practice," I said.

"Why did we not bring Margot, Courtney, and Millicent to Mytilene?" asked Clitus. "They would be in no danger. They would be safe with their branded hides and their locked, neck-encircling collars."

"I feared naval warfare," I said. "Their collars would not protect them from fire or the high, cold waves of Thassa."

"You have solicitude for them," asked Thurnock, "such dishonest, wicked, treacherous beasts?"

"In their collars they cannot be such," I said.

"Still," insisted Thurnock.

"If you wish," I said, "it is irrational to risk the loss of property, particularly when it might have some monetary value, however negligible."

"True," said Thurnock, "why risk the loss of even a vulo, a verr, or tarsk?"

"Females are the slave sex," said a man. "They are never fulfilled until they are collared."

"Beware of saying that before a free woman, particularly one of high caste," I said.

"They know it is true, in their hearts," said a man.

"They are no different from others," said another, "when they are stripped and on their knees, in their collars."

"I know a world," I said, "where women are expected to repudiate themselves, to be pretend men, or neuters, or steriles."

"What world is that?" asked a man.

"One you would doubt exists," I said.

"What sickness is that?" asked Thurnock.

"An improbable malady," said Clitus.

"I cannot believe such things are possible," said Thrasymedes.

"One can do much with prescribing, teaching, and training, with controlling the means of communication and education, with the judicious distribution of praise and blame, with reward and punishment. If power is seized, one may do strange things, twist women into the image of men, twist men into the image of women, in effect, to outlaw biology."

"Who would wish to do so miserable and unnatural a thing?" asked Thrasymedes.

"Some," I said, "the restless and discontented, the miserable and unhappy, those who fear nature and perhaps themselves, those who seek social, political, and economic power by pretending that nature does not exist."

"Even the mighty Tur tree," said a man, "if denied sunlight, minerals, and water, if poisoned, can be stunted and enfeebled."

"Or slain," said another.

"Nature denied does not cease to exist," I said. "It exacts its vengeance in a thousand ways, in plagues of confusion and guilt, in the disordering of society, in the propagation of ignorance, illness, hypocrisy, and hatred."

"Surely no such world can exist," said a man.

"The tyranny of pigmies does not bode well for the strong and healthy," I said. "The suppression of free speech and thought, aside from its implicit claim of infallibility, restricts change and limits progress."

"It would surely seem so," said a man.

"Shackling the mind does little to improve a species," I said, "no more than its charming concomitants, disseminating hatred and instilling guilt."

"I find this hard to believe," said Thurnock, "so egregious a catalog of horrors."

"It is hard to believe," I said.

"What is really going on there?"

"Striving for power," I said.

"'Power'?" asked Thurnock.

"Power," I said, "delicious power, sought secretly."

"The true aim of such things then," said Thurnock, "is hidden?"

"Certainly," I said. "The calculated inculcation and manipulation of values is a subtle technique for seizing power and ruling others."

"I pity so troubled a world," said a man.

"It is far away," I said, "far away."

"Good," said Thurnock.

"It is late," I said. "I shall check the watch."

"I shall gather the relief and follow shortly," said Thurnock.

* * *

The evening was cool, and I wrapped my cloak about myself, and looked about. I hoped the night air would clear my head. It is one thing to look ahead to the morrow, having in view the prospect of victory. It is quite another thing when the likely prospect is defeat. "But better surely," I thought, "to go forth to meet the enemy, with determination and a good heart, be he ever so overwhelming and implacable a foe, than to stay within our walls another four or five days, clinging to life, only to subside in hunger and weakness, to the point where we could mount no more than a token resistance."

I turned toward the gate.

"Commander," I heard.

I stopped.

"Commander," a man said, "an anomaly!"

"What?" I said.

"An arrow," said the man, reaching within his cloak.

"We can use it," I said.

"No," said the man. "There is a strangeness here. It is blunt. It did not strike at the wall. It fell from a height. Others, too, have been found. I do not understand what is going on."

"It is dark," I said, "let me see it."

"See what is fastened to it," said the man.

"A wrapping of oil-soaked rags, not ignited," I asked, "a message?"

"No," he said.

"Let me see it," I said.

He handed me the long shaft.

"Bread," I said, "a piece of bread."

"What does it mean?" asked the man.

"There are others, as well?" I asked.

"Yes, Commander," he said. "What does it mean?"

"It means," I said, "that the siege is over."

CHAPTER FORTY-SEVEN

How the Siege Came to an End

The rising of the Peasants rendered the issuing forth of the men of Mytilene and their allies unnecessary. Within two days, the mercenaries, surrounded and beleaguered, harassed, shut off from the countryside, and sustaining dreadful losses, had withdrawn to the seven ships of the corsair fleet. Initially, in alarm and consternation, surprised by the swarming of peasants, their far camp burned, they had fled to the ground within the inner and outer ditch, taking what refuge they could within a circular shield wall. The hostile Peasantry, naturally, would not, nor would they ever intend to, attack ready infantry in such a position, descending into a steep ditch and trying to fight their way upward and out of such a ditch in the face of ensconced, armored resistance. The mercenaries, on the other hand, in such a position, were effectively pinned in place, denied access to supplies which might otherwise have been seized in the countryside. When contingents of mercenaries would leave their ditched fortress to attack the peasants, they found they could not close with them, for the peasants would withdraw before them, leading them farther from their fellows and isolating them from support, where, soon, ambushed and wearied, surrounded and outnumbered, picked off one by one, few of the would-be attackers could manage to do as little as make their way back to their fellows. Exacerbating the predicament of the mercenaries was that the range of the peasant bow exceeded that of the crossbow, allowing the peasants to, in effect, remain out of range of the shorter, heavier, quarrels while being able to discharge their own weapons with comparative impunity, and the almost indefinite quantity of ammunition at their disposal, arrows borne

less in quivers than bundled into carts. This plenitude of striking force was applied both singly and randomly and, occasionally, in thick volleys, falling like a dark, torrential rain of death.
I, and others, my men and the fighters of Mytilene, from the
town walls, watched the mercenaries' harried retreat to the sea,
through a corridor flanked by lifted shields. The corsair ships
did not risk coming within range of the peasant archery but
sent forth a small fleet of longboats to ferry their mercenaries to
the safety of the ships. These boats were few and overcrowded,
and largely exposed to arrow fire. We saw two swamped and
overturned. Men killed one another for a place on the thwarts.
Several cast aside helmets, weapons, and shields and tried to
swim to the waiting ships. Several may have drowned but others
were clearly drawn under the water, the churning and frenzy
in the water apparently having attracted marine predators, presumably sharks or the snakelike sea tharlarion. Many others,
hundreds, backs to the sea, shields lifted, must stay indefinitely
in place, trusting to the return of the crews of the longboats, few
of which, it seemed, cared, for their fees, to hazard a second trip.
Some four Ahn after the beginning of the evacuation, the beach
was empty save for bodies and equipment. The last survivors,
say some two or three hundred men, crowded together, abandoned by the longboats, were set upon by irate peasants, armed
with staves and axes. At that point I had turned away.

I descended from the parapet and made my way to the town
gate, which had now been opened, to allow the ingress of carts,
filled with produce. In time, I was joined by several men, Clitus,
Thurnock, Thrasymedes of Mytilene, and others.

"Commander," said a man, "the leader of the Peasant coalition
would speak with you."

"He is a man called Aktis," I said.

"How did you know?" asked the man.

"Sometimes," I said, "good fortune attends one's conjectures."

"He is with another, one called Xanthos," said the man.

"The son of Seleukos, of the Island of Seleukos," I said.

"You know such a man?" asked the man.

"And proud to do so," I said.

"Shall I bring them to you?" asked the man.

"No," I said, "bring me to them."

"I shall accompany you," said Thurnock.

"And I," said Clitus and Thrasymedes.

"My dear Thrasymedes," I said, "it seems Mytilene owes much to the simple, rude, benighted, ignorant Peasantry."

"Let us drink with them," said Thrasymedes, "let us sing and feast together. The town needs the land and the land needs the town."

"You should now think twice," I said, "before you tell Peasant jokes."

"Only if they think at least once before telling town jokes," he said.

"Never," said Thurnock. "We should lose too many of our merriest jests."

Another cart filled with food trundled past.

"One cannot but respect one with the great bow," said Clitus.

"I suspect that even Cos will learn to do so," I said.

"It had better," growled Thurnock.

"It seems," I said, "that Aktis did not desert."

"Of course not," said Thurnock. "I knew he would not do so."

"Oh?" I said.

"Certainly," said Thurnock.

"How did you know?" I asked.

"He is of the land, the Peasantry," said Thurnock.

"This way," said the man who had informed us of the presence of Aktis and Xanthos.

CHAPTER FORTY-EIGHT

The Field of Battle; The Feasting of Jards; Tarchon; The Lyre; We Prepare to Leave the Vicinity of Mytilene

Three days later a small party, of which I was one, examined the battleground about Mytilene. One could still smell smoke from the burned tents of the enemy. The bodies of the dead mercenaries, gathered together by men wearing scarves about their faces, had been, or would be, stripped, placed in small boats, and carried out to sea, to be disposed of in locales soon to teem with welcoming sea life. In this way, they need not be burned in gigantic pyres, costly of valuable timber, or, with a sorry expenditure of time and effort, buried in nearby, perhaps revered, land, certainly not within the *pomerium* of Mytilene. The wealth, valuables, coins, rings, jewelries, garments, cloaks, weapons, helmets, shields, and such, of the slain enemy would be considerable. This would be divided amongst representatives of the dozens of villages, some from as far away as Thera and Daphna, who had participated in the liberation of Mytilene. The tunnel leading from the enemy camp beneath the town walls, opening in what had been the dwelling of Tarchon, and the two ditches about Mytilene, the inner and outer ditch, would be gradually filled. The disrupted turf, seeded, refreshed by rain, would gradually renew itself as had the fairgrounds near the town.

"Some feared you had deserted," I said to Aktis.

"Understanding the obvious peril of Mytilene, its isolation and subjection to siege, I hoped to rally relief," said Aktis. "Accordingly, I returned to the ruins of Nicosia, where I encountered

Xanthos, and others. Given the fair, that seemed the best point from which to initiate an insurgence. The attack on Nicosia and other villages had already produced outrage, and made clear the menace posed by organized, unchecked marauders. Danger was obvious, distant perhaps but real. Who could be safe? Who could be sure the storm would not fall upon them? Doubtless probabilities suggested that one's own village would be spared, but what if it were not? Xanthos and I made our way to several villages, and soon, abetted by others recruited along the way to our cause, our message, our summons and solicitation, was conveyed to many other villages. Two incidents, considered, helped to stir thought, one, the destruction of the large, prosperous village of Seleukos on Thera itself made it clear that little, if anything, might deter the marauders. What could stand against their skills and numbers? Desperation, ugly and gloomy, fell like unlit, unwelcome night. Did not shadows encroach even upon Home Stones? And Cos remained inert, indifferent, disinterested, perhaps even intimidated by the marauders, perhaps even in league with them. Who could help villagers but villagers themselves? To whom else could they look? Then, second, a startling torch, an unexpected, glad victory, suddenly flamed in the darkness. The battle of Zeuxis proved the marauders could be not only withstood but defeated. No longer were they deemed invincible. Too, by this time, the great bow, if only in stealth, was becoming known in the villages. Had such a weapon not proved its formidable worth at Zeuxis? Might not it do so again?"

"Yet," I said, "villages are proud, muchly autonomous, and seldom do they see beyond their own fields."

"We expected no succor from Peasants," said Thrasymedes. "They are tied to the cycles of the year and the seasons of custom. They are like the mighty Tur tree, rooted in place, slow to grow, and slow to change."

"Attend to the ancient myths, the stories told about the fire pits," said Thurnock. "Should the Tur tree anger and draw up its roots, it is much to be feared."

"An attack on one village is an attack on no single village alone," said Aktis. "It is an attack on the caste itself. To attack one Home Stone is to attack all Home Stones. To defend one Home Stone is to defend all Home Stones."

"Peasants have arisen from time to time," said Thurnock. "More than one town has awakened in terror to discover a wooden shoe nailed to its gate."

"But at Mytilene," said Thrasymedes, "it was otherwise. The fields came to the walls not with rage and fire, but with hope and bread."

"It required will, organization, planning, training, arrows, hundreds of arrows, and supplies," I said.

"Much had preceded our message," said Aktis. "The lessons of the fair and Nicosia were better understood than we realized."

"Victory is ours," said a man.

"Not while corsairs rule the sea," I said.

"The ships of the corsairs have withdrawn," said Clitus, shading his eyes, looking out to sea.

"We know only," I said, "that they are not now seen."

"Surely they are bound for Sybaris," said Clitus.

"Let us hope so," I said.

"After the rout of Mytilene, why should they linger?" asked Clitus.

"Why, indeed?" I asked.

I might mention that I had taken my men out of Mytilene, and bivouacked them a pasang west of her walls. I had done this so that our departure for the *Dorna* and *Tesephone*, both waiting in their secret hiding place, a departure which was imminent, might be accomplished, if not in stealth, at least discreetly. Men talk, and even worthy men may be careless.

"Commander!" said a man. "Behold!"

"I see," I said.

"What is it?" asked Thrasymedes.

"You need not look upon it," I said.

For an instant I had not been sure what it was.

"Foul," said Thrasymedes.

"I fear," I said, "it was to have been expected."

At first I had taken it to be a stunted tree, with thick, uneven branches, then a trophy pole. But it was neither.

It had been put in place several yards beyond where had stood the remoter tents of the enemy. One supposes they did not wish to have such a thing within their camp, a camp now little more than refuse and ashes.

When a battle has been successfully fought, and the enemy driven from the field, it is not uncommon for the victors to mark the field in such a way as to commemorate their victory. If a tree is available, suitably situated, and of an appropriate size, it is cleared of bark, leaves, and smaller branches, and then used as a mount or frame on which to hang paraphernalia proclaiming the victory, usually helmets, shields, insignia, banners, standards, broken weapons, and such, taken from the enemy. Such displays, if not destroyed, stolen, or removed, sometimes in later battles, for certain places and fields, given their location and favorable properties, have been the scene of more than one battle, can remain in place for years, even generations, until wind, rain, ageing, heat, cold, and rust have their way. If a tree is not available, a trimmed, barkless pole may serve the same purpose, which is then denominated a trophy pole.

What was before us, however, as noted, was not such an object.

When we approached the object, a clutter of small birds, scavenging jards, took flight with a reproachful burst of wings. Earlier there had been such clusters of jards elsewhere on the field, as well, from a distance looking like restless, crawling heaps.

The thin necks of the small, hook-billed birds were bare, lacking feathers. This had perhaps to do with minimizing contamination, which might be incurred in their feedings.

"He was a citizen of Mytilene," I said.

"He betrayed his Home Stone," said Thrasymedes.

The naked body, now much fed upon by jards, had been impaled horizontally on the short, thick pole, which was no more than some five feet in height. The body had been placed on the sharpened point of the pole, facing upward, and then dragged downward, worked downward, wrenched downward, slowly, bit by bit, perhaps by four men, until the pole's sharpened terminus, red with blood, now a dried stain, was visible, protruding some eighteen inches above the abdomen. The eyes, what was left of them, were still open, as though staring wildly at the sky.

At the foot of the pole a lyre lay broken, its strings cut.

"It is an ugly way to die," I said.

"An appropriate way for one such as he," said Thrasymedes.

"It must have been extremely painful," I said.

"Let us hope so," said Thrasymedes.

"At least," I said, "it would have been relatively quick."

"Unfortunately," he said.

"Do you hate him so?" I asked.

"Yes," said Thrasymedes.

"It is true that he was a murderer," I said. I recalled the guard at the tunnel opening, whom he had killed.

"He betrayed his Home Stone," said Thrasymedes.

I shuddered, more aware at that moment than ever of the ways of Gor. I recalled another who had betrayed her Home Stone.

"Shall I close the eyes?" I asked.

"I will do so," said Thrasymedes.

I watched him perform this action.

"Why should such eyes be open?" asked Thrasymedes. "They are unworthy to look upon the glory of the sky, even in death."

He then, with one foot, thrust the pole down. The body half slid from it.

"He was of Mytilene," I said. "Some wood can be found, enough for a small pyre."

Thrasymedes turned to the side and called to two men who, their faces half covered with scarves, had been clearing the field of the dead.

"Take this carrion," said Thrasymedes, "put it in a cart, take it to the beach, get it on a boat, and see that it is disposed of at sea."

I lifted the broken lyre from the ground.

"He was skilled at the lyre," I said.

"He betrayed his Home Stone," said Thrasymedes.

I watched while the two men wearing scarves worked Tarchon's body free of the pole. It was then added to others on a small cart. Shortly thereafter, the cart, drawn by the two men, left for the beach.

"Why would Tarchon have been killed by the mercenaries?" I asked. "He served them well, by obtaining access to Mytilene by means of the tunnel, and doubtless, too, by providing them with information as to the straits to which we were subjected."

"One may speculate," said Thrasymedes. "The affair of the tunnel turned out badly for the mercenaries, costing them men and, soon, by means of the same tunnel, in your attack, the loss of the great catapults. On whose side was Tarchon? How could the mercenaries know? Might he not be a patriot of Mytilene? He doubtless told them of our shortage of supplies, but their scouts doubtless, too, reported the sounds of singing and feasting from within the walls. Too, the same night, the Peasants closed in, merciless and determined. Had Tarchon known of the gathering and rising of the Peasants? Was he trying to falsely inspirit the mercenaries, lulling them into patience and quiescence, holding them in place to be slaughtered?"

"Interesting," I said.

"I suspect that they, under the circumstances, as matters unfolded, viewed him as a spy for Mytilene, and, accordingly, to his dismay and horror, treated him as such."

"War," I said, "has not only its secrets, but its surprises and ironies."

"Too," said Thrasymedes, "who, mercenary or not, blames themselves for anything? What is more common than to blame others for one's own faults, failures, and lacks? Why assign blame to oneself when it is so easy to ascribe it to others?"

"I fear it is common," I said.

"And the hapless Tarchon was at hand, to be deemed responsible, at the mercy of lawless, desperate, frightened, imperiled men."

"Such would not have been good fortune for him," I said.

"He betrayed his Home Stone," said Thrasymedes.

I turned the lyre about in my hands, its frame broken, its strings dangling.

"Give it to me," said Thrasymedes. "It did not betray a Home Stone. I shall wrap it in soft folds of scented silk and have it burned in honor."

I handed the instrument to him.

In some cities it is against the law to deface a scroll or damage a musical instrument. That is, I suppose, because Goreans respect such things.

"How shamed it was, to have been touched by a hand so unworthy of its strings," said Thrasymedes.

"I do not think that Tarchon would have injured the instrument," I said. "He took it with him in his escape. He loved it, if not his town, his Home Stone."

"Mercenaries, in their vengeance, in their haste and fury," said Thrasymedes, "did this dreadful thing."

I did not doubt that mercenaries had been guilty of destroying the instrument, probably before Tarchon's very eyes, before his impalement.

"It was innocent," said Thrasymedes. "No longer will it whisper, cry, and sing."

I was silent.

A musical instrument had been destroyed.

Goreans are unlikely to forget such things.

Many Goreans, as I understand it, though such things are seldom made explicit, being more taken for granted than pro-

claimed, more understood than expressed, have a view of the
world and reality which might be found surprising by the average individual of Earth. It is difficult to find words for this as
the feelings and attitudes tend to be pervasive, or nearly so,
and thus tend to be so obvious or familiar that they are seldom
articulated or named, particularly by the Goreans themselves.
One sees and breathes, but seldom does one notice or state that
one is seeing or breathing. In any event, I can do little more than
gesture or point at such things, with some clumsy, dull, hap-
lessly inadequate words. It does not occur to the average Gorean,
for example, that nature is divided into two distinct substances
which somehow, incredibly, one in space, the other not, inter-
act with, and affect, one another. Nature is one, it is thought,
and worthy of existence. The world is what it seems to be, one
place, its own place, mighty and glorious. Desire, hope, fear, and
thought, though not measured in pounds or centimeters, are no
less real than wind and grass, than mountains and stars. If the
world is one, then the Gorean, as part of the world, is one with
the world. He is not estranged from it, but is its bred and living kin. His relationship to his encountered reality is thus likely
to be far more personal than that of the average individual of
Earth. He is likely to see nature not as alien and different, but as
congenial and animate. Do not tides come and go, and seasons
change; does not water rush over rocks, and snow fall and melt;
does not night follow day and day night? It is not unusual for a
woodsman to ask forgiveness of the tree he intends to fell; or a
hunter to respect the animal he hunts, or which hunts him. Such
feelings and attitudes may be entertained, as well, even toward
objects, particularly those with whom a close or personal relationship may be sustained. "Serve me well," says the assassin to
his dagger, the woodsman to his ax, the fisherman to his net and
trident, the scribe to his pen, the warrior to his sword.

I looked upon the broken lyre in the grasp of Thrasymedes,
and, oddly, felt sorrow, and that a wrong had been done.

"It is only an artifact," I reminded myself, "only a meaningless
object."

"We are done here," said Thurnock. "Let us go to our camp,
gather our men, trek to our ships, and put to sea. There is dark
work to be done, the work of blades, work to which we must address ourselves in Sybaris."

"I fear so," I said.

"Tab and Sakim will be ready," said Clitus. "The *Dorna* and *Tesephone* wait, concealed to the south."

I had not ordered them to the harbor at Mytilene, for I feared, despite our victory, that the harbor might yet be under surveillance.

"The voyage will be uneventful," said Thrasymedes.

"I shall hope so," I said.

"The horizon is clear," said Thrasymedes.

"What," I wondered, "might be beyond the horizon."

"Mytilene," said Thrasymedes, "will be forever grateful to you, your men and the noble Peasantry which wreaked such slaughter amongst the cohorts of the hateful Bosk of Port Kar."

"Thank, too," I said, "yourself, the brave and august Thrasymedes, Administrator in Mytilene, and the noble citizens of Mytilene who withstood the terrors of a long and hard-pressed siege, even the harrows of incipient starvation."

"It is done," said Thrasymedes.

"I wish you well," I said.

"I wish you well," he said.

We grasped wrists, in the fashion of the sea.

Thrasymedes then took his leave, carrying the broken lyre, wrapped within his robe.

"Let us go to our men, gather them, and march to the ships," said Thurnock. "The sooner we put to sea the better."

"No," I said. "We will not put to sea until dark."

Thurnock was silent, and, I fear, troubled.

Commonly Gorean mariners stay within sight of land and beach their vessels at night. Few captains and crews care to be at sea in the darkness.

"Uneasy is the ship that dares the night," said Thurnock.

"I trust that the enemy will be of that opinion," I said.

"The corsairs have withdrawn," said Thurnock.

"I shall hope so," I said. "I do not know so."

"Defeated, sustaining dreadful losses, driven from the field," said he, "they flee to Sybaris, to lick their wounds, perhaps even to disband in humiliation and chagrin."

"We shall hope so," I said.

"We owe much to Xanthos and you," said Thurnock, turning to Aktis.

"More than we can ever repay," I said.

"It is nothing," said Aktis.

"Xanthos is already returning to the Isle of Seleukos," said Thurnock.

"He is losing little time," said Clitus.

"He is anxious to rejoin his Companion," said Thurnock.

"Cuy," I said.

"I believe that is correct," said Thurnock. "But how would you know?"

"Perhaps he mentioned the name," I said.

"That must be it," said Thurnock.

"What of you, Aktis?" asked Clitus. "I suppose that you are now going to return to Nicosia."

"Not yet," said Aktis. "I have business in Sybaris."

"We all do," said Thurnock.

"We will go now to our camp," I said. "Then, after dark, we will join Tab and Sakim at the *Dorna* and *Tesephone*."

"And thence," said Thurnock, "to the Cove of Harpalos, and then to Sybaris."

"None will see us leave," said Clitus.

"We cannot be sure of that," I said.

"True," said Clitus. "A spy might have been left behind, in the guise of a Peasant."

"No," said Thurnock. "Each must have a village, and each must be recognized by his fellow villagers."

"But there could be other spies," I said, "landed pasangs north and south of the harbor at Mytilene, each with a caged vulo."

"It is possible," said Thurnock.

"The horizon is still clear," said Clitus, shading his eyes, looking out to sea.

"The corsairs' living island, the Brigand Island, may be about," I said, "too low to see, with cots of vulos which will home to at least the flagship of the corsair fleet."

"But we will leave at night," said Clitus.

"And be visible by day," I said.

"Surely the corsair fleet has fled," said Clitus.

"Were I Admiral of that fleet," I said, "shamed and disgruntled, eager for blood, aching for vengeance, with seven fine ships, not one of which has borne a scratch, I would not have done so."

CHAPTER FORTY-NINE

The Beach; A Rendezvous is Not Kept;
Tab and Sakim Return; The Horizon is Clear

I closed the panel of the dark lantern.

"Hold," I whispered.

"What is wrong?" asked Thurnock, softly.

"Perhaps nothing," I said.

"You hesitate," he said.

"Why have we not been challenged?" I asked.

We had moved about the side of the rise above the beach.

I had kept all but a handful of men back. The column behind, at a horizontal movement of the opened lamp, would break ranks, fanning out, forming an extended skirmish line. A forward circular movement betokened advance, a reverse circular movement withdrawal. The closing of the lamp's panel signified halt. The panels of the dark lamp are adjustable in a variety of ways, by means of which the beam may be controlled, reduced or enlarged, shielded on one side or the other. Similarly, by means of the opening and shutting of a single panel, and the manner in which this is done, light being shown for a shorter or longer time, these changes corresponding to letters, messages may be transmitted, even over considerable distances.

"Perhaps," said Thurnock, "there are none to do so."

"I fear you are right," I said.

"May I reconnoiter?" asked Aktis.

"Wait," I said.

In a few moments the yellow moon emerged from the clouds and, briefly, illuminated the bare, broad half-circle of the beach.

"The beach is empty," said Thurnock. "The *Dorna* and *Tesephone* are gone!"

I unshuttered the dark lamp, and waved it horizontally four times, and then rotated it forward, slowly, three times.

In a few Ehn we had descended to the beach.

"The beach is now secured?" I asked Aktis.

"And the local area," said Aktis.

"What has occurred?" asked Thurnock.

"Examine the beach," I said. "There is no sign of struggle, no evidence of war."

"There are furrows in the sand where the *Dorna* and the *Tesephone* were launched," said Clitus.

"Note," I said. "There is no sign of an incursion or surprise, nor of enemy troops about."

"None that I can see," said Thurnock.

"They did not attack here," I said.

"Apparently not," said Clitus.

"Nor did they intend to," I said.

"Possibly not," said Clitus.

"We are their quarry," I said, "their nemesis, their coveted foe, the core of the defense of Mytilene, more so than the *Dorna* and *Tesephone*. Had they attempted to attack us here, or nearby, here on land, they would have risked losing us. Presumably outnumbered we might have scattered, slipped from their grasp, even withdrawn to the safety of Mytilene."

"But the *Dorna* and *Tesephone* are gone," said Thurnock.

"We are abandoned," said a man.

"No," said another.

"If so," said another, "to no stern fate. Mytilene is free, the siege lifted, the garrison relieved. Allies, armed peasants, hold the field."

"I see no treachery here," said another.

"Nor I," I said.

"Captains Tab and Sakim would not desert us," said Clitus.

"No," I said, "but how is it that they are gone?"

"They were to await us here," said Clitus. "They must have had reason to depart."

"Undoubtedly," I said. "Let the beach be examined for messages, papers pinned to a stake, a marked board, weighted in place by a stone, words drawn in the sand."

Several torches were lit, and men, in lines, made their way about the beach.

"Nothing," said a man later, reporting on the results of this disciplined perusal of the sand.

"Where then are Captains Tab and Sakim, where the *Dorna* and the *Tesephone*?" asked a man.

"I am puzzled," said another.

"Night is filled with mystery," said a man. "It is the way of night."

"It can be the way of day, as well," I said. "Night does not own mystery. The sleen is nocturnal, but it prowls at will. Mystery does not eschew the sun. Even in the light of day, much may be unseen, much may be invisible."

"Conjecture, Commander," said a man.

"To begin," I said, "we accept that our brethren are both brave and loyal. We thus dismiss both cowardice and treachery as an explanation for their absence. Accordingly, we attribute their departure, their failure to keep our rendezvous, to the presence of the enemy. The enemy would have made their appearance either by land or sea. Given the victory of Mytilene and the control of the fields by our Peasant cohorts, we may rule out an attack by land. This leaves us with an attack by sea, but there is no evidence of such an attack, no bodies or equipment, no signs of disruption or bloodshed. But one might well have assumed, mistakenly, in the heat of the moment, given an appearance by the enemy, that the corsair fleet intended to attack the beach."

"'Mistakenly'?" asked Thurnock.

"As Tab and Sakim left no message of any sort to explain their departure, we may infer that the appearance of the corsair fleet was sudden and unexpected, perhaps emerging from darkness in the vicinity of dawn, a situation calling for instant action, getting the *Dorna* and *Tesephone* to sea before an enemy landing took place, presumably to be followed by the destruction of both vessels."

"'Mistakenly'?" urged Thurnock.

"I think so," I said.

"Would you have done differently?" asked Thurnock.

"I do not think so," I said. "The mistake was intelligent and natural. Who would willingly risk the ships?"

"But it was a mistake?" pressed Thurnock.

"Yes," I said. "Consider the enemy's intentions. He is zealous for our total destruction. Suppose he had made a landing. We might lose the ships, but he would lose us. We could easily withdraw to the safety of Mytilene and, if he dared to follow us, he would encounter our allies, much to his peril. His victory on the beach would have been slight and, for most practical purposes, empty. There are always other ships."

"He would not have landed?" said Thurnock.

"Not if he were as intelligent as I fear," I said.

"He would wait then, blockading the harbor," said Thurnock.

"Briefly," I said, "for show, then he would withdraw, apparently giving up the chase, apparently resigning himself to failure, apparently returning in dudgeon to Sybaris."

"He wants us at sea," said Thurnock.

"Subject to his presumed invincible force," I said.

"It is clear," said Clitus, "they want us held in place, confined to our ships at sea, with no hope of escape, want us trapped in vulnerable prisons of wood."

"Yes," I said. "They wish to have us at sea."

"We could remain indefinitely here, on Chios," said a man.

"Under surveillance by one means or another," said a man.

"But what then of our project, our purpose and mission," said Clitus, "stopping the depredations of corsairs burning, slaughtering, and looting in the name of Bosk of Port Kar?"

"I think that Tab and Sakim will return," I said. "First, they will be puzzled that they have not been pursued and attacked. Second, they will return, sensing the plan of the enemy."

"Let the enemy beware," said Thurnock. "We are swift and dangerous."

"So, too, is he," I said.

"One who grasps the fur of a sea sleen or the tail of a shark is unwise," said Thurnock.

"But sometimes less unwise than at other times," I said.

"Listen," said a man. "I hear muffled oars."

I listened for moment. "The *Tesephone*," I said.

The lighter ship would approach the shore first, stern forward, and discharge scouts to survey the beach. If all seemed safe, the larger vessel, the fifty-oared *Dorna*, would follow. Both vessels would, in this place and time, beach stern first, permitting a quicker return to the water. The lightness and shallow draft of most Gorean vessels makes beaching and half-beaching possible. Stakes and ropes are sometimes used as well to anchor ships in place, particularly 'round ships', which have somewhat broader beams than 'knife ships'. This can be done, too, with knife ships, where the ebb and flow of the tides warrant such a precaution.

"The night is dark," said Clitus.

"Listen," I said.

"Yes," said Clitus.

We sensed, rather than saw, the narrow shape off shore, a darkness within a darkness. There was then no more sound of oars, but, given the silence, they had not yet been drawn inboard. By now two or more men would have slipped over the side and would be wading to shore.

"Let us meet our fellows," I said, and, followed by Thurnock, Clitus, Aktis, and some others, I descended the beach.

I heard a sword half freed of its sheath.

"Hold," said a voice some yards before us. "Stand and be recognized."

"I recommend you do so as well," I said.

"Captain?" said a voice.

"Port Kar," I said, "is the scourge of the sea."

"She is the jewel of gleaming Thassa," said the voice.

"Welcome," I said.

"You hold the beach?" asked the voice.

"It is held," I said.

Shortly thereafter, oars were drawn inboard, crews disembarked, and, with intermittent, soft, sliding sounds, the *Tesephone* and *Dorna* were thrust partly onto the beach.

Tab, who had captained the *Dorna*, and Sakim, who was captaining the *Tesephone*, soon joined us.

"We feared for you," said Tab.

"And we for you," I said.

"Mytilene?" asked Tab.

"Stressed and bloody," I said, "but whole and free."

"My caste," said Thurnock, "the mighty ox on which the Home Stone rests, strung its bows and arrows spoke."

"Mercenaries suffered grievous losses," said Clitus, "and soon, as they could, under fire, those who could, sought to avail themselves of the hospitality of the corsair fleet."

"Longboats were sent forth to ferry them aboard," said Aktis, "but few such boats, given clouds of arrows, hazarded a second trip."

"The shore ran with blood," said Clitus.

"It is getting light," said a man.

"Report," I said to Tab and Sakim.

"Seven ships appeared, two days ago, early, emerging from the mists," said Tab. "At first sight of them, lest landing parties should disembark and trap us ashore, we put to sea, intent on fighting our way to open water."

"But," said Sakim, "no effort was made to hinder our escape, nor to follow us. The enemy was inert, like mountains in the sea, between which we might pass, undeterred, unmolested."

"Why, we wondered," said Tab, "are they, in their numbers and might, letting us pass."

"Surely we could easily have rowed on, saving ourselves," said Sakim.

"They knew you would not do so," I said.

"How could they have known that?" asked Sakim.

"They know well what they themselves lack," I said. "They scorn honor themselves, but recognize it in others, and seek to exploit it to their advantage."

"I was terrified, and seized with a desire to flee, even be it across the waters of the hith," said Sakim.

"We crossed those waters earlier," I said. "We proved them not only passable, but safe."

"You do not believe the hith exists," said Sakim.

"I do not think it exists," I said.

"I have seen it," said Sakim.

"Many people," I said, "think they have seen many things. In moments of alarm and stress, or given lights, shadows, and reflections on shifting water, one may imagine what they have not truly seen."

"I lost a ship," said Sakim.

"When ships are lost," I said, "the cause is not always clearly understood."

"In any event," said Sakim, "when we passed unhindered through the gathered ships of the corsairs, and might make for Thera, I did not flee. I could not do so. I returned, despite my terror."

"The enemy knew you would," I said.

"I did not know myself," he said.

"You see," I said, "the enemy knew you better than you knew yourself."

"It is well that you did not issue orders of escape," said Thurnock, "for your oarsmen would have broken your back and cast you into the sea."

"Such are the men of Bosk of Port Kar?" said Sakim.

"They are such," said Clitus.

"To a man," said Thurnock.

"We returned," said Tab.

"Of course," I said. "To the honorable, not all options are available."

"Honor," said Sakim, "would seem to be something of a tactical handicap."

"One must choose how one will be," I said, "what one will do, how one will live, for what one will fight."

"Honor," said Thurnock, "is what parts men from the urt and ost."

"I think I know," said Tab, "why we were not attacked at sea."

"I am sure you do," I said.

"They wish to have their vengeance complete," said Tab. "They wish to take us all together."

"And can accomplish that," I said, "only at sea."

"What are your orders?" asked Tab.

"Rest," I said, "eat and sleep."

"Respite will be welcome," said Tab. "And then to sea."

"Not immediately," I said.

"You will dally some days," asked Tab, "hoping the corsair fleet will grow impatient and depart?"

"Possibly," I said.

"I do not think the corsair fleet will be so accommodating," said Tab.

"Nor do I," I said.

"Should we not leave soon?" asked Tab.

"We have something to do first," I said.

"What is that?" asked Tab.

"Paint the ships white and yellow," I said.

"Why?" asked Tab.

"Is it not suitable?" I said. "Are we not simple, innocent Merchants?"

"I do not understand," said Tab.

"I have my reason," I said.

"Tonight we will put to sea," I said.

"Tonight?" asked Tab.

"I do not think the enemy will expect that," I said.

"Night is filled with hazards," said Sakim. "Who but the bold and desperate will risk Thassa in the darkness?"

"It is light now," said Aktis.

"The horizon is clear," said Thurnock. "There is no sign of the enemy, not for days."

"It seems he has withdrawn," said Clitus.

"Yes," I said, "so it seems."

CHAPTER FIFTY

Impact at Sea; Fog; A Situation is Desperate; Sakim's Proposal

"Rudders right!" I cried.

The impact had been totally unexpected. There had been no sound of alien oars, no warning, no cries.

"Reef!" called Thurnock.

But these waters were free of reefs. And if a contact of this size had been made with a reef, there would have been a hideous tearing and splintering of wood, like thunder at one's ear drum, a swift inrush of cold water rising to the gunwales.

"We are aground!" cried Sakim.

But ground seldom rises and shakes, recoiling. The contact had been made neither with rock or wood, not with stone, nor beach, nor grating sand. It was as though the *Tesephone* had inadvertently struck, or had been struck by, some enormous living mountain, a mountain which could live and breathe, could lift itself and then, trembling, subside, and draw away.

The *Tesephone*, tilted, slid down the side of the living island, splashing into the water. At the same time, I heard cries from the island. "We have found them!" we heard. "Spears and shields! Arm your bows and slings! Release the vulos."

"The enemy!" shouted Thurnock.

"Away!" I called to the helmsmen.

Most Gorean vessels south of Torvaldsland are double-ruddered. This makes the vessel more responsive and agile than a single-ruddered vessel, a feature important in naval warfare, both in attack and flight. The two rudders, each with its own helmsman, are commonly engaged with one another, or coupled, in such a manner that they move in unison. Uncoupled, each is independent of the other, which feature, particularly should one rudder be damaged or destroyed, permits the vessel to proceed unimpaired.

Almost at the same time as the impact the early morning fog parted and, briefly, I glimpsed several tents, many men, some seizing up weapons, some great heaps of stone blocks, of the sort which had been used in the great catapults of the mercenaries near Mytilene, and a flare of fire to the right. Too, water began to rumble beneath the surface suggesting an agitation or a disturbance of some sort. At the time I did not understand the likely explanation of this seeming subsurface tumult or thrashing. Too, I did not understand, then, the meaning of the flames to the right. I thought they might be igniting bundles of pitch for use as missiles, but I saw no visible catapults, or any means for delivering such missiles. Then the fog closed in again, and I could see little or nothing through the fog save for the dim incandescence of the fires being lit or stoked to the right.

"Away!" I called again. "Stroke! Stroke!" I heard the mallets of the *keleustes* strike the cadence drum, first one blow, and then, after several Ihn, the next.

The *Tesephone*, turned about, sped into the fog, leaving the Brigand Island behind.

I went back to the low stern castle, accompanied by Thurnock, Sakim, and Clitus.

"We are discovered," I said, looking astern. I could still see the dim glow of the fire behind us, through the fog.

"How could the enemy island be so far from Mytilene?" asked Clitus.

"I think it was not close to begin with," I said.

"It was probably waiting for us," said Sakim.

"At least," said Clitus, "the corsair fleet is still far behind."

"I doubt it," I said.

"But we left in darkness," said Clitus.

"So, too, I think," I said, "did they."

"I heard shouts of having to do with releasing vulos," said Clitus.

"Seven ships will soon know our position," said Thurnock.

"To encounter the Brigand Island was a great misfortune," said Clitus.

"How could it have come about?" asked Thurnock.

"A lamentable coincidence," said Clitus.

"Lamentable, yes," said Sakim, "but I think it no coincidence. First, it was doubtless clear in Mytilene that we had come from Thera. Many, including Tarchon, would have known this. Accordingly, it would be conjectured that we, in leaving Chios, might be returning to Thera."

"Even so," said Thurnock, "the sea is large."

"Do not forget," said Sakim. "They would know our point of departure. Knowing our point of departure and our likely destination, and our likely haste to reach our destination, suggesting a straight course, would considerably reduce the likely area to be covered in a search."

"The sea is still large," said Thurnock.

"Living islands, as sluggish as they may seem," said Sakim, "are alive and in some respects very aware and sensitive, that having to do with detecting fish, locating desirable feeding grounds, and such. Too, the behavior of living islands, like that of other forms of life, those of a sufficient degree of sensitivity, is susceptible of modification, even training of a sort. I would guess that the mercenaries associated ships with feedings, an easy enough thing to do. In this way, the island would tend to seek out ships, this behavior, when successful, being rewarded by the mercenaries."

"The sea is still large, very large," said Thurnock.

"The living island," said Sakim, "can detect the sound of an oar striking the water at a distance of pasangs."

"In the moment the fog parted," I said, "it was clear the island was heavily freighted."

"Stone blocks, many men," said Thurnock.

"How many men?" I asked.

"I would guess four hundred," said Thurnock.

"At least," I said.

"Perhaps some there were evacuated from Mytilene," said Thurnock.

"Quite possibly," I said.

"Given the numbers evacuated from Mytilene," said Clitus, "most of those evacuated would still be aboard the ships."

"Unfortunately," I said.

The corsair fleet constituted a formidable foe at sea not only in virtue of its size, its number of vessels, but in virtue of its number of men, this enhancing its capacity both to board and resist boarding, and to mount frequent shifts of oarsmen, this enabling the vessel to maintain a high rate of speed almost indefinitely.

"It is not only ships we must fear," said Sakim.

"How so?" I asked.

"It is the island, as well," he said.

"I do not understand," I said.

"Surely you saw the fire kindled on the island, noted the turbulence in the water," said Sakim.

"Speak," I said.

"The great beast was in excruciating pain," said Sakim.

"How is that?" I asked.

"You saw the fire," said Sakim.

"Surely," I said.

"Those who inhabit the living islands or have their camps on them," said Sakim, "move and guide the islands, when they wish, by gentle pressures, from which the beast withdraws."

"True," I said.

I had learned that much from my brief time on the Island of Seleukos.

"The mercenaries are heartless and cruel," said Sakim. "You saw the fire. They do not respect the island or care for it. They goad it. They spur it to do their bidding; they exploit it, pitilessly, mercilessly, by sharp instruments and blazing irons."

Thurnock growled in fury.

"See how low the beast was in the water," said Sakim. "Consider the weight with which it is still burdened, the huge blocks of stone, inhumanly not discarded, even after the destruction of the catapults."

"Would we had a hundred ships," said Thurnock, "to go back and free the beast, to scrape the parasitical scum from its hide."

"We can do nothing for the beast," said Sakim.

"We must think of escape," I said.

"We can easily outdistance a living island," said Clitus.

"Do not be too sure," said Sakim.

"The danger is the corsair fleet," said Clitus, "should it detect us, given its armament and its presumed changes of oarsmen."

"Do not underestimate the effects of jabbing, pointed metal poles, serrated blades, and white-hot irons affecting the Brigand Island," said Sakim, "nor the willingness of the mercenaries to kill it in their attempt to overtake us."

"The corsair fleet is faraway," said Clitus.

"Perhaps not so far," I said. "We do not know."

"Even now," said Clitus, "we are slipping away in the fog."

"The fog will lift," said Thurnock.

"By that time," said Clitus, "we will have disappeared."

"You forget one thing, my friend," said Sakim. "Should the mercenaries lose touch with us, they need only give the Brigand Island a temporary surcease of its pain, and, soon, it will seek us of its own accord."

"The behavior of seeking ships for food," said Thurnock.

"Abetted by the acuity of its senses," said Sakim, "senses capable of detecting the entrance of an oar into water, the creaking of rudders, from pasangs away."

"Raise the mast and yard," said Clitus.

"There is little wind," said Sakim.

"Yet we will do so," I said.

"But, Captain," said Sakim, "that, in itself, given the height of the stem decks of the corsair fleet, and the glass of the Builders, will make us visible from pasangs away."

"That is the point," I said. "We have been detected. We must now signal Tab on the *Dorna* to separate from us and proceed alone. We cannot in wisdom, the two of us, engage the corsair fleet. If one ship must be lost, and we hope none will be lost, better the smaller *Tesephone* than the larger, more crewed, more formidable *Dorna*. If it escapes, it can still continue our work."

"You will lead the corsairs away from the *Dorna*?" said Sakim.

"That is my hope," I said.

"And what of us?" asked Sakim.

"We may have an opportunity to transfer you to the *Dorna*," I said.

"Do not insult me, Captain," said Sakim.

"Forgive me," I said. "I spoke foolishly."

"You expect to entrust us to the hands of fortune?" said Sakim.

"Yes," I said, "in a way."

"I see no point in leaving all things to fortune," said Sakim.

"What do you have in mind?" I asked.

"Marking a card, chipping a game stone, weighting a die," he said.

"I attend your words," I said.

"Turn back to Mytilene," he said.

"The Brigand Island and the corsair fleet are both between us and Mytilene," I said.

"I know these waters," he said. "Turn back to Mytilene."

"We would not be able to reach Mytilene," I said.

"I know," he said.

"The fog is lifting," said Thurnock.

CHAPTER FIFTY-ONE

Incident off the Coast of Chios

"There is the coast of Chios," said Thurnock, pointing forward, toward the thin brown line, half visible over the water.

"They have cut us off," said Clitus.

We had been under sail, the sail now limp on the long, sloping yard.

"That was my intention," said Sakim.

"There are only three ships there," I said. "Where are the other four?"

I had hoped to lead the corsair fleet, all seven fifty-oared ships, away from the *Dorna*. Clearly this stratagem had been unsuccessful. I had no doubt that the other four corsair ships, possibly in communication by means of message vulos, were in pursuit of the *Dorna*. If the *Dorna* had been detected, possibly in virtue of the activity of the Brigand Island, I did not think it could long elude its pursuers, given the numbers of rested oarsmen on which they could draw, heavily crewed as they were with large numbers of draftable, evacuated mercenaries. There was the possibility, of course, that the *Dorna* had somehow escaped and was now bound for the Cove of Harpalos.

Thurnock eyed the three ships between us and the coast. "The oars are still," he said.

"They know they have us," said Clitus. "We have failed to reach the coast."

"It was not my intention to reach the coast," said Sakim.

"You know the waters we are in?" I said to Sakim.

"Of course," he said.

"We passed these waters, safely," I said, "and under oars as well, when we first came to Chios, to warn Mytilene of the intentions of the corsairs."

"I think we were fortunate," he said.

"Many ships must pass this way," I said, "and under oars."

"Fewer than you think," he said.

"There is nothing to fear here," I said.

"Do not taunt fortune," he said, "do not presume on her patience, do not treat her with contempt."

We had come to this point under sail, oars inboard.

"The *Tesephone* is swift," I said. "I think we could give our friends a splendid chase."

"Until our oarsmen, exhausted and aching, could no longer draw an oar," said Sakim, "and our friends, with ten shifts of oarsmen, their pursuit never abated, could draw abeam, cast out their hooks, and swarm aboard."

I looked at the three corsair ships, each a vessel of fifty oars, the coast of Chios behind them. "What will you have of us?" I asked.

"Bring us about," said Sakim, "as though we, dismayed at our position, would risk all in a run for the open sea."

I gave the orders.

"Now," said Thurnock, "their oars are outboard."

"Our men are strong, the *Tesephone* is swift," said Clitus. "Out our oars and race east."

"No," said Sakim. "Keep the oars inboard. We will rely on the sail."

"They will wonder about that," I said to Sakim.

"Let them wonder," said Sakim. "I do not think the High Admiral of the fleet will be aboard one of those vessels, each surveying the *Tesephone* like a hungry sleen eyeing a cornered tabuk. The High Admiral would be after bigger game, the *Dorna*."

"There is very little wind," I said.

"Keep the oars inboard," said Sakim.

"We cannot allow them to come within grappling distance," I said.

"Keep the oars inboard," said Sakim.

"We are moving," said Thurnock, looking on the half-filled sail.

"Use the oars," said Clitus.

"In passing the den of a larl," said Sakim, "it behooves one to tread softly."

"The corsairs stir," I said. Even at the distance it was easy to see the oars were not only outboard but now in the water.

"The birds of prey spread their wings," said Thurnock.

Then, from across the water came the dim sound of a cadence drum, and then another, and another.

The sight of a galley's oars, such graceful, mighty levers, drawing, and lifting, in unison, water running from the wood in sparkling rivulets, is a beautiful sight, one that those of my former world had not seen in centuries.

"They will have us in an Ahn," said Clitus.

"By that time we will be well from shore," said Sakim.

"If they are on the point of closing with us," I said, "I will resort to oars."

"Be patient," said Sakim.

"Would that the breeze might freshen," said Clitus.

"Our sail thirsts," said Thurnock. "Would it could drink the paga of the wind."

"Hear the drums," I said.

"The beat increases," said Thurnock.

"They do not spare their oarsmen," said Clitus. "In half an Ahn, with chains and hooks they will be upon us."

"Clearly," I said, "they are eager to finish their work."

"Bloody work, to be brought to a quick finish," said Thurnock.

Shortly, the first of the three ships was within forty yards of us. We could see files of helmeted men, mercenary warriors, not mariners, doubtless mercenaries embarked from the beach near Mytilene. Sunlight was reflected from helmets, from the metal bosses of rounded shields, from the blades of spears. We heard the rustling of looped chains terminating with short, thick metal rods, each of which, as though exfoliating, seemed to blossom into three metal hooks.

"We must act," said Clitus.

"Patience," urged Sakim. "There are three pursuing ships, three, large and heavy, each laden with supplies and men. Each has fifty oars. These oars, hastening, strike the water, again and again. They are fools, or do not know the waters they ply."

"Ready oars," I called to the benches.

"Be gentle, I beg of you," said Sakim. "Be silent as the fog, glide like the cloud, float like the petal of a flower."

"There is no time," I snapped.

"Give me another Ehn," said Sakim, "another Ehn!"

"Only that," I said.

I raised my hand, and began to count the eighty Ihn which compose an Ehn.

All eyes were upon my raised hand.

The nearest ship was now within twenty yards of the *Tesephone*, preparing to draw alongside.

At seventy Ihn I tensed, preparing to slash my hand downward, at which signal the oars would be thrust outboard, be poised, would enter the water together, and the *keleustes*, his mallet already lifted, would deliver his first blow to the metal-headed drum.

A moment before the eightieth Ihn, a gigantic snakelike form with a diameter of some ten feet burst some forty feet upward from the water like some living geyser, and, in the midst of screams and tumult, fell heavily, laterally, across the deck of the enemy ship, and wound itself, with incredible rapidity, coil after coil, about the ship. After the third coil the great head of the beast caught the left side of the stem deck in its fanged jaws, and bit into it, as though to fasten itself in living prey, as though the ship might be alive, and attempt to free itself, splintering planks and railings. We then, to our terror, watched the ship being crushed in those mighty coils, board by board, plank by plank, until the water was filled with debris and men.

"You see, Captain," said Sakim, "so much now for Sakim the delusional, Sakim the mad, Sakim the liar, Sakim the fraud."

"It is horrible," I said.

"The hith, nearly exterminated on land," said Sakim, "took to cover and plenty, to the vast world of the sea."

"It breathes air," I said.

"Of course," said Sakim.

"Like the living island," I said.

"Yes," said Sakim.

There was much screaming and splashing in the water.

"Horrible," I said, "horrible."

"It takes prey of many dimensions," said Sakim. "Its largest natural prey is sea tharlarion, of various kinds."

"It seized the ship in its fangs," I said. "It cannot eat a ship."

"I think that is a biological reflex to anchor prey," said Sakim.

"Why would it attack a ship?" I said.

"It is within its prey rage," said Sakim. "It may think it is an animal of sorts. It is, in any event, the ship, a moving object, with oars like appendages, and, I suspect, more seriously, an intruding object, an object invading what the beast presumably takes as its territory."

"It is territorial," I said.

"That seems so," said Sakim. "Large land animals, of which the hith was one once, given the amount of food needed to sustain a large organism, tend to be territorial."

"Perhaps that hith is the same beast which once attacked your ship," I said.

"It is possible," said Sakim. "One does not know."

I found it difficult to take my eyes away from the confusion, the blood, the terror, and carnage in the water.

The hith's jaws had closed on a screaming swimmer; then the swimmer was drawn underwater, the place marked with bubbles exploding to the surface.

"Another theory," said Sakim, "is that the hith scents warmth and blood, and its attack is not so much to destroy an intruder as to get at possible food."

"I think the defense-of-territory theory is more plausible," I said. "First would come the movement of oars, particularly of several oars, the disturbance in the water, alerting the hith to the presence of an intruder, then the discovery of a large, dark shape entering his domain, and then, only after the attack, would it be likely to sense possible prey, thrashing in the water."

"I much agree," said Sakim, "and such is my view, but surely you will grant that once food has been associated with an attack, that attacks might be thus encouraged?"

"Surely," I said.

I guessed that there might be two hundred and fifty to three hundred men in the water, as the corsair ships were crowded with evacuated mercenaries.

I saw one fellow trying to crawl onto a narrow plank. It could not support his weight. I saw a helmeted figure slip beneath the water, seemingly drawn under the surface, one hand raised, as though it might be grasped by someone. I recalled that it was not far from this point that, in clearing the battlefield, bodies of dead mercenaries, as that of Tarchon, had been disposed of at sea.

The two enemy ships, given the sudden appearance of the hith, coiling about their fellow, had held up like frightened animals, and had then, frenziedly, and awkwardly, out of rhythm, begun to back oar. They now stood half a pasang away, hull to hull. One of them had put out longboats, four longboats, which were now approaching the scattered, splintered wreckage of the first vessel. The other vessel had declined to risk its longboats. Captains differ with respect to such matters.

Another man screamed and disappeared under the water.

"Sharks," said Sakim, "jubilant sharks, rushing to the feast."

Sharks will follow food wherever it may be found, as in following a ship for days, to feed on discarded garbage, but most tend to stay in shallower water, where sunlight can nourish rooted, aquatic plants, which can nourish small fish, which, in turn, can nourish larger fish, such as sharks.

I witnessed two coils of the gigantic hith encircle a swimmer and constrict. There was a sound as though of snapping sticks. I looked away, as organs began to be expelled through the victim's mouth.

"The hith," said Sakim, "being a cold-blooded reptile, has a slow metabolism. Once it has gorged itself, it becomes inert. It may not eat again for months. In that time it would be relatively safe to ply these waters."

"Do you think the corsair captains are aware of this?" I asked.

"I would suppose so," said Sakim. "It is in the legends."

"Then the other two ships will follow us," I said, "even through these waters?"

"I do not doubt it," said Sakim.

One of the four lifeboats had now reached the wreckage of the first corsair vessel. Seventy to eighty men, like frenzied lelts, were now trying to reach it. I watched it capsize, men swarming then like insects on the overturned hull.

The second longboat was now amongst the floating debris, but four mercenaries, with spears, were thrusting at those trying to clamber aboard. The boat seemed to float on a scarlet sea. Several dorsal fins began to cut toward the boat. We watched a few men drawn aboard, while others were repelled at the point of bloody spears.

"They are saving officers," said Sakim.

"What of the others?" I asked.

"The others are not officers," said Sakim.

"I know that man," I said, "he just drawn aboard! It is Ctesippus, a colleague of Glaukos, proprietor of the tavern, *The Living Island*, in Sybaris!"

"Does it surprise you?" asked Sakim.

Ctesippus now stood in the boat, shuddering, drenched and dripping. He regarded us, shaking his fist.

"He is displeased," said Sakim.

"Does it surprise you?" I asked.

Ctesippus was now apparently issuing orders to the crew of the longboat. It turned about and, the mercenaries with spears continuing to fend off desperate swimmers, began to make its way back toward the two unharmed corsair ships, waiting closer to shore.

"The boat could hold several more occupants," I said.

"It seems that Ctesippus has no wish to take on further passengers," said Sakim.

One fellow was clinging to an oar of the longboat but lost his grip, a spear jabbed into his face.

The third lifeboat, like the first, overloaded, awash, capsized; the fourth lifeboat, like the second, bore policing spearmen and, in the midst of shrieking swimmers, seemed determined to take on only elite passengers, presumably officers and special persons. As it turned out, its intentions, despite an undoubted adherence to orders, were frustrated, three, massive, whiplike coils of the monstrous hith wrapping themselves about the boat and, tightening, reducing in as little as a dozen Ihn the boat and certain occupants to little more than floating debris.

"The hith, the sharks," I said, "it is a slaughter."

"Nature is so bred," said Sakim.

"Many," I said, "despairing of rescue, swim for the corsair ships, the shore."

"It is a long swim," said Sakim.

"Surely many will make it," I said.

"Perhaps," said Sakim, "if they can get outside the compass of the feeding. It is a gauntlet."

"If some reach the shore," I said, "they may fall into the hands of the Peasants, or of those of Mytilene. That is a fate I would not envy them."

"Many men, terrified, confused, blinded by sea water, swim toward the open sea," said Sakim.

"I would we could turn them toward the shore," I said.

"Do not be concerned," said Sakim. "Those on the corsair ships can see. They will have the glass of the Builders."

Hardly had Sakim said this than the oar drums on the corsair ships began to sound, the reverberations carrying over the water.

"The mother vulo calls to her chicks," said Sakim.

Suddenly the huge, wide head of the hith, slick, wet, shedding water, rose more than twenty feet out of the water, some ten feet aft of the *Tesephone*, a body grasped in its jaws.

"It is looking at us," I whispered.

"Do not move," said Sakim.

Then it, with its prize, disappeared under the waves.

"I think," said Sakim, "that this would be a good time to take our departure."

"Let us wait a little," I said.

"Why?" asked Sakim.

We could still hear the oar drums of the corsair ships carrying over the water.

"What do you think would happen if we took our departure now?" I asked.

"The corsair ships would pursue us, but presumably under sail," said Sakim.

"Not picking up the survivors, their men, but abandoning them to the sharks, to the sea, to the Peasants, to the citizens of long-suffering, beleaguered Mytilene," I said.

"Of course," said Sakim.

"Let us wait a little," I said.

"Why?" asked Sakim.

"Codes," I said. "Codes."

"They are mercenaries, killers," said Sakim.

"Some are caste brothers," I said.

"You would save a fellow whom in battle you would think nothing of driving a sword into his heart?" said Sakim.

"Yes," I said.

"Codes?" said Sakim.

"Yes, codes," I said.

An Ahn later, shortly before sundown, oars inboard, we brought the long, sloping yard into the wind.

"The corsairs will follow us," said Sakim.

"We will have the cover of darkness," I said.

"But there is the Brigand Island," said Sakim. "It can trail us, like a sleen of the sea."

"It may have already led the balance of the corsair fleet, four ships, to the *Dorna*," I said.

"I fear so," said Sakim.

"We did our best," I said. "We tried to draw attention away from the *Dorna*."

"Sometimes one's best is not good enough," said Sakim.

"We will try to rendezvous with the *Dorna*," I said.

"Her eyes may no longer see," said Sakim.

"There might be wreckage," I said.

CHAPTER FIFTY-TWO

We Rendezvous with the *Dorna*; Enemy Ships; Masts are Down

"Look!" cried Sakim. "The *Dorna* can see!"

"She lives!" cried a man, and cheers rang from the benches.

"She lists," I said. "She has taken on water. She is crippled. She must have lost oars."

Normally the *Dorna* has twenty-five oars to a side. From my current position I could see but seven on what we may refer to as her port side, these presumably matched by another seven, plus or minus one, on what we may refer to as her starboard side.

Our mast was still raised.

We had been proceeding under sail, to spare oarsmen whose strength we might soon need, and sorely.

The mast of the *Dorna* was not visible. The mast is always lowered when battle is imminent.

I had stationed Thurnock on the stern deck, with a glass of the Builders, to scan the horizon aft.

I was sure that the two unharmed corsairs we had sighted near the coast, their masts now down, now that they would be past the waters in which the hith was feared, must be close. But, masts down, it can be difficult amongst the waves of gleaming Thassa to detect the presence of a swift, shallow-drafted Gorean fighting ship. This feature, naturally, conditions naval actions. It facilitates advantages to be found in stealth, for example, in stalking, surprise, and evasion.

"Our rendezvous is kept," said Clitus.

He was beside us on the stem deck with a second glass of the Builders. "I see Captain Tab, at the railing," he said. "He is gesturing us away."

"We may be able to effect simple repairs," said Sakim. "Too, we have spare oars."

"The *Dorna* must have had spare oars as well," said Clitus. "Where are they?"

"The *Dorna* has been in action," I said, "doubtless more than once."

"Captain Tab is waving us away," said Clitus.

"The enemy must be about," said Sakim.

I called back to the helm deck, to draw alongside the listing *Dorna*.

"Captain Tab is agitated," said Clitus, peering through the glass of the Builders. "He declines converse. He is vehement. He waves us away, fiercely, plaintively."

"He warns us of a trap," said Sakim.

"And the *Dorna* is the bait," I said.

"He wants us to depart," said Clitus. "He demands to be deserted, to be left behind."

"With not even a transfer of personnel, not even a taking on of the injured and wounded?" said Sakim.

"Clearly the enemy is close," I said.

I called to the stern deck, that Thurnock might join us. I wished him to hear what might ensue. Surrendering his glass of the Builders to Aktis, he was soon at our side.

Not long thereafter the *Tesephone* rocked gently against the hull of the *Dorna*.

"You might have escaped," said Tab. "You might have had at least a slim chance of survival. But now you are lost."

"Then," I said, "we will be lost together."

"Why did you not flee?" said Tab, angrily.

"We are short of paga," I said. "We hoped that you might have some."

"You are mad," said Tab.

"Or thirsty," I said.

"It seems we shall die together," said Tab.

"Perhaps," I said, "we will live together."

I supposed that there were worst places to die, if one must, than in the midst of ringing metal on a goodly morning, on the deck of a fine, if disabled, ship, on the bright waves of Thassa, amongst friends, in the light of Tor-Tu-Gor.

But death will take care of itself. It is life which requires attention.

"Dear Captain," I said, "I had hoped, mast high, posing as a tempting prey, to draw the corsair fleet away from you. But my plan failed of fruition. I sorrow. It is much to my regret."

"Regret nothing," said Tab. "Rather it is I who should lament, had I profited from the risk you took, the sacrifice you hazarded."

"Four ships of the corsair fleet followed you," said Sakim.

"How did you know?" asked Tab.

"We sighted the other three near Chios," said Sakim.

"Only two of the three remain," said Thurnock.

"Surely the tiny *Tesephone* did not engage a fifty-oared vessel," said Tab, "let alone manage to sink such a foe."

"Sakim, with a little help, possibly from an old friend, managed it," I said.

"I do not understand," said Tab.

"One should not sing in the vicinity of a sleeping larl," said Thurnock. It was a Gorean saying, not unlike many others. Gorean, like most languages, furnishes many such sayings, almost one of which is likely to be applicable in any conceivable situation.

It seemed clear that Tab's puzzlement was not much dissipated in the light of Thurnock's observation.

"Sakim brought us to waters in which there lurked a territorial hith," I said. "We trod softly, the enemy did not."

"The hith," said Tab, "is a creature of mythology."

"But not, it seems," I said, "of mythology alone."

"It does not exist," said Tab.

"The hith itself," I said, "was unaware of that."

"Two of the three ships, then," said Tab, "remain."

"They search for us," I said, "I am sure."

"They may be near," said Thurnock.

"Four corsair ships followed me," said Tab, "even in darkness, unerringly. It is uncanny. It speaks of the hands of Priest-Kings. I could not slip away."

"It is done by means of a living island," said Sakim, "that island we speak of as the Brigand Island, a pathetic, enormous aquatic beast under the control of corsairs and mercenaries. It is that which has followed you. As a sleen, tenacious and swift, can follow scent on land, tenacious and swift, a living island can follow sounds, disturbances, stirrings, in the water, schooling fish, the wake of a passing vessel, and such. The enemy has taught the island to associate feeding with ships, so it seeks ships."

"Why would it leave the corsair ships?" asked Tab.

"They will not feed it," said Sakim. "So it seeks another ship."

"And it would lead them to the *Dorna*," said Tab.

"It is so," said Sakim.

"It will get no feeding from the *Dorna*," said Tab.

"The island does not know that," said Sakim.

"For Ahn we rowed swiftly," said Tab.

"The corsairs torture the island with pain, spurring it to greater and greater speed," said Sakim. "I wonder that they have not killed it by now."

"Clearly the *Dorna* has seen action," said Clitus.

"Twice," said Tab. "In the first engagement I used the tactic of the 'separation of foes'. I pretended to flee and the enemy hastened after me, the fastest enemy naturally closest to me, the second-fastest enemy behind him, and the third-fastest behind him, and so on. Thus I hoped to engage in a series of single combats, one against one, rather than finding myself surrounded and overwhelmed."

"You could not outdistance the foes?" said Clitus.

"It seemed they were tireless," said Tab.

"They were doubtless heavily crewed," I said, "and had the services of transported mercenaries, making possible frequent shifts of rowers."

"I turned about," said Tab, "and, circling, and charging, for the *Dorna*, for her size, is like a tabuk, stove in the hull of the nearest pursuer, but the ram anchored itself athwart the keel of the enemy, and before I could disengage it, my oars were being sheared, rudders torn away, and planking ruptured at the waterline."

"You sank one of the enemy," said Clitus.

"Yes," said Tab.

"But the foes did not finish you off," said Thurnock.

"No," said Tab. "As I soon realized, they had a use for me."

"As bait in a trap," said Thurnock.

"I tried to warn you away," said Tab.

"Ho!" cried a mariner on the stern deck of the *Dorna*, pointing abeam, to his starboard side, "a mast, a mast!"

"That is a signal," I said, "the raising of a mast."

"Doubtless," said Tab.

Whereas the typical shallow-drafted Gorean vessel, low in the water, mast down, as noted, can be difficult to detect, its presence is much more easily marked when its mast is raised. Much depends, of course, on a variety of factors, the height of the mast, the type of sail on the yard, say, a fair-weather sail or storm sail, or such, and the point from which the observation is made, say, from the main deck or the height of one's own mast, and so on.

"There is another!" called the mariner pointing abeam, past the *Tesephone*, to his port side.

Shortly thereafter he had called out thrice more.

Five masts had now been raised. The raised mast of the first ship, which doubtless had the Admiral of the corsair fleet on board, had signaled the readiness for action. The other four ships had then raised their own masts, acknowledging the signal.

"The net is cast," said Clitus.

"Five ships," said Thurnock. "Now they are moving. They approach."

"They close the net," said Clitus.

"Lower your mast," said Tab, tensely. "Flee. Your oarsmen are rested. You may have time. There may be a chance. Flee!"

"But we have not yet had our paga," I said.

"They lower their masts!" called the mariner on the stern deck of the *Dorna*.

The Gorean warship lowers its mast before entering battle.

"Mast down!" I called to my men.

CHAPTER FIFTY-THREE

We Find our Position Perilous; A Stratagem; We Seek Darkness and Open Water

"Why do they not charge?" asked Clitus.

"Steady," I said to the benches. Oars were in the water. The *keleustes* grasped his mallet. I was on the stern deck, the common position of command when battle is imminent or in process. This position provides a height sufficient to survey action and provides immediate communication with the helm deck. Captain Tab was similarly ensconced on the stern deck of the crippled *Dorna*. We had now drawn away from the *Dorna* to where we might come about, unimpeded.

Five ships, quiet, were within fifty yards of the *Dorna* and the *Tesephone*.

"Perhaps they wish to parley," said Clitus.

"They give no sign of that," I said.

"For what then do they wait?" asked Thurnock, impatiently.

"Be patient," I said. "We do not yet know."

"They are in a position to impose harsh conditions," said Clitus.

"Their position is such that they need not impose conditions, at all," I said.

"Then why do they not attack?" said Clitus.

"They have lost two ships," I said. "I think they do not care to risk another."

"It is some sort of standoff then?" said Clitus.

"Hardly," I said.

"Should we not attack?" asked Thurnock.

"Which ship could we attack without being outflanked and rammed by another?" I asked.

"The *Dorna* is lame," said Sakim. "We might support her, but she would be of little help to us."

"I do not understand," said Clitus. "Why do they not move? Why do they not act?"

"The answer to your question approaches," I said, pointing.

"Tents in the sea, like sails, men with ladders?" said Thurnock.

"They are using the island, the living island!" cried a man.

"It is like land, living land, rushing upon us!" cried a helmsman.

"Steady," I said. "Steady."

"Tragic, innocent, overloaded, abused beast," said Thurnock.

Men with burning irons were thrusting them into the body of the island, while it, as if it would escape from the pain, was driving toward us. I caught the scent of living, burning flesh.

"Thus," said Thurnock, "they turn a dumb animal into a weapon."

"It must be in agony," said a man.

"Perhaps such things cannot feel," said another.

"It will find no food here," said Sakim, "only pain."

"That is perhaps to our advantage," I said.

The *Dorna* was between us and the onrushing behemoth, the living island. On its present trajectory it would make contact with the *Dorna* full on her starboard side. The mercenaries on the island, swarming forward, were intent to bring their ladders into play a moment after the island's impact on the *Dorna*'s hull, perhaps then stove in. But Tab, by oars and rudders, was already struggling to bring the prow of the *Dorna* toward the island, which maneuver would minimize the width of the expected impact.

"Good Tab!" I cried.

The iron-shod ram, mounted in such a way as to withstand the grievous shock of tearing through reinforced planking, cut a short, sharp, linear, bloody furrow in the hide of the living island and then, as it was riding over the beast, the beast, reflexively, reared upward, like a hill of muscles, as though to dislodge some predator, which caused the *Dorna*, given its inertia, to ride over the crest of this hill, pause for a moment, and then plunge downward, slicing through the massed mercenaries, dividing and disrupting their formation, and crushing several. There was much screaming, much confusion, a splintering of ladders, a tumbling of rectangular blocks of stone, intended originally to be ammunition for the great catapults, the tearing loose of tent pegs which had been pounded into the flesh of the island, and a scattering of tents rising from the back of the island like startled birds. At the same time the island, with a great roaring noise, exhaled a towering, violent spume of warm air and water. This rose a hundred feet into the air, and droplets fell like warm rain, drenching the island.

The flesh of the island then began reacting to the trauma of its wound, to shudder and ripple, contracting and expanding, its edges, or coasts, disappearing on one side or the other for a moment and then rising again, shining and dripping. Some parts of the island, more central parts, remained dry, but elsewhere, like tides, water washed its surface to a man's knees and then his waist.

"The island is sinking!" screamed a man.

The faces of many of the mercenaries were pale with horror.

Several, here and there, fought, and slew one another, to attain a place, sometimes no more than a yard high and wide, on one or another of the modest prominences in the flesh of the beast, a footing on certain irregularities, corrugations, blemishes, sealed lesions, and layers of twisted, knotted scar tissue.

Given the unexpected action of the *Dorna*, its inadvertent plunging into the ranks of the mercenaries, scattering all and crushing many, and the ensuing behavior of the injured, perhaps maddened, beast, war was far from the minds of most of the mercenaries, that despite the urgings and howling of certain officers, some of whom were knee deep in water.

Nature herself, it seemed, had declared a truce.

The hill-like mound of flesh which had risen under the *Dorna*, reacting to its inadvertent, bloody intrusion, had shrunk down, considerably, almost immediately, a moment after the *Dorna*'s plunge amongst the mercenaries. The ship was now rocking, its planking holding, the ship responsive to the continuing agitation of the surface beneath it. The few serviceable oars of the *Dorna* were out from the thole ports, almost like narrow wooden legs to keep the tormented craft from pitching on its side. Several oarsmen had leapt over the gunwales and were trying to force the *Dorna* back into the churning water, that it might once more find itself in its proper element. At the same time I had had the *Tesephone* brought to a position where it would be abeam of the *Dorna* should that craft manage to extricate itself from its current position and require assistance, and if it could not do so, we would be close enough to take swimmers aboard. Many Gorean vessels, when not in port, beach, or half-beach, themselves at night, where a camp is made, one sometimes rudely fortified. I mention this lest it seem surprising, or improbable, that portions of the *Dorna's* crew were outboard, attempting to free their ship from the shore of the living island. Their travail was brief, however, for the shore of the island drew back under them, and inclined downward, as though, water rushing in, it would so rid itself of an unwelcome visitor. Men clambered back aboard the *Dorna.*

I cupped my hands to my mouth and called to Tab, "Back, back into open water!"

"Flee!" he called back.

"We decline to do so," I said.

"Consider," he cried. "Confusion abounds. Two enemy ships are blocked by the island. The island itself is injured. It may not be able to lead ships to you. The *Tesephone* is swift! You may be able to elude the enemy, even with his shifts of rowers, until dark. In the night you may slip sway!"

"Back," I called, "free yourself in the open water."

"The *Dorna* is crippled," he said. "She ships water. She cannot keep up with you. Flee!"

"Come aboard," I said, "you and your crew."

"No," he said. "We decided that matter, long before you arrived."

"Speak," I cried.

"While the *Dorna* sees, while the *Dorna* lives," he said, "we will not leave her."

"We will not leave you!" I said.

"Abandon us!" he demanded.

"It cannot be done," I said.

"Why not?" he said.

"The *Dorna* sees, the *Dorna* lives," I said.

Tab had the *Dorna* backoared from the Brigand Island, whose tremors had now subsided, and whose pilots were already struggling to rekindle fires in which irons might be heated, enabling them to control the course and speed of their vast mount. Mercenaries, outraged but no longer discomfited, shouted, brandished their weapons, and shook their fists. Thurnock brushed them a kiss from his fingertips as we withdrew, which gesture doubtless incensed them further. As I knew Thurnock, the massive, wily peasant, this was no idle, childish gratification but a movement designed with war in mind. It is a foolish and often short-lived enemy whose steel is subject to hatred and blinding emotion; beware more the blade subject to the wary mind, the blade whose lightning is patient and cunning. The thought of Pa-Kur, Master of the Black Caste, the Assassins, briefly crossed my mind. Soon I had come about in such a way that the *Dorna* was between the Brigand Island and the *Tesephone*. In this way I hoped to shield her from the two corsair vessels to port and the three to starboard.

"Prow to Thera," I told the helmsmen.

In a moment the mallet of the *keleustes* rang on the drum.

"You are rushing into the jaws of the larl," said Sakim.

"I do not think so," I said.

"You cannot withstand the attack of three knife ships," said Sakim.

"True," I said. Certainly that was the case without the support of the *Dorna*.

"Fly to Chios," said Sakim.

"That is impractical, given the condition of the *Dorna*," I said. "We would be intercepted by the two corsair ships to port, and possibly the Brigand Island. Then, engaged, we would be at the mercy, as well, of the three corsair vessels in our wake."

"I see little to choose from," said Sakim.

"The three corsair vessels to starboard are, for the moment, inert," I said. "I do not think they realize what has occurred here. Their strategy, I suspect, was to take the *Dorna*, either by further damaging her or beaching her on the Brigand Island. Clearly the mercenaries, given their ladders and formation, were intending, if possible, to board her in one way or another, either from the Brigand Island or the beach."

"They want the *Dorna*?" said Sakim.

"And possibly the *Tesephone*," I said.

"Why do you think this?" asked Sakim.

"Because we found the *Dorna* alive," I said. "She was crippled. If they wished, they could easily have sunk her."

"But they did not," said Sakim.

"I think they were waiting for the *Tesephone*," I said.

"So they could have two ships," he said.

"I think so," I said.

"And both crews," he said.

"I would suppose so," I said.

I listened to the pounding of the drum.

"Why are the corsair ships waiting?" asked Sakim.

"They will move shortly," I said. "I suspect they were not immediately aware of what occurred near the island. Perhaps they could not believe their strategy had failed. They may have thought, seeing the *Dorna* and *Tesephone* together, that we had been boarded and captured, that their plan had been success-ful."

"They will not think so for long," said Sakim, "as our oars taste Thassa and our prows are set for Thera."

Clitus, who had a glass of the Builders, and was on the stem deck, called back, "Three ships, to starboard, oars outboard!" And a moment later the sound of a drum, and then two others, carried over the water.

"Burdened with the *Dorna*," said Sakim. "We cannot escape."

"Shall we leave her?" I asked.

"No," said Sakim.

"How do you see things?" I asked.

"It would be easy for them, given our handicap," he said, "to ram us abeam, or at stem or stern, or to shear away oars."

"At the possible loss of one or two of their vessels?" I said.

"Possibly one, it seems clear," said Sakim. "The *Tesephone*, in free water, is like a flighted javelin."

"And in this very act, that of making our strike, we would pre-sumably be rammed by one or two other ships," I said.

"Presumably," he said.

"But in such an action at least two ships would be lost," I said, "the *Tesephone* and at least one of theirs."

"Yes," he said.

"The enemy has already lost two ships," I said, "one to the *Dorna* and one to the hith."

"What are you thinking?" asked Sakim.

"I am thinking the enemy would be reluctant to risk more ships, and would much prefer to replace his losses with two prizes, the *Dorna* and the *Tesephone*."

"Ah," said Sakim, "as you said, the *Dorna* was not destroyed when she was at the mercy of the corsairs."

"No," I said, "and they waited, it seems, for the *Tesephone* to join her."

"A second ship," said Sakim.

"I do not think the enemy wishes to use his rams and shearing blades," I said.

"He wants to board," said Sakim.

"And he has many fighting men ready to do so," I said, "skilled soldiers, evacuated from Chios."

"It is much easier to ram than board," said Sakim.

"And less dangerous," I said.

Consider the maneuvering required to draw alongside, the employment of fending oars, the closure with the enemy, facilitating the use of missiles at close range, the shifting gap between hulls, the uncertainty of footing, the sea destabilizing the two platforms involved, the temporary exposure of attackers, the resolution and desperation of defenders.

"I do not think the enemy will mind expending his mercenaries in that endeavor," said Sakim.

"I am sure he will be generous in their application," I said.

"They will earn their pay," said Sakim.

"I fear there is little booty for them here," I said.

The pay of mercenaries is often much in the form of whatever booty they can manage to seize and carry. Sometimes they are apprehended and slain in retreats due to their own unwillingness to cast aside earlier obtained spoils.

"I suspect that few of them have ever fought at sea," said Sakim.

"They will expect a small land action, only in a different venue," I said.

"A tiny land of wood, possibly awash, shifting beneath their feet," said Sakim.

"Steady," I called down to the *keleustes*, "slow, be as if on some excursion."

"Is this a suitable beat?" inquired Sakim. "The *Dorna*, even crippled, can manage more than this."

"Let the enemy rejoice," I said. "Let them think we can do no better. Let them think they can have us when they please."

"You gamble for time," said Sakim.

"Hopefully," I said, "they will do no more than keep us in sight until they are joined by the two ships to port."

The ideal for an enemy contemplating boarding was clearly, if possible, to utilize two ships and draw alongside the target vessel on both the port and starboard side, thus permitting a simultaneous, coordinated attack, analogous to a land action in which an enemy can be attacked both on the front and rear, or on both flanks. To do this in one maneuver the enemy would require four ships, two for the *Dorna* and two for the *Tesephone*.

That necessitated being joined by at least one of the two ships to port.

I looked to the sun, Sol, Tor-tu-Gor, the common star of Earth and Gor, of dozens of orbiting bodies, from massive to miniscule.

"It is two Ahn until darkness," said Sakim.

"At least," I said.

I hoped that it would take at least an Ahn for the enemy to bring his consolidated forces into a position where an attack would be possible.

For the next twenty Ehn, the *Tesephone* and the *Dorna* rowed abreast, like a larger and smaller waterfowl, the beat set by my charge to the *Tesephone's keleustes*.

Thurnock lowered the glass of the Builders. "Five ships, now joined, like birds of prey, pursue," he said.

Captain Tab and I, given the proximity of our two ships, had had no difficulty in communicating.

I had issued certain orders. One dealt with a deep coil of rope on the stern deck. The second order was to mount a ship's lantern, unlit, on the stern deck of both the *Dorna* and the *Tesephone*.

"At this pace," said Sakim, "we shall be overtaken well before darkness."

"I trust the enemy believes so," I said.

"Thus he proceeds at his leisure?" said Sakim.

"Exactly," I said.

Some ten Ehn later the coiled line on the stern deck was deployed. Though the *Dorna* and *Tesephone* were still abreast, the line was fastened to the stern of the *Tesephone* and the prow of the *Dorna*. This action would likely pass notice with the enemy, given his distance. If not, I expected that it would give him little concern.

Fifteen Ehn later I signaled the *keleustes* to cease the beat, and the *Dorna* and the *Tesephone* rocked on the water.

"Surely you do not intend to capitulate?" said Sakim.

"There is little point in capitulating," I said, "if it means the death of every man aboard the *Dorna* and the *Tesephone*."

"You would seek more time?" said Sakim.

"While Tor-tu-Gor goes about his business," I said.

"The five ships of the enemy pause," said Thurnock. Clearly their oars were at rest, blades submerged.

They were now within several yards of us.

I had the speaking tube brought to the stern deck. "Terms!" I called. "Terms!"

Laughter drifted across the water to us.

"Prepare to die!" we heard.

"We have a hundred stone of gold aboard," I called back. "At the first sign of hostility we shall cast it into the sea!"

There seemed some confusion on the stem deck of the nearest vessel, which I took, mistakenly, as it turned out, to be the flagship of the corsair fleet.

"Shall we now give the gold to the waves of mighty Thassa?" I called.

"Let it be the price by means of which you purchase your lives," came back. "Transfer the gold to this ship and your lives will be spared."

"Do not believe them," said Sakim.

"Thurnock," I said, "can you see who speaks?"

Thurnock lifted the glass of the Builders. "We know him," said Thurnock. "It is Laios, from the tavern of Glaukos, *The Living Island*, in Sybaris."

I had thought it would have been Nicomachos, Admiral of the Fleet of the Farther Islands, posted in Sybaris. Was he not a familiar of Archelaos, governor of Thera? Would he not be the plausible commander of the corsair fleet?

"Laios?" I asked.

"Laios," said Thurnock.

"Not Ctesippus?" I asked.

"No, Laios," said Thurnock.

"In the tavern," I said, "Ctesippus had primacy over Laios. Thus I conjecture that the ship sunk by the hith, the sinking of which Ctesippus survived, was the designated flagship of the corsair fleet."

"And Ctesippus was the Admiral?" said Thurnock.

"He was deferred to and his orders were promptly obeyed," I said, "even to abandoning men to the risk of drowning."

I then turned back, with the speaking tube, to the nearby ship.

"I will deal only with he who is first amongst you," I said, "else the gold goes in the sea."

"I am first," called Laios.

"One ship," I called, "reposes in safety, concealed behind four ships. Doubtless that brave vessel is your newly designated flagship."

"No!" called Laios.

"Have it launch a longboat, and bring your Admiral, Ctesippus, forward, to negotiate."

"Show us the gold!" called Laios.

"Bring your Admiral, Ctesippus, forward, to negotiate," I said, angrily.

"Madness!" cried Laios.

"Then you accept responsibility for the loss of the gold?" I asked.

"Hold, do nothing," called Laios. "I will consult."

"That will take time," said Sakim.

"I trust so," I said.

We watched a longboat enter the water and begin to make its way back between enemy vessels to the farthest ship back, the presumed flagship of the corsair fleet.

"Tor-tu-Gor descends," said Sakim.

"I did not know we had a hundred stone of gold aboard," smiled Thurnock.

"The enemy," I said, "cannot be sure that we do not."

"Surely," said Sakim, "we have a hundred stone of imaginary gold aboard."

"Two hundred," I assured him.

"You did not specify that it was imaginary gold," said Thurnock.

"They did not ask," I said.

"We will make our move presently, will we not?" asked Sakim.

"I think that would be advisable," I said.

"When?" asked Sakim.

"When Ctesippus is well on his way forward, in a longboat," I said. "I do not think the fleet will care to leave him behind."

I then gave orders that the two stern lanterns, these on the *Dorna* and *Tesephone*, be lit.

"It is still light," said Sakim.

"I want the enemy to see that the lanterns are lit," I said.

"I am not sure we can make it to darkness," said Sakim.

"Nor am I," I said.

"If we are so fortunate," said Sakim, "the enemy will think it madness that such lanterns are lit."

"Let them deem it rather a device to keep our ships together in the darkness," I said.

"They would give away our position," said Sakim.

"They would give away a position," I said, "but not ours."

A few Ehn later, Thurnock reported that a longboat had been launched from the last ship.

"So, when?" asked Sakim.

"In a bit," I said. "Let it get farther from the mother ship, say, midpoint between the mother ship and the four closer ships."

"In that way," said Thurnock, "there is likely to be confusion as to who should take the Admiral aboard."

"And the ships will hold their places, awaiting orders," said Sakim.

"Let us hope so," I said.

"I trust, fellows," I said, calling down to the benches, "you are well rested."

Eager assent greeted this speculation.

"The longboat is midway between the mothership and the forward ships," said Thurnock.

"Now, lads," I called down, "we will see if you row faster for your lives than the foe for his pay."

I then slashed my hand downward, and the *keleustes* brought his mallet down on the great drum.

The *Tesephone* leapt forward, slipped past the *Dorna*, tautened the line between herself and the *Dorna*, was arrested by the line, and then, smoothly, forcefully, began to draw against it, giving impetus to her fellow. At the same time, the rowers of the *Dorna* bent to their oars, and the *Dorna*, partly towed, partly under its own power, fell into place behind the *Tesephone*. The enemy had not anticipated the suddenness of our motion, as we stole a start, nor, I think, understood the speed which we could achieve, even with the imperfect condition of the *Dorna*. We profited, as well, from the confusion and delay attendant on recovering their Admiral. These factors gave us the start we needed to slip into the lowering dusk. Shortly thereafter, as darkness fell, I had the two lanterns removed from the sterns of the *Dorna* and *Tesephone* and mounted on two separate buoyant frameworks, fastened together with some sixty or seventy feet of line. These I set adrift, that pursuers might mistake them for lights mounted to assist the *Dorna* and *Tesephone* to remain in proximity despite the darkness. Needless to say, once we were ahead of the pursuers, and had established a sufficient interval, the *keleustes* put away his mallet and, descending to the benches, called the beat by voice. At the second Ahn, we raised the mast, lowered the yard, loosened the sail, relieved the helmsmen, and rested the oarsmen.

"Well done, Commander," said Sakim. "I think we are safe now. We should reach Thera and the Cove of Harpalos without difficulty."

"I am afraid," I said.

"Why?" asked Sakim. "We have eluded our pursuers."

"Men," I said.

"Then what is there to fear?" asked Sakim.

"That which is not man," I said, "that which pursues and does not know it pursues, that which is guided, and does not know it is guided, that which serves and does not know it serves."

"Do not fear the Brigand Island," said Sakim. "It was wounded, torn, and burned. It was abandoned near Chios. It was left there. You saw it left behind. The mercenaries fear it. They want nothing more to do with it. Could it follow us, it would have done so. It may be dead."

"Do you think," I asked, "that it can feel?"

"Surely," said Sakim.

"Really feel?" I asked.

"Yes," said Sakim. "It must have some rudiments of feeling, however simple and primitive, else it could not respond to irons, to gouging instruments, to fire."

"It must be a patient beast," I said.

"I do not think it knows that men exist," said Sakim, "only that pain and pleasure exist."

"The course and watch are set," I said.

"Thurnock is already asleep," said Sakim.

"Dear Thurnock could sleep in a kennel of hungry sleen," I said.

"He sleeps soundly," said Sakim. "May you do so as well."

"Have me awakened at the first light," I said.

"I shall notify the watch," said Sakim.

CHAPTER FIFTY-FOUR

We Fail to Elude the Enemy

It was the tenth Ahn, the Gorean noon.

At dawn we had lowered the mast and yard, thereby decreasing our visibility.

We moved at first beat.

"It seems," said Sakim, "that we have Thassa to ourselves."

Hardly had Sakim spoken than the lookout on the *Tesephone's* stern deck called out, "Sails! Five sails astern!"

His cry was echoed a moment later by the lookout ensconced on the stern deck of the *Dorna*.

"Mast up!" I called.

This cry was raised, too, on the *Dorna*.

We ascended to the stern deck and were shortly joined by Thurnock and Clitus.

"Second beat," I called to the *keleustes*. "Second beat," he responded.

The beats vary from ship to ship. My ships, the *Dorna* and *Tesephone*, and those others at sea or docked in the arsenal at Port Kar, used a five-beat system. The first beat is the least taxing for the oarsmen whereas the fifth beat is the most taxing. The fifth beat cannot be satisfactorily maintained over more than twenty or so Ehn. Muscles ache, men tire, and rhythm, so essential for oared vessels, is impaired or lost. Accordingly, the fifth beat is usually reserved for situations in which ramming or shearing is imminent. A good *keleustes*, like good helmsmen, is invaluable, particularly in battle. Some ships use a mechanical device, rather like a metronome, to guide the *keleustes* in his work, in governing his striking on the metal drum, but most captains of knife ships do not avail themselves of this aid, regarding it as of little worth. Too often it is, in its thoughtless way, unrelated to the reality of the moment, sometimes dangerously so. They prefer a living *keleustes* who can see the benches and heed the action of the oars and, consequently, adjust the beat, subtly, as necessary, to optimize the performance of the vessel, subject to actual conditions.

An Ahn later our lookout reported that the pursuers had gained.

"We cannot outrun them," said Thurnock.

"Not at second beat," I said.

"The *Dorna* cannot keep up with us if we go to third beat," said Thurnock.

"Attach the towing line," I ordered.

"It will slow the *Tesephone*," said Thurnock.

"Then," I said, "the *Tesephone* will be slowed."

The line was attached and the *Dorna* fell in behind the *Tesephone*.

"Third beat," I called to the *keleustes*.

"Third beat," he responded.

An Ahn following the transition to third beat we had maintained much the same distance between us and the foe.

"Overnight, last night, they followed like sleen," said Sakim.

"In darkness, how could it be?" asked Clitus.

"I had hoped," I said, "that our tactic of the buoyed ships' lanterns might have led them astray."

"It did not do so," said Sakim, moodily.

"Their success in pursuit was their good fortune," said Thurnock.

"And our ill fortune," growled Clitus.

"I do not think this was a simple matter of fortune," said Sakim.

I did not speak, but I shared Sakim's doubt.

"Thassa is wide, and ships are small," said Thurnock.

"Yet five sails mark the horizon," said Sakim.

"We are holding our lead," said Thurnock.

"They are permitting us to do so, as of now," I said.

"Could we not, at third beat, do so indefinitely?" asked Thurnock.

"Possibly," I said, "if matters now were as they commonly are."

"But they are not, mighty scion of the Peasantry," said Sakim. "Consider the crewing involved. They could bring fresh oarsmen to the benches every ten Ehn if they wished, even at the fifth beat."

"They are content, at present," I said, "merely to keep us accessible."

"Our lads are strong and skilled," said Clitus. "I would match them for a time against any on Thassa."

"For a time," I said. "That is the point, time."

"Captain?" asked Clitus.

"Our lads," I said, "however strong and skilled, cannot match frequent shifts of oarsmen."

"But until darkness?" said Clitus.

"I think until then," I said.

"You hope to slip away in darkness?" said Sakim.

"I do not think that will be possible," I said, "for a reason which I suspect you can divine."

"Then let us then turn about now and do battle," said Thurnock.

"We would be destroyed," I said.

"But nobly," said Thurnock. "I do not care to rush into meaningless, unavailing darkness, like some quivering urt."

"Sometimes a clever urt can escape the descending paw of the larl," I said.

"I do not understand," said Thurnock. "But I know my captain. He is not a coward."

"Have you something in mind, Captain?" asked Sakim.

"Yes," I said.

"You know something we do not?" he asked.

"Possibly," I said.

"You have a plan?"

"There is a chance, a slim chance," I said. "It goes back to Sybaris, before we left for Mytilene."

"Are you sure of it?" asked Sakim.

"No," I said. "Not at all."

"Take courage, dear Thurnock," said Clitus. "You can die tomorrow as well as today."

"I do not like being thought a coward," said Thurnock.

"Why should you concern yourself," said Clitus, "if the enemy entertains a mistaken notion?"

"Such might work to your advantage," I said.

"Shall we maintain our present course, to the Cove of Harpalos?" asked Sakim.

"No," I said. "Set our course for Sybaris, straight for Sybaris."

"Is that wise?" asked Clitus.

"We have no choice," I said.

"It has to do with the 'chance'?" said Sakim.

"Of course," I said.

"Would you tell me more of this chance?" asked Sakim.

"I do not think so," I said. "If I did so, you would realize how slim it is."

"To Sybaris?" said Sakim.

"Yes," I said.

"I shall inform the helmsmen," he said.

"Do so," I said.

"The corsairs could overtake us in the night," said Thurnock.

"That is possible," I said, "but I do not think they would care to engage at night."

"In the morning, shortly before first light," said Thurnock, "I shall have the mast lowered, that we seem to disappear."

"Keep it up," I said, "and have the sail full."

"Captain?" said Thurnock.

"It is important that we be seen," I said.

"And thus we show our boldness, our contempt for the foe," said Thurnock.

"Doubtless," I said.

"Five sails hold steady in our wake," said the lookout, lowering a glass of the Builders.

"Would we had brought along Margot, Millicent, and Courtney, the worthless slaves," said Sakim.

"No woman in a collar is worthless," I said. "Only free women, being priceless, are worthless. Margot, Millicent, and Courtney are all comely. Stripped and exhibited on a slave block, each would bring at least a silver tarsk."

"Would they were here," said Sakim. "We could hand them about tonight, and, in the morning, use them as human shields."

"That would be a waste of slave," I said. "All domestic animals have some value and comely slaves are no exception."

"It is pleasant to have absolute power over a beautiful woman," said Sakim.

"That is why they are enslaved and put in collars," I said.

"They love their collars and hunger to be owned," said Sakim.

"I know a world where many slaves starve, denied their collars," I said.

"Still," said Sakim, "I would that Margot, Millicent, and Courtney were here."

"Other than the obvious, what would we do with them?" I asked.

"When we were finished with them, bind them naked, hand and foot, and leave them on the deck," said Sakim. "They are property. They are loot. They are slaves. In that way they would abide the outcome of the action, will wait to see what is to be done with them, their fates dependent on the doings of men, must wait to see who will own them."

It might be noted, in passing, that neither I nor Sakim, nor others, considered the possibility that, should the corsairs be victorious, they might recognize Margot, Millicent, and Courtney as former allies and free them. In Gorean thinking such an option is absurd. The women had been collared. Thus, they were slaves, and would stay slaves. There is a Gorean saying, "Once a slave, always a slave." This is a saying to which Gorean free women, in their hatred of female slaves and in their contempt for them, interestingly, also subscribe. The notion is that a woman who has once been in the collar is spoiled for freedom. Thereafter she can be naught but a slave. Another saying, whispered about by slaves, is that they would not trade their collars and the freedom they know in their collars for a ubarate. The emotional freedom of love, service, and chains, and the fear of the whip, which will be assuredly used on them if they are not pleasing, is inordinately precious. In bondage they find their wholeness and fulfillment.

"Sakim," said I, "inquire of our stores, and of those of the *Dorna*, what quantities of sip root we have on board."

Sip root is the active ingredient of slave wine. It is ground, and added to a brew of scarlet meal and water. It is used to control conception in female slaves for, obviously, the reproductivity of the female slave, as that of many other forms of domestic animals, is subject to the discretion of the owner. I am told the taste is horrid. Commonly the female, always a slave or a woman soon to be enslaved, is knelt naked, with her hands braceleted or tied behind her. Her head is then held back and her nostrils are pinched shut. The brew is poured into her mouth, filling it. After a time she must breathe, and, to do so, she has no choice but to swallow the brew. It is felt that two things are hereby accomplished. First, conception is blocked, until a master might decide otherwise, and the woman is well reminded, so treated, that she is, or will soon be, a slave. The effects of slave wine may be removed by a drink spoken of as a Releaser, which is aromatic and delicious. When a slave is knelt and ordered to imbibe that drink, she realizes, perhaps to her misery, that her Master has decided that she will be bred. It is common for Gorean war ships to have sip root or prepared slave wine amongst their stores. Captured women are commonly enslaved. Gorean men tend to prefer the woman in a collar at their feet to a ransom.

"I will do so," said Sakim. "But may I inquire for what purpose you wish to undertake such an inventory?"

"It will become clear in the morning," I said. I then turned to Thurnock and Clitus, who were at hand. "Thurnock," I said, "we will need screening which, when brought into play, will be capable of shielding bowmen and resisting arrow fire."

"We have no materials for such an effort," said Thurnock.

"You are mistaken," I said. "Take what planking you need from the stem and stern decks." I then addressed Clitus. "Clitus," I said, "the enemy will use grapnels. As we are grievously outnumbered, we must do our best to limit boarding."

"I shall have axes ready to sever the ropes," said Clitus.

"The grapnels," I said, "are likely to be, close to the hooks, on lengths of chain."

"We must then chop the rails away," he said.

"That will take our fellows time," I said, "time during which they will be exposed to enemy fire."

"How can it be helped?" asked Clitus.

"By rendering the grapnels useless, or largely so," I said.

"I do not understand," said Clitus.

"We will arrange the matter," I said. "Too, gather together some small vessels of tharlarion oil and a supply of small nails. That done, please call to the *Dorna*. See that Captain Tab is brought aboard. I would speak with him."

CHAPTER FIFTY-FIVE

Engagement is Imminent

"There they are," said Sakim, viewing the horizon with a glass of the Builders.

"We expected they would be, did we not?" I asked.

"Of course," said Sakim. He lowered the glass.

"Again," said Clitus, "even from afar, they have somehow followed us, unerringly through the darkness."

"Sakim," I said, "speak to Clitus."

"The matter, hitherto speculative, is now clear," said Sakim. "The Brigand Island, in all its simplicity, enormity, and inert sluggishness, has been trained to associate ships, some ships, randomly selected, with a reward, a feeding. Accordingly, it follows ships, hoping to be fed."

"The corsair ships will not feed it," said Clitus.

"No," said Sakim, "but it is easy for them to follow the beast while it seeks a different vessel, hoping to be fed."

"But we will not feed it," said Clitus.

"The beast does not know that," said Sakim.

"And who knows," I said. "Perhaps we will feed it."

"Yes!" whispered Sakim.

"I do not understand," said Clitus.

"Captain," called Thurnock, upward from the main deck, "the plankage has been prepared. It can be raised at your command."

"Let the enemy not know it exists," I said, "not yet."

"I have seen to the railings, following your instructions," said Clitus.

"On the starboard side of the *Tesephone* and the port side of the *Dorna*," I said.

"As specified," said Clitus.

"Thurnock," I called, "signal the *Dorna* to come alongside, and see to the lashing of the ships together."

"You will have a fort in the sea," said Clitus.

"One may then, in battle, by means of a single platform, apply men as needs be," I said.

"So joined, tied together, many oars unavailable, speed is lost, maneuverability is nullified," said Sakim. "We will be an easy target for ramming."

"I do not think the enemy will care to ram, at least at first," I said. "As they outnumber us considerably in men, and presumably want our vessels as prizes, they will elect to board."

"You will fight a land battle at sea," said Sakim.

"And what is joined can be disjoined," I said.

Shortly thereafter, the *Dorna* and the *Tesephone*, oars inboard, were lashed together. In this way, we now had not only a single platform for combat, but only two, not four, sides of our ships would be exposed to the risk of boarding.

Sakim again lifted the glass of the Builders. "It seems," he said, "the enemy has vanished."

"Should we not, the *Dorna* and the *Tesephone*, lower our own masts, as well?" asked Clitus.

"No," I said.

We were then joined by Thurnock.

"All is ready, Captain," he said.

"I see them now," said Sakim. "They are at beat four."

"They are eager to close," I said.

"With them," said Sakim, "is a darkness in the water, a plateau in the sea."

"The Brigand Island," said Thurnock.

"I see smoke," said Clitus.

"From the fires by means of which they torture the beast to do their bidding," I said.

"It does not even know the source of its pain," said Sakim.

"I rage," snarled Thurnock.

"Doubtless, in its pursuit of the last two nights, it was not goaded by fire and iron," I said. "Its pursuit would have been painless, it not having been necessary, or expedient, to alter its course or hasten its progress."

"After surcease, the sudden return of agony must be excruciating," said Clitus.

"It is a dumb beast," said Thurnock. "It is not like a reluctant slave girl who, to her misery and tears, grasps, with a single stroke of the whip on her stripped fair body, that she will henceforth obey the least of commands and suggestions with perfection, instantly and unquestioningly."

"One no longer needs the glass of the Builders," said Sakim. "I can make them out, clearly now."

"As can we all," said Clitus.

"How will they proceed?" asked Thurnock.

"I expect them to do what is simplest, and exposes their ships to the least risk," I said.

"They will bring the Brigand Island alongside, and we shall find our floating citadel besieged," said Sakim.

"I expect they will be lavish in expending their mercenaries," I said.

"The more who die the more loot to be distributed amongst survivors," said Clitus.

"And those in the ships, the elite, risk nothing," said Thurnock.

"We cannot withstand dozens of ladders and hundreds of men," said Thurnock.

"The Brigand Island will move to the starboard side," said Sakim. "It is being so goaded."

"The oars of the enemy ships, save those of one, rest," said Clitus.

"That ship," I said, "will be the ears and eyes of the corsair fleet. It will approach more closely, not closely enough to be in danger, but close enough to monitor developments and, if need be, intervene and direct operations. It, by signals, will remain in contact with the main body of the fleet, the four ships held in reserve."

"Its oars now rest," said Clitus.

It lay some hundred yards astern of our small 'fort in the sea'.

"The Brigand Island approaches," said Sakim.

"We are taking aboard fellows from the *Dorna*," said Thurnock.

"That was the plan," I said, "given an attack on a single flank."

"We can use every man," said Sakim.

"Thurnock, if you would," I said, "please inform our fellows that engagement is imminent."

CHAPTER FIFTY-SIX

One Makes Use of What Means are at Hand

A dozen ladders struck against the starboard-side hull of the *Tesephone*.

A trumpet blared, hundreds of voices screamed cries of war, metals clattered, wood creaked, helmeted visages appeared, eyes wild, ladders sagged, swords thrust, quarrels and arrows passed in flight, men bellowed, men screamed, shields were pressed back, ladders were thrust back and to the side.

Once again a trumpet sounded and ladders were drawn away.

The deck was awash with blood.

"We cannot withstand another such onslaught," said Sakim.

"They know we are finished," growled Thurnock.

"Then," I said, "they know more than we."

At this point the massive, heavy body of the Brigand Island had slipped some seven or eight feet back, away from the side of the *Tesephone*. I did not know if this was intended, and wrought by iron and fire, or if it were the result of some movement internal to the beast itself.

"That attack," said Clitus, wiping his bloodied trident, "was no bare probe."

"They have tested our defenses and assessed our numbers," said Thurnock. "Their officers are heartened; they are sanguine with victory; they can feel it in their grasp, they can smell it in our shed blood, see it in our weakness and paucity, hear it in the groans of our wounded, note it in the confidence and jubilation of their troops."

"The observation ship of the corsairs, forward from the balance of the fleet, is closer now," said Clitus.

"It wants to observe the kill," said Thurnock.

"I want it closer," I said, "and I want the mercenaries to mass together, crowded, shield to shield, intent on naught but war, each hoping for his place on a ladder, each eager for a kill."

"Dear Captain," said Thurnock, "I fear you will soon have your wish."

A violent tremor shook the beast.

"They are bringing it against the hull again," said Clitus. "The irons glow, the spikes gleam; the enemy churns agony once more into its gaping wounds."

"How can a beast stand such torment?" asked Thurnock.

"Perhaps it has no feeling," said Clitus.

"If it had no feeling, it could not be goaded, or guided, by such means," said Sakim.

"But it may not know feeling as we know it," said Clitus.

"Perhaps not," said Sakim.

"It does not even know the source of its misery, only its misery," said Thurnock.

"In a moment the beast will be once more against our hull," said Clitus.

"The enemy advances, massed," said Thurnock.

"The ladders are like a forest," said Sakim.

"The beast has found us, but has not yet been rewarded," I said.

I raised my arm, looking to the stem deck, where, at the very prow, two mariners stood, amidst baskets.

The *Tesephone* seemed to shudder as the left flank of the Brigand Island slid against its side.

The war cry of the mercenaries was deafening.

Ladders struck once more against our gunwales.

I brought my arm down swiftly, savagely, and the mariners at the prow emptied basket after basket into the sea.

Shortly thereafter, scarcely had war sandals been pressed on the first rungs of the braced scaling ladders, than a sudden, hideous tremor shook the beast, a violent stream of air and water exploded upward from its breathing hole, and its enormous body reared a dozen feet from the water, scattering ladders and men. Then it submerged, and the water was filled with startled, struggling men, ladders, tents, supplies, and a camp's debris. Steam and bubbles had hissed up as the water flowed into the fires and drenched the spurring, heated irons by means of which its movements had been controlled.

"It may be under the ship!" cried Sakim.

"No!" I said, pointing. "See the water, to starboard!"

Then the water seemed quiet.

Might not that monstrous body move beneath the ship?

I then feared Sakim's alarm might soon be warranted.

"Where is it?" said Clitus.

"I do not know," I said.

"It is gone," said Clitus.

"I do not know," I said.

"The observation ship of the corsairs approaches," said Thurnock.

It was clearly its intent to succor and retrieve goods and men, these scattered like detritus in the water.

Suddenly, without warning, violently, like a massive, discharged, living quarrel, threatening the sky and clouds, the immense body of the Brigand Island hurtled upward, vertically, twisting, from the water.

In that terrible moment I saw what few men had seen, even those accustomed to camp upon and inhabit living islands, the monster beneath the placid surface, hundreds of tentacle-like filaments, tiny eyes, and a sharp, hooklike beak.

It could well be that, in that brief moment, it was the first time the eyes of the Brigand Island had risen above the surface.

Then it returned to the water, falling, like a mountain, and the residue of this great splash descended like rain on the *Dorna* and *Tesephone*, and the closest of the five corsair ships.

"The eyes!" said Sakim. "I would not care to be seen by such eyes."

"We are not moving," I said. "We are large. We are a fortress in the sea. Conjoined with the *Dorna*, we might be taken to be a natural object. We might not be registered as something deserving attention, if at all."

"It is rising to the surface," said Sakim, "but on its back, under the swimmers."

"It cannot breathe so," said Clitus.

"The head of the island seldom submerges," said Sakim. "But when it does, as in scouting fish, mating, or territorial conflict, the breathing hole closes. The head can remain under water for better than an Ahn, and the body, as well, should the beast so choose."

There was a startling crackle of sound and flashes coming from the water, and the screams of men.

"Thus," said Sakim, "the beast shocks and paralyzes prey, commonly fish."

I took the matter to be the result of an organically generated electrical charge.

"You may not care to look," said Sakim.

The victims, stung, or shocked, or numbed, could not speak or move, but the horror in their eyes could be easily read as the tentacle-like filaments conveyed them to the hook-like beak.

"The corsair ship is back-oaring," said Thurnock. "They are no longer concerned with their fellows."

Most of these, shields, weapons, and helmets discarded, were still in the water. Several, half visible, had doubtless drowned. Some thrashed about, in terror, to flee the tentacle-like filaments. The wisest remained as still as possible, the tentacle-like filaments, like snakes, feeling about in the water.

"The captain of that ship," said Sakim, "is a fool."

"Perhaps only ignorant," I said.

We had all by now had evidence of the capacity of the Brigand Island, and perhaps other such islands, to detect motion in the water. Had we not been followed unerringly, even in the night?

"He abandons his fellows," said Clitus.

"He should rest his oars," said Sakim.

"It is unwise to wake the sleeping larl," said Thurnock.

"Or the fierce bosk," said Sakim, looking at me.

"I wonder if a mountain can hate," said Clitus.

"If so," said Thurnock, "I would not care to be the object of its wrath."

"Do you think," asked Clitus, "that it now understands what was done to it, that it now associates its pain and misery with a visible, independent, identifiable source, something that can be dealt with, another form of life, an enemy, men?"

"I do not know," I said.

"I think so," said Sakim. "Moreover, I think it, in some way, feels it was misled or betrayed."

"How is that?" asked Clitus.

"It was trained to expect, as a result of certain behaviors, rewards, at least occasionally," said Sakim. "Then, following the behavior, there was not only no reward, but dreadful, disgusting, keen disappointment."

"The ringing of the bell signifies food to the animal," I said, "and it welcomes the sound of the bell and salivates. Then, after a time, the ringing of the bell is followed not by food, but by unexpected disappointment and pain. The animal is confused. It goes insane."

"What animal?" asked Sakim.

"It is not important," I said.

"What is this about ringing bells?" said Sakim.

"Nothing, my friend," I said, "nothing."

"Look!" said Clitus. "The island rolls over and submerges!"

"The observation ship turns about, it flees," said Sakim.

"It wishes to join its fleet," said Thurnock.

"I do not think the fleet will be pleased about that," I said.

Some Ihn passed, perhaps nearly an Ehn.

"Aiii!" screamed Clitus.

I gripped the rail of the *Tesephone*.

Once more, the enormous living weight of the Brigand Island exploded up from the sea and then, from some sixty to eighty yards above the surface, plunging downward, it fell athwart the retreating corsair ship, snapping it in two.

"What is going on now?" asked Clitus.

Sakim disengaged a glass of the Builders from his belt and trained it on the divided sinking corsair ship.

"Where once was a fine ship," said Sakim, "there is now debris."

"No, not that," said Clitus. "What of the beast?"

"I think it is calm," said Sakim. "It is going away. It moves slowly, peacefully, toward the horizon."

"It is now free," I said.

"In time its burns and wounds will heal," said Thurnock.

"What did you have cast into the sea, from the baskets?" asked Clitus.

"What I hoped the island would take for its long-anticipated reward," I said, "bundles of sip root."

"Disappointment and betrayal, horror and disgust," said Clitus.

"That was my hope," I said.

"So the bell of pleasure became the bell of pain," said Sakim.

"Something like that," I said.

"Sometimes a tarsk-bit, cast into the scale," said Sakim, "can unbalance the weight of mountains."

"That was my hope," I said.

"The island gone, the corsair fleet will set itself to rescue survivors," said Clitus. "Should we not then unlash our ships and attempt to withdraw?"

"No," I said. "It is early. We could easily be overtaken."

"What shall we do then?" asked Clitus.

"Care for our wounded," I said, "and prepare to resist boarding."

CHAPTER FIFTY-SEVEN

War at Sea

"They are coming!" called the lookout.

I lifted my hand to Captain Tab on the stern deck of the *Dorna*, and he returned this salute.

Following the sinking of the forward ship, or observation ship, by the maddened living island, which we commonly spoke of as the "Brigand Island," the corsair fleet was reduced to four vessels, two of which were now drawing close, one to attempt drawing alongside the port side of the *Dorna*, and the other intending to draw alongside the starboard side of the *Tesephone*.

The grapnels of the enemy, as I had anticipated, had some seven or eight feet of chain between the eye of the grapnel and the normal casting ropes. This arrangement made it impractical to chop away the casting rope, thus rendering the grapnel ineffective. The usual negative effect of this arrangement was to shorten the distance the grapnel could be cast by one individual, necessitating then greater proximity, the use of an engine, or the vulnerable clustering of two or more individuals. More importantly, in understanding the nature of the grapnel, with its customary three or four hooks, one recognizes that it must have an accessible, independent anchoring point to render it effective, such as the top of a wall, the girth of a branch, a railing, or such. If the grapnel is denied purchase, its utility to the enemy is nullified.

We surveyed the ship approaching our starboard side.

"The decks are crowded with mercenaries!" said a man.

"How can we resist such steel?" asked a man.

"Take heart," called another, stringing his bow. "How could you miss, even you, firing into that throng."

"Pick your targets," I said.

"Attend the captain," roared Thurnock. "You do not aim at a herd of tabuk, you aim at one tabuk."

"Shields will be raised," I said. "Keep swords, knives, bludgeons, axes, ready."

On the other side of our small 'fort in the sea', Tab and the crew of the *Dorna* were similarly observing the approach of a corsair ship and readying themselves for action.

The enemy would, to the best of his ability, attack simultaneously at the port side of the *Dorna* and the starboard side of the *Tesephone*, but this maneuver, given a choppy sea, intermittent gusts of wind, the difference in vessels, a disparity of helmsmen and command, and the rocking of the target is more easily planned than executed. Ideally, from our point of view, the enemy vessels would be unable to attack our 'fort' at the same time, this permitting us to concentrate our forces in such a way as to match, or nearly match, the width of at least a first boarding party on one side. As suggested earlier, the lashing together of the *Dorna* and *Tesephone* made this possible, permitting a rapid, judicious distribution of men and resources, allowing them to be applied when and where most needed.

As the prow of the corsair ship at our starboard side slipped past our stern deck, like a long, gliding sea tharlarion, her port oars were withdrawn. She ground against our side. As she did so, I called, "Oars outboard," and the oars of the *Tesephone*'s starboard benches thrust out, trying to force a distance between the *Tesephone* and the corsair. Given the weight of the corsair and surge of the sea, several oars snapped, but others, some bending and others half broken, interposed themselves between the two hulls. Some of the corsair mercenaries had leapt between the ships at the moment of contact, but these, isolated from their fellows who could not follow them, were cut down or forced back over the rail, some of whom were being crushed between the vessels in our battle to force the hulls apart. Then, in the wash of the sea, the corsair was separated from our proximity and rocked some ten feet to the side. Clearly the enemy must strive to close with us. He must strive to draw our ships together, or draw back and bring his beak or ram into play.

"Bold fellows," called Thurnock, admiringly.

"Bold for an additional bounty of gold," hissed Clitus.

Several mercenaries had plunged into the sea with hand axes, and, reaching and climbing upward in the rolling sea, assisted by oars thrust forth from the corsair, dipping and rising, had clambered onto the few remaining oars of the *Tesephone* which were still holding the corsair at bay. These they were frenziedly attacking with their axes. "Stay back!" I cried to our fellows. Given the railing of the *Tesephone* we could not well interfere with their work without unduly exposing ourselves.

"The grapnels are next!" I cried. "Fire on any who touch them!"

Bows were leveled.

On the corsair ship, several who held the casting ropes hurled them down.

One was killed by a screaming officer, and then men with shields rushed to the rail, that those who would cast the grapnels might loft them from behind shielding. Suddenly dozens of these devices, heavy with seven or eight feet of chain, most cast by two men, hurtled toward the *Tesephone*.

A cheer went up from the corsairs.

As much as seven or eight men would drag on each grapnel rope, to pull the corsair ship and the *Tesephone* together.

I heard an oar snap and then another.

I also heard screams from the water between the vessels. The oars of the enemy, to which the mercenaries had clung, had been withdrawn, forcing them from the oars, into the water. It was more than apparent to these brave fellows that their position, as the ships' hulls began to approach one another, was not an enviable one. Some swam desperately to make their way to and about the prow or stern of the corsair vessel. Some dove under its hull, and would hope to be reboarded on its starboard side. Others were crushed.

A grapnel is ineffective without purchase.

For example, it cannot fasten itself to the side of a vertical wall. Similarly, it cannot hold on a smooth flat surface. In such applications it can do little more than slide and scratch.

The sides of the two vessels were coming closer and closer to one another.

"Pull," I heard from the corsair vessel, and then, again, "Pull!"

The two hulls, rocking in the sea, approached one another, more and more closely.

The grapnel chains and ropes were taut.

Then, suddenly, there was a splintering of wood in several locations and the grapnels leaped backward with force, several even striking the corsair ship itself, others disappearing between the hulls, splashing into the water. Simultaneously, strings of men who, behind shields, were hauling on the grapnel ropes, lost their balance and spilled backward onto the deck of the corsair.

The ideal points of purchase for grapnels, the likely targets of their application, had been partially sawed through, and, given the stress imposed by the straining ropes, these points, mostly railings, broke loose.

Thus, for most practical purposes, the grapnels, denied purchase, were useless.

Freed of the grapnels, the two ships, responsive to the physics of the sea, once more rocked apart.

"Archers, shields!" blared a hand-held speaking tube on the corsair ship.

"Screens up!" I cried.

Scarcely had I cried than the plank screens, hitherto unnoticed, were raised and set.

Across the water, the speaking tube fell to the deck and Thurnock refitted another arrow to his string.

Quarrels like a rain of metal struck the shaken screens. Had it not been for the screens I fear the deck would have been raked with death. The planks bristled like the back of the poison-spined urt.

"Men for the *Dorna!*" cried a voice from behind me.

I looked about, wildly. "Every other man to the *Dorna*," I shouted. The other corsair ship, that addressing itself to the port side of the *Dorna*, had, despite the general neutralization of grapnels, grated alongside her, and, in the moment, was held in place by the sea. Mercenaries were trying to clamber over the corsair ship's railings, to force themselves to the muchly leveled deck of the *Dorna*. I was sure that the doubling of defenders could hold back at least a given wave of attackers. Should another and another wave mount to the railings, I had no doubt a boarding could be forced, that requiring that we must meet the enemy on our own decks. On our side of the 'fort', the storm of quarrels had lessened, and then cleared.

"Their quarrels are spent," called a man.

"Glory to the screens!" cried another.

"Do not neglect cover," I called.

Surely they did not think that an enemy would expend all his ammunition so early in battle. A trick as old as war itself, whether

waged with rocks or bullets, is to pretend the paucity or absence
of resources and then suddenly unleash them on a startled, unex-
pecting foe. To be sure, the cessation of fire was doubtless connected, at least in part, with the recognition that little was to be
gained by wasting ammunition on stout wooden screens, an im-
pervious target.

"The foe is quiet," said Clitus.

"He rests," said another, gratefully.

"Can it be?" asked Clitus.

"No," said Thurnock. "They are preparing a boarding party."

"Grapnels have failed," said Clitus.

"They will try to close with us, as the other ship with the
Dorna," I said.

"That is precarious," said Clitus.

"We are content that the risk be theirs," I said.

"We are half manned," said a seaman, apprehensively.

"They are doubtless well aware of that," said Thurnock.

"Recall our fellows from the *Dorna*," said a man.

"They are needed there," said another.

"We cannot meet them at the rail," said a man. "We are now
too few."

That was true. They could, sooner or later, overextend any line
we could bring to the rail.

"We will meet them on the deck," I said. "The screens are
ready. It takes but a moment to spread the oil. Our footing will
be secure."

"It will be a slaughter," said Thurnock.

"If all goes well," I said.

"We shall make it go well," said Thurnock.

"The foe! The foe!" cried an oarsman.

"Steady, steady!" I called. "There may be a shock. Keep the
screens steady."

And there was a shock, long and grating. The screens tottered
but remained in place.

"Oil!" I called.

It was cast from buckets on the deck.

Almost at the same time dozens of mercenaries, unopposed,
uttering war cries, leapt over the rail of the corsair ship on our
starboard side, and landed on the smooth, glistening deck, only
to cry out in dismay and alarm, as they slipped, skidded, and lost
their footing.

At the same time our men, bearing swords, axes, knives, and even clubs, rushed out from behind the screens, sure footed from the bits of nails fastened in their sandals and boots, and fell, like butchers on verr, on the numerous discomfited and often helpless foes, most unable to regain or maintain their footing.

Other mercenaries, dozens on the corsair ship, milled behind its railing, unwilling to follow their fellows, much aware of the hazard of placing themselves on so treacherous a surface.

Without grappling holding the ships together it was difficult for the corsair ship, given the sea, to retain its position, and soon, pitching and rocking, it was no longer at the side of the *Tesephone* but lay abeam of her by some seven or eight feet.

In this interval several of our men, moving the screens forward like walls, thrust mercenaries from the slick deck. Some other mercenaries, comprehending their predicament, had already cast aside their shields and weapons and had crawled or rolled to the railless edge of the *Tesephone* and plunged overboard, preferring the jeopardy of Thassa to the near certitude of extermination.

"Victory is ours!" cried a man.

"Cover!" I cried.

A volley of quarrels struck screens, penetrated the raised mast, skidded or tumbled across the deck, even to the *Dorna*.

"They will come again," said Thurnock.

"And the deck, next time, will be no surprise to them," said Clitus.

"Perhaps it will be," I said.

"Perhaps they will not come again," said a man.

"I think they will," said Thurnock. "They cannot be unaware that, on this side, we are still grossly undermanned."

"Mercenaries can take only so much," said Clitus, folding his net. "They fight for gold, not death."

"What mercenary shrinks from a fight he deems easily and profitably won," asked Thurnock, "a fight in which he risks little and is likely to gain much?"

"It is true," I said, "the corsairs have four ships to our two, and the *Dorna* is crippled."

"They are coming again!" cried a man, pointing.

The corsair ship was maneuvering to come alongside once more. It was a beautiful ship, low in the water, with fine lines, with the eyes on either side of the graceful, concave prow. I re-marked how the beak, mostly submerged, divided the water before its passage. It reminded me a little of the dorsal fin of the nine-gilled Gorean shark, so much like those of Earth, a graceful, efficient, savage form of life, presumably selected for efficient predation, just as the Earth shark in similar environments.

"They will beware the deck," said Clitus. "They will wrap leather or rags about their boots and sandals. They will test their footing. They will step with care."

"They are land fighters," said Clitus. "Under the best of conditions, the rhythms of a deck, with its pitching and rolling, however subtle and gentle, is not to their liking."

"I hear no war cries," said a man.

"See the helmets and faces," said a man.

"They are proud, dangerous men," said Thurnock. "They have been surprised and humiliated. They seek blood and vengeance."

"Draw back, behind the screens," I called. "Do not contest the boarding."

"The lamp is ready," said Thurnock.

"This time there will be no reckless, mad charge," I said, "no attempt to intimidate a frightened foe. They will assure themselves of footing. They will form rows for the advance, which would then proceed, step by step. We shall wait until they have four such rows."

"Then the lamp," said Thurnock, igniting the wick.

"On my signal," I said.

The helmsmen of the corsair ship were skilled. In a moment the length of the corsair ship, oars swiftly brought inboard, the vessel then obedient to inertia, would slide parallel to the starboard side of the *Tesephone*.

"No!" I heard, a long scream from the water, presumably from one of the mercenaries forced from our deck, or one of those who had earlier preferred the risk of Thassa to that of our crew.

I heard two more screams, both of which were suddenly stifled or cut short, as the corsair ship slid along our hull, scoring planking.

Given the movement of the decks, and our changes to the starboard side of the *Tesephone*, minimizing or eliminating points of purchase, the passage between ships was precarious. Too, I did not think the corsair could hold its current position for more than a few Ihn at a time. Accordingly, the passage between ships would be dangerous, brief, and intermittent. The two ships, the corsair ship and the *Tesephone*, were literally against one another only briefly, but the gap between them, ranging from a few inches to a yard, held for almost an Ehn; then it widened to four to five feet, and then, once more, was such that it could be easily bridged. After some two or three Ehn, the fourth row was in place, each row consisting of some ten men. We had not yet, muchly concealed behind the screens, attacked the boarders, nor had they, as yet, shields lifted, weapons poised, charged us.

"Surely we are now rich enough in foes," said Clitus.

"Others, behind them," said Sakim, "are preparing to board."

"There will be too many," said Clitus.

I brought my arm down, swiftly, and Thurnock dashed the flaming lamp onto the oiled deck before the screens. Instantly spreading fire, like a striking, scarlet snake, raged about the ankles and legs of the mercenaries.

"Now!" I cried, and I, and my men, some thrusting screens before them, rushed forward. We knew, as the mercenaries presumably would not, that on a flat deck coated with a layer of oil, that the flames, after their initial flaring, would provide little impedance to the business of war. One might fight amongst them, as they subsided, even with them about one's ankles. The primary effect of the flames would be psychological, disconcerting and alarming. Despite this, several of my men had soaked their footgear with water and wrapped their lower legs with water-soaked rags. I did not object to this. It allayed fear in some of my men and the sight of them being presumably so protected against fire would most likely further alarm mercenaries, realizing they lacked such putative protection. What I had not anticipated was the alarm amongst the officers and seamen of the corsair ship. They did not realize the nature of the fire, its extent or violence. Some thought that our ship was genuinely afire, either by accident or that we had deliberately fired the ship, certain that all was lost, to immolate our vessel and the corsair ship in a common conflagration.

Few unfamiliar with maritime matters realize the seaman's terror of fire at sea. One of a mariner's worst nightmares is to awaken at night to the cry of "Fire!" Fire at sea is quite different from fire on land, say, in a house or village. There is nowhere to run. Flames burn and water drowns. If one is fortunate, one might people a longboat, a small vulnerable craft, with limited water and food, on a wide, lonely sea.

"Oars out, thrust away!" I heard from the corsair vessel.

Oars from the corsair ship thrust out, striking our hull, trying to move their ship from our proximity.

"Back, back," cried a mercenary officer on our deck, looking behind him, and men began, sustaining our determined, fierce attack, to back away. Some lost their balance and fell backwards into the sea. Others threw away their shields and weapons and leapt from the *Tesephone* to the water now separating us from the corsair ship.

Ropes were cast down from the corsair ship, which were grasped by struggling men. One man, screaming, was pulled away from a rope by a shark. This was surprising as sharks are not normally found in deep, open water, far from the shallower water housing the banks of flora fed upon by smaller fish. The shark in question was presumably one the few who will follow a ship in open water, sometimes for days, feeding off garbage cast overboard.

"Shall we fire on the survivors?" asked Thurnock.

"No," I said, "they are sword brothers."

"I do not understand the scarlet caste," said Thurnock.

"Nor I the caste upon which the Home Stone rests," I said.

"The foe spared," said Thurnock, "may one day kill you."

"It is a matter of codes," I said.

"The flames subside," said Clitus.

"They might rise again," I said.

"Oil is left," said Thurnock.

"The enemy draws away," said Sakim.

"He fears fire," said Thurnock.

"Perhaps he has had enough," said Clitus.

"That is my hope," I said.

At that point there was a cheer from behind us, across the decks, from the *Dorna*.

"I take it that the *Dorna* has repelled boarders," I said.

"It seems so," said Thurnock.

I detected, briefly, a wisp of burnt oil.

We were then joined not only by those men we had sent to assist the *Dorna*, but by several from the *Dorna* herself.

"Those on the corsair ship will not be pleased," said Clitus.

"Not only are we no longer undermanned," said Sakim, "but now we are reinforced."

We watched the corsair ship take aboard her mercenaries, one by one. Not long afterward, she drew farther away, and was joined by the ship which had attacked the *Dorna*. Both then lay to.

"We are victorious," said a man. "There is paga on the *Dorna*. Let us celebrate."

"We are now in our greatest danger," I said. "Boarding was intended to secure our vessels, to garner the *Dorna* and *Tesephone*, valuable, fine ships, as prizes. Boarding was unsuccessful."

Thurnock, Clitus, and Sakim exchanged glances.

"Unlash the *Dorna* and *Tesephone*," I said. "We will not be taken and slaughtered like penned verr."

"We are short even on oars," said Sakim.

"Two of their ships have not even been engaged," said Clitus.

"The *Tesephone* is light," said Sakim. "The *Dorna* can scarcely limp at sea."

"We will do what we can," I said.

"It is now that the ram speaks," said Thurnock.

"Their rams," said Sakim.

"I fear so," I said.

CHAPTER FIFTY-EIGHT

The Arithmetic of Battle

"Take in the sail, lower the yard and mast," said Sakim. "You must maneuver as you can. You must be able to turn short, in an Ihn to shift course, to backoar at a blow on the drum. How can you fight when the wind has its hand on your tunic? You cannot fight the wind. It may be your foe. It impedes helming!"

Sakim's advice was sound.

It is for just such reasons that knife ships lower the mast, yard, and sails before entering combat.

"At least, Captain," said Clitus, "would it not be desirable to take down the mast, that we be less easily seen at sea."

"See the sail," said Sakim. "It is swollen with wind. It can be seen for pasangs."

"Our position is known to the enemy," I said.

"Let our mast stay high, let our sail remain full," said Thurnock. "Thus we show our scorn of the enemy."

"It will be difficult to fight with the sail so," said Sakim.

"It is no fight we can win," I said.

"We repelled boarders," said Sakim. "We then freed the *Dorna* and cast her a towing line. We have tried to outdistance the enemy. We have failed. Now, Captain, lower the mast, turn about, and meet the enemy."

"There are worse ways to die," said Clitus.

"Cut the towing line," I said.

"Captain Tab," said Sakim, "has urged you to abandon the *Dorna*."

"I do not choose to do so," I said.

"You can take Captain Tab and his crew aboard," said Thurnock.

"That we would all die together, crowded on one ship?" I asked.

"The towing line is cut," said a seaman.

"Good," I said. "The *Dorna* will be safer, free."

"We will guard her flank," said Thurnock.

"And who, mighty peasant, will guard ours?" asked Sakim.

"In battle," I said, "there are many turns and twists."

"I am curious, Captain," said Sakim, "why you have persisted in holding our course for Sybaris and not the Cove of Harpalos, which is closer."

"Do not concern yourself, friend," I said. "We could not have reached either before being overtaken."

"But you had a reason?" said Sakim.

"Yes," I said.

Sakim, Thurnock, Clitus, and myself were on the stem deck of the *Tesephone*. I surveyed the horizon with a glass of the Builders.

"Captain Tab," said a seaman, from below us on the steps of the stem deck, "as he deems battle is imminent, has signaled for permission to lower his mast and sail."

"Convey my regards to the captain," I said. "Permission is not granted."

"Thus we scorn the foe," said Thurnock, grimly.

"Dear friends," I said, "the enemy has recently shown, by preferring boarding to ramming, that he would like to obtain our ships, the *Dorna* and the *Tesephone*, as prizes, and doubtless most the *Dorna*. What then would you think of the following proposal? I mention it for your consideration. We trade our lives for our ships. The enemy obtains our ships and we retain our lives."

I lowered the glass of the Builders.

I was not pleased with what the glass had revealed.

"I think the enemy would be most happy with that proposal," said Sakim.

"Perhaps we could add a demand for some coin in the bargain and be guaranteed a free passage to a safe port," I said.

"They would grasp at such a bargain," said Clitus.

"As would a hungry urt or a cunning ost," said Thurnock.

"Precisely," I said.

"We would depend, of course, on their honor," said Sakim.

"Of course," I said. "Who doubts the honor of liars, villains, murderers, and hypocrites?"

"Should we not just present our throats to their knives?" asked Thurnock.

"I gather," I said, "that my proposal does not meet with your approval."

"That is correct, Captain," said Sakim.

"I thought it might not," I said.

"The battle clearly lost," said Clitus, "we might fire our ships, and charge the enemy. Flames might thusly spread to one or another of our foes."

"The *Dorna* could be easily avoided," I said.

"We could turn the *Tesephone* into a torch," said Thurnock. "For an Ahn I would match her against anything on the sea, regardless of the enemy's frequent shifts of oarsmen."

"She will not be so swift if stove in, her decks buckled, her hold heavy with water," I said.

"We could fire her before action begins," said Thurnock.

"Defeat," I said, "is not to be purchased prematurely."

"You have hope, Captain?" asked Sakim.

"Why not?" I said. "It is free."

"You think somehow to outdistance the enemy?" asked Sakim.

I handed the glass of the Builders to Sakim.

"What do you think?" I asked. "Look ahead, then to the sides, and then astern."

A bit later, Sakim returned the glass of the Builders.

"We are surrounded," he said.

"And have been, for some time," I said.

"How is it possible?" asked Thurnock.

"We were towing the *Dorna*," I said.

"She is free now," said Clitus.

I called down to the main deck. "Oars, rest," I said. "Heave to."

"You will make your stand here?" said Sakim.

"Yes," I said.

It is wise to assume that one's opponents are shrewd and competent. Underestimating the foe is a mistake few swordsmen, or commanders, will make.

Similarly, when possible, one declines engagement when one is at a disadvantage. Unfortunately, this is not always possible.

The most common form of disadvantage, assuming a parity of weaponry and skills, is to be outnumbered at a given time and place.

This is most simply illustrated in swordplay in which two blades are set against one. A swordsman can engage but one oppo-

nent at a time, and this renders him vulnerable to the other, however brief the engagement. If, instead, he defends himself against
one, with a particular parry, however swift, he is exposed to the
thrust of the other.

Something very similar to this occurs in Gorean naval warfare, where, commonly, the ship is the weapon. Let us suppose,
for example, two ships are matched against one ship. In attacking
a given ship, the attacker is commonly vulnerable to the attack of
the other.

"The *Tesephone* is swift, Captain," said Thurnock. "Would that
we could pretend flight, separate pursuers, and then turn about
and engage them, one at a time."

"Would indeed that it were practical," I said. "But even if we
were willing to abandon the *Dorna*, we are short of open water.
We could be cut off. The enemy is about us."

"Too," said Sakim, "the *Tesephone* is light. She would need a
long, clear course to accumulate enough speed to break through
the timbers of a fifty-oared vessel."

"Which course," I said, "is not likely to be permitted her."

"Foe to starboard!" called Clitus.

"Her ram is set for the *Dorna*!" cried Thurnock.

"The parry, the parry!" I called to the helmsmen.

At the same time the mallet of the *keleustes* pounded on the
metal drum.

This maneuver borrows its name from swordplay. My antici-
pation of its utility had motivated my current position *vis-à-vis*
the *Dorna*. The point of the parry is not to directly block a blow
but to move it from its course, to cause it to deviate. If we were
to interpose the hull of *Tesephone* directly between her and the
attacker we would save the *Dorna* but only at the expense of the
Tesephone. It was my hope that we could, with harrowing but
acceptable damage, bring the forward starboard side of the *Tesephone* against the side of the attacking ship in such a way as,
given the attacker's speed, to force his thrust wide of the *Dorna*.

There was a screech of metal at our forward starboard side
where our bow and ram had struck against the port shearing
blade of the enemy.

This impact caused the enemy to veer to starboard.

"She is wide of the *Dorna*!" cried Thurnock, jubilantly.

"Another against the *Dorna*, abeam of her!" called Sakim.

"We cannot protect her!" I said.

"Enemy astern!" called Clitus.

I spun about to see a great ship looming behind us.

"Away, to port! To port!" I called to the helmsmen.

The mallet of the *keleustes* rang on the metal drum.

There was a brutal shock and a sudden, ear-shattering tearing of wood behind us and Clitus, Sakim, Thurnock, and myself fell to the remaining boards of the stem deck. We saw, rearing above us, slipping past to starboard, the stem castle of the enemy.

We struggled to our feet, the ship rocking to port.

"The starboard rudder, gone!" called a helmsman.

"There are two now, aligned against the *Dorna*," said Sakim.

That would be the attack ship and her guard ship.

Meanwhile, the ship which had torn away our starboard rudder was slowly coming about, for another attack.

"We are lost," said Sakim. "Prepare to fire the ships."

"Ready oil and flame," I said.

"So signal the *Dorna*," said Sakim.

"No, my friend," I said. "Tab stands as captain of the *Dorna*. At such a moment that command is his alone to give or withhold."

There are commonly two justifications for so desperate a measure as to fire one's own ship. The first is to guarantee that the ship does not fall to the enemy; the second is to attempt to take the enemy down with one. Given the proximities inevitably involved in ramming and shearing it can be highly dangerous to approach a flaming ship. From the point of view of the incendiaries, the torching of the ship must be arranged in such a manner as to put the enemy at the highest risk possible. This means either that one takes the flaming ship to the enemy, or fires the ship unexpectedly when the enemy finds himself in a position from which it is difficult to withdraw.

At this point I was reasonably sure, despite the loss of one of our rudders, that we could bring the *Tesephone*, aflame, against one of the enemy ships. Over a short distance I would have matched her in speed against anything on Thassa. The *Dorna*, on the other hand, was crippled, and slow in the water.

Which of the enemy ships, I wondered, now served as the enemy fleet's flagship?

The position of the four enemy ships was now as follows. Two were aligning themselves against the *Dorna*, which had now come about to face them. Another, she who had broken away our starboard rudder, was now poised to renew her attack. We had come about to face her. The fourth enemy ship, which lay a quarter of a pasang ahead, off our bow, was now approaching.

"Captain Tab," said Clitus, pointing to port, "is preparing oil."

"If it be his order," I said, "be it so."

"He knows it is the end," said Sakim.

"I would prefer to die in a field at harvest time amidst ripening, golden sa-tarna," said Thurnock, "but this will do."

"Where one dies is not important," said Clitus. "What is important is how one dies."

"It is my hope that we shall die well, with courage," said Sakim.

"May it be so," said Clitus.

Who knows about such things, I wondered. Sometimes the strongest, bravest man is seized in the claws of fear. I recalled an afternoon long ago, in the delta of the Vosk.

Thurnock looked down to the main deck.

"Oil is ready," he said. "Lamps are lit."

"See that the sail is drenched," I said. "Aflame, we may be able to topple the mast onto the deck of an enemy."

Thurnock gestured to the sail, loose on its yard.

I saw the sail darken, absorbing the oil.

"Captain," said a seaman, "the enemy forward will close."

"Keep our bow to his bow," I said. In this fashion one presents a narrower target and allows for a swift move to either side.

"Glass of the Builders," I said, and Sakim handed me the instrument. I trained the glass on the oncoming vessel.

"It is not circling," said Sakim, his eyes half closed against the shimmering brightness of Thassa.

"Odd," said Clitus.

Ideally, a ram ship takes the enemy amidships.

"It is closing," said a seaman.

With the glass of the Builders I had no difficulty in making out individual figures on the approaching ship.

"It makes no sense," said Sakim. "It is oncoming, at ramming speed."

"It intends a ram stroke to the bow," said Clitus.

"The commander must be a fool," said Thurnock.

"He is not a fool," I said, looking through the glass of the Builders. I could see men busied amidships on the enemy vessel.

"Prepare for impact!" called Thurnock down to the benches.

"There will be no impact," I said.

There were cries of wonder as the enemy ship sped past to starboard. We could hear the pounding of the drum of its *keleustes*. It was at full ramming speed. Clitus looked after her. "She is raising her mast, her yard, unfurling her sail," he said.

"To make greater speed," I said.

"I do not understand," said Sakim.

I handed him the glass of the Builders, and pointed forward. "Look," I said.

"Sails," he gasped.

"I count twenty," I said, "every ship in the fleet of the Farther Islands."

"I do not understand," said Sakim.

"Nicomachos, Admiral of the Fleet of the Farther Islands, returned from patrol, and received my message," I said.

"What message?" asked Sakim.

"Where he might encounter the corsair fleet," I said.

"You have arranged this?" said Sakim.

"From as long ago as the fair at Mytilene," I said. "But I did not know where his allegiance lay."

"It lies, I wager," said Sakim, "with himself."

"That was my hope," I said.

"That is why you kept your course directly between Mytilene and Sybaris," said Sakim.

"I hoped Nicomachos would return sooner from his patrol and encounter the corsair fleet at Mytilene," I said.

"The other corsair ships withdraw," said Clitus. "They follow the first. They depart, masts now high, sails filled with the wind of fear, like terrified urts."

"And well might they do so," I said.

"How was this done?" asked Sakim.

"At the fair at Mytilene we arranged a mode of communication," I said, "how intelligence, if obtained, might be shared."

"You learned in Sybaris that the corsair fleet would attack Mytilene, naturally enough to seize the wealth accrued from the fair," said Sakim. "But how, given the absence of Nicomachos, could this be transmitted to him?"

"One required confederates to do so, in this case plausible but unwitting confederates," I said. "Aktis, from Nicosia, our valued oarsman and archer, was instructed to watch for a dancer on the street, one he recalled and had earlier found of interest, one who, as we learned, had been named 'Sylvia'. She was owned by Glaukos, proprietor of the tavern, *The Living Island*. He then charged this slave to deliver a short, somewhat cryptic message to her master, Glaukos. This message was, "Falarian is to be found at Mytilene." Glaukos, in turn, as I expected he would, conveyed the message to Archelaos, who, in turn, could be counted on to bring it to the attention of Nicomachos. Glaukos and Archelaos would be keen to obtain the falarian if it were at all possible. Nicomachos, on the other hand, would understand the true import of the message, which was to deliver to him the location of the corsair fleet."

"Archelaos would expect Nicomachos to send a single ship to Mytilene, under the command of one of the governor's loyal minions to investigate the claim," said Sakim.

"Presumably arriving after the destruction of Mytilene and the withdrawal of the corsair fleet," I said. "But, happily, Nicomachos departed with the entire fleet of the Farther Islands, eager to wipe the fleet of Bosk of Port Kar from the sea, and thereby restore himself to station and favor with Lurius of Jad, Ubar of Cos."

"Aktis did well," said Sakim.

"If all goes well," I said, "I will give him the dancer, Sylvia. I expect she will do nicely, carrying water and hoeing in the fields shackled and naked and spending her nights chained by the neck to a floor ring in Aktis' rebuilt hut."

I did not think that Lais, who had been discomfited in the tavern by the dancer, would object to that. Even if she did, it would not matter, as she herself was only a slave. One does what one pleases with slaves. They are slaves.

"Look," said Clitus, "one of the pursuing ships signals us."

"Signal that all is well," I said.

"It seems we are rescued," said Thurnock.

"Let us hope they do not look too closely," I said.

"I am pleased we painted our ships white and yellow," said Sakim.

"What else could we do, given that we are innocent, harmless merchantmen?" I said.

"They resume the chase," said Clitus.

"May they be successful," said Thurnock.

"Extinguish all lamps, carefully," I said. "Let not the least spark escape. Seal the canisters of oil. Wash the oil from the sail."

"It will be done," said Thurnock.

"We are safe," said Clitus.

I suddenly began to shake with fear.

"Captain?" asked Thurnock.

"I think I am afraid," I said.

"Do not concern yourself, Captain," said Sakim. "Sometimes one is most afraid, when the danger is past. It is only then that one realizes, in harrowing recollection, how great it was, and what might have been."

"Perhaps that is true," I said.

"It is," said Sakim.

"I understand now," said Thurnock, "why you kept the mast raised, that we might be the more easily seen."

"It would not have been well had the Fleet of the Farther Islands passed us, unknowingly," I said.

"I think the *Dorna* has paga," said Thurnock.

"Break it out," I said.

"Next afternoon," said Sakim, "when the lights are no longer too bright for the crew, when the noises are no longer too loud for them, when the slightest move no longer torments them, when the clouds no longer scream and beat on their heads, what course shall we set?"

"Sybaris," I said, "there are dry docks there, needful for the repair of our ships."

"And thence to Port Kar?" asked Clitus.

"We would not wish to miss the triumph of Nicomachos, naval hero, victor over the fleet of the notorious pirate, Bosk of Port Kar," I said.

"Surely not," agreed Sakim.

"And thence to Port Kar?" said Clitus.

"I think not," said Thurnock. "Do we not, Captain, have unfinished business in Sybaris?"

"That is my view," I said.

CHAPTER FIFTY-NINE

The Corridor; Events Have Rushed Forward; The Triumph of Nicomachos; We Chat with Glaukos, Proprietor of *The Living Island*

I caught the scent, in the dim corridor, lit by widely-spaced, tiny, tharlarion-oil lamps, in the back precincts of the tavern, *The Living Island*, of a voluptuous perfume, a slave perfume.

She was approaching.

Then, irritated, she stopped, for I blocked her path.

"Stand aside," she said. "I have been summoned."

"Why are you standing?" I asked.

A slave, when addressed by a free man, instantly kneels. Thus she acknowledges that she is of the submitting sex.

"Out of my way," she said.

Speaking so is permitted to free women, who may say and do much what they wish. It is not permitted to slaves.

Freedom is for men. They are the owning sex; the female is the owned sex. Once a female is suitably mastered, she no longer desires freedom. She is grateful for, and revels in, her submission. She basks in her bondage. In the collar she has come home to herself and her sex.

Four days ago, I had stood before the public boards, set up near the palace of the governor. The gate to the governor's palace was less than fifty yards away.

"Noble merchant," said a short fellow, squinting up at the boards, "I am no Scribe, no learned man, nor one familiar with figures and accounts, such as yourself."

"What would you like read?" I asked.

"You are of the white and yellow caste, the gold caste," he said. "white for the records you keep, yellow for the gold you gain. I am a poor man. What would you charge?"

"Nothing," I said.

"But you are of the Merchants," he said.

"Today is a holiday," I said.

"May the Priest-Kings look with favor on the cheating and chicanery of your caste," he said.

"Thank you," I said.

"Those letters," he said, "the large ones," pointing.

"I shall render the gist of matters," I said. "Due to the valor and skill of the noble Nicomachos, Admiral of the Fleet of the Farther Islands, all hail to the sublime Lurius of Jad, Ubar of Cos, the fleet of the notorious pirate, Bosk of Port Kar, predator to shipping, burner of villages, ravager of towns and cities, has but recently been surprised, captured, burned, and sunk fifty pasangs off the coast of Chios."

The matter seemed to have unfolded as follows. The Theran fleet under Nicomachos, anticipating land action on Chios near Mytilene, had embarked with numerous Cosian regulars aboard, which allowed frequent shifts of oarsmen, an advantage which the corsair fleet had itself hitherto exploited, this now, however, enabling the Theran fleet to equal, if not exceed, the speed of the corsair fleet. Further, the position of the Theran fleet cut the corsair fleet off from its base in Sybaris, and the width of its line prevented an escape to the side. The corsair fleet then, fleeing toward Chios, had either been caught near Chios or had tried to land on Chios and, encountering the hostile, armed Peasantry on the beaches, fresh from Mytilene and its vicinity, had put once more to sea, where it eventually fell to the pursuing Theran fleet, say, some fifty pasangs off the coast of Chios.

"Is there no mention of the glory and prowess of the noble Archelaos, the governor?" asked the short fellow.

"I see none," I said.

"Surely he should claim credit for this magnificent victory," said the man.

"Perhaps he was not there," I said.

"What difference would that make?" asked the man.

"None, I suppose," I said.

"He does not proclaim his involvement in large red letters?" said the man.

"It seems not," I said.

"Nicomachos advised the scribes what to post," said a by-stander, who had overheard our conversation.

"The noble Nicomachos does not attribute victory to the wisdom, astuteness, guidance, and leadership of the governor?" asked the man.

"Apparently not," I said.

"I think that bodes ill for the noble Nicomachos," said the fellow. Then he pointed again to the boards. "What does it say there?" he asked.

"In two days, a triumph is to be accorded to Nicomachos," I said.

"It could not be denied," said my small interlocutor.

"There will be a parade," said the bystander. "There will be banners and streamers on the houses, perfume in the air, flowers cast by free maidens in the streets."

"Drums and trumpets," said a fellow.

"Free *ka-la-na* and paga, too, I hope," said another.

"And what there, kind and noble master?" asked my small interlocutor, again pointing.

I paused. The print was smaller, but still easily enough read.

"What?" pressed my interlocutor.

"It is another benefit of the victory," I said. "It is the claim that prisoners of the corsairs, even some notables of Sybaris, were liberated."

"Splendid," said my interlocutor.

I remembered the siege of Mytilene. The corsairs did not take prisoners.

"What of the leader of the pirates," asked my interlocutor, "the nefarious Bosk of Port Kar? Is there nothing of him there?"

"I see nothing," I said.

"He was captured," said one of the bystanders. "He is a jab-bering fool. He claims to be an actor hired to impersonate the true Bosk of Port Kar."

"What is to be his fate?" I asked.

"I do not know," said the man.

"Is there more?" asked my small interlocutor.

"That is pretty much it," I said. "I wish you well."

"I wish you well," he said.

I then turned away from the public boards. The repairs on the *Dorna* and *Tesephone* were nearly complete. Tomorrow both would be freshly repainted.

She stamped her small, sandaled foot, with its slim, bangled ankle.

"Out of my way," she said. "I have been summoned!"

She did not remember me, of course, only one, and long ago, amongst the many patrons of *The Living Island*. And, even were I familiar to her, the dimness of the corridor might have impeded recognition. Nor did she sense Thurnock and Clitus behind her, each having emerged from the shadows. We had employed a simple, well-known stratagem for gaining admittance to the corridor. I had pushed between the two guards, intruding myself behind the curtain. Naturally the two guards, startled, affronted, and angered, followed me, to seize me and eject me from the tavern. In following me, who had monopolized their attention, they neglected to be sufficiently aware of the entire situation. Thurnock and Clitus followed them and each dealt one of the guards a heavy blow, sufficient to render them unconscious, until they should awaken, to find themselves bound, hand and foot, and gagged.

"I know you," I said, "you are Sylvia, the comely dancer."

"Merely dancer!" she said. "Merely comely!" she said. "I am the finest dancer in Sybaris and the most beautiful woman in all the Farther Islands!"

"You will do for the Farther Islands," I said. "As a dancer you might not be noticed in Ar or Turia, or Brundisium, or Port Kar. And as for beauty, I know at least four, locally, who are your superior." I was not being quite candid. She was quite pretty and might do for one of the lesser taverns in Ar. I did think that Lais, Margot, Millicent, and Courtney were her superiors, or, might, at least, bring a better price off the block. To be sure, with respect to writhing naked at one's feet, one's foot pressed gently, firmly, on her belly, she would not be displeasing, no more so than other slaves.

"Out of my way, bumpkin," she snapped.

"You might do well in a peasant's field," I said.

"I am not a bred slave," she said. "I was a free woman!"

"So, too, were most slaves," I said.

"A free woman!" she said.

"All women are slaves," I said. "It is only that not all are fortunate enough to be put in collars."

"Get out of my way," she hissed.

"Of course," I said, and stepped aside.

As she brushed past, with a flutter of silk, I seized her from behind, pulling her back against me, my right hand capped over her mouth. Shortly thereafter, with the assistance of Clitus and Thurnock, she sat on the stone floor of the corridor, gagged, looking up at us, in fury, her hands thonged behind her.

I bent down and, with one hand, my left hand, lifted her ankles up, which caused her to go to her back on the floor.

She twisted on the floor, fuming, unable to speak.

I slipped her sandals off with my right hand, and tossed them to the side.

As is well known, slaves are animals, and, as animals, need not be clothed. How slaves are clothed, if they are to be clothed, is up to the free. The slave owns nothing, not even her collar. It is she who is owned. She is dependent on the free, fully, even to be fed.

"Sandals are a privilege," I said. "I doubt that you have earned them."

Even to be permitted on the surface of a master's couch, after kneeling, head down, and humbly kissing the furs, is a privilege to be earned by diligence and pleasingness.

"She has small feet," said Thurnock.

"Yes," I said.

"And slim, trim ankles," said Thurnock.

"They would look well in shackles," said Clitus.

The slave twisted angrily.

"I am not sure that this little beast has yet learned her collar," I said.

"It might be pleasant to teach her her collar," said Thurnock.

I regarded the slave. "How beautiful are women," I thought, "so extraordinarily different from men, almost another form of life, so precious, desirable, and exciting. It is no wonder that men wish to own them."

And what woman does not wish to be collared and owned by the Master of her dreams?

"Are you angry?" I asked the slave.

She half reared up, and shook her head fiercely, affirmatively.

"Do you object to having had your sandals removed?" I asked.

Again she nodded, fiercely, affirmatively.

"Remove her clothing," I said, "even the ribbon binding her hair, and spread her hair out, widely, and brush it behind her shoulders. And kneel her before me, back on her heels, her knees widely spread."

This was done.

My hand reached to my belt.

I saw fear come into her eyes, not the fear of a free woman, but slave fear.

At that point, a small gong rang, the sound emanating from behind a closed door farther down the corridor. A moment after, we heard a man's angry voice cry out. "The slave, where is the slave?"

"Glaukos," whispered Thurnock.

I looked down at the frightened slave. "As I recall," I said, "you had been summoned." I then held my left hand open, at my left hip.

She struggled to her feet and, bending over, placed her head at my left hip, and I fastened my hand firmly, deeply, in that pelt, by means of which such a lovely beast may be easily, conveniently, and efficiently guided and controlled.

The gong, sharply, rang again.

"The slave! Where is the slave?" demanded Glaukos, the voice angry, half muffled, coming from behind the door.

Thurnock, Clitus, and I, then, the slave beside me, conducted, bent over in leading position, made our way toward the door from behind which had come the sound of the gong and the voice of Glaukos, proprietor of the tavern, *The Living Island*.

"It is very loud, is it not," had asked Thurnock, "the music, the cheering, and all?"

"Quite," I had said, being shoved about somewhat, as a fellow squeezed by, intent on getting more to the front of the crowd.

"Too noisy," said Thurnock.

"Parades are seldom quiet, sedate affairs," I assured him.

"It is not every day," said a fellow near me, "that the fleet of the notorious Bosk of Port Kar is sunk and its very commander, the cruel and monstrous Bosk of Port Kar himself, is apprehended."

"I would suppose not," I said.

"See the ribbons and streamers from the windows," said Sakim, "the flowers, the observers lining the roofs."

"They have a better vantage than ours," I said, being jostled.

"How many bands have you counted?" asked Clitus.

"Eleven," I said.

"I saw at least thirty-seven floats," said Thurnock.

Many of these, drawn by draft tharlarion, were surmounted by tableaux, several showing valiant Cosians, mariners and ground forces, triumphant over a variety of perhaps once-formidable, but now whimpering and cringing, foes. One float judiciously portrayed grateful citizens acclaiming an enthroned figure representing Lurius of Jad, the Ubar of Cos, presumably expressing their thanks for the privilege of flourishing under so just and beneficent a rule. Some others celebrated and advertised various organizations and businesses. One establishment advertised was *The House of the Golden Urt*, which was now, apparently, under new management. It had once been managed, as I recalled, by three women, the 'Three Ubaras', Melete, Iantha, and Philomena. Interestingly, there was no float, at least as far as we now had noted, for *The Living Island*, which was surely one of the better-known taverns of Sybaris. Too, interestingly, no float, at least as yet, had proclaimed the glory of the governor of Sybaris, Archelaos. Two of the 'business floats' advertised slave markets, *The Golden Shackle* and *The Ta-Teera*. In each of these, samples of the merchandise were displayed in such a way that there could be little doubt about its charms. Also, apparently unwilling to be left out, certain castes had contributed their own floats to the parade, among them, the Shipwrights, Bakers, Distillers, and Metal Workers.

"Captain," said Sakim, who now stood at my elbow.

"How are things at the wharf?" I asked.

Recently the *Dorna* and *Tesephone*, in dry dock, after having been repaired, had been repainted.

"Rigged and provisioned," said Sakim, "a whisper and both can slip free."

"I hope both may do so, and soon," I said.

"You missed the free maidens casting flowers," said Clitus.

"There will be more toward the end," said Thurnock.

"How were they?" asked Sakim.

"Too young," said Thurnock. "Give them five years."

"Remember they are free, even then," I cautioned him.

"They are town girls," said Thurnock.

"That is true," I admitted.

"I smell perfume," said Sakim.

"That is not surprising," said Clitus. "It drenches the streets. It runs like rain water in the gutters."

I thought that something of an exaggeration, but it was clearly detectible. It was perhaps a bit more obtrusive after the passing of the slave-market floats.

"Drums, trumpets!" said Thurnock.

"Nicomachos is near!" said a fellow nearby.

"I see pennons and banners," I said.

I heard a roar from the crowd, some hundred paces or so to our right.

"What now?" I asked.

"Some noble citizens of Sybaris," said a fellow near me, "freed from captivity, liberated by Admiral Nicomachos from the foul clutches of Bosk of Port Kar."

Shortly thereafter a festooned float trundled by.

On it were some ten or twelve fellows, dressed in celebratory garments.

"Ctesippus!" said Thurnock.

"Laios!" said Clitus.

"Amongst others," I said. I presumed that the 'liberated prisoners' were high men amongst the corsairs. As the net of Nicomachos had drawn tight, it seemed probable that they had somehow managed to portray themselves, perhaps even to having themselves laden with chains, as captives of the corsairs. This would be most easily managed if some of the corsairs had managed to reach the coast of Chios near Mytilene, and then fallen into the power of locals, or the armed Peasantry, which had lifted the siege of Mytilene.

"Another float approaches," said Thurnock.

"What is it?" pressed Clitus, who was nearly a foot shorter than Thurnock.

"I do not know," said Thurnock.

Cheering now shifted, like a mood of mighty, capricious, rolling, thundering Thassa, into cries of rage and voluble threatening imprecation, into violent jeering and hooting, into torrents of insult and ridicule, into a storm of scorn and mockery.

"I see little but chains," said Thurnock, "and two soldiers, with shields."

"It is the villain, Bosk of Port Kar," cried a man near us.

He shook his fist at the approaching float.

The crowd roared with hate.

The central figure on the float was swathed with chains. It was difficult to see how more chains could be placed on a single body. The two soldiers with the prisoner on the float shook their shields warningly, menacingly, at the crowd, presumably to discourage it from clambering onto the float and tearing the prisoner apart. The shields did little, however, to protect the prisoner from the fruit, garbage, and debris which was cast upon him.

"In Sybaris," said Sakim, "it seems there are many zealots after justice."

"Guard him well!" cried a man.

"What is to be done with him?" I asked the man.

"Torture and impalement," he said. "Lengthy torture and slow, gradual impalement, lasting perhaps five days."

"Tear him to pieces!" screamed another man.

"No, no!" cried another. "Let not the torturers be cheated of their sport! Let not the impaling spear be denied its due!"

"He seems to be crying out something," I said.

"Over and over," said Thurnock.

"It is hard to make out," said a man.

"The float passes," said a man.

"I am not Bosk of Port Kar!" cried the figure on the float. "I am Bombastico, an actor. I am not Bosk of Port Kar! I am Bombastico, an actor, an actor!"

"What is he saying?" asked a man.

"He is denying he is Bosk of Port Kar," said another man.

"Who could blame him?" said another man.

"What a meretricious coward, what a loathsome, lying coward," said the first.

"Should he not have a trial?" I asked.

"Of course," said a man. "We are a civil society."

"It will not take long," said another man.

"It should be over by supper," said another.

"When one is guilty, a trial is a waste of time," said a man.

"I have unwelcome, grim news for you," said yet another. "He is to be transported to Jad, on Cos, for his trial, sentencing, and execution."

"No, no!" cried men about me.

"Not Cos, but Thera, Sybaris!" screamed a fellow, clearly distraught.

John Norman

"His blood belongs on the Farther Islands," said another. "It is here he indulged his roguery! Let him suffer torture and execution here, one ugly, villainous corpuscle at a time! Thera, Daphna, Chios will have it no other way!"

"Yes!" cried a man.

"Seize him," cried another. "Drag him from the float!"

"The float has passed," said another.

"There are only two guards," said a man. "Spread the word!"

"Look," said Thurnock, pulling at my sleeve. "The last float approaches!"

"Hail, Nicomachos!" cried a man.

I heard the jangling of instruments and the beating of drums, and then a fanfare of trumpets.

"Here, friend Sakim," said Clitus, "are more free maidens, joyously dancing in flowing garments, casting flowers, mostly dinas, talenders, and veminium, before the wheels of the final float. Do not miss these."

"Are these as good as the earlier ones?" asked Sakim.

"Better," said Clitus.

"Town girls," scoffed Thurnock. "It would take four to pull a plow."

"Or one," said Clitus, "if the tiller had a whip."

"These are older, somewhat," I said.

"Excellent stock," said Thurnock, "seizable and marketable."

"They are free," I reminded him.

"That is a defect in a woman," said Thurnock. "It can be remedied."

I reminded myself that Thurnock did not share a Home Stone with the lissome dancers.

"Look!" said Clitus. "The float is constructed to look like a ship, with a prow and all!"

"And Nicomachos on the seeming stem castle, bowing and smiling, lifting his hands to the crowd."

Cheers were deafening.

"Hail, Nicomachos!" cried men.

I saw tears of gladness shed.

The last float was followed by several ranks of Cosian spearmen.

"I hope there is free food and drink in the taverns," said a man.

"It is easy enough to see," said another.

"A fine parade," said Thurnock, "—for the Farther Islands."

"Better than most put forth in a peasant village, even on the continent," said Clitus.

"Listen!" I said.

"What?" asked Sakim.

I pointed to my left. "Down there!" I said.

"I hear it," said Thurnock.

About us the crowd had begun to dissipate, men wending about, in one direction or another, but farther down to our left, we could still see clusters of people, some sort of roiling crowd.

"Disturbance," said Clitus.

"Rioting!" said Thurnock.

"What is going on?" asked Sakim.

"A float is being stopped," I said. "Men swarm to its surface! It is being stormed! The crowd is out of hand!"

"I see confusion, I hear shouts and cries!" had said Clitus.

"Turmoil," had said Sakim.

"Follow me," I had said, hurrying toward the disturbance.

I kicked open the door in the narrow, dimly lit corridor in the private precincts of the tavern, *The Living Island*, from behind which had come the sound of the small gong. Startled, Glaukos, short and thick-bodied, thick-legged, proprietor of the *The Living Island*, spun about to face me.

"Touch a weapon and die," I said.

I hurled Sylvia, stripped, bound and gagged, to her knees. "Head to the floor," I said.

She needed not see what men would do. Rather, she, a slave, would wait to see what would be done with her.

Glaukos still clutched the small hammer which he had applied to the gong. I looked at it. He dropped it to the floor and backed away.

"You have no right here," he said. "Who are you? What are you doing here? What do you want?"

"My presence here," I said, "is by right of the sword. I am known variously. Perhaps you do not recall me. You knew me once by the name, 'Fenlon of Ti'."

In his eyes I saw quick recollection, and apprehension.

"I was drugged in your tavern," I said, "and a map was stolen."

"I know nothing of that," he said.

"I see," I said, "that the sword must speak for me."

"No!" he said. "The map was worthless!"

"I will declare its worth," I said.

He cast his eyes on the kneeling slave, her head pressed to the floor.

"Why is the slave stripped?" he asked.

"It pleased me," I said. "She is beautiful enough to be stripped."

"I am not accustomed to seeing her so," he said.

"How is that?" I asked.

"Kneeling so," he said, "head to the floor, naked, well gagged, hands tied behind her, so small, so soft, so vulnerable, so helpless, so submissive, so slave."

I nudged the slave's thigh with the toe of my boot. "Whimper, she-tarsk," I said.

She whimpered, instantly, fearfully.

"Ahh," said Glaukos, softly.

"You can get much from a female," I said, "once she learns her collar."

"Perhaps," said Thurnock, "she has not been much hitherto in the hands of a true Master."

Glaukos threw an angry glance at Thurnock.

"Shall I break his neck now?" asked Thurnock.

Glaukos turned white.

"No," I said, "at least not yet."

"I shall call for help," said Glaukos.

"There will be none capable of assisting you," I said. "That has been seen to."

"The map was useless, and was burned, in fury and chagrin," he said. "But, as you say, it is yours to declare its worth. It was a meaningless scrap of rence paper, but I will compensate you for its loss. I trust that a hundred gold staters of Brundisium, or a dozen gold tarns of Ar, will be acceptable."

"How much is your life worth?" I asked.

"More than I can pay," he said.

"Let the cost be," I said, "a single gold stater of Brundisium."

Relief flooded the countenance of Glaukos, but, almost instantly, this expression changed to one of fear.

"Then," he said, "you have not come here to rob me, have not come for gold?"

"No," I said.

"For what then?" he asked.

"Information," I said.

"I know little or nothing," he said.

"Ctesippus, Laios, and others," I said, "are now in Sybaris."

"Happily, liberated from the corsairs," he said.

"They were one with the corsairs," I said. "It seems they succeeded in deceiving Nicomachos, perhaps on a beach of Chios, presenting themselves as prisoners of the corsairs."

"Surely you are mistaken," he said.

"Your life will be in less jeopardy," I said, "if you are candid."

"You are interested in such men?" he asked.

"Only indirectly," I said. "They were your employees and they stood high amongst the corsairs. Through them you are linked with the corsairs."

"No," said Glaukos.

"Shall I break his neck now?" asked Thurnock.

"Wait," I said.

"I was given no choice," said Glaukos, sweating. "Strong dark forces lurk in the shadows of Sybaris."

"Through Ctesippus and Laios, you are linked to the corsairs," I said. "But with whom are you linked?"

"Let us forget such matters," he said. "The corsairs are defeated. Bosk of Port Kar was captured and later torn to pieces by an angry crowd. All is done."

"The body was not found," I said.

"He was chained, and heavily so," said Glaukos. "There could be no escape."

"Still," I said, "the body was not found."

I recalled an incident in Ar. It had taken place long ago. In that case, too, no body had been found. That had been of interest, later, to a friend, on the Plains of the Wagon Peoples, Kamchak, of the Tuchuks.

"I know nothing," said Glaukos.

"Perhaps you might recall," I suggested.

"I know nothing," said Glaukos.

"Very well," I said to Thurnock. "You may break his neck."

Thurnock, wide hands open, took a sudden, savage step toward Glaukos.

"No!" cried Glaukos. "I recall! Archelaos, Archelaos!"

"Of course," I said, "but it is pleasant to hear it from a minion's mouth."

"I was threatened, I am blameless!" said Glaukos.

"Do you not owe me a gold stater, of Brundisium, in compensation for the loss of a map?" I said.

"As agreed!" stammered Glaukos, reaching into his belt pouch, extracting such a coin, and pressing it into my hand.

"In the parade," I said, "I saw no float proclaiming the glory of Archelaos, nor did I see one representing *The Living Island.*"

"There is bad blood, jealousy, between Archelaos and Nicomachos," said Glaukos. "Archelaos declined to contribute to the triumph of Nicomachos, by implicitly saluting the glory of a rival, and Nicomachos did not wish his triumph diminished by implicitly accrediting any share of his glory to the governor."

"And thus," said Thurnock, "even enemies may find solidarity on sensitive matters."

"And I," said Glaukos, "in deference to the possible feelings of Archelaos, did not place a float in the parade."

"It all hangs together," said Clitus.

"Things often do," I said.

"It is unfortunate," said Glaukos. "My float would have been the finest of the tavern floats."

"I am sure of it," I said.

"Perhaps you wish a written confession," he said, "one in which I specify a crime, that of conspiring with the dreaded Bosk of Port Kar, and name the governor as its perpetrator?"

"That will not be necessary," I said. "Its authenticity could be challenged, as having been forged, or its validity nullified, as having been exacted under duress."

"Thus time, paper, and ink may be spared," he smiled.

"Do you truly believe," I asked, "that the governor conspired with Bosk of Port Kar?"

"Of course," he said.

"And you recruited on behalf of Bosk of Port Kar?"

"I, and others," he said. "We were well paid."

"How came it about," I asked, "that Nicomachos, Admiral of the Fleet of the Farther Islands, encountered the corsair fleet near Mytilene on Chios?"

"I do not know," he said. "It was unfortunate. The sea is vast. Yet such things can happen. The governor was much distressed."

"You have been helpful," I said.

"I detected little choice in the matter," he said.

"I take it," I said, "that you will not report our small discussion to the governor."

"Certainly not," he said, eyes glinting. "Should I learn more, or recall some item inadvertently omitted, where may I contact you?"

"Perhaps," I said, "at the Inn of Kahlir."

"Of course," he said.

He would know, of course, that the Inn of Kahlir, by supposed rioters, had been torched and looted months ago. It was now no more than rubble and ashes.

I put my boot against the left shoulder of the kneeling slave and thrust her to her right shoulder on the rug. She remained in this position, not having been given permission to move. She looked up at me. Her eyes, over the gag, were frightened.

"What do you want for her?" I asked.

"She is worth at least two silver tarsks," he said.

"Here," I said, flipping him the gold stater of Brundisium.

"Yours!" he said, snatching the coin in flight.

The slave went gladly to her belly and humbly, fervently, pressed her lips to my boot.

Perhaps she had not been thrilled to be the property of Glaukos. But then a slave has no choice as to whom she will belong. That is one of the pleasant things about slaves. Does it not help them to understand that they are slaves?

I gestured that she might kneel before me, and she struggled to that position.

"Would you like to belong to a peasant?" I asked.

She shook her head negatively, fiercely.

"Shall I sell you to a peasant?" I asked.

She shook her head pleadingly, "No."

"Very well," I said. "I will not do so."

Joy flooded her features.

"I will give you to one," I said.

She shook her head wildly, "No." Tears burst from her eyes. She shuddered in misery.

"Do not be concerned," I said. "I have had you in mind for him, for some time. Indeed, you have met him before, though you might not have been told his name. He charged you with giving a message to your Master."

She looked at me, her features startled.

"I see you remember," I said. "His name is Aktis, and he is of the village of Nicosia, on Chios. You will be well worked during the day, and, I expect, well used whenever it pleases your master, day or night, in the furrows, or, chained, on a hut mat."

"I have spoken to Aktis," said Thurnock. "He will chain her naked, outside, in the weather, until she begs to be pleasing. If that is insufficient, he can break her to the whip."

"That will not be necessary," I said. "She will soon be as helpless as a she-tarsk in heat. Slaves are the prisoners, and victims, of their own needs. She will soon crawl to him on her belly, begging for slave use."

"It seems," said Glaukos, "the slave has fainted."

"Yes," I said.

"What is this business about a message?" asked Glaukos.

"It is not important," I said.

"About falarian?" he said.

"Possibly," I said.

"Nothing came of that," he said.

"Oh?" I said.

"It was a hoax," he said.

"Such things often are," I said.

"I trust I may no longer be of service," said Glaukos.

"I do not think so," I said.

I lifted the blade of the short, double-edged weapon, the Gorean *gladius*.

"Do not kill me!" he cried.

The hilt of the weapon clutched in my right fist, I delivered him a heavy blow.

"I could have struck him," said Thurnock.

"He asked not to be killed," I said.

"What of the slave?" asked Thurnock.

"Gather her up, gently in your arms," I said to Thurnock. "And outside, in the corridor, wrap her features in her removed garments, that she not be recognized."

"Why did you mention the Inn of Kahlir?" asked Thurnock.

"As soon as he recovers consciousness," I said, "he will hurry to report our conversation to Archelaos. In going over the conversation, detail by detail, my mention of the Inn of Kahlir should be recalled. That will remind Archelaos of his attempt to rid himself of Kenneth Statercounter, troublesome merchant of Brundisium. That will suggest that the supposed Fenlon of Ti, of the recent conversation, is either Kenneth Statercounter, or someone in league with him."

"Then Archelaos will be searching for Kenneth Statercounter," said Clitus.

"And he should not be hard to find," I said, "as he has two ships in the harbor."

"You risk much," said Thurnock.

"We cannot storm the palace," I said. "How else can we arrange an interview with the governor?"

CHAPTER SIXTY

We Await a Messenger from the Palace

"You see them?" asked Clitus.

"Yes," I said.

"The tridents make them fishermen," said Thurnock.

"My dear friend," said Clitus, "it takes more than a trident to make a fisherman." His eyes were narrow. He shook out his own net, and unstrapped his trident.

"There are two of them," I said.

We were standing on the dock, near the *Tesephone*. The *Dorna* was moored within fifty yards. Our men were not at the ships. Most were in Sybaris. I had wanted to make it easier, and less intimidating, to be approached by a messenger from the palace. Let it seem we were few in number, and, perhaps, open to dialogue. Who were we, really? What did we want? What did we know? Did we have a role in these dark games? Might we not have something to sell the governor? Information? Silence?

"There are six more, hooded, farther away," said Clitus, "those fellows carrying *amphorae*."

"Deep enough to hold swords," I said.

"I will fetch my staff," said Thurnock.

This was the peasant staff, less an accessory to walking than a stout weapon, some six or seven feet in length, some two inches, or so, in thickness. In the hands of a strong, skilled man it is a formidable weapon.

"What are those two doing?" I asked.

"I inquired, when they were less close," said Clitus. "Supposedly they seek to clean the harbor, in particular, to reduce the number of serpentine spined tharlarion in the harbor. They cast garbage into the water and spear the tharlarion when it rises to the surface to seize the garbage."

"I see," I said.

Something very much like that was done in Port Kar, as well, only a tethered, swimming slave is used to attract the canal urts.

Thurnock then joined us, staff in hand.

"Perhaps they are what they seem," said Thurnock, "hunters of the spined tharlarion."

"No," said Clitus, loosening his net further. "They hold the tridents improperly. They hold them like they were spears. The trident is light. It is not hurled; it is darted."

"They are coming closer," I said. "Seemingly paying us no mind."

"Seemingly," said Clitus.

"The others with the *amphorae*, drift closer, too," I said.

The two closer men stopped now and then, began to cast scraps into the water, these extracted by handfuls from canvas sacks worn at their belts.

"I had hoped to be contacted civilly, by messengers from the palace of the governor," I said.

"Perhaps the governor is not granting interviews today," said Thurnock.

"Their guise," I said, "would have been more convincing if they had a cart with them, heaped with their kills."

"That would be dangerous," said Clitus. "The spines are deadly, for days, even when the thing is dead, and it is not always dead, and, for some time after death, it may, like the ost, toss and twitch. The least scratch can lead to a swift, terrible death."

Thurnock, turning away, spun his staff, twice, and thrust at some imaginary foe. Such a thrust, with the force of a man of the size and strength of Thurnock, can, lifting a fully-grown man, plunge through the belly to the backbone.

"Thurnock practices," I said.

Clitus walked to the edge of the dock. I joined him there. "Look," he said, pointing down, into the water.

"I see nothing," I said.

"Wait," he said. "Another is coming."

"Yes!" I said. The slender, serpentine body, a yard long, surfaced for a moment, eyes beady, drawing air, and then slipped beneath the surface, the water raked by its double array of brightly colored spines.

"I have seen at least four," he said.

"It is the garbage," I said.

"It is not only the spined tharlarion which seeks food," he said.

He then looked down the dock, to the two fellows with tridents and bait sacks. They were still some yards away. "I wonder if they know what they are doing," he said.

"One supposes so," I said.

"I trust they are well paid," he said.

"Why is that?" I asked.

"Because the risk is great," he said.

"Why is that?" I asked.

"I think they are ignorant," he said.

"How so?" I asked.

"I do not think they know what else is in the water," he said.

"What?" I asked.

"Something far more dangerous than the passive spined tharlarion," he said, "something small, numerous, mindlessly aggressive, and hungry."

"Of course," I said. "Harbor sharks!"

These are a breed of sharks which, as far as I know, are found only in the Farther Islands, small sharks, seldom more than a foot in length, but they can vary from three or four inches, a size one could hold in one's hand, to a foot and a half.

"I see no harbor sharks," I said.

"They are there," said Clitus.

"Perhaps we should chat with our friends, with the tridents," I said.

"Why not?" agreed Clitus.

The two fellows with tridents and bait sacks were now quite close, but seemingly unconcerned with us, seemingly intent only on their fishing. The six others, hooded, with *amphorae*, were a few yards behind them, down the dock.

"Tal," I said, to the two fellows with tridents.

"Tal," said they, as though surprised to have been addressed.

"It is a strange day," I said.

"How so, Master?" asked one.

"Behold the six fellows down the way, with *amphorae*," I said. "Surely they are not bringing water to ships."

"That does seem strange," said one.

Amphorae are familiar vessels on Gor but, given their shape, as they cannot stand by themselves, they are commonly used buried, to keep contents fresh and cool, or mounted in racks, which, on ships, is something of a waste of space. Water on ships is commonly stored in barrels or leather bags.

"Perhaps they are porters, and intend to take on water," said the second of the trident bearers.

"The water of Thassa?" I asked.

Thassa was not a fresh-water sea. Hundreds of rivers and streams, for centuries, had been bringing salt into its deep, turbulent waters.

"That does seem strange," said the first trident bearer, warily.

"Perhaps," I said, "the *amphorae* themselves are trade goods, to be stored aboard certain ships."

"That must be it," said the first fellow.

"But they seem rather plain, rather common stuff, for trade goods," said Clitus.

"It is indeed mysterious," said the second trident bearer.

"How goes your hunting?" I asked.

The six hooded fellows were drifting closer now.

"We have had little luck," said the first trident bearer, "—as yet."

I saw a large shadow in front of me, to the right. Thurnock, with his staff, as though curious, had joined us.

"Perhaps it will improve," I said.

"I think it will," said the first trident bearer.

"It is hard to say," I said.

"Not so hard as you might think," said the second trident bearer.

By this time the six hooded fellows with the *amphorae* were quite close, so close that they might easily overhear our conversation.

"What do you think is in the *amphorae*?" asked the first trident bearer.

"I do not much care," I said.

"Perhaps it is wine," he said, "or perhaps it is oil."

"Perhaps," I said.

"But it is neither," he said.

"How would you know?" I asked.

"It is swords!" he cried, and, at the same moment, the six hooded fellows flung off their hoods and drew forth swords, discarding the *amphorae*.

Two of these earlier hooded fellows were minions of Archelaos, proprietor of *The Living Island*, Ctesippus and Laios.

"Why, you are right," I said, "swords."

"You are amazed!" laughed the trident bearer.

"Who would not be?" I asked.

"Such things are cumbersome sheaths for steel," said Thurnock.

"What is the meaning of this?" I asked. I thought it an appropriate question, surely one to be expected.

"You will have little time to ponder that," said the second trident bearer.

"Perhaps longer than you think," I said.

"Watch out," said Ctesippus, "he has a sword."

I had withdrawn this from within my cloak, but I had called no attention to this move, fixing my attention elsewhere, and, it seems, the second trident bearer noticed this just now. I had picked up this trick from an old friend, the impresario, rogue, and magician, Boots Tarsk-Bit.

"It matters not," said the second trident bearer. "He is a Merchant. His weapons are the abacus, ledger, and scales."

"I trust that you are not threatening us," I said. "In any event, be warned. I can summon the harbor guard."

"You may summon them," said Ctesippus, "but they will not come."

"They have been withdrawn," said Laios.

"By order of the governor?" I asked.

"As it happens," said Laios.

I stepped slightly to my left, near the edge of the dock. In this way I could be approached only frontally, or on my right, and on my right was Thurnock, with his weighty, formidable staff. I did not think this subtlety was noted by our visitors.

"Your array," I said, "could easily be construed as hostile."

Laios laughed, and glanced at Ctesippus, which glance informed me of what I had long suspected, that Ctesippus was first between them.

"On whose behalf do you brandish your weapons?" I asked.

I recalled the codes.

It was not inadmissible to make such an inquiry.

"On behalf of the noble Glaukos of Thera," said Ctesippus.

"Surely there is some misunderstanding," I said. "I am Kenneth Statercounter, a simple merchant of Brundisium. What fault has the noble Glaukos to find with me, or I with him?"

"You are inconveniently about too often," said Ctesippus. "You appear too frequently in surprising places. You are either a conniving villain or a spy on behalf of Brundisium. You ask too many questions. You guess shrewdly at too many answers. Uninvited, unauthorized, you seek truth, an enterprise often fraught with peril. Have you not guessed that some knowledge is less safely grasped than an ost?"

"Are you sure," I asked, "that the harbor guard has been withdrawn?"

"Yes," said Ctesippus.

"Good," I said, "then there will then be fewer questions to answer."

"I do not understand," said Ctesippus.

"I now accord you the opportunity to lower your weapons and leave," I said.

"You are mad!" said Ctesippus.

"You decline," I said. "I grant you but a moment more to accept."

"Kill them!" cried Ctesippus. "Attack! Kill them!"

I do not think the first man realized the throat thrust when it happened, perhaps not until he turned about, as though puzzled, and then, gasping, coughing blood, fell into the water. Where he fell, the water churned, erupting in a frenzy of tiny bodies. The second man had intended to coordinate his attack with that of the first, but he failed to reach me, the front of his skull broken in by a thrust of Thurnock's mighty staff. Almost at the same time, Clitus' net flashed over our heads and fell gracefully over the two fellows with tridents. Before they could free themselves of the net's toils, Clitus drew them from their feet and punched twice with the butt of his trident, the first blow to the temple of one of his foes, the second splintering ribs into the lungs of the other. They rolled, tangled in the net. A second pair of foes advanced on Thurnock and myself, but then, seeing our guard, drew back, not certain of themselves.

"Attack, attack!" screamed Ctesippus.

"Kill!" cried Laios.

In this lacuna of battle, Clitus drew his net about and emptied it into the water. One man had already died, he struck in the temple. The other man tried to seize a paling of the dock but was pulled away from it, and disappeared, screaming, in a cloud of water and blood.

"What are you waiting for?" demanded Ctesippus of the two fellows more forward.

"Attack!" urged Laios.

"For this," said one of them, "we were not paid."

"This is not easy game, a Merchant and some clumsy bump-kins," said the other.

"Attack! Kill!" said Ctesippus.

"Did you not see the sword work?" asked the one. "It is the stuff of the red caste."

"Kill!" screamed Ctesippus.

"You kill!" cried the first of the two closer fellows, backing away, not taking his eye off Thurnock and myself.

"I shall!" cried Ctesippus, striking the man across the back of the neck with his sword, following which blow the head lolled half to the side, dangling, and fell to the planks with the body.

This left the other closer man, and Ctesippus and Laios.

They looked about.

Clitus was now behind them, with net and trident.

"Perhaps you should call the harbor guard," I said.

"You killed him," said the minion to Ctesippus, looking at the body on the planks, the head still attached to the torso.

"Face the fisherman," said Ctesippus to his colleague. "Guard our back."

The minion faced Clitus, frontally, trembling.

"Three to three," I said. "The odds are now more evenly distributed."

"You are no Merchant," said Ctesippus. "Who are you, really?"

"One who awaits your advance," I said.

A few yards down the dock, Clitus moved to the edge of the dock, to my left, to his right, his net dangling from his left hand, the trident in his right hand, seemingly, oddly, unengaged in matters at hand. I trusted that he could note and deal with any sudden charge by the minion. But the minion did not move. He eyed the trident, the net. Doubtless he would have given much for a shield. Ctesippus, Laios at his side, was facing myself and Thurnock.

"I am not unskilled," said Ctesippus.

"I did not think that the commanding officer of the corsair fleet would be," I said.

"Let us meet," he said, "sword to sword."

"As you wish," I said.

"But you are two and I am one," he said. "Ask the lout with the large, clumsy pole to stand aside."

"So that it will then be one against one, only one against one,"
I said.

"That," said Ctesippus.

Behind Ctesippus and Laios, and before the minion, I saw Clitus dip and sweep his net in the water.

I paid him little attention.

I made nothing of his action.

My concern was Ctesippus, and his fellow, Laios.

An Ihn can divide life and death.

"Move away," I said to Thurnock.

"Better not," said Thurnock. "Two will charge as one."

"I know," I said.

Clitus had now withdrawn his net from the water and the net
seemed alive, thrashing and squirming. I caught a flash of roiling color within it, saw teeth cutting at its fibers, saw part of a
body, short, serpentine, and muscular, bulging and distending
cords, and saw a cord severed and a triangular head, viperish,
thrust through torn mesh, followed by half a body, when Clitus
cried out, "Ho!" and flung the entire net and its contents over the
head of the terrified, screaming minion. At the cry of the minion,
Laios and Ctesippus, startled, looked back, over their shoulders,
and Laios howled in horror, the net and its half-freed contents
falling about his head and chest. Laios threw down his sword,
screaming, and tried to pull the net and its occupant away from
his face. There was blood about his eyes and throat. The net and
the spined tharlarion, torn away, were then on the planks about
his ankles. Ctesippus cast me a wild look, perhaps fearing that I
might attempt to exploit this confusion, and rush forward. But I
was as startled as he, and, in any case, would have been unwilling to approach the half-netted death which squirmed at his feet.
He did not move. I did not know if he were frozen in place, paralyzed with fear, or was merely afraid to move, unsure of where to
place his feet, where or how to move, or that any movement, the
thing so close, so agitated, so distraught, might trigger a blind,
defensive, attack reflex. At his feet, Laios, weeping, clawing at his
own face with his fingernails, was expiring. In the intensity and
confusion of the moment, no one, unless Clitus, was aware of the
minion. Then suddenly he was behind Ctesippus, and thrust his
sword fiercely, deeply, into his back. "For my friend, Keos!" he
cried. "Now, dear Keos, you are avenged." The short, serpentine
tharlarion, meanwhile, flopping on the planks of the dock, had

half slipped from the severed net, and, in doing so, squirming to the side, had changed its position. The minion, sword in hand, not realizing this, spinning about, to run back, away, down the dock, stumbled over the net and its still-partially-trapped beast. He slashed down at the tharlarion but his blow was blocked by the interposition of the prongs of Clitus' trident. The minion then, a long scratch on his leg, ran past Clitus, and fled down the dock.

"Pursue him!" cried Thurnock.

"There is no need to do so," said Clitus. He then lifted and shook the net, and the tharlarion squirmed free. Almost at the same time he slid two of the trident's three prongs toward the tharlarion, wedging the creature between the two prongs. He then lifted his catch up, for us to see.

"Get rid of it!" urged Thurnock.

"Few have an ally so colorful," said Clitus.

"Or so loathsome," said Thurnock.

"It is inoffensive," said Clitus.

"But deadly," said Thurnock.

"You could bathe with it," said Clitus. "Just avoid the spines."

"I would prefer my bathing with naked, collared slave girls," said Thurnock.

In Sybaris, as in many Gorean cities, there were public baths which provided such amenities. Ar was famous for its baths. Its largest and most opulent was the Capacian.

"Get rid of it," said Thurnock, shuddering.

"The tiny harbor sharks are far more dangerous," said Clitus.

Thurnock growled.

"Very well," said Clitus, and he lofted the spined tharlarion free of the trident and into the water.

I looked down the dock.

Not twenty yards away, the minion was collapsed, and unmoving.

I watched Clitus walk slowly to the body, and then drag it to the side of the dock and thrust it over the side, into the water.

It would not do to leave bodies on the dock.

Presumably the harbor guard would eventually make its appearance, once their prescribed absence had elapsed.

One supposed they had been reassigned or directed elsewhere for a time, on some pretext or other. Certainly the governor would not have taken them into his confidence, thereby multiplying confederates.

Almost at our feet, Laios lay dead.

Thurnock, with his staff, rolled the body from the dock. There was a brief rage in the water. Harbor sharks, like their larger brethren, are very alert to certain anomalies in their environment, such as an unexpected splash or a thrashing in the water, or a trace of blood, a liquid streamer, sensed from afar.

I looked away.

Thurnock disposed, as well, of two minions, he whose skull he had broken with his staff and he whom Ctesippus had slain for insubordination. Then, staff in hand, he returned to my side.

"This one is still alive," he said, looking down at Ctesippus, who lay prone on the planks.

I turned then, and also looked down at the body.

I had seen the thrust, its location and depth. The assailant knew his work.

"The wound is lethal," I said.

Thurnock, with his staff, moved the body to its back.

Ctesippus' eyes were open.

"Finish me," he said.

"It will be over in a few Ihn," I said.

"Finish me," he said.

"I will put him into the water, alive," said Thurnock.

"Wait," I said.

Ctesippus looked up at me.

"You are no Merchant," he said.

"And you, I suspect," I said, "are no common killer."

"I betrayed my codes," he said.

"Once long ago," I said, "I betrayed mine."

He lifted his hand, weakly, to me.

"Warrior," he said, "do not let me die by a common felon's stroke."

I, troubled, did not speak.

"Let it be by your blade," he said.

"Do him no such honor," said Thurnock.

"Sword brother?" said Ctesippus.

"Sword brother," I said, and slid my blade into his heart.

"I do not understand," said Thurnock.

"It has to do with codes," I said. "And with those who have broken them."

Thurnock looked at me, and I nodded.

He then rolled the body into the water.

We were joined by Clitus.

"The supposed Bosk of Port Kar and his corsairs have been defeated," said Thurnock. "Thus our work is done and we may cast off for Port Kar."

"Perhaps our work is not yet fully done," I said.

"Glaukos, of *The Living Island*, Archelaos, the governor?" said Thurnock.

"Why," I asked, "would corsairs have pretended to be raiders from Port Kar, and have alleged themselves to be captained by Bosk of Port Kar? Why not from elsewhere, a hundred possible places, and why not otherwise captained, by anyone, even dozens of anonymous marauders?"

"Bad blood has long existed between Cos and Tyros, and Port Kar," said Clitus. "And Bosk of Port Kar is known."

"Perhaps we should think at least of Glaukos, the taverner," said Thurnock.

"He has failed the governor," I said. "Let the governor deal with him."

"I do not envy him," said Clitus.

"I had hoped," I said, "following our visit to Glaukos, to have been invited to the governor's palace, that in the guise of the mysterious Kenneth Statercounter of Brundisium, he somehow troublesomely implicated in recent events."

"Instead of heralds from the palace, bearing that invitation," said Clitus, "steel, suborned by gold, was sent against us."

"It is well known we are too few to rush the palace," said Thurnock. "Let me then signal the crews and ready ourselves for departure."

"Without bidding farewell to Archelaos?" I asked.

"How shall we manage so perilous an interview?" asked Clitus.

"By recourse to a key which will open a palace's gates," I said.

"And where," asked Thurnock, "will you find such a key?"

"We already have it," I said, "gagged, bound hand and foot, in a leather capture sack."

"The actor?" said Clitus.

"Of course," I said.

"Would," said Thurnock, "that the contents of that sack were instead a comely woman who might, stripped and nicely collared, kick and moan, and serve us well on the return trip to Port Kar, and then, if we wished, further, bring us a nice handful of copper tarsks off the block."

"Who could deny admittance, even to the governor's palace," I asked, "to stalwart fellows who had recaptured the escaped, notorious Bosk of Port Kar?"

"Who, indeed?" said Clitus.

"There would be rejoicing in the city," said Thurnock.

"What if our principal demurs, what if he declines participation in this small project?" asked Clitus.

"Then we feed him to the harbor sharks," said Thurnock.

"I think that will not be necessary," I said. "Our friend, Bombastico, is an actor. They strive for parts. They covet parts. They hunger for them. And what actor would not be eager to reprise his greatest role?"

"And if he is reluctant to do so?" asked Clitus.

"Then," said Thurnock, "the harbor sharks."

CHAPTER SIXTY-ONE

Bombastico

"I shall render such a performance," said Bombastico, "as will endure through the ages, as will be so memorable and splendid that it will transform the lore of the theater, so awesomely magnificent that others, should they dare to ascend the boards, made aware of it, will be plunged into despair, and will flee the premises in tears, deeming themselves unworthy of even witnessing such a triumph!"

"Mainly," I said, "you are to say nothing and look disconsolate."

"Dialogue and voice are but inessential accouterments," he said. "In saying nothing I shall speak volumes. My least expression will fill a hundred scrolls. A trembling of the lip, a blinking of an eye, a trickling tear, will speak of crumbling walls, of cities in flame, of cosmic conflagrations, of ruined, lost, and dying worlds."

"That should do nicely," I said.

"I am not one of those handsome, charismatic fellows who cannot act but merely portrays himself under different names," he said.

"As you wish," I said.

"I am an actor," he said. "I disappear in my roles. I vanish in my parts."

"How then," asked Thurnock, "can you become known?"

"I emerge at the end of the play," he said, "revealing that it was I, all the time, Bombastico."

"The audience is then enlightened, and dazzled?" I said.

"Inevitably," he said.

"I think I can see why the corsairs chose you to act the part of Bosk of Port Kar," I said.

"It may be hard to believe," he said, "but I have never actually met Bosk of Port Kar, and I know little about him. Accordingly, the role was a challenge, one which might not merely have daunted, but might have crushed, a lesser actor. I had to create a character, vivify a persona, on the basis of little or nothing. But, as you know, I managed to do so brilliantly. It was my masterpiece, to date."

"I know something of the theaters in Ar," I said. "I had not heard of you there."

"Ar," he said, "is not yet ready for me."

"Cultures mature," I said. "Perhaps later."

"I trust," said Bombastico, "it will not be necessary this time to swathe me in chains."

"It would add realism," I said.

"What has realism to do with the theater?" he scoffed. "Realism is the enemy of the theater. Let not the theater be flattened into the shallowness of the prosaic. The country of the theater is the world of the mind, of the imagination, of the heart, a world far more real than realism can dream, far more real than realism can comprehend."

"Very well," I said. "We shall omit the chains."

It is well known that a crowd, responding to the wisp of an idea, incited by a shout, stung by a cry, secure in its faceless anonymity, can easily and swiftly transform itself into a clumsy, mindless, many-headed monster freed of all civil and moral constraint. In a crowd it is not unusual for many a beast to discover itself untethered. When things became ugly in the triumph of Nicomachos and irate citizens saw fit to swarm the float exhibiting a prisoner, the supposed Bosk of Port Kar, to overcome his guards and tear him to pieces, Thurnock, Clitus, and I had rushed to the tumultuous scene. There was much confusion, much buffeting and trampling. Men impeded one another and struggled with one another and tore and clawed at one another. In the crush of bodies the two guards on the float were brushed aside as by a roaring surf and dozens of hands stretched out, grasping at the prisoner, whom few in the crowd, in the rush and press, even saw. Thurnock, Clitus, and myself, unlike the teeming jungle into which we thrust ourselves, striking, elbowing, and kicking, dragging at robes and tunics, shoving amongst bodies, had direction and purpose. We managed to reach the prisoner who was lost amongst bodies, strike him unconscious, cover him with my cloak, and make our way back, out of the press. "I see him!" I had cried, standing over the prone figure covered by my cloak. "There!" I had cried, pointing away. "There!" So directed, the crowd, stumbling, buffeting, tripping, trampling, hastened in the direction I had indicated. Several men were left behind, senseless, or groaning with broken limbs. "What fellow is that?" asked a man, pointing at the covered figure at my feet. "Sergius of Sybaris," I said. "I fear for his life. Help me get him to shelter!" "Others can help," he said, pointing to Thurnock and Clitus. "Citizens," I addressed them, "please help me with my friend." "Very well," said they. The man had then hurried after the crowd.

"They would not believe me," said Bombastico. "I told them I was not really Bosk of Port Kar, but no one believed me."

"Perhaps your performance had been too authentic," said Clitus.

"That must be it," said Bombastico. "I was foiled by the unsurpassable excellence of my own art. I was betrayed by my own talent. It was that which led to my downfall."

"Perhaps some believed you, but declined to admit it," I said.

"What is the nature of my imminent role?" he asked.

"Just be quiet and come along quietly," I said.

"I shall be so quiet," he said, "that none will even notice me."

"You do not have to be that quiet," I said.

CHAPTER SIXTY-TWO

The Governor Grants an Interview

"They have been searched, and all their weapons have been removed?" asked Archelaos.

"Yes," said he who was first amongst the guards.

"Admit them," said Archelaos.

Thurnock, Clitus, and I, with Bombastico, were conducted into the private audience chamber in the gubernatorial place. I remembered the chamber from shortly after my arrival, long ago, in Sybaris, in particular the map table.

"Leave us," said Archelaos, dismissing the guards.

They withdrew, but, I suspected, to no great distance.

"You are surprised to see us?" I said.

"As certain reports have not reached me," he said, "no." He stroked the long strings of a mustache on either side of his chin.

"You are gracious to grant this audience," I said.

"How could it be refused to one who has captured the famous pirate and outlaw, Bosk of Port Kar?" he said.

Bombastico straightened up, and looked properly chagrined, and fierce.

"It was thought he had been torn to pieces by the crowd," said Archelaos.

"I have read such on the public boards," I said.

"It is not too late to arrange that," said Archelaos.

Bombastico paled, and trembled, actions which I suspected were not feigned.

"That would save amending the public account," I granted him.

"I am not truly Bosk of Port Kar," said Bombastico, hastily, if unhelpfully.

"You will do," said the governor.

Bombastico cast me a frantic look.

"It is my surmise," I said, "that Glaukos, proprietor of *The Living Island*, was importantly involved in the recruitment, supply, and organization of the corsairs, and that it was he who engaged, or had engaged, the services of our friend, Bombastico."

"Incredible," said Archelaos, drily.

"In some quarters, too," I said, "it is conjectured that the noble Glaukos was little more than the tool of a higher, more obscure figure."

"As governor," said Archelaos, "I must look into this."

"Do not look too carefully," I said. "Glaukos knows much."

"In any snare he sets," said Archelaos, "he, too, would be enmeshed."

"You must rejoice," I said, "in the victory of your friend, Nicomachos, over the corsairs."

"Nicomachos is a noble fool," said Archelaos, "the naive dupe of honor and duty. He has dabbled in matters of which he knows not. He has gone to Cos, to be rewarded by Lurius himself, for clearing the seas of the dreaded Bosk of Port Kar. He will have his ceremony, and receive his decoration, and then, to his dismay, be put to what amounts to exile, be consigned to practical banishment, be sent to be again Admiral of the Fleet of the Farther Islands."

"A hero, he is not popular in Cos?" I said.

"Not in the court of Lurius," said Archelaos. "Heroes do not fit in. They are an embarrassment. They have no place in the vicinity of a throne. They detract from the prestige of their superiors."

"They may even accrue a populace's love which is more properly bestowed on a loftier object," I ventured.

"That is always a danger," said Archelaos.

"At least," I said, "the great Lurius of Jad, Ubar of Cos, regards the clearing of the sea with delight?"

"Doubtless," said Archelaos.

"It is my conjecture," I said, "that the resources of the corsairs were considerable, in both wealth and ships."

"It seems so," said Archelaos.

"Surely far beyond the means of Glaukos, a taverner," I said.

"And even beyond the means of the governor of Thera?" asked Archelaos.

"Yes," I said, "even beyond the means of the governor of Thera."

"Do you think you will leave this room alive?" he asked.

"It is my intention," I said.

"Who are you, really?" asked Archelaos.

"A simple merchant of Brundisium, Kenneth Statercounter," I said.

"And how much do you know, of dark things which you should not know, noble Statercounter?"

"Little more than other men," I said, "say, that he who employs a tool may himself be the tool of another."

"And you conjecture a higher craftsman," said Archelaos.

"Much higher," I said.

"How high?" he asked.

"As high," I said, "as the occupant of a throne."

"You have permitted yourselves to be disarmed, most unwisely disarmed," said Archelaos. "I shall summon the guards."

"Do not act in haste," I said. "There are three men in this chamber, other than our prisoner, any one of whom could kill you with his bare hands before guards could reach you."

"If I am slain, you will never reach the outer gate alive," he said.

"I can understand," I said, "why Lurius of Jad, fat with avarice, insatiable for wealth, corpulent with greed, would secretly organize, support, and protect marauders, that some percentage of loot would find its way to his private coffers, but why this pointless, extravagant hoax of attributing these raids and depredations to Bosk of Port Kar?"

"Why would you think?" he asked.

"At least," I said, "to associate such villainy with some figure, any figure, remote from the Farther Islands, that to divert suspicion from Thera, and, for such a purpose, Bosk of Port Kar, I suppose, would do as well as any other."

"Not quite as well as any other, my friend," said Archelaos.

"I see," I said, "he, selected, a hated enemy, would deepen the friction between Cos and Port Kar, an enmity valuable to, and exploitable by, say, the court in Jad."

"You see the footprint of the sleen," said Archelaos, "but you do not see the beast itself."

"Speak," I said.

"Have you something to do with Bosk of Port Kar?" asked Archelaos. "Much would become clear were that the case. Are you an agent for him?"

"I know him," I said.

"Those of my party," said Archelaos, "see in the defeat of the corsairs the hand of the true Bosk of Port Kar."

"Port Kar," I said, "is far off, on the continent itself, on the Tamber Gulf, on the eastern shore of Thassa."

"We think," said Archelaos, "he is somewhere on the Farther Islands, in any one of a hundred ports."

"Have you detected a foreign fleet in your waters?" I asked.

"We have noted over the months a dozen traces of his work," said Archelaos.

"Surely the defeat of the corsairs is the work of Nicomachos," I said.

"Who," asked Archelaos, "sped the coordinates of the corsair fleet to Nicomachos? Who led him at just the right moment to the waters of Mytilene?"

"Do you not conjecture implausibly, recklessly?" I asked.

"I am sure that he, the true Bosk of Port Kar, is somewhere in the Farther Islands," said Archelaos.

"Perhaps somewhere," I said.

"You know him, you said," said Archelaos.

"Yes," I said.

"Then know," said Archelaos, "and inform him, that he is a fool and a dupe."

"How is that?" I asked.

"Does he truly think that great Lurius of Jad, the glorious Ubar of Cos, would promote the fortunes of thieves and pirates for a mere percentage of their booty? Far more is afoot, cities and fleets, fields of diamonds, seas of gems, rivers of silver and mountains of gold."

"I do not understand," I said.

"Bosk of Port Kar was essential to our plans," said Archelaos.

"How so?" I asked.

"You have heard of Talena, the egregious traitress, the perfidious Ubara of Ar, she who betrayed her Home Stone, who did treason to her city, who brought proud Ar into vile subjection, who opened its gates to Cos and Tyros?"

"I have heard of her," I said.

"After the restoration of Marlenus of Ar, rightful Ubar of Ar, she disappeared from the city."

"I have heard that," I said.

"A reward was offered for her capture and return to Ar," said Archelaos, "a reward of ten thousand tarns of gold, tarn disks of double weight."

"An unbelievable fortune," I said.

"What you may not know," said Archelaos, "is that she was discovered far from Ar, in unlikely Port Kar, improbably and brilliantly hidden, kept as a publicly displayed tavern slave. Who would think of her other than a common paga girl? But she was noted by one of the few hunters, one of the few pursuers, who could recognize her features. Her false identity compromised, she was removed for safekeeping to the stout holding of Bosk of Port Kar, a veritable fortress on the delta." At this point, Archelaos regarded me, closely. "Are you disturbed?" he asked.

"No," I said.

"Bosk of Port Kar was feared," said Archelaos. "It was deemed perilous to storm the holding, a redoubtable feat in any case, while its master was in residence. Accordingly then, Bosk of Port Kar was duped, lured to the Farther Islands, to deal with raids and ravaging allegedly perpetrated by him."

"And what then?" I asked.

"Are you well?" asked Archelaos.

"I do not think Bosk of Port Kar would be pleased to hear these things," I said.

"The holding was stormed," said Archelaos. "In the confusion Talena slipped away with a man named Seremides, in the expectation of being carried away to riches and honor, liberty and safety, in the court of her former ally, Lurius of Jad."

"Then she is safe," said Bombastico.

"Lurius of Jad is now negotiating with Marlenus of Ar," said Archelaos, "arranging for the delivery of Talena, stripped and in chains, to Ar, and the payment of the reward."

"With such wealth," said Thurnock, "Lurius of Jad could not only build fleets but hire armies to ravage the continent."

"It seems," I said, "Bosk of Port Kar is indeed a fool and dupe."

"He could have done little but what he did," said Clitus.

"Should he have remained in Port Kar," asked Thurnock, "and permitted the continued burning of villages and the slaughter of hundreds?"

"Intervention was imperative," said Clitus.

"We had hoped, of course," said Archelaos, "that the intervention of Bosk of Port Kar would have proved unsuccessful."

"What is to be the fate of the Lady Talena?" asked Bombastico.

"Hideous tortures, publicly inflicted over several days, followed by a slow impalement," said Archelaos.

"What time is it?" I asked.

"Something past the twelfth Ahn," said Archelaos.

"I think then it is time for us to take our leave," I said.

"Gross bravado is but a sorry jest," said Archelaos.

"Recall," I said, "any one of three in this room could kill you before the arrival of guards."

"But you are fortunate," said Archelaos. "I am prepared to offer you an arrangement."

"Do so," I said.

"I am spared," he said, "and you are free to leave, safe and undeterred."

"A splendid proposal," I said.

"My life for yours," he said.

"Excellent," I said.

"Beware," growled Thurnock.

"Kill him now," said Clitus.

"We have your word for this?" I asked.

"Of course," he said.

"As a man of honor?" I asked.

"Certainly," he said.

"As soon as guards are between us," said Thurnock, "he will sound the alarm and have a hundred men set upon us."

"It is unlikely we could cut our way to the first gate," said Clitus.

"But we have his word," I said.

"Better the word of an urt or ost," said Thurnock.

"Civilization cannot survive without trust," I said.

"That is true, noble Statercounter," said Archelaos, whose forehead seemed damp, presumably with perspiration.

"I am pleased that we have reached this understanding," I said, "as it means that lovely Sybaris and its mighty harbor, and a thousand or more ships, will not perish in flames before nightfall."

"What are you saying?" asked Archelaos.

"I, too, have an arrangement," I said, "one which somewhat antedates yours."

"What is that?" inquired Archelaos.

"Surely your spies have informed you that my men were not at the ships this morning," I said.

"What arrangement?" pressed Archelaos.

"At the time," I said, "I did not realize you were a man of honor, so I arranged that if I and my companions were not back on the dock before the fourteenth Ahn, the city and harbor, the piers, ships, and all, would be set afire."

"I do not believe you," said Archelaos, one hand grasping and twisting one of the dangling strands of his mustache.

"Lurius of Jad would not be pleased," I said, "to learn that Archelaos, loyal and esteemed governor of Thera, was responsible for the destruction of the city, ships, and harbor."

"There is no such arrangement," said Archelaos. "You are bluffing."

"More than two hundred men, stationed about," I said, "are waiting with ignitable fire vessels and accelerants."

"I do not believe you," said Archelaos.

"Then let us maintain our small stand-off," I said, "until the Fourteenth Ahn, at which time we will kill you and, possibly, escape in the flames and confusion."

"Two hundred men," said Archelaos, "are not enough to enfire so much, a city, wharves, and ships."

"One is enough," I said. "Fire fathers fire. A pinch of burning oil can bring about the ruin of a warehouse, a brand of tinder the loss of a palace, a toppled candle the destruction of an impregnable fortress."

"Let us kill him now," said Thurnock, "and then take our chances at the fourteenth Ahn."

"That will not be necessary," said Archelaos, quickly. "I will have your weapons returned, and have you escorted in safety to your ships."

"I find that satisfactory," I said.

"I think you are bluffing," said Archelaos.

"But you do not know, do you?" I asked.

"No," he said angrily.

The guards left us at the dock where the *Dorna* and the *Tesephone* were moored.

Thurnock, Clitus, Bombastico, and I watched them take their departure.

"I played my part well, did I not?" asked Bombastico.

"Brilliantly," I said.

"You should have seen me in *The Trial of Hesius* and *The Four Secrets of Enrobion,* Baker of Turia," he said.

"I missed them," I admitted.

"The true actor prefers a good part to a good meal," said Bombastico.

"Only if he is not hungry," said Thurnock.

"Our enemies play a fine and cruel *kaissa,*" I said.

"Our moves were forced," said Thurnock.

"Our crews will be aboard shortly," said Clitus.

"It is near the fourteenth Ahn," I said.

"I wish to congratulate you, dear Captain," said Thurnock. "Your quick thinking and wily bluff brought us safely out of the palace. The governor feared to call your bluff."

"My dear friend," I said, "your compliment is much appreciated, but, I confess, undeserved."

"How so?" he said.

"I arranged with Tab to arm and distribute the crew of the *Dorna* and with Sakim to arm and distribute the crew of the *Tesephone* in such a manner as to fire Sybaris, the harbor, and ships, if we were not back by the fourteenth Ahn. Their absence, too, was intended to encourage contact with messengers from the governor. What I did not anticipate was the appearance of an assassination squad."

"Then I hope our crews will report soon," said Clitus.

"The sooner the better," I said. "We must cast off as soon as possible."

"I had not thought, hitherto," said Clitus, "that Archelaos was so great a hero."

"How is that?" I asked.

"He has saved a city, a harbor, and a great many ships," said Clitus.

"I see Tab approaching, and Sakim, and men," said Thurnock.

"Prepare to cast off," I said.

CHAPTER SIXTY-THREE

We Set Our Course for Port Kar

"Captain Tab has cleared the harbor," said Thurnock.

"Are there signs of pursuit?" I inquired.

"None, Captain," said Thurnock.

"Archelaos may fear incendiaries still in the city," said Clitus.

The *Tesephone*, smaller and quicker, more responsive, than the larger *Dorna*, lay a pasang out, south, beyond the harbor, that she might warn the *Dorna* of danger and, if necessary, cover her flank.

"You seem pensive, Captain," said Thurnock.

"I think of Ctesippus," I said.

"Put him from your mind," said Clitus. "His codes were betrayed, his scarlet was soiled."

"So, too, once, were mine," I said.

"I doubt that you took food from the hungry, or put the innocent to the sword," said Clitus. "You do not seem to me one who kills for sport, one who claws for power, one easily blinded by the brightness of gold."

"Do not blame yourself," said Sakim. "As in Thassa, there are currents, deep and swift. They carry one where they wish."

"We must not let that be," I said.

"All wisdom may not be in the codes," said Sakim. "There may be wisdoms unknown to the codes, wisdoms beyond the codes."

"Possibly," I said.

"Perhaps it would have been better, cleaner, less ambivalent," said Thurnock, "had you crossed swords with Ctesippus."

"Perhaps," I said.

"In the sport of steel," said Thurnock, "only one can be first. It is clean. It does not confuse things. Clarity resides in it."

"And simplicity," I said.

"The past is done with," said Thurnock. "Dismiss it."

"There is a darkness in me," I said.

"There is a lightness and a darkness in all men," said Thurnock.

"A wound heals," said Sakim.

"A scar may remain," I said.

"Ho!" cried Bombastico, from the *Tesephone*'s small stem castle. "Behold! See how my cloak flutters meaningfully! Note the wind in my hair. Regard the fierce serenity of my visage, my look of intent and far horizons!"

"Impressive," said Clitus.

"What are you portraying?" I asked.

"The Admiral of a mighty fleet," said Bombastico.

"There is still time to throw him overboard," said Thurnock. "He might be able to swim back to the harbor at Sybaris."

"I do not think he can swim," I said.

"So much the better," said Thurnock.

"As the acrobat, the czehar player, and the swordsman," called Bombastico, "so, too, must the actor practice. Already, today, I have been a pastry cook, a Ubar, a shrewd scribe of the law, a befuddled metal worker, and a sly, oily fellow soliciting patronage for a paga tavern."

"Excellent," I said.

"Can you portray an abysmal actor utterly devoid of talent?" asked Thurnock.

"Marvelous!" said Bombastico. "What a challenge! I had not thought of it! What a test of my limits!"

"What do you intend to do with him?" asked Sakim.

"Port Kar is short of theatrical talent," I said.

"Importing Bombastico is not likely to remedy that deficiency," said Clitus.

"Send him to Ar," said Thurnock.

"Turia is farther away," said Sakim.

We were now in the wake of the *Dorna*.

I looked astern, seeing the harbor at Sybaris falling behind. It was a large and beautiful harbor.

The *Dorna* and the *Tesephone* would proceed due south for some ten pasangs, and then, if we detected no other ships in the vicinity, part company. In this way, our courses would remain a matter of conjecture in Sybaris. I expected, given my pose as the merchant of Brundisium, Kenneth Statercounter, that the most likely surmise in Sybaris would be that we, both ships, would return together to Brundisium. The actual situation was to be quite different.

"Should we not have dealt further with Glaukos and Archelaos?" asked Thurnock.

"I did not think it necessary," I said. "I deemed it sufficient to leave Glaukos to Archelaos, and Archelaos to Lurius of Jad."

Soon, the *Dorna* and the *Tesephone* would rendezvous and then go their separate ways. The *Dorna* would proceed to the Cove of Harpalos, to pick up some of our men, those who had been left there, and board equipment, and various supplies and stores. I had also instructed Captain Tab not to dispose of the four slaves left there, Lais, Margot, Millicent, and Courtney, marketing them locally, but to add them, lovely articles of property, to the cargo manifest, and return with them to Port Kar. Each was of interest. I had arranged to have Lais placed with Ho-Tosk, master of the paga tavern, *The Golden Chain*. Having been a paga girl at *The Living Island* in Sybaris, she well knew the nature of the paga girl and what was expected of one. I did not think she would be frequently whipped. I would have had her taken to my holding in Port Kar but I did not expect to spend more than an Ahn or two there and did not know if I would ever see it again. I had specified that Margot, Millicent, and Courtney, the former Melete, Iantha, and Philomena, the former 'Three Ubaras' of *The House of the Golden Urt* in Sybaris, and the confederates of the corsairs, be sold in Port Kar. By now, as other slaves, they would be the helpless prisoners of their ignited slave fires. Enslaved, collared, wholly owned, utterly subjected to uncompromising male domination, their sexual needs liberated and exponentially intensified, they were now the needful possessions, pets, and toys of men. It would be pleasant to see them on the block, piteous in their need, zealous to attract buyers, desperate to be purchased, by any male.

"In a few days," said Clitus, "I expect Nicomachos, Admiral of the Fleet of the Farther Islands, to return to Thera."

"The fleet of Cos," I said, "is doubtless commanded by some sycophant of Lurius of Jad."

"Perhaps it is just as well," said Clitus. "Nicomachos is said to be a fine officer, well-organized, shrewd, and audacious."

"I fear he is short on the obsequious virtues of the courtier," I said.

"The better for Port Kar," said Clitus.

"I shall miss Aktis," said Thurnock.

"You miss competing with one whose skills with the bow match your own," said Clitus.

"More than that," said Thurnock. "He is a caste brother."

"More than that," smiled Clitus.

"Yes," said Thurnock. "He is a friend."

Aktis was aboard the *Dorna*, drawing an oar. In the unlit, low-ceilinged hold of the *Dorna*, on the damp sand used as ballast, stripped, her ankles chained to parted rings, lay his slave, Sylvia, former dancer at *The Living Island*. The last I had heard, she had learned to lick and kiss a whip well, even begging, in the darkness and on the damp sand, to be permitted to do so. After leaving the Cove of Harpalos, Tab was to lay a course for Chios and disembark Aktis and his slave on the coast near the ashes of Nicosia.

"I trust," said Clitus, "Aktis will be successful in organizing leagues of peasant villages."

"He will travel about, endeavoring to do so," I said.

"May he be successful," said Clitus.

"Villages, united and armed, would give pause not only to raiders but even to the predatory regulars of Cos," said Sakim.

"Few people understand," I said, "that the state is the most dangerous of enemies."

"It is cruel," said Sakim, "that his village, Nicosia, was destroyed."

"It was not destroyed," I said. "Only huts and fences were destroyed. Its Home Stone exists."

"And," said Thurnock, "some who escaped the attack of the raiders will drift back, and others, longing for a Home Stone, will drift in."

"One must have a Home Stone," said Clitus.

"Many do not," I said.

"Where?" asked Clitus, interested.

"Elsewhere," I said.

We watched the *Dorna* pull away, her course laid for the Cove of Harpalos.

"She departs," said Clitus.

"Yes," I said.

"But we do not accompany her," said Clitus.

"You will see her again, in Port Kar," I said.

"Surely all of us will see her then," said Clitus.

"One does not know," I said.

"I do not understand," said Clitus.

"Our course, I take it, is Port Kar," said Thurnock.

"Yes," I said.

"We will be in Port Kar days before the *Dorna*," said Thurnock.

"Yes," I said.

"I do not understand this, and I do not like this," said Thurnock.

"Sakim," I called.

"Captain?" he asked, coming aft.

"When we reach the arsenal at Port Kar," I said, "you will take command of the *Tesephone*."

"How is this?" he asked.

"It is my will," I said. "Do not question me. You are dismissed."

"I see, in your eye," he said, "there is a tear."

"No," I said. "It is the wind, a drop of ocean spray."

"Captain?" he said.

"Go," I said.

"What is wrong?" asked Clitus.

"Leave me," I said.

"Have I failed my captain?" he asked.

"No," I said. "One could not ask for a finer officer or a greater friend."

"What then?" he asked.

"I fear your loyalty," I said.

"I do not understand," he said.

"Go," I said.

He withdrew.

"Do you wish me to withdraw as well?" asked Thurnock.

"No, dear friend," I said. "It is to you that I must speak. It is in you that I must confide."

"You need not speak," said Thurnock. "I know the looming burden of your discourse. And I advise you, as a friend and as a disengaged observer, as a neutral judge of deeds and an impartial arbiter of honor, that it is not your concern. Cast the burden away. It is not necessary to bear it. It is, indeed, wrong to bear it."

"You know what I must do," I said.

"You need not do it, you must not do it," said Thurnock.

"She expected shelter and security," I said.

"She deserves neither," said Thurnock.

"I did my best to protect her," I said.

"Better you had turned your back," said Thurnock.

"She was sought by a thousand bounty hunters," I said, "sought in hovels and sheds, in palaces and citadels, from rocky Torvaldsland to the jungles of the Ua, even to the World's End."

"Unsuccessfully," said Thurnock.

During the confusion and terror attending the uprising and restoration of Marlenus, Talena had disappeared from Ar. In the months following her disappearance, many women suspected to be, or falsely represented to be, Talena had been brought to Ar.

"Have you no pity for her?" I asked.

"None," said he.

"She is much as a pathetic tabuk doe," I said, "pursued by swarms of larls and sleen, a vulnerable quarry universally sought, friendless and fleeing, nowhere to step, nowhere to hide, every hand turned against her."

"She was a traitress Ubara, a betrayer of her Home Stone, a subverter of law, an enemy to her own city, a puppet of foes, a duplicitous servant of blood enemies. Let her be taken, and promptly, to Ar; let her face the justice she denied others; let her face the wrath of an outraged Ubar; let her be put before vengeful Marlenus."

"She was once my free companion," I said.

"The companionship, not renewed annually, expired long ago," said Thurnock. "Now you are nothing to her, and she is nothing to you. You are unknown to one another. You are strangers."

"She is very beautiful," I said.

"No more than thousands of others," he said, "others who are not selfish, vindictive, arrogant, and cruel, others who have not bartered honor and betrayed friends, who have not betrayed Home Stones."

"Surely you see the hideous irony here," I said, "a piteous fugitive, widely sought for torture and impalement, living in terror, fearing each small, unexpected sound, each unfamiliar step, for months, and then, suddenly, she is given hope, senses the bright beacon of refuge, is promised asylum, protection, comfort, honor, and wealth, all at the hands of a former ally, a confederate, a supposed friend, an understanding, compassionate brother in strategy and policy, but behind the proffered aid, concealed behind the kindly word and welcoming smile, is treachery and greed."

"The irony I see," said Thurnock, "is that hundreds of hunters expended considerable effort, toil, time, and gold without success, that they sweated and exhausted themselves fruitlessly, for months, and all for nothing, while their prize drops itself into the lap of a sedentary, deceitful tyrant who had not bothered to stir from his throne."

"I wonder," I said, "if she is already on her way to Ar."

"Quite possibly," said Thurnock. "Lurius will want the reward as soon as possible."

"Will there be a trial?" I asked.

"She is guilty," said Thurnock. "What need is there of a trial?"

"Perhaps," I said, "that vengeance be decked in the colors of law."

"The Ubar makes law," said Thurnock. "He is thus above the law."

"Do you take the supremacy of law to be a myth?" I asked.

"Who makes the law?" said Thurnock.

"Even so," I said, "do not deny the power of myth. Even if a trial is no more than a theatrical gesture designed to conceal a foregone conclusion, such a gesture, even a meaningless farce, even a lie, takes time."

"We are days from Port Kar," said Thurnock.

"In Port Kar, a tarn may be obtained," I said. "The wings of the tarn are strong. The tarn cleaves the sky like a knife."

"I think you are already too late," said Thurnock.

"We do not know so," I said. "Perhaps the prisoner will be taken by sea to Brundisium and from Brundisium, transported not by tarn, but by overland caravan to Ar, that she be publicly exhibited, opprobriously scorned, lengthily humiliated, on her way to face the justice of Ar."

"Marlenus is impatient," said Thurnock. "And the city will cry for the blood of Talena. And few Ubars, even a Marlenus, can brook the will of a roused, clamoring city with impunity."

"There must be time," I said.

"She may be dead already," said Thurnock, "seared and torn by tortures, impaled with exquisite slowness, her body burned and her ashes cast amongst the dung of tharlarion."

"I must do what I can," I said.

"Do nothing," said Thurnock. "It is not your business."

"One must decide for oneself what is to be one's business," I said.

"The matter is worse than perilous," said Thurnock. "It is hopeless. Do not involve yourself."

"I tried to protect her," I said.

"You did your best, that is enough, far more than enough," said Thurnock. "Remain in Port Kar, frequent the markets, taste *ka-la-na*, swill paga, feast, served by naked slaves, feel the deck of a fine ship beneath your feet, pursue unfamiliar horizons."

"I must to Ar," I said.

"What difference could you make?" asked Thurnock. "What could you do?"

"I suspect—nothing," I said.

"Were you not banished from Ar?" asked Thurnock. "Were you not denied bread, fire, and salt? Do you think mighty Marlenus will welcome you? Does the verr challenge the larl? Might you not be slain the moment you stepped within the *pomerium* of Glorious Ar? Does the tarsk rush to knock on the door to the slaughter house?"

"I must to Ar," I said.

"I will come with you," said Thurnock.

"No, dear friend," I said. "Neither you nor others. I must go alone."

"I weep," burst Thurnock.

"No," I said. "Do not do so."

"We have done much, and have seen much," said Thurnock.

"And for that we are grateful," I said.

The great body of Thurnock shook, as he turned from me.

"Oars ready," I called.

"Oars ready," called the *keleustes*.

"Stroke," I called.

"Stroke," called the *keleustes*, and his mallet struck the metal drum, and oars, as one, dipped into the waters of gleaming Thassa.

CPSIA information can be obtained
at www.ICGtesting.com
Printed in the USA
JSHW041637290421
14083JS00001B/1